INSIDE STORY

SUSAN PAGE DAVIS

HARVEST HOUSE PUBLISHERS
EUGENE, OREGON

The author is represented by MacGregor Literary.

Cover by Left Coast Design, Portland, Oregon

Cover photos © David DeLossy / Photodisc / Getty Images; VisionsofAmerica / Joe Sohm / Digital Vision / Getty Images; Chee-Onn Leong / Shutterstock

INSIDE STORY
Copyright © 2009 by Susan Page Davis
Published by Harvest House Publishers
Eugene, Oregon 97402
www.harvesthousepublishers.com

Library of Congress Cataloging-in-Publication Data
Davis, Susan Page.
Inside story / Susan Page Davis.
    p. cm.
 ISBN 978-0-7369-2474-0 (pbk.)
1. Women journalists—Fiction. 2. United States. Navy—Officers—Fiction. I. Title.
PS3604.A976I57 2009
813.'6—dc22
                                                                    2008020672

Printed in the United States of America

09 10 11 12 13 14 15 16 17 / RDM-SK / 10 9 8 7 6 5 4 3 2 1

To my dear husband, Jim.
I thank God for the 32 years He has given us together.

Acknowledgments

I owe a big thank you to a man named Don Sparks, YNC(SS), U.S. Navy-Retired. Don and I have never met in person, but he read the earlier books in this series and kindly agreed to read through the *Inside Story* manuscript, watching for authenticity in anything Navy related. His faithfulness and humor encouraged me. Thanks, Don!

My son Jim and daughter-in-law Debbie also read through the manuscript. Thanks for all those booboos you caught! Jim, again your suggestions were invaluable.

Others who helped me with this book in a big way include my critique partners, Lisa Harris and Lynette Sowell. My husband, Jim, also read the manuscript and did the first line edit.

Thank you all!

"Because he loves me," says the LORD,
"I will rescue him; I will protect him,
for he acknowledges my name."

PSALM 91:14

ONE

"Uh, Claudia? That gorilla is *looking* at me."

Claudia Gillette turned to glare at the photographer who accompanied her on her most athletic adventures. "Hush, Tommy. I knew I should have left you in Bwindi."

She ignored the large male mountain gorilla Tommy was staring at and turned back to Dr. Bleeker, the veterinarian in charge of their expedition. Tommy was the best photographer on the magazine's staff, but in high-stress moments he exhibited all the valor of a field mouse.

"See how the snare has eaten into the flesh on her foot." The doctor knelt beside an adult female gorilla. "We'll have to cut out the wire, disinfect, and stitch her up. The injury is quite severe, but we may be able to avoid amputation."

"Will you come back again and check on her?" Claudia asked, bending over the comatose gorilla to observe the wound Bleeker exposed on the creature's left hind foot.

"Absolutely. I'll try to come back next week, but certainly within two weeks. If she's not healing well, we'll consider alternatives."

"Uh..." Tommy eased around to the opposite side of the makeshift operating theater in the jungle, putting the unconscious gorilla, Dr. Bleeker, and Claudia between him and the silverback he was eyeing.

"You said they're usually peaceful, right, doctor? 'Cause that one over there looks a little testy to me."

Bleeker glanced over his shoulder at the male, which was now only ten yards away. "Hello. Gotten closer, hasn't he? Curious, I expect. We'll work as quickly as we can." He gestured to one of the local porters, who had carried a pack of medical equipment up the grueling trail for the veterinarian. "Let's have a little light here, shall we?"

The man unpacked and set up a powerful, battery-operated light to give the veterinarian the extra illumination he needed in the shadowy rainforest floor. The tracking guide, who had helped them locate the gorilla group, and two more porters waited ten yards away, barely visible under the trees. One of the local men they had hired held a tranquilizer dart gun, but she knew Bleeker, the tracker, and the long line of administrators supporting their work wanted as little human interference in the animals' world as possible.

Claudia looked up. Through the canopy overhead, she could barely glimpse snatches of blue-gray sky. They were high in the Virunga Mountains—higher than she'd ever climbed before. She'd felt a little light-headed the last hour of the climb. Back in Maine she'd scaled Katahdin twice, nearly a mile high. There'd been snow at the summit in July. If they were higher here, shouldn't there be snow? Of course, they were much nearer the equator. She'd have to check the elevation before writing her article.

If not for the vegetation that closed them in, she'd probably have a view unparalleled in East-Central Africa. Volcanoes. Jungle spreading over the national parks, rivers pouring down steep precipices and frothing toward Lake Tanganyika.

Just for a second, she let herself absorb the thrill of being here. Few people were allowed to view the mountain gorillas in their native habitat, but here she was, not just observing them, but actually helping treat a primate patient. She reached out and touched the rough hair on the gorilla's side. This one must weigh double what Claudia did and could no doubt tear her apart without breathing hard.

Tommy was snapping photos and seemed absorbed in the job now. Good. She slapped a mosquito and glanced out toward the gorilla group. About a dozen animals were scattered within sight, eating and occasionally jostling each other. The juveniles chattered, now and then erupting into screams, but they kept their distance. All but the big male, who continued to watch them and pace on his knuckles and hind feet.

"Just hand me that thing that looks like a needle-nose plier, would you?" Bleeker said.

She seized the tool from his array of wrapped instruments laid out on a towel and placed it in his hand. "What do you call that?"

"Needle-nose pliers."

She laughed and wrote it down.

"They have built-in wire cutters, which come in handy out here. Don't worry, they're sterile." He snipped the wire embedded in the gorilla's foot. Using a steel instrument, he probed at the deep crease it had formed in the flesh. "Okay, there's a tool that looks like a little hook."

She found it and gave it to him. "Will she be all right?"

He shrugged, noncommittal. "I hope so. They get in these poachers' snares, and without intervention, they get infected. They can die from it, and it's a slow, painful death."

Claudia winced. "They're so…beautiful."

He smiled at that. "Most people don't think gorillas are beautiful, but I know what you mean. And their numbers are so low now that the loss of even one adult female, like this one, would be a serious blow to the population."

He finished the surgery and stitched the wound. Somehow Tommy managed to stay cool enough to swap lenses and keep taking pictures. Behind them the other members of the gorilla group chattered and barked as they ate the succulent bamboo and prickly nettles that grew lush in the area. The huge silverback, the dominant male of the group, still paced back and forth, watching the humans while the rest of his group fed.

"All right," Bleeker said at last. "If you'd just place the used instruments in this pack, I'll take hair and blood samples, and we'll fade back into the forest to watch until she comes to and rejoins her family." The porter began to put the light away.

Already the female was twitching. Claudia gathered the dirty tools. Raindrops found their way down through the dense foliage and spattered their clothing.

"Uh..." Tommy's uneasy utterance was drowned by a roar.

Claudia and Bleeker whipped around. The silverback stood on his hind feet, stretching to full height, rolling his head back and forth and voicing his wrath.

"Oops, let's move!" Bleeker lifted the heavy equipment pack with seeming ease, tossed it to a porter, and then grabbed his instrument case. The tracker gestured frantically from the tree line.

Tommy didn't wait for them but scurried for safety with his camera. As Claudia rose, she spotted a package of dressings and a towel on the ground and hesitated.

"Dr. Bleeker."

"Leave it!"

The silverback's roar escalated and undulated with an accompanying loud thumping. She looked back. He pounded his chest and bellowed, staring into her eyes.

She looked again toward the former operating theater. The groggy female gorilla lifted one hand and scratched her side. Near her head lay Claudia's notebook.

Claudia gasped. She'd gotten so caught up in the surgery that she'd laid the notebook down and forgotten it. She couldn't leave her notes behind. Even if the gorillas didn't destroy them, the rain would. In a flash she considered the work it would take to reconstruct her notes, not just from today, but also yesterday's session at the veterinary clinic in Bwindi.

The injured gorilla still lay prone, though she was stirring. The huge male had approached the female but was now turned toward the more distant members of his group and challenged them with his shouts. The others hopped about, chattering and feigning runs toward him and back.

Claudia sprang forward and lunged for the notebook. She had it in her grasp when the silverback swiped at her over the body of the female with his long arm. Claudia flew backward from the blow and sprawled in the brush. Her breath whooshed out of her lungs.

Dr. Bleeker and the others jumped out from the tree line, screaming and waving their arms. The tracker shouldered the tranquilizer gun.

"Hold off!" Bleeker seized Claudia's hands and pulled her to her feet. "Are you all right?"

She gulped in a deep breath. "I think so."

He grabbed her wrist and yanked her toward the trees. When they'd gone several yards into the forest, they stopped and looked back. The porters and the tracker came flitting between the tree trunks. Claudia leaned against the bole of large mulberry, panting and clutching her notebook to her chest. Tommy approached them from one side, roughly where they'd left him. He hadn't run forward with the others to scare off the silverback. That figured.

Now they could barely see the big gorilla, still posturing, but only yipping and barking.

"Sorry. That's the only warning we'd have gotten, I'm afraid," Bleeker said. "Are you sure you're all right?"

She wiped the perspiration from her forehead. "I'm fine."

"Where did he hit you?"

She put her hand to her shoulder.

"Sore?"

"Kind of. I'll probably have a bruise."

"Consider yourself lucky it's not worse. If they move away later, we'll go back and retrieve those other things. I don't like to leave any supplies or trash lying about. But it's better than sustaining a casualty."

Tommy gulped. "I *told* you he looked mad."

"We're safe here," the tracker said.

Bleeker nodded. "Everyone, just relax and drink some water. In a few minutes I'll go forward and see if the female has regained consciousness."

"Did you get all your samples?" Claudia asked.

"Yes. I'd have liked to observe the group a little longer and collect more data on their health status, but we accomplished what we mainly came for."

Raindrops pattered down through the foliage. Claudia slid her notebook into a plastic bag, tucked it into her backpack, and zipped her sweatshirt to her throat. She huddled in the shelter of the mulberry, thankful that no one spoke of her reckless act. They sat in the shadows for fifteen minutes, talking in low tones and slapping at bugs. The falling water increased, proving it was rain, not condensation from the trees. Claudia put her hood up, but then she broke out in perspiration. She lowered it again and let the light rain soak her hair. The veterinarian left them and crept toward the gorillas again to observe the patient from a distance. Claudia looked at her watch. The afternoon was waning.

"How long will it take us to hike out?" she asked the tracker.

He grinned. "Not so long as coming in. Maybe three hours."

She nodded. Already she was bone tired, but she felt good.

Tommy opened his pack and pulled out a granola bar.

The tracker held out his hand and shook his head. "Do not eat so near the animals. It is not permitted."

Tommy sighed and dropped the granola bar back into his pack.

"Can I turn on my phone now?" Claudia asked. *Global Impact* magazine provided her with a pricey, high-end satellite phone that enabled her to check in with her editor from even the most remote assignments.

The tracker shrugged. "You must be quiet. But I don't think you can get good service here anyway."

She smiled and dug out the device. "How about if I just check my text messages? That won't make any noise." Not that she was eager to contact her irksome boss, Russell Talbot, but she felt a little cut off from her usual bustling, high-tech world. She'd had the phone off for hours while immersed in the gorillas' world.

She zipped down the line of unread messages.

Russell. *We need you back by Wed.*

Mya, her assistant at the magazine's Atlanta office. *R. T. fuming over early deadline. Call if U can.*

Her sister Lisa, from home in Maine. *R U OK? U take 2 many risks.*

Russell again. *You can't chase apes forever.*

Pierre Belanger, her brother-in-law, from the Navy base in Virginia. Claudia's pulse thudded even faster than it had when the silverback roared. Pierre never called or texted her. That was her sister Marie's province. What was wrong? She quickly opened it.

It's a boy. Marie doing GR8.

Claudia pumped her fist and gave a silent cheer.

"What's up?" Tommy asked.

She glared at him. He was surreptitiously eating that granola bar.

"I'm an aunt. Do we have all the photos we need?"

He swallowed. "Hey, we almost got killed, but I have excellent photos. Everything from the droopy patient to Furious George."

Claudia smiled. "Terrific. I'm going home to see my nephew."

TWO

1900 HOURS, MARCH 7
NEAR ALGIERS, ALGERIA

Lieutenant Bill White took the cleanup spot. He hunched in the shadows at the end of the dock as the men of his unit dashed past him and leaped into the boat. As the last two in line—Lieutenant Junior Grade Heidi Taber and the commander—passed him, a burst of gunfire came from the trees seventy-five yards away.

Bill let loose with his M16 assault rifle as he ran backward along the dock and then hopped over the rail into the boat, just as Stu cast off and Brownie gunned the engine to full throttle. All but Brownie, at the helm, huddled on the deck against the bulwarks and listened for the popping of more small weapons fire over the roar of the motor. Ten seconds later a huge *crump* and a glow in the sky behind them told them their op was successfully completed, and they all relaxed.

When they were a mile off the Algerian shore with no sign of pursuit, they began to talk softly and soon broke out in laughter over their narrow escape.

Three hours later they rendezvoused with a Navy ship. Before they dispersed to quarters, Commander Dryden gathered them all in a closed room for debriefing. "Good job. Things went pretty much as we planned, except for that last little skirmish at the beach. What do you say, White?"

Bill cleared his throat. He was dog tired, but that was nothing new. "I say we accomplished our mission without any slipups. The undercover man was repositioned as planned, and we can't be connected to his reappearance in Algiers. It would have been better if we could have gotten out without being spotted, but they have no idea who we are or what we were doing there. Other than blowing up their munitions dump, of course."

Dryden pursed his lips and nodded, focusing on the far wall. "Next time we'll do better." He clapped Stu, the petty officer in charge of communications, on the shoulder. "Good work, Stuart. We had good contact all the time we were out. Taber, excellent job on reconnaissance. The drop point was exactly where you said it would be." He spoke to each member of the unit in turn, picking out some aspect of the mission they had performed well. "That's all. Turn in. And those who want to take part in Lieutenant White's charity op in Mali, we'll see you off at 0800 hours."

Bill nodded and rose. The commander allowed him and some others from the unit to carry out humanitarian acts between their demanding secret missions. For the next two weeks, he would be building a new wing on a school building near Bamako with Stu, Brownie, Taber, and Squeegee. The others would probably go home to their families or take R & R at some resort. Then they would meet again at their home base and prepare for the next op.

His smaller group within the military unit received no recognition for the hard work they put in unpaid during their leave time—even less than they received for their official, but unsung, duties. Bill liked it that way. It didn't matter if no one else on this earth knew how William Oliver White Jr. spent his off-duty time. He and God knew.

As he followed the others to their quarters, he felt only a fleeting desire to head for home. But home didn't exist anymore. His parents were both gone now, and his brother, Ben, was somewhere on the other side of the international date line on another ship, heading into a different situation. All he could do was pray for Ben and hope they'd meet up again sometime this year. Home was an elusive concept, a distant aspiration. Maybe someday he'd learn how to build a new home, form a family of his own. For now this unit was his family.

Heidi Taber slipped off down a different passageway toward another section of the ship's quarters. Her feet dragged, and her helmet hung from loose fingers, almost scraping the deck.

"Sleep tight, Taber," Stu called after her.

She lifted her free hand in a halfhearted wave without turning around.

We're all exhausted, Bill thought. But that was normal, after a tense operation. Give him a week or two working on the school building, and he'd be fit and refreshed, ready for a new assignment. He crawled into his bunk knowing he would be asleep within seconds. *Thank you, Lord, for getting us all out safe.*

THREE

Claudia rang the doorbell and looked around while waiting impatiently on the steps. Base housing. Oh well, Marie and Pierre had given it their own flair. The small flower beds on each side of the stoop looked well cared for. Probably by summer they'd be bursting with colorful blooms. Beside the door hung a slate, hand-painted with a spray of wild blueberries. Marie's handiwork. Attaching it solidly to the siding so no one could steal it was Pierre's contribution, Claudia was sure.

The door swung open, and Pierre greeted her with a laugh and feigned shock. "Well, well! Look who finally decided to show up. We'd about given up on you."

Nostalgia deluged Claudia, and she threw herself into her brother-in-law's arms. "Can it, Pierre. I came as fast as I could. My editor had a new assignment lined up for me before I even got back from Uganda, and I had to write up and edit my gorilla story." She stood on tiptoe to kiss his cheek. "Now, where's my nephew?"

Pierre returned her hug. "At the moment, he's sleeping. But if you don't lower your voice, I'm sure he'll be awake and reporting for duty any second."

"Oh, sorry." She dropped her voice to a stage whisper and scrunched her shoulders in imitation of a turtle retreating into his shell. "No one told me nap time was at 1400 hours."

He laughed and led her into the living room. "Nap time is whenever the skipper says it is."

"The skipper? You mean Edward Georges Belanger? Is that what you call him?"

"Oh, yeah. He's the one giving orders around here. A week old, and he's calling all the shots." Pierre ran a hand through his dark hair, and Claudia noticed the dark circles beneath his eyes.

"Why didn't you just name him Admiral?"

"Ha! I'm telling you, I love him to pieces, but he's way too independent."

Marie came from the hallway, her brown eyes gleaming. "Claudia! It's so good to see you!"

More hugs, this time gentler. Claudia found her eyes misting. "So, you're okay?" She and Marie settled on the brown plush sofa.

"I feel good. If I can just lose the twelve pounds that appeared when I wasn't looking, I'll be great."

Claudia sat back and eyed her critically. "You look terrific."

"Well, thanks. And Skipper's already gaining weight."

"A real bruiser, eh? You said he was more than eight pounds when he was born."

"Oh, yeah," Pierre chimed in. "This guy doesn't do anything by halves. Eating, crying, diapers…"

She laughed. "I can't wait to get my hands on him."

"Where's your luggage?" Marie looked toward the door.

"Still in the rental car."

"I'll get it." Pierre stood, and Claudia tossed him her keys.

"Thanks. It's in the trunk. A duffel and a laptop."

"Aye, aye, ma'am." He went out whistling.

Marie flipped the footrest up on her end of the couch and leaned back into the cushions. "So tell me about the gorillas. Was it scary?"

"Only for a few minutes. We hiked for hours, tracking them. When we finally caught up with them, it was pretty intense. But you can read all about that in the magazine next month. Tell me about Skipper. I want to know everything!"

"Here." Her sister leaned toward the end table and picked up a digital camera. "Pierre's been snapping pictures all week. He got some really cute ones when I was giving the baby his bath yesterday."

Claudia found the control for the slide show feature and laughed aloud. "Oh, precious!" The snapshots kept her riveted to the tiny screen. "What a gorgeous kid. But then, look at his parents."

"Yeah, yeah." Marie smiled and watched her sister's expressions as she viewed the pictures.

"Awww!" Claudia looked at her and sighed. "I want one."

"Well...you know it takes two."

"Oh, yeah. Well, someday." The inkling that she was missing something of infinite value teased at her subconscious. She was still flipping through the shots when Pierre came in with her luggage.

"I'll put these in your room." He headed for the hallway.

"Tell me when you want to freshen up, and I'll show you where," Marie said.

"Am I sharing with the baby?"

"No, he's in a bassinet in our room for the time being. We'll move him into the other room when he stops getting up to nurse seventeen times a night."

Claudia clicked through a few photos quickly. "Guess I'm back to the beginning. You've got some great shots there."

"I'm going to have a few made for Mom and Dad," Marie said. "Pierre's going to show me how to download them onto the computer too, so I can send them to the whole family."

"That should be simple." Claudia set the camera on the coffee table. "I can show you, if he doesn't have time."

"Great. Maybe when Pierre goes to the office tomorrow?"

"Sure." Claudia leaned toward her and stage-whispered, "Does he really work at a desk now? I can't believe he's given up secret missions and all that cool stuff he used to do."

Marie's smile froze, and she hesitated a fraction of a second too long.

"I knew it! He's still in special ops, isn't he?" Claudia jumped and wiggled in triumph. "I want to write a profile of him."

"Oh, no, you can't do that." Marie's brown eyes darkened in dismay. "And he's not in special forces. Not exactly. He's a training officer now."

"Oh, got it. He's training other guys to do secret missions. I love it!"

"No, Claudia." Marie frowned and laid a hand on her arm. "Please don't ask Pierre to let you write about him. He would hate that. I'm serious. And his boss would say no anyway. So would *his* boss and *his* boss."

Claudia scrunched up her face. "Phooey. You're such a killjoy!"

"I'm glad you're staying a whole week," Marie said.

"Changing the subject, aren't you?"

"Well, yeah. We're not going back there. I mean it."

"Okay, I give up. For now. What are our plans? Besides lots of baby time?"

"Let's see, I can take you shopping at the PX, and there's a concert on the base Friday night..."

Claudia wrinkled her nose.

"Just kidding. There's a fantastic mall ten minutes away, and we're having some friends over tomorrow night."

"Are you up to it?"

Marie's eyes widened. "I am very up to it. Pierre has a long weekend too. It's been ages since he had a day off, so we're going to the beach. I *love* Virginia. The beach in March."

"Wow, I'll bet they're still shoveling snow back home."

"Yeah. I talked to Mom yesterday, and it was about twenty degrees."

Claudia shivered. "New York was bad enough, thank you."

Pierre came from the hallway just then, with a fuzzy, blanketed bundle nestled against his shoulder. "Look what I found."

"Did you wake him up?" Marie asked in an accusing tone.

"No! I just peeked in at him, and he peeked back. He was kind of babbling to himself, just lying there, looking up at the mobile."

Claudia jumped up. "Oh, let me see him. Gimme, gimme!"

Pierre laughed and laid the warm bundle in her arms. She stared down into a pert little face. Dark blue eyes stared up at her.

"Hey, Skipper!" Pierre bent over his son. "That's your Aunt Claudia, but you can call her Clod."

"Ha! Don't you dare, you precious little chunk. You could become my sole heir, you know." She lifted him up and ran her lips lightly over his fuzzy hair. He smelled deliciously warm, a little like soap and milk. "Ohhh! What a darling." The baby blinked at her and flexed his tiny fingers. Claudia knew she was fully and irrevocably in love.

FOUR

Bill hopped out of the Jeep and walked swiftly up the path to Lieutenant Belanger's house. He hated disturbing him during his time off, but orders were orders.

A snazzy red coupe with rental plates sat in the driveway. The lieutenant and his wife must have company. Bill was a little disappointed. He'd hoped to spend a few minutes talking to Belanger. They'd worked together a few times—Pierre helped ready Bill's unit for fieldwork. They'd discovered a common interest in fishing and had become casual friends. But the bond of faith had drawn them to each other even more strongly; they attended the same church when they were in their home port.

He rang the bell, and a stunning woman opened the door. She had the rich, dark brown hair that Pierre's wife Marie had and eyes the color of strong coffee. She was taller than Marie and looked older. More sophisticated somehow, though she wore jeans and a simple pullover.

"Hi. I'm Lieutenant White, and I have some papers for Lieutenant Belanger."

She smiled. "Sure. Would you like to come in?"

He stepped inside. Marie came to the kitchen doorway. "Oh, hi, Bill! I didn't know you were around." She turned and called over her shoulder, "Honey, it's Bill White." When she looked back at Bill, her expression turned cautious. "This doesn't mean you're taking him away, does it? He's off duty today."

"No, I don't think so. I'm just a courier tonight." Bill smiled in an attempt to reassure her. "I understand you have a new little one since the last time I was here."

Pierre appeared behind Marie and grinned at him over her shoulder. "We sure do. Hi, Bill." Marie stepped aside, and Pierre walked toward Bill, his hand extended. "Want to see the little guy?"

"Sure. And congratulations."

He'd lost track of the other woman for a moment, and from somewhere she produced an infant. Bill looked down at the mewling little fellow. The baby's face was scarlet as he turned his head back and forth and let out a caterwaul. The woman guided a tiny fist toward his mouth, and the baby slurped it. Bill laughed.

"He's hungry, I'm afraid." Marie reached for her son and held him up against her shoulder, bouncing him gently. "Bill, this is my sister, Claudia Gillette. She's been visiting us this week and getting to know Skipper."

"Pleased to meet you." She held out her hand, and he took it, noticing how soft her skin was. Her scarlet nails were trimmed quite short, though, and he wondered if she did a lot of typing.

The two women made a striking pair. Marie was always attractive, with her slightly exotic bobby-soxer air, but she looked tired tonight. Her rumpled jeans and T-shirt, with stocking feet and a ponytail, added to the juvenile aura.

On the other hand, Claudia's heeled clogs complimented her designer jeans, and her hair was expertly styled. She wore makeup too, though he hadn't noticed before. Just a hint of glimmer on her eyelids, and long lashes, thicker than nature would bestow. She could have stepped from the pages of a casual—but expensive—women's wear catalog.

"If you'll excuse me, I'm going to feed Skipper." Marie headed through the living room. "Make yourself at home, Bill. Pierre, get him something to drink."

Pierre grinned and gave a shrug. "So...iced tea? I think there's some soda in the fridge."

"Uh, well..." Bill stole another glance at Claudia and decided he definitely wanted to stick around for a while. "Sure. If it's no trouble."

"Not a bit." Pierre led him into the small kitchen. "If you're not in a hurry, you can sit down and tell me about your last operation. I heard it went like clockwork." He called over his shoulder, "Hey, Claudia, you want something?"

She hesitated in the doorway. "Sure, if this isn't a top secret meeting."

Bill and Pierre looked at each other and laughed.

"She thinks I'm a spy," Pierre said in a confidential tone.

"No, merely a secret agent." Bill winked at her, and she smiled and shrugged.

She accepted a cold can of diet cola from Pierre. Bill chose a glass of iced tea, and soon all three were sitting in the living room. Claudia kicked her shoes off and curled her long legs under her in an armchair. Bill had to tear his gaze away and remind himself not to stare. Although she didn't seem to mind. He had a feeling she was sizing him up from beneath those mile-long eyelashes, and he was glad he was in uniform.

Pierre stretched out his legs and sipped his tea. "So, the commander said you took a leave in Mali after your op. Get a lot done there?"

Bill couldn't help grinning. He loved talking about his humanitarian projects with the few people who knew about them.

"Yeah, it was great. We built a whole wing on the school in Bamako. Four new classrooms and a multipurpose room. The kids were so excited. It was fantastic." He looked over at Claudia, and she seemed interested. "You know, people here take everything for granted, but not in Africa. Those people...the teachers, the parents, the kids...everyone was so thankful. And they have next to nothing, but they would bring us gifts. Little pieces of food. Meat roasted on a skewer or a handful of nuts."

"Wow, that's great," Claudia murmured.

"One of the women brought Heidi a head scarf. You should have seen her face when Heidi put it on. She was so happy and honored. Heidi let her show her how to tie it right, and that woman acted like the queen had just kissed her."

"Who's Heidi?" Claudia asked.

"Oh, she's…one of the people who was on the project." That sounded evasive, even to him. He didn't want Claudia to think he was in love with Heidi or anything, but he had to be careful how much he spilled about his unit.

Pierre said, "Bill and several people he works with do these projects whenever they get a chance. They call it 'leave,' but it's hard work. Right, buddy?"

"Absolutely, but it's worth it."

"How many of you went there?" Claudia asked.

"Five of us, and there were two missionaries nearby who helped us, and several local men. One of the missionaries set it up for us."

"You know, Claudia just came back from Uganda," Pierre said. "You two must have been in Africa at the same time."

"Really?" That surprised Bill. He'd been back all of eighteen hours, and the first civilian he met had been in Africa too. "What were you doing there?"

"She was tracking gorillas, if you can believe that." Pierre shook his head. "Claudia does all kinds of crazy things."

"Gorillas?" Bill was hooked now. He loved animals but hadn't had a pet since he was a kid, and turtles didn't count for much. Gorilla tracking sounded like a dream vacation. "Were you working on a scientific project, or did you go as a tourist?"

"Neither. I'm a journalist."

He nodded, fitting that into his first impressions of Claudia. Gorgeous. Smart. Now he added athletic, savvy, and cultured to the list. Probably independent as all get out. "That's great." In spite of the caution flags his brain waved at him, he found himself leaning eagerly toward her, wanting to know more. "Broadcasting or print?"

"Print. I write for *Global Impact* magazine."

He whistled. "Impressive."

"Thanks."

"So, what's the article about? Gorillas, I guess, huh?" That sounded stupid, but she didn't sneer at him.

"Actually, I was shadowing Dr. Ian Bleeker who is with the Mountain Gorilla Veterinary Project."

"I think I've heard of that."

"It's a group that monitors the health of mountain gorillas and gives them medical care in the wild when it's needed. They also do research with as little intervention as possible."

"And you got to go with them into the jungle?"

"Yeah, it was great." Claudia's face lit up, and he could see that her enthusiasm extended to the subject, not just the job of writing about it. "One of the guides for a tourism outfit had spotted a female gorilla that had gotten into a snare."

"People still trap gorillas?"

"Poachers go after them in the reserve—smaller game too. This gorilla had stepped into the snare, and the wire had bitten into her foot. She seemed to be in a lot of pain—limping, not eating like she should, fussing over the wound. The guide reported it, and Dr. Bleeker made arrangements to try to locate the animal and perform surgery to remove the wire."

Bill blinked. "Huh. Operating on her in the jungle? I mean, they didn't bring her out, did they?"

"No, we carried all the medical equipment—instruments, lights, dressings, all that—into the reserve and up a volcano. It took us half a day to get up there and find the gorilla group. Then he did the surgery. As soon as she was awake and on her feet again, we left, but it was after dark when we got back to civilization. One of those jobs you were talking about—exhausting, but definitely worthwhile."

"What was it like up there?" Bill asked.

She thought about that for a moment. "It was a different universe. So remote. So untouched. More than a mile above sea level. I was feeling the altitude a little. Damp and chilly, but the forest is unique. Lots of flora that doesn't grow anywhere else, and our guide pointed out several rare species. The Africans are serious about keeping the habitat intact. Only a few people get to visit the gorillas, and you can't go if you're sick. I felt…privileged."

He nodded.

"She took a photographer with her," Pierre said. Bill had almost forgotten his friend was in the room, he'd been so absorbed in Claudia's narrative. "The guy took some super pictures to go with Claud's article."

"Yes, although Tommy doesn't deal well with high altitude and wildlife. But he's given me a lot of prints of the pictures he took. It was an unforgettable experience." She smiled, perhaps remembering something she hadn't shared. "The mountain gorillas are so intelligent."

"I'll bet. I've read a little bit about them." Bill sat back in his chair, watching her. "I've been a lot of places and seen a lot of sights. But that sounds like something really special."

She nodded and tipped her soda can up.

Marie glided back into the room and sat down on the sofa between Pierre and Bill.

"So, did you guys talk Navy talk yet?"

"Oh, no, we haven't," Pierre said. "What have you got for me, Bill?"

"Instructions for what our unit needs from you. I think we're going to spend some time with you next week." Bill reached for the folder he'd brought and handed it to Pierre. "I was going to apologize for bothering you at home, but I'm glad I came tonight." He shot a glance at Claudia. "And, of course, the commander ordered me to."

Pierre chuckled as he opened the folder. "Right." He glanced at the papers inside, then closed it. "Want a refill on that tea?"

Bill took that to mean Pierre wanted a private word with him about the unit's next assignment, so he picked up his empty glass and followed Pierre to the kitchen.

"Looks like more of the same-old and a few new skills you guys will need," Pierre said. "Help yourself to more tea."

"No, thanks. Always furthering our education," Bill said lightly.

Pierre frowned over the printed orders and flipped through a couple of loose pages. "This wasn't sealed. I assume you know where you're going."

Bill nodded. "We seem to be spending a lot of time across the Atlantic this year."

"Well, keep your head down. That's a hot spot they're putting you in."

"That's why we're going, right? They need us to help cool it off a little."

"Okay. We've got some new eavesdropping equipment you guys need to train on. I think you'll like it. And I'll bring in the chief of your delivery unit the first day to nail down your transport."

"Sounds good."

"How long since you guys had a refresher on resistance to interrogation?"

"We're not going to get caught."

"I know. But that's something you need to be prepared for. Always."

Bill eyed him pensively. "Maybe I shouldn't mention it, but there's a rumor in my unit that we might go to the Philippines before long. Not this trip, but after."

"Nothing I can tell you." Pierre's features remained neutral.

"But you know about that scientist who was kidnapped outside Manila?"

"Of course."

"It's the type of thing we're best at. I mean, we *are* the best. We want to help."

Pierre laid a hand on Bill's shoulder. "Don't worry. A lot of people are looking into it. You're right that it's important—not just the research Dr. Gamata was doing, but we don't want to lose his family."

"But the Abu Sayyaf snatched him. If we could go in with a strong enough force, we could clean them out."

"And maybe lose the Gamata family. The Philippine government wants to try to recover them on their own. If they fail, they'll be happy to accept any assistance we can give, but we have to give them first crack at it. Trust me. As soon as we get the word they want us involved, we'll hammer out a plan."

Bill nodded. He'd have to live with that for now, but the minute he'd heard the news report about the aerophysicist's abduction, he'd had a feeling his future and Dr. Gamata's would intersect. The United States and its allies would suffer if Gamata was put to work for the wrong side. Bill prayed that God would deliver the man, his wife, and his son from the radical Muslim insurgents who kept the rural areas of the Philippine islands in terror.

"Besides, we're not even sure it was the Abu Sayyaf," Pierre said. "They haven't claimed responsibility."

Bill eyed him carefully. So his chain of command was watching the situation closely. That made him hopeful that his unit would sooner or later get into it.

"Right. Could be the Moro National Liberation Front. They use any tactics they can to promote their cause too." The radical group had fought for years toward the formation of an independent Muslim nation in the southern part of the Philippines. Bill found the prospect of seeing one of America's allies torn apart a little scary. He wanted to get in there and help. But until they knew the Gamatas were alive and where they were held, and until the Philippine government officially invited them in, American special forces could do nothing.

A few minutes later, he and Pierre rejoined Claudia and Marie. Bill wondered if he should make his excuses and leave, but Claudia spoke to him, and her smile was well nigh irresistible.

"And what do you do, besides build schools in third world countries?"

Bill sat down in the chair on the other side of the sofa. Her

mesmerizing brown eyes were fixed on him, and he swallowed. "Uh…
I'm a lieutenant, and I'm second in command in my unit."

"Which does what specifically?"

"Uh…" Bill shot a glance at Pierre. "I'm not at liberty to say,
ma'am."

She smiled.

"He's a man of many talents," Pierre said. "You know…commu-
nications, logistics…"

"So, Bill, are you coming to church tomorrow?" Marie asked with
a bright smile. "I'm trying to convince Claudia to go with us—"

"It's my last day here," Claudia said. "Can't we just snuggle the
little skipper and laze around?"

"Our friends at church are dying to see him," Marie said.

"Oh, yeah, we've got to take the little guy." Pierre's glowing face
left no doubt.

"I'll be there," Bill said.

Claudia opened her mouth and then closed it.

"So will you come, Claudia?" he dared to ask.

"I might."

FIVE

Bill had been gone only a few minutes when the phone rang. Marie answered it and at once squealed with excitement.

"Claudia, it's Lisa! Quick! Go pick up the other phone."

Claudia rushed to the kitchen and picked up the receiver. Less than a year had passed since the three sisters had been together, but it seemed like forever.

"I'm so glad I caught you," Lisa cried. "Mom said you're leaving soon."

"Yeah, I'm flying out tomorrow night," Claudia said.

"Where are you headed?"

"A quick stop in Atlanta and then off to cover a hot story in Norway."

"Norway?" Lisa's voice curdled. "I'm so jealous."

Claudia chuckled. "I'll send you a postcard."

"How's the skipper?" Lisa asked.

"He's great," Marie told her. "His daddy's holding him right now. Pierre is trying to keep him awake for a while, so he'll sleep longer tonight."

"You guys must be exhausted."

"Kind of."

"Well, listen…" Lisa paused, and Claudia knew something important was coming.

"What? Spit it out."

"André is here with me."

"Oooh," said Marie. "Does he want to talk to Pierre?" André was one of Pierre's four younger brothers, and he had begun spending a disproportionate amount of his spare time with Lisa the summer before.

"No. Not yet. Maybe after a while."

"So what are you guys up to?" Marie demanded.

Claudia grinned, though she couldn't see either one of her sisters.

"Not much. Just getting married."

Marie's ear-splitting scream temporarily deafened Claudia. She yanked the phone away too late. After rubbing her ear and waiting until she could hear Marie's excited voice from the living room without benefit of the telephone, she cautiously put the receiver back to her ear.

"When?" Marie demanded.

"We haven't set a date yet."

"We'll need to know as soon as possible so Pierre can arrange leave."

"All right. As soon as André figures out his vacation schedule, we'll let you know. He has to work it so that the post office is covered while everyone else has vacation too, and…"

Claudia could almost see the gleam in Lisa's toffee-colored eyes. She was happy for her sister. Lisa had always been considered the awkward one. She definitely fell heir to "middle child syndrome." Always doubting herself, always sure no one liked her. The fact that she wasn't conventionally pretty hadn't helped. While Claudia could objectively state that Lisa's features were less appealing than gorgeous Marie's or even her own, Lisa was smart and loads of fun. And apparently she'd become a good electrician and businesswoman—her company was thriving.

But let's face it, Claudia thought, *her chin is too long, and her eyes are too far apart, and her skin never was that great*. But André didn't seem to mind. There was some satisfaction in that—a discerning man had seen the gem beneath the plain exterior. At the same time, it made Claudia feel a little glum and…well, left out.

They'd all known Marie would get married first, although she was the youngest. Pierre had staked his territory early. And that was fine. Everyone loved Pierre, and he took good care of Marie. But now Lisa was getting married too. She was in love, as head-over-heels crazy about unassuming André as Marie was about Pierre. She'd have a cozy home in Maine and raise brilliant but homely children who would probably wind up on the U.S. Ski Team or invent a better lightbulb or…

"So will you, Claudia?"

She jerked back to the present at the sound of her name. "Huh? I'm sorry. What were you saying?"

"I said, will you be my maid of honor?"

Tears pooled in Claudia's eyes and spilled over, dripping onto the scarred gray-green countertop. Cheap base housing. She sniffed. "Of course I will, honey."

"Great! We'll try to let you know the date as soon as we can."

"Hey," Claudia said, "don't you worry about that. I will be there, no matter when you have the wedding. That's a promise. No matter what Russell Talbot tries to schedule for me, I will be in Waterville, Maine, on your wedding day. You can take that to the bank."

"Thanks, Claud. I love you."

That did it. "Love you too." She lunged for the tissue box in the corner, where the counter met the wall.

"So what color dresses are you thinking of for us?" The lilt in Marie's voice said she was ecstatic. *So am I,* Claudia thought. *Only I show it in different ways.* She laid the receiver down while she blew her nose.

When she picked it up again, Marie was saying, "…and we're taking him to church for the first time tomorrow. I'm going to feed him right before we leave, so he won't cry. I don't think I could bear to put him in the nursery yet."

Claudia blinked away more tears. Why was she getting all sentimental over weddings and babies? *I like my life. It's exactly the way I dreamed about it, all those years ago when I chafed to get away from Maine and earn my way into a more exciting world. I'm right where I wanted to be at age twenty-seven. Exactly on target. Bull's-eye.*

A sound began as a tiny whimper over the phone, but escalated into a wail, and she realized Skipper was crying. Pierre's voice came, hopeful but willing to tough it out, "Chérie, I think he needs a new diaper."

Marie laughed and excused herself and went off to change the baby so her husband wouldn't have to change two wet diapers in a row. Then Pierre came on the line with delighted congratulations, and Lisa passed her phone to André. Claudia hung up and leaned against the counter, staring across at the crack in the sheetrock on the opposite wall, beside the refrigerator. Marie had unsuccessfully tried to cover it with a calendar.

Crummy base housing.

SIX

Pierre watched Bill and Claudia with amusement on Sunday. Circling and sniffing like a couple of stray cats who'd met up in an alley. With Claudia you could never tell if she'd start purring or spitting. But she'd been quite docile all week and seemed to truly dote on the baby. Where Bill was concerned, Pierre was betting she'd purr. Which might not be so great for old Bill.

At the moment Claudia was cuddling Skipper, and Bill was watching with the eyes of a jealous man. Pierre wandered out to the kitchen, where Marie was putting frozen pizza into the oven.

"Need any help?"

"Thanks, honey. You can get the silverware out if you want. Claudia offered, but I told her I could manage. It's her last day, and I hated to tear her away from the baby."

"And Bill."

"Well, yeah." Marie grinned at him. "Cute couple, hey?"

Pierre frowned as he counted out the forks. "You know, Claudia doesn't believe in..." He turned to face her. "She's not saved."

Marie's face fell. "You're right. I guess I've avoided thinking about that. I love Claudia."

"Of course."

"And Bill's a great guy."

"Yeah, he is. So...maybe we're not doing him any favors by

35

throwing him together with Claudia. No offense intended." He studied her face carefully, hoping he hadn't said too much.

"You're right." Marie sighed and opened the refrigerator. "I tried to talk to her a couple of times this week, but she's not interested in God. She thinks she's got her life all mapped out and nothing can stop her."

Pierre slipped his arms around her and turned her toward him. "Makes me glad I'm not still dating."

"Yeah. It's too hard." Marie leaned against him for a moment and then pushed away. "I'll make the salad, and we're ready."

"Okay. I'll tell them." He walked to the doorway and saw Bill and Claudia sitting on the couch. Bill was leaning over very close to Claudia, peering down at the baby. Both cooed and googooed at Skipper, trying to keep his attention. For just a second, Pierre wanted them to fall in love. Claudia was lonely. She wouldn't admit it, but she had the classic signs. Bouts of depression and self-doubts. A too vehement denial that she was missing out on anything.

And Bill? Great guy but at loose ends. He rattled around the globe completing his ops and finding more work to do to fill the lonely leave time. Every time he visited, Pierre sensed his deep longing for a place where he belonged. Guys in that stage were prone to latch on to the first woman willing to go to the altar.

"So why won't you let me interview you?" Claudia asked, shooting a sidelong glance at Bill.

He sat up straighter. "Well, I can't just talk about my work, you know. My CO would have to approve it. But he wouldn't. We don't do media ops."

"Ever?"

Bill shrugged. "Once in a while we get filmed while we're training or something. But not often. Security, you know?"

"I'd think it would be good PR for the military. It would give civilians a better understanding of what you do and why you're needed."

"Well, that's a good thought, but I just can't do it."

"Hmmm. We'll see."

Pierre wondered what she meant by that. She probably saw Bill's refusal as a temporary setback. She was ambitious, and he knew that. She'd landed interviews Barbara Walters would have killed for. She'd won several prestigious awards in the last two years, and when she went home to Maine, she got celebrity treatment.

Yes, there were lots of reasons for Bill to stay away from her.

All he had to do was keep a damper on things until she left for the airport tonight. Tomorrow he and Bill would go back to work. Pierre's job entailed making sure the elite force was ready for the next harrowing operation, which was coming up all too soon.

Claudia nuzzled the baby. "I don't know how I'm going to get along without this little guy."

"He's a keeper, all right." Bill's voice was husky, and his eyes softened as he watched her.

Pierre stepped forward. "Hey, you two, lunch is almost ready. How's Skipper doing?"

"He's fine. Wide awake." Claudia smiled at Pierre. "I suppose you want to hold him again."

"Well, I've got to stock up on baby hugs. I go back on duty tomorrow."

"Yeah, but what about me? I fly out of here in—" Claudia glanced at her watch. "Five lousy hours." Her lip curled. "Man, I hate to leave. This has been the best week I've had in a long time, Pierre. You guys have been great." She transferred Skipper into Pierre's arms.

Bill cleared his throat. "Say, Claudia, I could take you to the airport if you like. I'm not busy tonight, and it would give Pierre more time to be with Marie and Skipper."

No, Pierre thought. *No, no, no. Don't do that, Bill. You'll be sorry.*

Claudia's smile was one watt short of dazzling. "Why, thank you, Bill. That's awfully sweet of you, but I've got a rental car."

"Oh, right." Bill's face actually flushed. One of the toughest men in one of the world's most intrepid special forces, and he blushed.

Pierre sensed that it was a losing battle. Of course, the two were about to embark for destinations thousands of miles apart. If he could just keep Claudia from completely bowling Bill over in the next few hours, she'd be gone, and the poor sap would be safe.

"Say, you mentioned someone in your unit named Heidi," Claudia said as they walked to the kitchen.

"Uh…yeah." Bill looked at Pierre, as he had the first time Heidi Taber's name came up.

"She's a woman Bill works with," Pierre said.

"A woman in a special forces unit."

"I never said—"

"Oh, come on, Pierre. We've known for years that you were in special ops. It may be a secret, but it's no secret, if you know what I mean." She wiggled her eyebrows at Bill. "He almost got vaporized out in the Pacific right before he and Marie got married. Everybody knows about that now."

"What on earth…?" Marie stared at her sister. "Claudia…"

Her sister shrugged. "I'm not going to blab any government secrets. I was just thinking what a great article it would make to shadow a woman in special ops for a week or two. Show the world what American women are made of. What they're sacrificing for their country—for the rest of us."

"Well…" Bill looked helplessly at Pierre.

"No."

"Oh, come on." Claudia sat down and reached for a slice of pizza. "You know I'd be professional. And I can be discreet."

Pierre felt annoyance beginning to bubble in his stomach. He didn't want his dinner ruined, but he was starting to recall how obnoxious Claudia could be when she wouldn't let go of something. He shifted the baby in his arms and looked pointedly at Bill. "Would you please ask the blessing, Bill?"

SEVEN

Funny how Pierre's friend stuck around all afternoon, taking a turn bouncing the baby and swapping travel stories. Claudia had no doubt she was the cause of Bill White's persistence. She didn't mind. He'd shaped up to be an interesting diversion. Good looking in a clean-cut, all-American way. Short, sandy-colored hair, blue eyes, broad shoulders and muscles built the hard way. The uniform was a bonus. Oh, yeah. She wouldn't mind showing him off at an office party.

Beyond that, he kept her attention. He had an innate talent for connecting important bits of information. His probing questions about the gorilla medical project showed her that. She rarely met a man who had the combination she needed to hold her interest: smart, well spoken, concerned about conservation, and taller than she was. And he'd seen more foreign ports than she had. That was another anomaly—someone who could top her travel itinerary. Bill had some great stories about past jaunts to far-flung locations.

He occasionally clammed up, and she knew then that he was treading on the border of classified information. It only fueled her desire to write an article about his unit—whether featuring Bill himself, the entire outfit, or the shadowy figure of Heidi Taber, she wasn't sure.

She realized Heidi's story attracted her simply because Pierre and

Bill had said such a project was taboo. And Heidi probably was not glamorous. She was more likely to be dressed in mud-spattered camos than a designer gown. But Claudia loved that type of profile. Heidi had to be intelligent and quick-witted to be a part of this branch of the service. She must have passed grueling tests that would make gorilla tracking look like a picnic. And she had the same altruistic attitude Bill had. She must. She took part in his charitable activities. Just the kind of woman Pulitzer-prize-winning stories were made of.

While Claudia flirted with Bill, she let her subconscious percolate the idea of interviewing Heidi Taber. She had no doubt it would happen. The question was when. And how would she bring that about?

"What's the worst place you've ever been to?" she asked.

Bill rolled his eyes and pretended to ponder that. "You mean after Iraq, I assume. Afghanistan? No, Algeria. Wait, wait. I think maybe Somalia. Yeah, Somalia was bad. But I think the worst experience I ever had was in the Philippines."

She drew back, frowning over that. "The United States hasn't had a military presence in the Philippines for years."

"You're right," Pierre said, almost too quickly. "We don't. Just an advisory and supportive capacity."

"Oh, right." Claudia filed that away for future exploration and smiled at Bill. "So were you advising or supporting? Or did this escapade have to do with your...missionary endeavors?" His rapt attention to the sermon that morning had given her the idea that his benevolent projects had something to do with his religious beliefs.

"Well, this incident was part of an official assignment gone wrong. We, uh..." He glanced at Pierre, but Pierre only shrugged and looked away. "Some of us got stuck in the jungle in the pouring rain for three days with no food. It was the pits."

"But you're trained to survive anywhere," Claudia said, sensing that he was glossing over a much deeper story.

"We can. We do. See? I'm here, aren't I?" Bill laughed.

Claudia made a mental note to research America's current military role in the Philippines. There was a lot going on there…communists, she thought, and maybe Muslim nationalists too. In the back of her mind something about a terrorist training camp festered.

At three thirty Pierre reminded her that her departure time was near. Bill offered to carry her bags out to the car. Claudia could see that he was in the stage between initial attraction and blind adoration, thinking everything about her must be as wonderful as the small part she'd let him see so far. She smiled and thanked him profusely. When she gave him her key ring, she wrapped her fingers around his hand and gave it a squeeze.

"Thanks, Bill. I'm really glad we met."

"Me too." He gazed down at her with a smile of wonder for a full five seconds, then jumped as if recalling where he was and hurried out with her laptop and duffel bag.

Pierre was on his feet in an instant. "Claudia, if you interfere with Bill's unit, I will call down the wrath of the Pentagon on you and your magazine."

She whirled and gaped at him, with what she hoped was an innocent stare. "Interfere? Pierre, I like him. Is that a criminal offense? The last thing I'd want to do would be to interfere with the business of a military force that is protecting our nation."

Pierre's hot brown eyes wavered. "Yeah, well, you've got him wrapped around your pinky. I can see that. Don't you dare ask him for any professional favors. I mean it."

"That's a low blow. You think I'd start a relationship with a man to get a story?"

Pierre said nothing, but with clenched jaw, he held her gaze.

Marie stood and passed Skipper to Claudia. "Hey, come on, you two. Nobody's doing anything out of line here, and nobody's going to. Are they, Claud?"

"Absolutely not." She smiled down at her nephew, who slumbered peacefully in her arms. Marie would rake Pierre over the coals after she left, she was certain, for accusing her sister of being unscrupulous. Let it be that way—Marie would make him feel a little guilty, and then they'd make up. Claudia would leave on a friendly note. She'd stay out of Pierre's hair for a while, and he'd forget about it. She had other ideas of how to get the story she wanted, and she would bypass Pierre completely.

Bill came in and handed her the car keys. "I think you're all set. You know how to get back to the airport, right?"

"Yes, thanks." She snuggled the baby and kissed his velvet-soft cheek. "Goodbye, little love. I'll come see you again soon." She handed him back to Pierre and stood on tiptoe to kiss his cheek.

Pierre returned the kiss and smiled sheepishly. "Come anytime you can, Claudia."

"Thanks." She embraced Marie for a long moment. The latent longings for all her sister enjoyed hit her again, and tears gushed into her eyes. She blinked them away. "'Bye, sweetie. You're a wonderful mother. Take care of your two guys."

"I will. I love you, Claud."

She pulled away and nodded, trying not to sniff. Nope, she was beyond the point of no return. The tissue box on the end table beckoned her, and she dove for it. After a quick swipe at her eyes and a judicious wiping of her nose, she shoved two more tissues into her pocket.

"Thanks again, guys. I'll be in touch."

"Call me when you get back to Atlanta," Marie called.

With unspoken consent, Bill walked her out to her car.

"Have fun in Norway." He swung the car door open for her.

"Thanks. I'm sure I will. I've always loved Vikings, and I'm going to get to see the latest archaeological finds."

"Wish I was going along."

"Oh, don't worry." She turned and grinned at him. "You'll have a great adventure in...wherever it is you're heading tomorrow."

"Oh, I'll be right here on base tomorrow and for a few more weeks. Extra training before we head out."

"For...that place."

"Yeah." He laughed. "That place. Maybe we'll meet up here again sometime, and I can tell you about it then." He hesitated and then stuck his hand out. She shook it, and their eyes met. Bill brought his other hand up and held hers. "Take care, Claudia."

"You too." She gently disentangled her hand and drove away.

Rats! I really *like him.*

Was she ready for that? She wondered just how close Bill and Heidi Taber were. She was guessing they were just friends and co-workers, or he wouldn't have spent practically the whole weekend at the Belangers' making eyes at her. Had she overstepped some invisible line by encouraging his interest? She couldn't see how. No rule said she couldn't start something with a military man, though it would involve logistical challenges.

She'd deliberately avoided tying herself down in a romantic relationship while she established her career. But now…maybe now was the time.

Why hadn't she given Bill her phone number or slipped him a business card? No, better to wait a while. Let him think about her. She could call Marie in a couple of weeks and tell her, "I just read an article that I thought would interest Pierre's friend, Bill. Can you give me his e-mail addy?"

As she exited the highway and drove toward the airport, she knew she would miss the slice of home she'd enjoyed this week. The intensity of feeling she'd experienced while holding her nephew had caught her unawares. Maybe when she got back from Norway, she'd propose a story on motherhood. Oh, not here in the U.S. of course. Indonesia, maybe. One of the few places she had yet to see. The problems new mothers encountered in Jakarta…

She pulled a ticket from the machine at the entrance to the parking lot for rental cars. Bill White's cheerful smile slammed into her psyche. *Take care, Claudia.*

She didn't usually daydream about men. She was too old for crushes, and she didn't need the distraction. This couldn't be good. *But I like him.*

EIGHT

Bill came out of the coral cave on Okinawa with Brownie, Stu, and Squeegee. He blinked in the brilliant sunlight. A crowd of sailors pushed past them and headed for the bus stop.

"That was something," Stu said.

"Yeah, Heidi would have liked it," Brownie added.

Bill laughed silently. Brownie's regard for Heidi was well known in the unit. But Heidi treated the petty officer the same as she did all the other men—as friends, but not overly friendly. When they'd invited her to visit the caves, she'd opted instead to attend the Japanese puppet theater in Naha.

"Where to now?" Stu asked.

Bill pulled a couple of brochures from the pocket of his work uniform. "There are ruins of some castle or something…a fortress, I guess. It's not far from here. What do you think?"

"Why not? Nothing better to do."

Bill nodded. They'd pull out tomorrow and be on their way home from another completed operation in the Pacific. He'd been glad to get out of the Middle East and Africa theaters for a change, but they'd been sent to an area experiencing the worst of its rainy seasons. Bad weather helped them do their jobs without being seen, but it also made them miserable. Three weeks in the dripping jungles of western Mindanao. Now they had a two-day layover in Okinawa, waiting to catch a Navy transport flight to Pearl Harbor and San Diego. He and the others had taken advantage of the down time to sleep late, do laundry, and see a few sights on the island.

When they reached Norfolk, they were supposed to have a full month at the base before shipping out again. He hoped he'd be able to connect with his brother during that time. Ben's ship was due in from its West Pac tour at the end of the month, and they'd e-mailed tentative plans to meet in San Diego if Bill could get a flight and leave at the right time. Almost a year and a half had passed since they'd seen each other, and Bill felt the yearning for family again.

"Looks like someone's setting up a photo shoot," Brownie said, tugging him to one side.

A new group of tourists walked past them toward the cave entrance. Bill looked in the direction Brownie had gestured. A short young man with spiky blond hair was adjusting a camera tripod, and a woman, at least six inches taller, seemed to be giving him instructions while poring over a brochure.

Brownie gave a whistle too soft for the woman to hear. "Let's hope it's a fashion shoot for the swim suit issue. Think she's American?"

"Yeah," said Stuart. "That or a Brit."

Bill watched the woman's dark hair swirl in the breeze off the ocean. Designer jeans and an embroidered kimono style tunic that might have been bought locally. She turned her head a few degrees. His heart caught and then raced on.

"It's Claudia."

"Who?" Stu asked.

Bill bit his upper lip, quickly deciding how much to give away. "She's Lieutenant Belanger's sister-in-law. I met her in Virginia a few months ago. Writes for a swanky magazine."

"Wow," said Brownie.

Stu elbowed Bill. "You gonna talk to her?"

Bill's throat went dry, but he managed to get out, "Sure." But he stood rooted to the ground, watching her. He could still hear Pierre's words the day Claudia had driven away from the cookie cutter house where the Belangers lived.

"You know Claudia's not a Christian."

Bill had thought about that for several seconds. It hit him hard. He'd spent an evening and most of a day trying to learn everything he could about her. He wanted to know every tiny thing. But he hadn't picked up on that. Or had he? Maybe he'd deliberately ignored any signs that should have tipped him off. At last he'd nodded and looked Pierre in the eye. "Thanks for telling me. I'll pray for her."

He'd prayed all right. Mostly that the Lord would help him forget her. But her lovely face returned to his memory at the most inconvenient times—like when he was huddled under an improvised shelter in the Philippine jungle, wondering if their contacts would betray them to the Muslim insurgents.

It's better not to have any contact with her, he'd told himself a bajillion times. But he still pictured her clearly…saw her bending over to place a whisper-soft kiss on Skipper's forehead. Saw her laughing at his most feeble joke. Felt the warmth of her fingers on his when she'd said goodbye.

And here she was in Okinawa, out of the blue. He couldn't not speak to her. Yet he hung back. Once he made himself known to her, he'd be caught up in the giddy excitement she'd generated in Norfolk. Did he want that, knowing she was off-limits? She lived for fame, money, and prestige. She didn't believe in Christ. Deep down he knew he didn't want to encourage his feelings for her, or Claudia's for him either. He was flying out tomorrow morning. At best they could spend the rest of the afternoon and the evening together. Then what? She'd haunt his memories even worse than she had for the last three months.

She looked up and scanned the people near the mouth of the cave. Her gaze slid over his group—four men in Navy working khakis. Her eyes widened, and she homed in on Bill. Someone's strong hand shoved him in the back, and he stepped forward with trepidation.

"Bill? Bill White?" She laughed a musical, enticing laugh. Her hair floated around her face as she shook her head in disbelief. "Incredible!"

She met him halfway between the photographer and Bill's cluster of friends. He took her hand and stood staring at her. Tourists detoured around them.

"Claudia. What a surprise. You're...doing a story here?" He glanced beyond her. The photographer seemed to be setting up for a shot of them. Bill turned his back and eased her around so that her face was toward the camera, not his. "Wow."

Her smile was infectious. "You know, I almost tried to contact you a while ago. I thought of it several times, but I always seemed to be on the run. I thought you were going back to Africa."

"We did. We get moved around a lot. Wherever they need us."

She nodded, and her dark eyes sobered. "So they need you in Okinawa this week?"

"Uh, no. We're just on our way back from..." He hesitated, but it wasn't as if they'd gone after the Abu Sayyaf. This was just a practice run. "Well, I guess it's all right to tell you now that it's over. We took part in a joint exercise with the Philippine armed forces."

"That sounds exciting. But don't tell me anything you shouldn't."

"No, it's okay. They send out press releases after it's all done. We—I mean our troops, not specifically my outfit but different arms of the American military—go and train with the Filipinos now and then. Make sure we can operate well together if we need to."

"What sort of things do you do?"

"Oh, landing exercises, patrolling, jungle operations, oil platform protection."

Her eyes widened. "Sounds like a full agenda."

Yeah, Bill thought. *And a show of force to the insurgents.*

"How long were you there?" she asked.

"A couple of weeks. My buddies and I are doing a little sightseeing here while we wait for our ride back to the States."

"Say, I don't suppose you're free tonight?"

Bill looked toward where his friends stood. Squeegee had left the group and was trotting toward the bus stop. "Yeah. In fact, we're just killing time now."

Claudia grimaced. "I've got to put some time in on this story. We made special arrangements for Tommy to take photos inside the caves. It took some gymnastics to set it up, so I can't blow it off. Otherwise I'd love to drop everything right now."

"Sure. I understand. Look, where are you staying? We could meet later. I don't have to check in until midnight."

The smile that had bowled him over in Norfolk lit her face. It almost hurt to think a woman this beautiful and sophisticated wanted to bum around Okinawa with him. He ignored the warning Pierre had given him. It was just an evening, not a lifetime together. They could be friends. It would boost his reputation within the unit, for sure. The guys would spread it around that he'd had a hot date with a knock-your-socks-off woman. Not that it mattered what the others thought. Much.

"We've got a hotel in Naha." She rummaged in her jeans pockets and pulled out a receipt and a pen. On the back of the receipt she scribbled the name of the hotel and her room number.

"Great." Bill stared down at it. "I don't have any civilian clothes."

"That's okay."

"What time should I pick you up?"

"Uh..." She looked back toward the photographer.

"Bill!" Stu grabbed his arm. "Hey, the bus is leaving. Are you coming, or..." He glanced significantly at Claudia.

"Yeah, I'll be right there."

"Six thirty, if we're eating dinner," she said.

"Terrific. See you then." He smiled down at Claudia, unable to tear his eyes away from her lovely, wistful face.

"Hey, Bill!" Brownie gave an ear-splitting whistle from the steps of the tour bus, and all the tourists meandering about the parking lot and cave entrance looked and scowled at him.

Bill jogged for the bus and hopped aboard as the driver hit the accelerator. He slammed against the barrier in front of the first seat.

His buddies laughed and pulled him back to where they'd saved him a place.

"Hubba-hubba," Stu said, shaking his hand as though he'd just touched a hot stove.

"You jerk," Bill said, but he couldn't wipe the grin off his face. "You guys are on your own tonight."

They all groaned and slapped him on the back, making more wisecracks as they rolled toward the ruins.

NINE

In her room at the Marriott Okinawa, Claudia prepared carefully for the evening. She and Tommy had squeezed every minute they were allowed in the breathtaking coral caves and then flitted about gathering information and photos of walls and various other structures built of coral. It had tired her out, but a shower had revived her. Bill was leaving in the morning; she'd have three more days on the island to catch up on sleep and write her story. Nothing could spoil tonight.

She wasn't certain how to dress and opted for a filmy white gauze pants set that would hold up under scrutiny in any restaurant and keep her after-dinner options flexible. And she'd let Tommy know without question that he could find his own dinner and entertainment tonight. She just hoped he wasn't so hungover in the morning that he couldn't work.

She applied her makeup carefully. Not too much. She'd learned the first time she met Bill that he was a small-town guy. If their meeting in March was anything to go by, he didn't require glamour to bowl him over. The natural look would suit him better.

Her throat prickled a little as she stared into the mirror while wielding the mascara wand—which was silly. She hadn't been nervous when she met the president of India or a notorious convicted forger in a Marseilles prison. But the people she interviewed put on a façade for her, as she did for them. Claudia Gillette, the professional.

She didn't want that with Bill. She hoped they could be genuine with each other. The authentic Bill White, that's what she wanted. If he couldn't stand the authentic Claudia, then he wasn't the man she thought he was. And better to find out now than after another three months of daydreaming about him.

Was that what she'd been doing? She frowned at her image in the mirror. Part of her wanted to scrub off the makeup and let him see her face unadorned. Show him the Claudia no one else had seen in years. Another part wanted to hide all her flaws—physical and temperamental.

A quiet rap on the hotel room door told her it was too late. *Okay, Bill, what you see is what you get.* She rose and went to the door, taking the prerequisite moment to look through the peephole and steady her breath.

Oh, yeah. Tall, blond, and khaki uniform. Maybe she should have worn the cobalt blue cocktail dress. But that might have shocked him. No, the white outfit was better.

She opened the door.

He froze in the middle of inhaling a deep breath, met her eyes, and smiled, almost in relief.

"Hi."

"You found me."

"Yeah. Pretty snazzy place." He glanced over his shoulder, and she realized he might never have seen the inside of such an opulent resort.

"The magazine's picking up the tab."

"Lucky you." He looked back into her eyes, and Claudia felt almost seasick looking into those blue irises. "Here. I picked these up at the train station." He held out a small bouquet of red hibiscus.

"How beautiful! Thank you."

He looked away, smiling as though pleased with her reaction but eager not to seem too happy about it. "You all set?"

"Yes. It'll stay warm this evening, won't it?"

"It's cooler than it was this afternoon. You might want a jacket for later."

She nodded. He was still nervous, and his feet seemed nailed to the hallway floor, through the thick carpet. Maybe he was afraid she would try to entice him into her room.

"Just let me put these in water and grab my purse and a sweater." She dumped the contents of the ice bucket in the bathroom sink, filled it with water, and plunged the flower stems into it. When she returned to Bill, he looked less stiff, and he'd moved a few inches to the side, allowing her room to pass him into the hallway. "So, where are we going?"

"I looked up a couple of restaurants. If you want to try the native cuisine—"

"I do."

He grinned. "All right. And afterward…I'm not sure. There's a storytelling performance at the National Theater tonight." They walked toward the elevators together. "It's not far from the train station. Or, if you'd rather, there's a skating rink a few blocks from the restaurant."

"Ice skating? Here?"

"Yes, it's promoted as a way to beat the heat. I understand there are actually several rinks on the island." He punched the button for the elevator.

"We used to skate on the lake at home," Claudia said. "I won't tell you how long ago that was." She remembered little Marie skating circles around her and Lisa.

He smiled at that. "Not so awfully long, I'm guessing. I'm no expert, but I think I can stay upright on blades if you want to try it."

"Sure. But it will probably make me homesick."

The doors opened, and they stepped into the car. "Just seeing a friendly face in a foreign country has set me off." He hit the button for the lobby.

"How long since you've been home?" she asked. "I don't mean Norfolk. I mean *home* home. Your folks…"

"That home is gone. Ben and I sold the house after our parents died. Neither of us has a permanent home now, and we saw each other in April for the first time in a year and a half. Never take for granted the family you've been blessed with."

"I'll take that to heart." As they left the hotel, she said, "Do you want to take my rental car?"

"Sure. That would be more comfortable than public transportation, I guess."

She could tell he hadn't expected it. Maybe he thought it extravagant, renting a car in a country where using public transportation was patriotic. "We needed it to haul our equipment around."

"Right."

He followed her across the parking lot. She didn't like the stiffness between them. So much for the candor she'd envisioned.

"Listen, Bill, would you like to drive?"

He eyed her carefully for a moment. "I can if you want me to. I won't squirm if you drive though."

"Here." She tucked the keys in his hand.

She was glad she'd made that decision. Bill seemed to know exactly how to get to the restaurant he'd chosen, and he navigated the heavy traffic with seeming ease.

The restaurant was crowded, mostly with Asians. The décor looked authentic to her. Paper screens, scrolls, sculpted lion figures. Low, candlelit tables with mats to sit on.

The waiter handed them a beverage list. Bill glanced at his card and handed it back. "Bottled water, please."

The waiter nodded and looked at Claudia. She hesitated. Was Bill saving money or avoiding alcohol? She'd bet on the latter. "Diet cola, please."

The waiter took her card and faded away.

"I like this place," she said.

Bill smiled. "Thanks. Someone at the base recommended it."

"I don't see many sailors in here."

"It's probably a little sophisticated for most of them."

She wondered if she should offer to pay the check. She was sure her salary was at least five times as much as Bill's military pay. No, he was the kind of guy who would bridle if she suggested it. Unless she were tactful...

"Say, Bill, I don't want to cause an awkward scene or anything, but it occurred to me that you might not have much for funds, since you're on your way home from one of your expeditions. So if—"

He waved his hand. "Not a problem, I assure you. I'm delighted that we ran into each other, and I want to treat you. I rarely get a chance to spend money on a woman."

She accepted that with a nod. Just as she'd suspected. Traditional man. It was refreshing, considering some of the whackos she'd met in the last few years. The last man she'd had dinner with—a mistake, on her Oslo trip—had actually stuck her with the bill. "Thanks."

"Have you eaten Okinawan food before?" Bill asked.

"I can't say that I have." She looked over the menu that displayed headings in Japanese and English. "No sushi, please. As much as I've tried, I can't like it."

"How about stir-fry?"

"Oh, yes."

"Try the goya chanpuru. Lots of veggies, bitter melon, a little meat."

She took his advice, and they chatted about her assignment while waiting for their food.

"I'm interviewing a Chinese scientist tomorrow," Claudia said. "She's the main reason I'm here. She's been studying the corals around these islands for twenty years."

"I've always thought it would be interesting to go diving here."

"We're actually going on Wednesday. Tommy's done some under-water photography before. I've been diving a couple of times. I'm no expert, but I enjoyed the little I've done so far. And they say the corals are spectacular here."

He nodded and sipped his glass of water. "Wish I could stay and go with you."

"I've got three more days here. It beats some of the places I've been lately. How about you? Have a successful journey?"

"To a point. It was more of a preparatory op, to pave the way for another." He shrugged apologetically. The less said about their hopes to rescue the kidnapped scientist the better.

"Is that woman still with your unit—Heidi Taber?"

Bill's eyebrows drew together in a frown. "Yes. Why do you ask?"

"She intrigues me. I'd like to meet her. I still think she'd make a wonderful subject for an article. Is she here on the island now?"

"I don't think that would be such a good idea. Our CO would definitely say no."

"I did a little research. Most special operational forces don't admit women."

"That's true."

Their plates arrived, and Bill steered the conversation to other topics, so Claudia let it rest. The food exceeded her expectations. After the meal they walked to the ice rink and rented skates. Bill insisted on buying her a pair of pompoms to tie onto her laces.

"A souvenir of Okinawa."

She liked that. They glided onto the ice together, and he grabbed her hand. He was a better skater than he'd let on, and she suspected he'd played hockey in school. Their speed snatched her breath away, and she found herself choking for air to laugh on.

An hour later they walked hand in hand back toward the parking lot where she'd left the car. Claudia had tied the pompoms through a buttonhole on her sweater, but she carried the sweater instead of putting it on. The air outside seemed overly warm after the ice rink.

Bill insisted they stop for iced fruit drinks. They sat side by side on a wall overlooking a moonlit topiary garden, slurping like two kids. Claudia watched him covertly. Who would have guessed two sober people could have so much fun?

His gaze collided with hers, and he arched his brows. "What?"

"Nothing. Just...thanks. Today turned out so much better than I thought it would."

"Yeah? What would you have done tonight if we hadn't met up?"

She sighed and looked out over the park. "I don't know. Probably gotten a burger with Tommy and maybe caught a movie."

"You spend a lot of time with Tommy?"

"Some. Out of necessity. We tolerate each other when we're in a strange place and don't know anyone. But we're total opposites on a lot of things."

"How so?"

She thought about Tommy's penchant for rap music, professional wrestling, and German beer. "We probably wouldn't be friends if we didn't work together. Sometimes we're the only two Americans within a thousand miles."

Bill nodded. "I'm blessed with some good people in my unit."

"I'm glad. That must make what you do easier."

"It does." He slipped his arm around her. "So, is there anyone special in your life, Claudia? I mean…"

"No." She leaned toward him and rested her head lightly on his shoulder. The cotton uniform cooled her cheek. "I don't stay in one place long enough to have a boyfriend. What about you?"

"Ditto. I'm too conservative for most of the women I work with."

"What about…"

"Hmmm?" He sounded sleepy. "Oh, Heidi?"

"You read my mind."

"It wasn't hard. You're obsessed with her."

"Maybe."

They sat in silence for a long moment, and then Bill said, "Brownie has his eye on her. One of my buddies. They'd make a good pair."

"Does she like him?"

"I think she's considering the ramifications. If they got serious, one of them would be transferred out of the unit."

She sat up and stared at him in the dimness. "Really? That's pretty crummy."

"That's the way the military works."

"Huh." She wished she hadn't left her cozy spot. But if she cuddled up to him again, he might peg her as aggressive. Or would he? He was watching her pensively. What was he thinking?

He inhaled suddenly and jumped down off the wall. "Come on, we'd better get you back to the hotel."

"How long will it take you to get back to the base?"

"Longer than I'd like. I'll cut it pretty close."

He drove mostly in silence, but once they were on the highway heading for the Marriott, he reached over and took her hand. "Tonight was super, Claudia. Thanks."

"I had fun. Too bad we can't do it more often."

"Yeah." He squeezed her hand.

He insisted on walking her up to her room, despite her protests.

"I figured on enough time to make sure you got in safe, provided we don't waste it arguing." He grinned and hustled her across the lobby to the elevators. Several other hotel guests crowded in with them, so they didn't speak on the way up, but Bill again reached for her hand.

She felt her eyes tear up as they got out on her floor. That was irrational. Yes, she was sorry the evening was ending and that he'd be gone in the morning, but it was only another parting. She'd had so many in her life.

She fumbled in her purse, but she didn't seem to have a tissue. She pulled out her key card instead. Bill took it, fitted it into the slot on her door, and then pushed the door open a few inches.

"I guess this is it."

She nodded and dashed away the errant tear that had betrayed her. "Sorry. Ever since that last time I visited Pierre and Marie, I seem to have these bouts of…I guess you'd call it homesickness. Not for Maine or for them specifically. Just…for family, I guess. The old ties. The familiar things."

"And I'm it tonight."

"Yes. You're it for me. I guess I'll always associate you with Okinawa."

"I hope it will be a happy memory."

"It will be. Except this part. Saying goodbye."

He reached for her, and she glided into his embrace, thrilling as his arms folded around her. Was this the real thing? The elusive future she'd longed for? It could be, if only...

He kissed her, a warm, lingering caress. She closed her eyes and let herself catch the dream for a few seconds. When he drew back, she looked up at him through more tears and put her fingers up to stroke his cheek.

"You don't want to miss your bus."

"Claudia, can I call you after you get stateside again?"

She nodded. "Please. Call me. E-mail me. Send me Morse code. Wait just a sec."

She hurried into her room, tore her briefcase open, and grabbed one of her business cards. Her smiling, airbrushed face with the magazine's logo and address. She flipped it over, scrawled a note, and then darted back to the doorway. Bill had stayed circumspectly outside.

"My private e-mail's on here." Breathless, she stuck it in his hand.

"Thanks!" Before she could get out another word, he was gone. She retreated into her room and rescued the hibiscus from the sink. The light, pleasant smell filled the bathroom. She set them on the nightstand so she would see them first thing upon awakening and arranged the bright pompoms at the base of the ice bucket. For a full minute, she sat staring at her impromptu still life. She wouldn't see Bill again for who knew how long, and yet, she wasn't lonely.

TEN

All the way to San Diego, Bill brooded. Mostly he thought about Claudia. Then he pondered the situation in the Philippines. They had to leave things alone for a while, that was obvious, and trust their native contacts to ferret out information. When the time was right, he hoped the Philippine government would call on the U.S. Navy's Gold Team to go back and complete the job. There were a couple of insurgent leaders he was itching to take on—especially the notorious Juan Cabaya, who led a large band of Abu Sayyaf terrorists in the southern islands. Meanwhile, the team might be off to Siberia or Nicaragua or Angola...anywhere, really.

Back to Claudia. What was he thinking of, kissing her? She was all wrong for him.

No, his heart protested. She was all *right* for him, except for one small detail. She didn't share his faith. And that was huge.

The men in the row behind him had started a lively poker game. Bill closed his eyes and tried to shut them out. He wanted to pray, but he wasn't sure he could take this to the Lord. After all, Scripture was clear on the topic. Why ask for wisdom, when he knew what he should do?

Okay, maybe I can just stay friends with her. A kiss isn't a lifelong commitment. And what are the chances we'll meet up again, unless we arrange it deliberately?

He touched his breast pocket. Through the material of his uniform, he could feel her business card. He couldn't ignore her now. That would be despicable after last night. So he'd e-mail her and keep it brief and friendly. Not too friendly. Yeah, that would be best.

"Hey, Lieutenant, why so glum?"

He looked up. Commander Dryden stood in the aisle.

"Just tired, sir."

Stu, beside him in the window seat, chuckled. "He left his girl behind in Okinawa, that's what's wrong with him."

The commander frowned. "What's this?"

"Nothing," Bill said quickly. "I ran into an old friend, that's all."

"Old! I doubt if she's thirty, and she seemed very friendly," Stuart put in. Bill scowled at him.

Dryden's eyes took on a faraway, fuzzy look. "I met an old friend once in Kiev. We called her 'Cathy' in high school, but in Kiev she called herself 'Katarina.' That was a wild weekend." He shook his head. "Great posting, the Black Sea."

Bill stared at him, unable to come up with a suitable reply.

Dryden clapped Bill on the shoulder. "I can always count on you to keep steady, Bill." He moved on down the aisle.

Great, Bill thought. *I'm the stodgy one of the unit.* Part of him wanted to fling regulations and his conscience aside and prove to them all that he was, indeed, capable of having a "wild weekend." But he knew he'd regret it. Already he wallowed in guilt over one kiss. One sublime kiss. He sighed and leaned back, closing his eyes again.

ELEVEN

9:00 A.M., JULY 2
ATLANTA, GEORGIA

Claudia hurried into the office on Thursday morning. She had a lot of catching up to do. Other than her one stolen evening with Bill, her trip to Okinawa had been constant work. She'd even conducted interviews during dinner on the other nights. Tommy, meanwhile, had snapped headshots of her interviewees and then excused himself for who knew what pastimes. At least she'd pieced together the major points of the magazine spread on the trip home, using her laptop. She could finish it up today and tomorrow.

Unless Russell handed her something she hadn't planned on. He entered the room from the elevator and paused at the receptionist's desk, but she could bet he was headed toward her office, a cubicle inadequately separated from the others by chest-high acoustic walls. She wasn't here often enough to warrant a private office, but she'd give a lot for one right now. Russell Talbot might be her editor, but he was far from her favorite person. She sat down in her chair and scooted close to her computer desk, knowing he would still find her within seconds.

The woman in the next cubicle called, "Hey, Claudia! Welcome back and congratulations."

She flinched and looked up. Salli Buxton peered at her over the divider on the other side of her cubicle.

"Thanks. For what?"

"The award," Salli said.

Claudia just looked at her, blinking as she mentally cataloged her writing awards. Nothing she'd call new.

"You didn't know?" Salli's face lit, and she glanced over the dividers toward where Claudia had last seen Russell. "R.T. made the announcement yesterday. He seemed a little grudging."

"Salli, what are you talking about?"

"The IPET. You're a finalist. Oops. Talk to you later. Love your blouse."

Claudia looked down at the subtly flowered gauze top she'd bought in Okinawa. It was a bit more frilly than her usual style, but it reminded her of Bill and the hibiscus he'd brought her. Was it only last Saturday? Less than a week. She hurried to bring up her e-mail program. Maybe there would be a message today. She'd looked for one every day since he left, but he probably hadn't had access to a computer for several days.

Receiving message 1 of 32.

She watched them gush onto the screen. There it was, in the middle. Number 18 or so. She grabbed the mouse.

"Well, you made it back in one piece." Russell's attempts at geniality always made her grit her teeth, and today was no exception. They both knew he didn't like her.

She nodded at him, but didn't rise. "Russell. Your observation is accurate, as usual."

"When can we expect to see your article on Dr. Chen? We'd like to finalize the layout this afternoon if possible."

"If Tommy's got the art ready, that shouldn't be a problem." She'd have to scramble, but she wasn't about to admit it.

"I have a couple of projects I'd like you to take a look at."

"Do I have a choice?"

"Of course. But the one on exotic pets seems right up your alley. A lot of human interest there."

Claudia wrinkled her nose. The gorilla article had instigated more reader mail than any other story they'd run in the magazine's ten-year history. So now Russell thought she should do an animal story for every issue. He didn't get it. It wasn't just the animals, though she had to admit Tommy's photos were spectacular. His portrait of the silverback, taken with a close-up lens, had made for a superior cover.

"I'll look at it," she said, deleting the junk mail. If he would only go away, she could open her message from Bill.

"And then there's that item we talked about last month, the alternative energy on Cape Cod."

"Really, Russell! I looked into that. It's old news. That story's so dead it stinks."

"Claudia! I didn't see you come in." Her assistant, Mya, appeared at Russell's side and peeked under his arm at her. "Did you hear about the IPET?"

"Uh…Is it that time already?" The International Periodicals Excellence Trophy was awarded annually, and Claudia was well aware that the time for the revelation of the finalists had arrived. But it didn't pay to appear too excited about something like that. Still, if what Salli had said was true…

"You're a finalist!" Mya grabbed Russell's arm and swung him around. "Haven't you told her yet? Claudia, your story about the president of India and his family is in the top five! And Tommy's got a photography nomination for his monkey pictures."

Claudia let her breath out. "Those were mountain gorillas."

"Whatever. You're one of the best, girl!" Mya shoved past Russell and hugged her.

Claudia smiled. "Thanks. That's fantastic."

Russell didn't look too happy. "I suppose you'll have to fly to Chicago for the awards ceremony next month."

"Is that a problem?" She knew it was, as far as Russell was concerned. It meant she'd miss a couple of days of work, and arranging her schedule would be a major headache, but she'd delegate that to Mya.

"No, no. We're—" He cleared his throat. "The magazine is very proud of you." The unspoken comment was loud and clear. That's what we pay you so much for. How could we not be proud when you come through for us? "Well, I'll see you after lunch. One o'clock, in my office."

She nodded. She'd well nigh kill herself to have the article finished by one.

"Oh, Claudia, I'm so happy for you." Mya grinned and bounced on her toes. "This is such an honor!"

Claudia let herself grin back. "Thanks! Are those stories he wants me to do anything worthwhile?"

"I'm not sure. You'll have to look at the files. Someone higher up thinks we need a story on Peruvian textiles."

"What sort of textiles?"

"Ummm, something about Inca women high in the Andes. They weave their history into textiles."

"I'll do it."

Mya pulled back and eyed her. "Just like that?"

"Yes, it sounds hard to get to, and it will keep me away from Russell for a week or two."

Mya chuckled. "All right. I'll bring you the preliminary research file. You'll want to go during the dry season, though. Hey, don't let Russell get you down."

"I don't. He's very good at running this business, but he's horrible at getting along with people."

"Well…" Mya sneaked a look over her shoulder. "I concur, but don't quote me."

Claudia nodded. "So I do my job and stay out of his way."

"You're good at that."

"Yes, I am."

"I think Russell is a little intimidated by you. Like most men."

Claudia swiveled her chair and stared up at Mya. "What's that supposed to mean?"

Mya leaned close. "He used to be a writer, you know."

"No, I don't think I knew that, but it makes sense. He worked into the editorial side."

"Because his writing was mediocre. But you didn't hear that from me. You scare him. I don't think he's ever felt very secure in his job." Mya clamped her lips together and nodded.

Claudia rocked her chair back and forth a couple of times. "All right, bring me the file, and then leave me alone. I've got to get busy or I'll lose my reputation for always making a deadline without sweating."

"You sweat plenty."

"Yeah, but I never let the management see it. Get out of here."

Mya scooted out of the cubicle. At once Claudia tapped on the mouse, and Bill's e-mail opened.

Hey, Claudia! It was great seeing you in Okinawa. I'll look for your magazine article in a month or two. Looks like I'll be on base for a couple more days, and then I'm out of here again. If you're not too busy, drop me a line. Bill.

No "I miss you." No "When can we get together again?" She chewed on her bottom lip, trying to read what he hadn't said.

"Here's the file." Mya stepped into the cubicle.

Claudia closed the e-mail and turned to take the manila folder. "Thanks."

"Russell was going to give this to Rick Spaulding."

"He was?" Claudia flipped the file open. It looked like a great opportunity. "This is exactly the type of story I excel at. Why would he give a textiles story to a man?"

Mya winced and looked around again. "Office politics. Shhh."

"You mean he doesn't want to give me a chance at another possible award-winner, so he hands me a proposal for an article on people buying smuggled pythons for pets?"

"Could be. Of course, the publisher loves you. The editorial board as a group loves you."

"But Russell hates me."

Mya shrugged. "Maybe he's a teeny bit afraid you'll replace him? A man in his fifties doesn't like to feel he's expendable."

"Nobody likes that feeling. And besides, I don't want his job. I like the one I have, thank you."

"I can't explain it, but he's wound up tight every time you're in the office. So…watch your back, hey? Need anything else?"

"Coffee and a Do Not Disturb sign."

TWELVE

Claudia sat at a small table in the hotel's café, watching Tommy eat the local version of home fries and waiting for an officer from the tourist police to arrive. They'd gone to the police station that morning only to be told the official they needed to see was away from his desk. They'd been instructed to go to the city hall and file paperwork, and the officer would come to the hotel to find them as soon as he could be freed from his duties. That was three hours ago.

"This is so stupid," Claudia muttered, looking at her watch for the hundredth time. "I think we should go back over there. He probably came in five minutes after we left, and the clerk forgot to give him the message."

Tommy shoved a bite of greasy potatoes into his mouth. Claudia grimaced and looked away.

"More likely he's waiting for a bribe." Tommy picked up his beer bottle—his third, but who was counting?—and took a swig.

Claudia hoped none of the other people in the café heard him. Only a few lingered over coffee and snacks, and none seemed to pay any attention to the two Americans, except for the waiter. He grinned at Claudia every time she glanced his way. "That's it. I'm going back over to the police station." She grabbed her tote bag and stood, just as a uniformed man entered the café. He looked around, squinting at the change in lighting. His gaze landed on her and then slid to Tommy. He swerved between the tables, walking toward them.

"Mr. Knowlton?"

"Right here." Tommy raised his hand and shoved his chair back. "Are you from the tourist police?"

"I am. Forgive the delay. We are making preparations for a visit from the Minister of International Cooperation." The officer's gaze lingered on Claudia for a moment, and then he turned his attention to Tommy. "I am Officer Vargas. I have read your report. As I understand it, you believe your passport was stolen last night in a bar."

Tommy smiled sheepishly. "That's correct."

"Which one?"

"Well now, that's a problem. It could have been one of several."

"And you have thoroughly searched your belongings?"

"I have, señor."

The officer nodded and turned to Claudia. "You are Mrs. Knowlton?"

"Good grief, no. I'm his coworker. Claudia Gillette."

His eyes narrowed. "What type of work do you do? You are here on a tourist visa, are you not?"

"Yes, but we work for *Global Impact* magazine. I'm doing an article about the Quechua women in Pacchanta. Tommy will photograph them to illustrate the story."

"I see. And you were leaving for Pacchanta today?"

"That was our plan."

Tommy laughed. "Some mule outfitter told us yesterday it was a weeklong trek. Good thing we didn't listen to him."

Vargas shrugged. "If you hike the Ausangate circuit—around the mountain, that is—then it takes you five to seven days. A lot of people come here to do that. But if you only wish to go to Pacchanta…"

"We do," Claudia assured him. "I'm sure the trek is lovely, and if we had unlimited time, we'd enjoy doing that, but we have deadlines, and so we're taking the bus to Tinqui—"

"Yes, that is best. From there it is only one day to the village. But most people go the other way, and Pacchanta is their last stop before they return to Tinqui."

Claudia rested her bag on the table. Her Spanish wasn't very good, and she was glad to get a second opinion on their travel route in English. "But what about Tommy's passport?"

He fixed his gaze on Tommy once more. "You have filled out the application for a new passport?"

"I surely have." Tommy burped. "'Scuse me."

"And you have the necessary identification with you?"

"Yes, he gave all that to them at city hall," Claudia said. Tommy gave her an injured look. He hated it when she spoke for him, but she was tired of waiting around. They should be halfway up to the mountain village.

"And was anything else stolen?"

Tommy shook his head. "No, sir. Claudia wasn't going out last night, so I left my camera equipment with her. I should have left her my passport too, instead of keeping it on me."

"Your hotel room was not vandalized?"

"No, sir."

"And would you say you were…inebriated last night?"

"Well…" Tommy looked away. "I might have been a little less on my guard than normal."

The officer's lips twitched. "I see no reason why you should not continue with your plans. I will personally see that your application is sent to the embassy in Lima today. You go one day to Pacchanta, a few days there…"

"One," Claudia corrected him.

He nodded. "And one day back here. Your new passport should be here by then."

"Wow." Tommy blinked at him. "That fast?"

"Sometimes a temporary document is issued to allow you to travel back to the United States. But usually they rush the duplicate passport through. And because you had the passport number and all the documents required with the application, it should be very quick. Come to my office on your return. If your passport has not arrived by then, I will see if I can help you."

Tommy stuck out his hand. "Thank you very much, sir."

Vargas shook his hand and then looked at Claudia again, a long, penetrating look. "Of course, if you wish to stay longer in Cusco and perhaps visit the ruins at Machu Picchu…"

"Thank you," she said. "I've done that before. Breathtaking. But not this trip."

He ducked his head in a nod that was almost a bow. "Enjoy your trip."

"Say, you mentioned the Minister of International Cooperation. He's coming here?"

"Yes. On Monday. He will be meeting with the department officials."

Claudia's brain whirred through the possibilities. She glanced at Tommy, but he was digging in his pockets for money to pay his tab. "How accessible is the minister?"

The officer frowned at her. "What do you mean, madam?"

"I mean, would it be possible for a journalist to get a word with him?"

"A journalist?"

"Me. Remember? *Global Impact?* It's a high-profile magazine, and I'd love to get even a sound bite from the minister."

His eyebrows almost morphed into a shaggy, black caterpillar. "I don't think he would have time to chat with a magazine model."

She wanted to slap him, but she managed to keep her smile intact. "You must have misunderstood me earlier, sir. I told you, I am here to write an article about the weavers in Pacchanta. I am not a model. I'm a writer."

She could almost feel his urge to look her up and down, but he kept his gaze riveted to hers.

"And a very good one," Tommy said.

After a prolonged moment, Vargas licked his lips. "Pardon me, please. My error."

Tommy laughed and slapped him on the shoulder. "That's okay, old boy. She *could* have been a model, but she's too smart for that."

Vargas looked toward the door as though he longed to escape. "Even so, I do not think the minister could…his schedule is full, you see."

She nodded. "But if we go up the mountain tomorrow, stay in Pacchanta Saturday, and come back Sunday—"

"The office is not open on Sunday."

"Exactly. So we'll come by to pick up Mr. Knowlton's passport Monday, the day the minister will be here…" She arched an eyebrow at him, waiting for him to make the leap.

"Oh, I don't think you will be able to do that. Security will be very tight for the minister."

"But we have to get the passport that day. Our plane leaves Tuesday morning."

"We will not be conducting business while the minister is actually in the building."

"Oh. And…how long will he be in Cusco?"

"All day."

"But we will be able to get the passport?"

"I suggest you be there when the office opens, at eight o'clock. The minister is expected later in the morning." He bowed as though ready to take his leave.

"Good," Claudia said. "That's good. He has to eat lunch, I presume?"

Vargas eyed her cautiously. "There will be a banquet in the evening for departmental officials."

"But lunch?"

The officer's jaw moved, but no sound came out for a second. He smiled and shrugged. "He has requested to mingle with the people and eat at a local establishment, madam."

She leaned toward him and smiled. He caught his breath and smiled back.

"Which restaurant?" she whispered.

"I...do not know."

"I think you do."

He shook his head. "No, señorita, if I did, I would tell you."

She believed him. He was so flustered he'd all but abandoned his careful English. She pulled back. "We'll come to your office early on Monday."

He nodded. "As you wish. Have a safe journey."

She watched him leave the café. "Come on, Tommy. Let's get out of here. We can get the bus to Tiqui in half an hour."

"Don't you want to wait until tomorrow—"

"No, I don't want to wait another day. I don't want to wait another minute. Go get your things, and let's move!"

She had to hurry Tommy along, but they caught the next bus, barely. Tommy sprawled on the seat and slept, snoring. She poked him a couple of times and finally gave up. An empty seat two rows back enticed her, and she left him.

There would be no computer service in the high mountains. She turned on her satellite phone long enough to check for text messages. There were three, but none from the person she wanted most to hear from.

Marie. *How R U? Miss U*

Russell. *How could U let T lose passport?*

Mya. *Did U get hold of embassy? R fuming over TK passport.*

She sighed and turned it off. Better save the batteries. The four-hour drive gave her ample time to think about Bill. His e-mails were short. Friendly, but short. She'd started out sending him longer, chatty messages, and he seemed to like getting them, but after the third one, she'd decided she was trying too hard. They didn't progress beyond friendship. And then he'd disappeared.

His last e-mail had arrived before she and Tommy flew to Peru. In it he'd said, "I'll be gone for a while. Don't worry about me. I'll let you know when I'm back on base." Another secret op. She'd quickly replied with the number for the sat phone, but he hadn't responded. She had no way of knowing if he'd received it before he left. Well, he knew she and Tommy were traveling. She'd given him her itinerary in advance. If he wanted to contact her and was able to do so, he would. The ball was in his court.

She clicked the button that let her view the photos she'd stored on the phone. One was a shot of her and Bill. Tommy had taken it the day they'd met at the cave entrance in Okinawa. Bill was turned mostly away from the camera, but she could see the back of his head and part of his face. Sort of a quarter profile. And beyond him, herself. She looked good. Hair loose and waving in the breeze, her mouth curved in a delighted smile. She'd never realized her eyes were that vivid brown. Must have been the natural lighting.

She'd always thought of Marie as the pretty one of the Gillette sisters, but she wouldn't complain about what she'd been doled. Maybe Tommy was right, and she really could have been a model, though she would never have believed that as a teenager. The tourist police officer seemed to think so. She chuckled. Did he think they would trek all the way up to an obscure mountain village for a fashion shoot?

She clicked off the photo viewer and leaned back in her seat. Where was Bill now? "That place" he'd been to before Okinawa? She could call Pierre and ask where Bill had been shipped to. Fat lot of good that would do. Pierre would give her some drivel about knowing better than to ask.

Was Bill in danger while she bumped along the old Inca Road on a bus that needed shock absorbers? Or was he playing tourist with his buddies in some tropical port? Every day she'd stared at that photo and wondered if she'd ever see Bill again and if he cared whether or not they ever met up again. But the answers to her questions continued to elude her.

THIRTEEN

1600 HOURS, JULY 16
MEDITERRANEAN SEA

The trip to the Lebanon coast was a quick one, in and out. Bill and his friends had returned to their transport ship sooner than expected. That's what they liked—a successful mission with no loose ends. For twelve hours they goofed off, staying out of the crew's way while Commander Dryden waited for new orders. They assumed at first that they'd go directly home, but then rumors began to fly that they would be sent on to Iraq. Bill hated Iraq, but if that was where they needed to go, he'd pitch in as he always did. The ship sailed south. Were they headed for the Suez Canal?

His turn came for computer access, a rationed perk when they were aboard a large ship. He sent an e-mail to Claudia's address. She and Tommy Knowlton were probably still in Peru. She'd tried to explain to him why the native weavings fascinated her, but he didn't exactly get it. Somehow the Quechua women wove their history and heritage into their cloth, using designs that held special meanings in their world. Lakes, streams, valleys, mountain peaks. It was a sacred art as well as a practical craft. He supposed it was like the samplers American girls made in colonial days.

Claudia seemed to genuinely care about the people she interviewed. Her articles told their stories in beautiful prose. He was certain that after he read this one, he would understand perfectly how precious those woven textiles were. He'd subscribed to *Global*

Impact after he'd met her in March, even though the glossy magazine was a little pricey.

She always seemed to show great respect for the religious beliefs of the people she wrote about, yet she saw no need for faith in her own life. There must be a way he could show her how important—no, critical—believing in God was.

He prayed before he began writing his e-mail. "Lord, I don't have the verbal gifts Claudia has. Help me to get through to her anyway."

Hey, Claudia. I'm sort of between tasks at the moment, stuck on a ship waiting for a new assignment. I hope your trip has gone well. Wish I could be with you for the llama trekking. The scenery must be spectacular. I dreamed about you the other night. We were skating on a glacier. Don't ask me where the glacier came from—not Okinawa!

I hope it won't offend you if I tell you that I'm praying for you. I'm asking God to keep you safe and open your heart to Him. Send me a message when you're able. I might not get it right away, but it will catch up to me eventually. Yours, Bill.

He read it over again, not satisfied with what he'd written. Should he add that he missed her? Wished he could see her again? No, in their first few communications, he'd sensed that she would take it wherever he led. It had been almost too tempting. A woman like Claudia. If he encouraged her, would she really want to take the relationship to the next level with him? A humble sailor? Okay, a naval officer, but still… And what would the next level be?

That's what scared him most. Better to keep it friendly. He could easily fall hard for her, but he knew better than to let that happen. When he'd been with her in Okinawa, he'd found her almost irresistible. Not just her looks, but her wit, her intelligence, and her almost tangible loneliness. On top of all that, she'd acted as though he were the most important man on earth. He'd felt flattered. Privileged to be with her.

Now that he was no longer around her, he'd gotten back on track. At least he hoped he had. He prayed that God had a woman out there somewhere, waiting for him. He wanted a family someday. But Claudia wasn't the one. As perfect as she seemed, he knew she wasn't the one.

The right woman would have a faith in Christ as deep as his—maybe deeper, realizing how he'd faltered a little lately. Maybe he should cut things off with Claudia. But he couldn't bring himself to do that.

"Hey, Bill, are you done?" Brownie came up behind him.

"Almost." He frowned at his message. If he said anything that smacked of wishing he could see her again, Claudia would probably have it all arranged before he knew what hit him. *P.S. I read your story in the July issue. Excellent!*

He hit SEND.

FOURTEEN

Claudia fidgeted while Tommy paid the tour guide for his services and the use of the pack llamas to carry their equipment. Her story was as good as completed—in her notebook, on her battery-operated laptop, and in her head. Tommy's pictures would make it come to life.

If they hurried, they could catch the next bus from Tinqui and be back in Cusco tonight. If they missed it, they'd have to stay over in Tinqui, and she had no desire to see more of the shabby little town.

Tommy settled up with the guide and ambled toward her. He eyed their pile of gear resentfully. "Too bad he wouldn't pack all this to the bus stop for us."

"Maybe we can hire someone." She looked around. Several young men lounged about.

"I don't know..." Tommy had distrusted the locals since the loss of his passport.

"Oh, come on. We need to hurry."

He shrugged. "I'll get the camera gear and your laptop, if you can get our duffels."

Claudia sighed and picked up several bags, slinging the straps over her shoulders and settling the burdens around her body wherever they felt they would stay while she walked the quarter mile.

Other people were waiting for the bus, so she knew they hadn't missed it. She lowered the bags to the ground and sat on her duffel bag. She had a blister on her left big toe, thanks to the steep downhill hike from Pacchanta.

"I'll be so glad to get to the hotel tonight." She glanced around at the other people waiting. Most were foreigners who had come down the mountain that afternoon. "Think it would be okay for me to use the phone here?" she asked Tommy.

"I don't know. We sure don't want someone to lift that. We'd both be fired."

"We would not." She scowled at him and flexed her toes inside her hiking boots.

"Would too. Do you know how much that thing cost?"

"All right, I'll wait until we're on the bus." That way fewer people would see it, and she could at least check for text messages without drawing attention.

But the results disappointed her. The only message was from Russell, demanding a progress report. By the time they arrived in Cusco several hours later, her body was drained of every ounce of energy. She paid a bellboy to help get their bags to their rooms.

"You want to eat together?" Tommy asked as they fumbled to unlock their doors that faced each other across the hall.

"No, I'm too tired. I'm going to bed, but I'll get up and eat an enormous breakfast before we go to the police station."

A long shower was next. The grime from the trail, sleeping in the wild, and the miserable bus finally swirled down the drain. Her instincts told her to flop into bed, but she couldn't resist setting up the computer first. The hotel was one of a handful in the area with Internet service.

Yes!

She clicked on the message from WOW2—Bill's version of his initials—with a grin plastered across her face. She was so tired it hurt to smile that big, but she couldn't help it.

She skimmed the message, then read it more slowly and sighed.

He thought of her. He even dreamed of her, though it seemed a rather ho-hum dream, and he wished he could have gone climbing with her in the Andes. Was that the same as saying he wished they were together? No mention of when they might connect again or even when he would return to the States. He was on a ship somewhere. As long as he stayed on the ship, there was a pretty good chance he'd be able to check his e-mail again.

She tapped out a message, straining to make it sound light-hearted.

Hey, there, WOW2! You can't be having as much fun as I am. I got a truly fantastic story and met several awesome Indian women. They taught me bundles of stuff about weaving and the Inca heritage. Thanks for praying for me. I can use the safety. Don't know about the enlighten-ment. We had a safe trip, other than getting a blister. TK lost his passport before we left Cusco, and we hope to pick up a duplicate tomorrow. Should be touching down in Atlanta late Tuesday. I hope to see you soon. Call me if you get to a phone. That's it for now—I'm exhausted. It was really cold on the mountain and I didn't sleep well up there.

She hesitated and typed *Love, Claudia.*

After staring at it for several seconds, she changed it to *Love ya!* Not quite so definite. No one could construe that as flirtatious or pushy. Could they? She typed over it again. *Be safe!*

Russell called at seven thirty the next morning. They were in the same time zone. She loved that and at the same time hated it.

"Are you sure Tommy will be able to pick up the passport this morning?" Russell asked. "We need you back here."

"No, I'm not at all sure. The tourist policeman thought it would be here, but he made no guarantee."

"Make sure you're on the plane to Lima today. If Tommy has to wait for his passport, you come without him."

"What for?"

"The board of directors says you're logging too many miles and spending too much time out of the country."

"That's stupid. The board loves my work."

"Of course they do. But they'd like to see your face once in a while."

"I may have another story here in Cusco, and if I have a chance of getting it, I'll call Mya and have her rearrange my flight."

"Don't do that!"

"Why not?" She stood and hoisted her suitcase onto the bed and ruffled through it. The dress she wanted wasn't there. Oh, yes. She'd hung it in the closet before the mountain hike.

"I just told you. Claudia, I mean it. You get back here as planned. You know it costs a fortune to change your ticket like that."

"Trust me, Russell, the story I'm chasing will be well worth a few hundred extra dollars."

Disgruntled, she put on the cool sundress and made up her face, striving for allure. Not that she thought she could bowl the minister over, but a little glamour couldn't hurt. Of course, she'd freeze in this if she didn't cover up with a sweater.

She turned on the laptop and checked her e-mail.

Hey, Claudia! Great to hear from you. We got our orders, and we're heading home soon. I may get a chance to make a call. Is that satellite number you sent still good? Bill

She felt suddenly better. *Yes! Call anytime, Bill. I'll carry the phone with me today. I'd love to hear your voice.*

There, that wasn't too vampish, was it? She gathered her sweater and leather purse. It would be cool outside, even though they were in the tropics. After all, they were 11,000 feet above sea level. She went across the hall and rapped on Tommy's door.

"Tommy? Are you up?"

A moment later he opened the door and stood blinking at her, his eyes bleary.

She wrinkled her nose. "What did you do, sleep in your clothes?"

"Uh…"

"I was going to see if you were ready for breakfast, but you're obviously not. I'm going down to eat. Get a shower and be ready to go with me to the police station in forty minutes."

"Uh…"

She pulled the door shut with a bang and strode to the elevator.

By the time she'd finished her breakfast, Tommy still hadn't arrived. At eleven minutes to eight, she decided that if he didn't enter the breakfast room in one minute, she would march upstairs and drag him out of his room. She'd rather just leave without him, but what good would that do? They wouldn't give the passport to her, she was sure.

The minute expired. She shoved back her chair. In her leather bag, the satellite phone rang.

"Oh, Russell, not now!" She pulled it out and glanced at the incoming data. Not Russell. "Hello?"

"Claudia!"

She sat down hard in the chair. "Bill?"

"Yes!"

"You sound like your head is in a bucket in Mammoth Cave."

He laughed. "Where are you?"

"Still in Cusco."

"Ah. I'm surprised I could get you, up in the mountains."

"Yeah. I won't ask where you are."

"Not home yet. Actually, I can tell you that right now I'm in the Cairo airport. They're sending us home on a commercial flight."

"Cairo, as in Egypt?"

"Yes. Ever been here?"

"Once. Bill, I'm so glad you called!" She caught her breath. Her voice had held a note of pathos she hadn't intended to reveal, but it was too late now.

"What's wrong?" Bill, on the other hand, sounded concerned and gentle, even across an ocean and two continents with a slight delay in the relay.

She inhaled deeply. "Nothing really. We're all right. But Tommy lost his passport or had it stolen a few days ago. He reported it, and we're supposed to go and pick up the duplicate this morning. But Tommy's late coming down to meet me. He…he drinks too much, and I'm afraid he's going to land in serious trouble someday. And if you get thrown in jail in South America…well, I don't want to think about it."

"Claudia, you're not responsible for Tommy's behavior."

"I know. I just feel…he's three years older than me, but he acts like a kid. Oh, Bill, he's the best photographer in the world. I mean that. But he could be even better if he'd get a grip on his life. He's so irresponsible! My boss told me that if his passport didn't come through, I should just go off and leave him here alone, but…I'm not sure I could do that." She ran out of steam and exhaled, closing her eyes. Her heart felt heavy in her chest, and beads of perspiration had formed on her forehead.

"You okay?" Bill asked.

"Yeah."

"Maybe your boss is right. Maybe Tommy needs to be forced to take care of his own problems."

"You think I'm enabling him?"

"I don't know. I'm not close enough to the situation to say. Stay calm. Ask yourself what Tommy would do if you weren't there. Chances are he'd get out of this on his own."

"He might, I guess." She puffed out a little sigh. "Just talking to you helps a little, I think."

"Would you mind if I prayed for you? Right now, I mean."

She gulped. Prayer seemed too simplistic. But in Bill's world, as in Marie and Pierre's, it seemed to be the antidote to everything.

"I guess not." Her gaze swept over the entrance and rebounded to Tommy, sauntering in and grinning. "Oh wait, there he is! But if you think it will help…"

Tommy waved at her and veered toward the buffet.

"Claudia, my time's up," Bill said, "but I will pray about this. I pray for you every day, you know. And I'll pray about this passport thing and your relationship to Tommy. Hang in there, okay?"

"I will. Thank you so—" A lack of static told her the connection had been severed. Just to be sure she said, "Bill?" Nothing. She stared at the phone for a moment. All this talk of praying made her uneasy. Apparently this was a regular thing with Bill and an important part of his psychological makeup. She wasn't sure she liked being prayed for. And men who prayed all the time...could he really be as tough as she'd assumed he must be? In her mind prayer meetings and special forces somehow seemed incongruous. She shoved the phone into her bag and went to meet Tommy. At least he was dressed and mobile, and he didn't look too hung over. "Hey, let's go. The tourist policeman's office is open now."

"Let me get some coffee into my veins, Claudia." He scooped a huge spoonful of scrambled eggs onto his already brimming plate.

"If you sit down to eat all that, we might not have time to get to the office before they have to close again for the minister."

"Yeah, yeah."

She could feel the heat creeping up her neck and into her cheeks. So much for staying calm. "Oh!" She stamped her foot. "You make me so mad."

"Really?" He smiled.

She looked at him. What now? It wasn't her style to cry. But ranting did no good with Tommy. "Why are you acting this way? We usually get along all right."

"You're not my mother, Claudia. Just back off. You think I can't find my way to the police station without you?"

She gritted her teeth and discarded the first response that came to mind. "I'm going over there now. If there's a line, I'll stand in it. But you'd better be there in fifteen minutes."

"Or what?"

She narrowed her eyes, debating whether to slug him or not. They both knew she wasn't winning this argument. She turned away and marched out the door. Outside she paused on the sidewalk to pull on her sweater. More than anything, she was glad Bill hadn't been on hand to catch that scene. He made it sound so easy. Stay calm. Let Tommy fend for himself. Why couldn't she do that? Just go for a walk. Come back in an hour and see if he'd gotten the passport.

As if.

She knew she couldn't let it go, and she stepped toward the street. Get a taxi? It wasn't that far, and walking might help her work off some of this frustration. As she headed out, tears filled her eyes, and she blinked them back. She would *not* let a man, especially that arrogant shrimp, bring her to tears.

Why couldn't he be like Bill? Sympathetic. Practical. Of course, there was the prayer thing. She wasn't exactly comfortable with that. And his teetotal habits had surprised her. Not many servicemen would pass up a drink. But stacked up against Tommy's overindulgence, Bill came out way ahead. He seemed to have life figured out. Maybe there was something to the whole Christianity thing. She wondered if there was a Bible in the hotel room. If so, it would probably be in Spanish.

She hurried toward the police station but soon slowed her pace. If she raced down there, she'd arrive gasping. Cusco's elevation kept her feeling as though she couldn't get quite enough air. As she mounted the steps, she heard a commotion. Horns blaring, and then sirens. She looked up the street.

Oh, no. It couldn't be. A motorcade?

She dashed inside and up another flight of stairs to the office of the tourist police. Three clerks scurried about behind the counter, seemingly ignoring the half dozen people waiting for assistance. Trust Tommy to blow it. She had a sinking feeling that they'd be stuck in Cusco another night.

A man entered the work area from an inner room. Vargas! Her spirits perked up at once. He'd definitely eyed her with interest the other day, even in her hiking clothes. She took her sweater off and held it demurely in front of her with her purse.

Vargas rattled off instructions to his minions. Claudia caught the words "minister" and "hurry."

She tapped the tall, blond man in front of her on the shoulder. "Excuse me. Did you understand what he said?"

"Well hello, love. I think he said they need to hurry and close up shop." The heavy accent tipped her off. A Kiwi for sure.

"New Zealand?"

"Yeah. America?"

"That's right." She smiled and extended her hand. "Claudia Gillette."

The woman in front of him swiveled and glared at him. "What do ya think you're doin'?"

His smile became a grimace. "Sorry. I'm Jerry, and this is my wife, Peg."

Claudia smiled sweetly at Peg. "Hello. My Spanish is so poor, I have trouble understanding the locals."

"Hmpf." Peg faced front.

Jerry shrugged. "I just hope they help us before they close."

A clerk came through the swinging gate that kept the visitors from the work area and turned the sign in the door's glass window to "closed."

Vargas approached the barrier and donned his official smile. "You will be assisted, but no more. The office is closed. You, madam—" He focused on Claudia. "You will be the last. Oh…" He pushed through the gate and walked along the line to stand next to her. "Miss Gillette, is it not?"

"Yes, sir. I'm impressed that you remembered."

His eyes said, *How could I forget?* However, his comment was, "It was your friend, I believe, whose passport was stolen?"

"Yes, my coworker. Thomas Knowlton. He's on his way here now, but he was delayed a few minutes, so I stepped into line to hold a place for him."

Vargas frowned and looked back toward the counter. "I see."

"Are you able to tell me anything? Did the passport arrive?"

He hesitated. He looked at her and then back toward the office. "Excuse me, just a moment. There is a small technicality. But I must get downstairs. Let me just…"

He left her and hurried back beyond the counter and disappeared. Claudia's heart pounded. Technicality. Terrific.

Vargas emerged once more, carrying a large envelope. He walked past the others—the first two people in line were now being helped by clerks—and again approached her.

"Would you walk with me, Miss Gillette? I will explain as we go, if you do not mind."

"Oh, of course." She wondered if leaving the office would lose Tommy his place in line and if that would matter. Vargas opened the door and held it for her, and she scooted out into the hallway.

He headed toward the stairs. The noise from the street below filtered up to them.

"The Minister of International Cooperation is arriving, you see. I'm afraid I've missed the mayor's welcoming speech."

"Not on my account, I hope."

"No, no. It is always something. Business, you know."

She nodded.

"Well, your friend's passport."

"Yes?"

"The embassy sent the document along, with the notation that one condition of the replacement was not met, or at least it was not in the report that my office sent." He ducked his head, as though embarrassed. "You see, there have been several incidents of people falsely claiming theft of their passports. Later they find them. Oops. It wasn't stolen after all."

She smiled. "I suppose it happens fairly often."

"You've no idea. Because of this, the government has made a rule that in the case of a lost or stolen foreign passport, the holder's lodgings and belongings must be thoroughly searched. Unfortunately when Mr. Knowlton reported the theft, this was not done."

Claudia sucked in a breath. "But…how long will he have to wait?"

"Oh, not long, I assure you." Vargas opened the door and piercing brass music bombarded them. Down the block, in front of the city hall, a throng had gathered. "Look," he said, "if I had realized the agents did not conduct the search…but I did overlook this point, and then you were gone up Ausangate, and now…well with the minister's visit, it is too difficult. But I assure you that tomorrow morning—"

"We're flying to Lima tonight," Claudia said.

"That would be most inadvisable." As they talked, they walked along the crowded sidewalk toward the city hall. The music stopped and the people hushed. A man with graying hair stood before a lectern equipped with a microphone. "The minister," Vargas said softly.

Claudia wondered if this man, Fuentes, was his hero. Or perhaps he aspired to one day fill the minister's position. He stared with rapt attention at the speaker. Claudia listened too. If she showed no respect for the revered man, Vargas might be less apt to hear her pleas.

She caught the gist of the speech. The minister assured the people that his department was working hard to guarantee the greatest possible interaction between Peru and other nations, ensuring that Cusco and other areas in the country would benefit from increased trade, tourism, and cultural exchanges.

The people cheered, and the minister greeted members of the departmental government.

"I'm sorry, you must excuse me," Vargas murmured. "He will be meeting the local officials soon, and I must participate." Fuentes worked his way around the edge of the crowd, shaking hands with several people as he approached them.

"But—" Claudia grabbed Vargas's elbow. She wasn't about to let him out of her reach with that folder under his arm.

"Claudia!" She whirled at the sound of her name. Tommy was rushing down the sidewalk, sliding between people and bumping them out of his way.

Vargas half turned as well, and his eyes widened. "Your friend—"

Tommy tripped over a boy's bicycle and crashed into Claudia, sending her flying backward. She ricocheted off Vargas, who attempted to break her fall, but only succeeded in spilling his papers on the sidewalk.

Claudia slammed into and careened off someone, landing hard on her back. The thud sent the air whooshing out of her lungs. A woman squealed and sidestepped to avoid trampling on her, and the crowd went suddenly still.

Claudia looked up into the faces of two stern-looking policemen. A third man sat on the pavement beside her. He held his hand to his chest and panted. As she struggled for breath with which to apologize, Claudia realized she had barreled into the guest of honor.

FIFTEEN

Claudia entered the office to hear congratulations on every side. The receptionists, clerks, editors, and other writers greeted her warmly. Mya met her halfway to her cubicle and engulfed her in a bear hug.

"It's brilliant, Claudia! We're all impressed with your ingenuity. How you ever managed to snag that interview with the minister is beyond me, but we're getting it into next week's issue. The directors are so excited you can feel steam billowing out from under the door of the board room. And they want to see you at nine o'clock sharp."

"What for?" Claudia set her portfolio and purse on her desk and stared at the three bouquets of flowers sitting there. "And what's all this?"

"My dear, you are the toast of the town and the office. The big one with all the showy lilies is from the publisher. He's sure your interview with Señor Fuentes will rock the nation. In fact, it's hush-hush until it hits print, but you should be ready for television interviews immediately following."

Claudia inhaled slowly, trying to hold in her anticipation. Her pulse raced, and the scenes tumbling across the screen of her mind made her giddy, but she said coolly, "I'll take that under advisement. Thank you."

"I mean, Fuentes' statement that his department is ready to form a drug enforcement consortium with the United States is huge. And the fact that he told you, two weeks in advance of his planned announcement. Claudia, the Drug Enforcement Administration doesn't even know about it yet. We're going to press with it before *anyone*."

"Yes, rather heady, isn't it? When I explained my lead time, he told me to go ahead and use it. I did tell him we might not be able to get it in before he meets with the Secretary of Justice and the administrator of the DEA." Claudia smiled at the memory of Señor Fuentes' kindness. He'd invited her to eat lunch with him and several local and departmental officials and had spent most of the hour staring at her across the table. "What did Russell say?"

"He nearly hit the ceiling when you called. Tried to talk the big boss out of running it. He said you might have got it wrong, and it would embarrass them. Can you believe it?" Mya gritted her teeth. "But Mr. Shanahan told him to yank Salli's story on yoga and put yours on the page. He saw how important it would be to the magazine."

"It's nice to know your publisher has faith in you." Claudia reached for the tag on the dozen pink roses.

"That's from Tommy. He came in ten minutes ago with it and asked me to place it prominently on your desk—which is hard, when the publisher's offering is so gaudy. But Tommy said you saved his bacon on the passport issue."

"Well, I…"

"Oh, he told me all about it." Mya leaned close. "I'm not to tell a soul, even my mother, how he knocked you smack into the VIP. But he says you charmed the man in two languages and got him to tell the obnoxious policeman to give him his passport."

Claudia threw back her head and laughed. "That's not exactly what happened."

"Well, I won't tell anyone you made the minister of—whatever—get his suit all filthy. Tommy said that between your charm, your long legs, and a little cleavage, the minister practically begged to do you a favor in return for pushing him down."

Claudia winced. "I wasn't trying to..." She sat down in her desk chair and took instantaneous stock of her motives and methods of landing interviews. "Look, I truly didn't set out to...well, maybe I did, but I wasn't trying to sandbag him. That was Tommy's fault."

Mya nodded. "Well, anyway, that little posy over there is from someone named Wow. Want to explain that?"

"Wow?" Claudia fumbled with the smallest floral arrangement, a cluster of giant purple violets in a small container. Her heart pounded even faster than it had when she'd learned she had to face the board of directors in half an hour. *Got your e-mail—great going! Still laughing and still praying. WOW2.*

"What does that mean, anyway?" Mya asked. "Laughing about what? And praying? Is that for real? Did you meet a priest in Peru or something?"

Claudia smiled. Apparently Mya hadn't noticed the Navy insignia on the side of the mug that substituted for a vase. "No, it's from a friend."

"Pretty classy friend. I like that one best."

"I agree. And if I'm going to have any space to work in, this big vase will have to go. Maybe you could put that large arrangement out near the elevators, where everyone can enjoy them." She tucked the publisher's tag, with Bill's, into her top desk drawer.

"Sure." Mya hefted the vase and awkwardly balanced the bushy bouquet as she moved out into the aisle between cubicles. "Coming through."

Claudia plucked the tag from Tommy's roses and glanced at it. *Thanks a million. You know what I'm talking about. T.K.*

SIXTEEN

"All right, that's it for today," Pierre Belanger told the troops. "We'll be back for more of the same tomorrow."

"Yes, sir," The men and women of the special unit chorused.

"Your performance on your last op was exemplary. Clean infiltration, quick completion of the mission. Congratulations. But the next one will be a lot harder. You're going back to finish the job you started last month. We hope you can wrap that one up with a good outcome." He surveyed them with mixed feelings. He hated sending young men and women—all very intelligent, cream-of-the-crop Navy personnel—into high risk. But sometimes that was unavoidable, and it was what they trained for. "You've got several weeks of preparation ahead. Commander Dryden says that we'll be doing some intense training together here for a while. You can tell your families that much. If something critical comes up, things can change in a hurry, but you did a great job in Lebanon, and you can expect to be here for at least two weeks. Clear?"

"Yes, sir."

"Dismissed." The ensigns assigned to help him began removing the used targets and putting away the throwing knives and dummy grenades the unit had used to practice their skills during the last hour of the day. Pierre flipped over a couple of pages on his clipboard and scrawled a signature. "White, got a minute?"

Bill White joined him as the others dispersed. "Sure."

Pierre smiled at him. "I wondered if you'd like to join Marie and me for supper."

Bill's eyes lit. "Sure. If it's okay. I mean, I don't want to be a bother."

"Marie suggested I ask you, but I didn't have a chance earlier. Too many people around."

"Sounds good."

Pierre nodded. "Go get changed. I'll pick you up in twenty minutes."

Their ride home took another twenty, and by the time they entered his home, Pierre was hungry. But so was Skipper apparently. The baby's wails drowned out Marie's greetings.

"What's the matter?" Pierre stooped to kiss her and then bent to peer at the baby. "Hey, fella. What's wrong?"

"I'm sorry. I need to feed him. Can you guys wait just another— oh, fifteen minutes?"

"Sure," Bill said.

Pierre shrugged. "Do we have a choice?"

Skipper revved up the howling, and Marie carried him toward the hallway. "Well, you could fix the salad. Get yourselves a glass of tea. I'll be back."

A door closed, and Skipper's crying stopped almost immediately.

Pierre smiled at Bill. "If only all our problems could be solved as easily."

Bill chuckled.

"So…iced tea?"

"Sure."

Pierre got their drinks, and Bill settled on a high stool at the counter while Pierre scouted in the refrigerator for salad vegetables. "I don't suppose you heard about Claudia."

"What about her?" Bill asked.

"She's getting all sorts of attention for breaking the story about this new drug-busting team we're forming with Peru." Pierre found a head of lettuce, and when he pulled it out of the drawer, he saw a few tomatoes and a cucumber behind it.

"Oh, yeah, I did hear about that. Claudia told me."

Pierre closed the refrigerator and stared at him. "You're talking to Claudia?"

"Well, you know." Bill jiggled his glass, swirling the ice cubes in his tea. "E-mails. I call her once in a blue moon. Nothing regular."

"Right." Pierre hated that he felt uneasy because his sister-in-law chatted occasionally with Bill. He turned to the sink to wash his hands. "Uh look, Bill, you wouldn't ever... Oh, forget it. You wouldn't."

"Tell her something classified?"

"Yeah. Like that jerk of a Peruvian minister did."

Bill's eyebrows shot up. "What are you saying?"

"Nothing. But you gotta admit, Claudia has a way of getting info out of people. Fuentes wasn't going to tell anyone about the drug coalition until our Secretary of Justice flew down there and held a press conference with him. But Claudia not only found out about it, she got his permission to spill it to the world."

Bill eyed him cautiously. "Is that a problem? I thought it was a great coup for Claudia."

"Sure it is. But the bigwigs in Washington aren't happy about it. They're wondering if they can trust this Fuentes to keep secrets when they start going after Peruvian drug lords."

"Ah." Bill took a long swallow of tea.

"I just..." Pierre stopped. He had no right to tell Bill what to do with his personal life. And Bill wasn't a naïve kid.

"What? You think she'll worm some top secret information out of me and broadcast it to the world?"

"No, not really. It's just that..."

"I know she's not a Christian. We've had this conversation before."

Pierre clamped his teeth together. Easygoing Bill seemed slightly irritated. "Okay. Forget I said anything. We love her. I mean, Marie idolizes her. No, that's not the right word. But Claudia is her big sister, and Marie looks up to her." Pierre tossed aside the towel he'd dried his hands on and selected a large knife from the utensil drawer. "You've got to admit, she's successful. Personally, I liked her better when she played field hockey for the Waterville Panthers. But now she's slick, like that magazine she works for."

"I...didn't get that impression in the few times I've been around her."

"Of course not. You get only the impression she wants you to get." Pierre eyed the tomato, turned it just so, and sliced into it. "With you, she's the sweet, small town girl who made good in the big city. With that minister in Peru, she was the gorgeous, charming, and highly acclaimed writer who could make him look good to the American people."

Bill frowned at him. "You don't like her, do you? At all?"

Pierre sighed. "Yes, I like her. She's very smart. I admire her, and I applaud her efforts and her success. But Claudia...can be difficult. Since she left home, she's rocketed into a society Marie and I will never be a part of. And, how do I put this... I think she's led a bit of a wild life since she entered the big leagues of the media."

Bill set his glass down on a coaster. "Is this why you invited me over? To warn me away from Claudia again?"

"No. Marie and I thought you'd like a night off the base." Pierre reached into a cupboard for the salad bowl. "I'm sorry. This isn't fun for you, is it? I truly invited you here out of friendship. Look, let's not talk about Claudia anymore. Okay?"

"You got it."

"Good. While you were gone, the church had a missionary speaker. I wished you were there to hear him. His ministry is in Kenya."

"Too bad I missed it."

"Yeah. I asked him if they ever needed volunteers to do projects. You know, like you do."

Bill nodded. "What did he say?"

"Always. They never have enough help. And people like you, who are used to primitive conditions—well, that's even better."

"Great. Give me his contact information. If we have a chance when we're in that part of the world, I'll see if we can set something up."

"I'll do that."

Marie entered the kitchen carrying Skipper, who stared at his father with wide, brown eyes.

"Hey, buddy. You happy now?" Pierre laid the knife down and held out his arms. Skipper grinned and lunged for him.

Marie relinquished the baby with a chuckle. "Daddy's boy."

"Man, he's getting big," Bill said.

"Yes. Sorry about the welcome he gave you. He's not usually that insistent. Oh, thanks for doing the salad, chérie."

Pierre glanced up from his baby talk with Skipper. "No problem. Is everything else ready?"

"I think so." She put a pair of tongs in the salad bowl and set it on the table. "Bill, did you know Claudia's going to be on TV tomorrow morning? She's in New York."

Pierre plopped Skipper into a baby seat at one end of the table. "Yeah, he knows all about Claudia. We've agreed not to talk about her."

Marie's eyebrows shot up. "What?"

Bill smiled. "I did know about her interview on the morning show tomorrow, but thanks. I'm going to set my recorder to tape it for me."

"He and Claudia *communicate*." Pierre stressed the last word as though it indicated a mystic, significant event.

"Ohhh." Marie smiled. "What's wrong with that?"

"Not a thing." Pierre sat down and adjusted Skipper's seat so that he could watch them all while they ate. The last thing he wanted was to get into another discussion about Claudia with Marie present.

The next evening Bill arrived exhausted at the apartment he shared with four other Navy men. Only Parker was home, and he hustled around the kitchen as Bill walked in.

"Hey there, White! Good to see you for a change."

"You too." They usually missed each other on their stints in Norfolk. Bill couldn't recall seeing Parker in three or four months.

"I'm out of here, though." Parker grabbed his car keys off the table. "You going to be around?"

"Maybe for a couple of weeks or so."

"Great! Catch you later. Got a date."

Bill opened the refrigerator and stood staring into it for half a minute. Had he really expected the groceries he'd bought two days ago to still be there? He grabbed a cheese stick and went to the living room. At least the DVD recorder he'd purchased last winter was intact. He checked the settings and turned it on.

The morning news show filled the TV screen, and he cautiously fast forwarded. After a prolonged commercial break, he let it ease into the next segment at regular speed.

The introduction jump-started his pulse.

"…and this intelligent, magnetic young woman came home with a story much bigger than the one she went after. Welcome to the show, Claudia Gillette."

Bill caught his breath. Claudia was prettier than ever. He eyed her critically, wondering what was different. Of course, she was made up for the camera. But still…

"I was captivated by the Quechua women I interviewed in Peru," she told the host. "That story is dear to my heart. But when my photographer and I returned to Cusco and realized we had a chance to interact with the Peruvian Minister of International Cooperation, we knew that we'd stumbled onto a story of global significance—one that would bring hope to the people of the Unites States as well as those of Peru. This man, Juan Fuentes, has helped forge a joint effort to stop drug traffic between our countries."

Her poise made pride well up in Bill's chest. That was *his* Claudia.

"That is wonderful news." The host smiled. "But is the drug problem in Peru really that large? Isn't it bigger in, say, Colombia?"

"It's serious in several South American countries," Claudia said, "and right now Peru is willing to step up to the plate and do something about it. This consortium is intended to expand in the future and help many countries take their drug problems by the scruff of the neck."

Bill smiled at the fire in her eyes. But a few minutes later, as the questions got personal, he saw a different expression on Claudia's poignant face.

The most mundane question seemed to catch her by surprise.

"How do you juggle your exciting career with a home life?" The interviewer asked.

The sadness he glimpsed in Claudia's eyes for that split second wrenched Bill's heart.

She smiled ruefully. "To be honest, I have almost no home life."

"Do you wonder how much you've missed to build your career, as fabulous as it may be?"

Claudia looked into the camera and paused only a second. "All the time."

Bill sat staring at the screen long after the interview was over. Good thing she was hundreds of miles away. If she were as close as Atlanta, even, he knew he'd be driving toward her.

SEVENTEEN

As Claudia checked out of her hotel in New York, three military officers entered the lobby. They chatted as they approached the desk. She could tell one of them was a Navy man, about forty years old with an air of authority. The others' uniforms were different, and she pegged one for a Marine. The third one she wasn't sure about.

The handsome naval officer stepped up beside her, and a second clerk behind the desk began to help him. He looked familiar, but Claudia tried not to stare. A veiled glance showed her the name plate on his blue dress uniform—Hudson.

"Aren't you…" She looked at the bars on his shoulders, frantically trying to remember the rank Pierre's friend held. "Commander Hudson, isn't it?"

"That's right." He turned toward her with an engaging half smile. "Do I know you?"

She extended her hand. "Claudia Gillette. You helped save my sister's life last year."

He cocked his head to one side, "Marie Belanger."

"That's right. My family will never forget what you did."

"Well, thank you. A lot of people worked together on that case. I'm glad I was able to help."

Claudia nodded, eyeing him with speculation. She'd bided her time on the military story she really wanted. Maybe this was her lucky day.

"Commander Hudson, is there any chance I could spend a few minutes with you? I realize you're a busy man…"

He glanced at his watch. "Maybe this evening? My dinner meeting is supposed to end at eight, but maybe we should say nine?"

"Perfect." Everything was going her way. She could teleconference with Mya on rearranging her schedule and do some Fifth Avenue shopping this afternoon. "In the bar here?"

Hudson frowned. "Are you staying in this hotel?"

"Yes."

"Suppose we meet here in the lobby and find a place for coffee?"

"All right."

"Nine o'clock then." He nodded and turned to finish registering.

The clerk attending Claudia eyed her expectantly. "And your key, ma'am?"

Claudia shook her head. "I've changed my mind. I'd like to stay another night."

The clerk's jaw dropped. "I'll have to check and see if the room is available."

Claudia leaned toward him. "Move me to another room if you have to. I'm staying." She slid a twenty-dollar bill across the counter, covered with her hand.

The clerk palmed it quickly. "I'll do my best, Ms. Gillette."

"Oooh, Claudia! I would rather shave my legs with a butcher knife than tell Russell what you're doing." Mya's wail caused Claudia to shudder, even though it came via cell phone all the way from Atlanta.

"Fine. Go shave your legs. I'll tell him."

"Really?"

"Connect me."

Fifteen seconds later, Russell Talbot's voice snapped, "What do you think you're doing?"

"Getting another great story."

"Some military boys' club meeting?"

"No, that's not the story. That's the means to the end. The story I'm after will win us another IPET next year and maybe a Pulitzer."

"You say that about every story you chase these days. I'm sick of it. Get back to Atlanta and do your job here."

"My job isn't there, Russell. My job is global, remember? It's in the name of our magazine."

"What about that speaking engagement you're supposed to fill tomorrow night?"

"Oh." Her promise to address Businesswomen of Greater Atlanta had completely slipped her mind. "What time does it start?" She fumbled with her Blackberry to bring up her schedule. "I'll make it in time. Just let me talk to Mya again, before she rebooks my flight. I'll tell her to be sure I land by four o'clock."

"You'll miss the dinner."

"I will not. If I have to go straight from the airport, I will be there. Trust me, Russell."

"Well…"

"Have I ever let you down before?"

There was a long pause, and she could tell he was trying hard to come up with an incident.

"You know I haven't. I've never missed a deadline, and I've never missed an appointment that couldn't be rescheduled. The ladies of Atlanta can't be rescheduled, ergo, I'll be there."

"You can't call them ladies," he barked.

"Russell, I am a woman. Therefore, it's all right. I can call them ladies. You, however, are a man. You can't."

"Ha, ha."

"Just so we're clear. Goodbye." She hung up.

George Hudson came into the hotel lobby from the elevator, searching for her. He spotted her and strode to the sofa where she waited. The little lines at the corners of his gray eyes caught the light with unflattering clarity.

"Miss Gillette. Have I kept you waiting?"

"Not at all, Commander. Thank you so much for agreeing to see me. You must be tired."

"It's been a long day. Would you like coffee?"

"Actually, the coffee shop is closed, and you've probably been drinking it all evening."

He smiled, and she caught a glimpse of the rugged hero. "You're right. But that doesn't mean you can't be comfortable."

"We can talk right here, sir, if it's not too public for you."

"Not at all." He eased down beside her on the sofa, but he maintained the erect posture. Did he ever relax? His back was as straight as a poker, without giving the impression of stiffness. She'd never thought of Pierre that way. Maybe it came with experience—and rank. "It's been a while since I saw your sister. How is Marie doing?"

"Very well. She has a baby boy now."

Hudson's smile grew. "I was delighted to hear that. I'd love to see him."

"Do you and Pierre stay in touch?"

"Yes, we talk fairly often. But I'm still stationed in Hawaii, so we don't get together very often. Pierre came through Pearl once since Marie's adventure. He had dinner with my wife and me."

"That's nice. What brings you to New York?"

The commander's smile stayed on his lips, but his eyes took on a pensive look. "I'm here for a conference among military and civilian leaders of several countries."

Claudia smelled intrigue. "Why here, not at the Pentagon?"

"We've been asked to brief the Security Council of the United Nations." In the pause that followed, she waited for him to reveal more.

"On…?"

"Joint efforts on various projects. I'm sorry I can't discuss the particulars with you."

"But the Navy sent you, not an admiral."

Hudson cleared his throat. "Actually, they did send an admiral. I'm here to assist him."

Her mind buzzed. How would a man like George Hudson play into all this? "Perhaps it's time I told you what I do for a living, Commander. I wouldn't want you thinking I waylaid you under false pretenses."

"Oh?" He continued to watch her, no more or less on guard than before. She imagined he would be a difficult man to surprise.

"I'm a writer for *Global Impact* magazine."

"So I understand. Congratulations on your nomination for the IPET award. That was an insightful story on India."

She pursed her lips. Either he had an extraordinary memory, or he'd done a quick background check on her. "Thank you. Why do I have the feeling you know what I'm going to say next?"

He laughed, and she found herself smiling again. He was very attractive. The combination of charm, experience, handsome features, a trim physique, and the bearing of a born leader swept away any reservations she'd felt.

"Let's see if you're right. The conference I'm attending is being covered by the media, but it's a closed event. Only people with high security clearance have access. The news will report that we are indeed talking about international security, but it won't have any details of our agenda. I'm afraid there's nothing I can do for you and your magazine."

She squeezed her lips together and gave a little shrug. "Then I guess it's a good thing that's not why I wanted to talk to you."

"Ah. Just wanted to chat with a shirttail connection? It's always nice to meet old acquaintances when you're away from home. Keeps homesickness at bay."

"Oh, don't tell me you're homesick, sir."

"Very much so. My wife is back in Hawaii, and I don't like to travel without her."

"I'm sure you'll want to contact her later. I won't keep you long, Commander. I'll be honest—when I saw you, it brought back good memories and gratitude. What you did for Marie was wonderful. But I also thought of a knotty little problem I've been worrying at for several months now."

He arched his eyebrows and said nothing.

"Commander Hudson, I believe you're in the chain of command above my brother-in-law, Pierre."

"Not anymore." He shook his head ruefully. "Pierre left the Pacific command last year."

"But…don't you have something to do with his…you know, his line of work?"

"I'm not sure what you're getting at."

"Well, Pierre trains special operations sailors."

He hardly blinked, but she sensed a change in his demeanor. His openness was gone. Still friendly, still ready for small talk. But discuss special military operations? Double-lock-cast-iron.

"Please don't be alarmed, sir. I won't try to get any secrets out of you. It's just that I've wanted for some time to write an article about the women of the American special forces. I know there are a few, though probably only a handful. It's mostly men in those positions. But there are a sprinkling of women here and there. Women who have undergone arduous training, who've had to be better than the men to earn a place among them. And I think it would do the U.S. Navy a great deal of good if I were to profile one of these women for *Global Impact*."

George Hudson inhaled slowly. "We're always looking for ways to educate the public and to accurately portray the sacrifice our troops make."

She nodded. She'd said enough. Let him mull that over.

"Have you spoken to Pierre about this?"

"You do read minds."

He laughed again. "I couldn't imagine you not asking him, if it means so much to you. He must have turned you down."

"Actually, yes. You're right on the mark. I wouldn't say he was against it, but he felt it was beyond his authority to grant permission for something like that. Sir, I can promise you the utmost discretion. I would go anywhere in the world for that kind of an interview, and I would take extra caution not to reveal anything about her duties or her assignments that would jeopardize what she does."

He leaned on the arm of the sofa and rested his chin on his hand. "I read several of your articles on my lunch hour, Miss Gillette. You're a fine writer. I expected you to hit me for information about the special UN meetings. This is so…"

"Innocuous?" she prompted.

"Hardly. But it may be doable."

"Yes! Thank you, sir."

"Save your enthusiasm. My aide will scrutinize you more closely than an IRS auditor. If you don't pass muster, you can forget it."

"Great! I'll cooperate in any way I can to expedite that."

"I bet you will. Just tell me, what brought this on?"

"Once when I was at Marie's house, it came up in conversation."

"Pierre runs a tight ship."

She puzzled over that. "You mean…he wouldn't spill something like that? Well, the truth is, he didn't. Someone else mentioned a woman in connection with a charity project, and from the conversation, I gathered that she worked in the same unit with…with another Navy person who was there. Look, Commander, I'm not getting anyone in trouble just by telling you that I know you have women in special ops, am I?"

"No. We try to keep the composition of special forces units quiet, but if I get permission for you to run the story you're talking about, we'll be telling the world that a small percentage are females."

"Yes, sir. Is that a problem?"

He frowned. "I'm not sure. Let me run it by an admiral or two."

"You make it sound simple."

"No harder than interviewing mountain gorillas in the wild."

"You liked that story."

"Loved it. I e-mailed a copy to my wife. She's big on animals of all sorts. She—" He eyed her keenly. "If I tell you what she does, you'll want to fly to Hawaii and write about her."

Claudia hadn't felt so smug in years. "I already know what she does, sir. Your wife trains diving sea lions at the Marine Mammal Research Center."

He nodded slowly, his mouth twisted in an "I've been had" smile. Payday for cutting her shopping short this afternoon and spending two hours on the phone and computer.

"And I'd love to interview her," she added.

"Well, she's no longer with the Navy—just got out a couple of months ago."

"Oh? I guess I fell down on my research. I didn't know that."

"We're starting a family."

She eyed him in surprise. "That's wonderful. Congratulations."

"We're very happy about it. I plan to retire in about two years, and we'll probably move back to the mainland then." He glanced at his watch. "You know, there's a restaurant across the street. We could probably get some decaf. Or a glass of wine for you, if you want it."

"Thank you, but I know you need your rest. I appreciate your making time for me and agreeing to speak to the powers that be on my behalf." She stood, and Hudson leaped to his feet.

"Was there a particular unit you especially hoped to write about? Or perhaps that woman you mentioned has a name."

"She's in the same unit as Lieutenant William White Jr. They were training in Norfolk when I visited Pierre and Marie in March. Her first name is Heidi."

He shifted his gaze for a moment.

"You said no one would get in trouble."

"Oh, they won't. I was just wondering if this woman is an old friend of my wife's. They served together for a short time and made a lifelong friendship. If it's her, she'd make a good subject for your article." He held out his hand. "I'll see if I can cut some red tape for you. And I'm glad we connected, Miss Gillette."

"It's Claudia. So am I."

EIGHTEEN

All of the team members were aware of Commander Dryden's arrival on the shooting range. They kept on with their drills but took extra care to look good.

Bill watched from the corner of his eye as Dryden approached Pierre Belanger and huddled with him. His friend Edwin Brooks, nicknamed Squeegee, emptied his rifle's magazine and moved back, so Bill could have his turn.

"All yours, White. Let's see you beat that."

Bill adjusted his ear protectors, took his place on the firing line, and put the stock of his rifle to his shoulder. He focused on the target and let loose. Not bad at all.

Someone socked him on the shoulder as he lowered the gun. He looked around, and Squeegee gave him a thumbs-up.

In a momentary lull, Lieutenant Belanger called them all to gather around him and Dryden.

"All right, boys and girls," Dryden said with a humorless smile. "Change of plans. We're going to split you into two eight-man teams. One team will carry out the Algiers op, as scheduled, under Browne's leadership."

Bill straightened. His pulse picked up. Usually when they split the unit, he led the team with the less complicated assignment, and

Dryden led the other. The grouping was different today, and he didn't know what to expect.

"Group B will go with me to the Pacific. We've got intel out of Luzon. We're going in."

The sixteen men and women exhaled. The Philippine National Police's Special Action Force must have learned Dr. Gamata's location and called for help. That meant the situation was tricky. The nationals might have already botched a rescue attempt or two, alerting the insurgents. *We're ready,* Bill thought. *Bring it on!*

"You'll get your individual orders this afternoon," Dryden said. "White, I need you on this one."

Bill nodded, glad he hadn't been relegated to the Algiers team. Brownie could handle that.

"Browne, you know exactly what you need to do," Dryden said, "but we'll spend some time together going over the plan this afternoon."

Brownie nodded.

"All right. I have the rosters here. Group B pulls out at 0500 tomorrow. It will be made up of Teams 1 and 2. Group A, with Browne, will be made up of Teams 3 and 4." He handed a sheet of paper to Brownie. They crowded around, sorting out the two teams. It didn't take long. They always split into the same four-man groups. The team members quickly joined their leaders, separating a little from each other. Bill was always part of Team 1, which consisted of him, Jeff Stuart, Heidi Taber, and "Squeegee" Brooks, three of his closest friends. The other four who would go with them were good, steady men. All had different specialties that would help the mission succeed. Bill would miss Brownie on this one, but if his pal did well, it might mean a promotion, and that would be great for Brownie.

They would be hitting the islands in the middle of the rainy season, which might mean typhoons in addition to the usual jungle hazards and the Islamic guerillas that hid out in the rural areas. It wouldn't be a picnic, but he didn't care. They needed to rescue Dr. Alejandro Gamata from the terrorists, not only for the scientist's sake. If his captors succeeded in making practical applications of Gamata's research and, for instance, started turning out missiles, the Philippines could see a bloodbath.

"All right, Group B, you're dismissed to prepare for the op. I'll see you in the morning." Dryden's hearty voice pulled Bill back to the mundane tasks he needed to complete before morning. Laundry. Packing. Last-minute paperwork.

The desire to talk to Claudia flickered in his mind, but he suppressed it. Pierre was right—when Bill was around her, he wanted to tell her things. And he couldn't tell her much. Better not to even say he was leaving. He could e-mail her when the op was complete. Or maybe he could send a quick message tonight—*Hey, I'll be away again. Don't fret about me. I'll let you know when I'm back.* That ought to be enough. Just let her know why she wouldn't hear from him for a couple of weeks. With her nose for news, she might put it together when she read that Dr. Gamata had been freed by special forces. The Pentagon would want to brag if they were successful. And they would be. He couldn't think otherwise.

Stu slapped him on the back. "Hey, Billy Boy! We got the plum assignment, eh?"

Bill grinned at him. "We sure did."

NINETEEN

Tommy Knowlton stopped by Claudia's cubicle. He was too short to see over the partition, so he came in and sat on the corner of her desk and pretended to polish the crystal quill of Claudia's IPET statuette with his cuff. "Your award looks pretty good. Almost as good as mine."

"Doesn't it?"

"Think it was worth the heat and bugs and smells of India?"

"Absolutely. Are you doubting your calling, Thomas?"

Tommy shrugged. "I get sick of crummy hotels and restaurant food."

"You need a vacation." Claudia reached for her portfolio and slid a stack of file folders in it. "Follow my lead."

"You're really taking some time off?"

"Two glorious weeks in Maine, where I intend to loll on the beach, water ski, eat lobster, and loll on the beach."

"You said that."

"I'm doing it again. Every day."

"I heard the water's freezing cold in Maine, even in August."

She feigned shock. "One of the seven places you've never been? You should photograph the pristine paradise."

"If it's so great, why don't you live there?"

"Unfortunately, Tommy, there are few jobs in Maine that pay as much as you or I make here."

He chuckled. "Right. I'll see you in a couple of weeks, then." He stood up. "You want to have a drink when we leave here?"

"No, thanks."

"Oh, that's right. You're on the wagon now."

"Am I?"

"I haven't seen you take a drink in weeks—no, months. Not since… Okinawa, maybe. Yeah, sure. When you cut me loose and went off with Popeye the Sailor Man."

"His name is Bill."

"Oh, 'scuse me. Barnacle Bill."

"Ha, ha. You're right. I stopped drinking alcohol, but I'm not sure Bill had anything to do with it."

"Oh? I don't like the sound of that." He shot a glance toward the doorway and whispered, "You're not in a state of impending motherhood, are you?"

"Good grief, no."

Tommy puffed out a breath. "That's a relief."

"I just decided I like having all my faculties about me, unlike some people I could name."

"Oh, like I take one drink and I get stupid?"

She paused with her hands above her keyboard and smiled. "Well, there have been moments. Case in point, the passport episode."

He scowled at her. "It was stolen, for crying out loud! It's not like I was so drunk I left it in the hotel bar."

"Let's put it this way: If you'd been sober and careful, we wouldn't have had to beg the tourist police to get you a new one."

"You know, the new one has a notation that I lost it."

"Yeah, they keep track of stuff like that." Claudia clicked to print out an online article she wanted to take along and read.

"But it makes me look incompetent. I didn't—"

"I know, I know. You didn't lose it. It was stolen. We've had this conversation seventeen times already. Go home, Tommy. Visit your family."

"Can't. I used up all my vacation."

"What are you doing while I'm away?"

"Following Salli around New Orleans."

"That might be fun."

"It's not like it used to be."

"Well, natch. Neither is Salli." She moved her computer mouse, and the e-mail program came up on the screen.

Mya stuck her head into the opening of her cubicle. "Claudia, you've got a registered letter."

"That can't be good," Tommy said. "Bet it's a summons."

Claudia made a derisive face at him as she stood and reached for the envelope. The corner bore an embossed Navy crest. Her pulse skyrocketed. She could think of two possibilities. Bill had been incommunicado since her New York trip. Maybe he was back in the 48. But he'd never sent her snail mail. Or... She glanced over her cluttered desktop for a letter opener, didn't see one, and then tore the envelope open.

A single sheet of paper.

Dear Ms. Gillette:

It was a pleasure meeting you in New York. I spoke with Admiral Truax about your request yesterday, and he has agreed to have the necessary documents forwarded to your place of business. The unit you'll be profiling is headed for duty in Saipan. Enjoy! I recommend the Oleai Beach Bar & Grill. I look forward to reading a compelling article.

Sincerely,

Commander George Hudson, U.S.N.

She noted that the letter was mailed in Washington, DC. Commander Hudson must travel almost as much as she did.

"What?" Tommy snatched at the letter, but she pulled it away.

"Mya, cancel my flight to Maine."

"You're joking."

"Would I joke about giving up water skiing? I'm going to Saipan."

Mya stared at her for a long moment. "I'm not even sure where that is."

"You'll find out, though."

TWENTY

Bill studied the map, knowing the lives of his team could depend on how well he remembered it. Basilan Island, off the southwest point of Mindanao, in the Philippines.

They were sailing from Saipan on a small Navy amphibious warship, heading south and west. In the Celebes Sea, outside national waters, they would meet with a large fishing boat chartered by their Filipino contacts, and it would take them to Basilan.

Dryden gathered them in a cabin below deck as the ship moved out of the harbor.

"Our latest intel indicates the rebels will be moving the hostages soon. We hope to be in place when that happens. Otherwise, our allies will attempt a rescue."

"Can't we just jump in?" Squeegee asked.

"The timing is tricky. We may not get there soon enough." Dryden scowled at his notes. "They want the credit if they can do it alone. We'll try to meet up with them before they make their move, but if things start to happen before we're in place, we're to stand by in case they need us. If they get the package and pursuit is too hot, we'll take the victims, bring them to the boat, and move them away from Basilan *rapido.*"

Bill kept quiet, but he didn't like it. They might have come all this way for nothing—or worse, to see the locals botch the job when the

Gold Team could pull it off without a hitch. If they would just give the Americans the hostages' location and stand back...

"This is your last chance to send a message home," Dryden continued. "Your e-mail will be monitored. Then we go silent except for official communications until we're off the island and land in Guam."

Bill thought about writing Claudia another message and decided against it. No sense sending her any last words. He knew he'd let himself become far too attached to her. Maybe a quick note to Ben? No, he'd talked to his brother before they left the States. Ben prayed for him all the time. They understood each other. If things went wrong, Ben would get the word from his commanding officer. And Claudia? She'd hear about it from Pierre. He didn't like that thought, so he pushed it aside. Claudia didn't need him or any man. What she needed was Christ. Instead of sending another futile message, he'd pray for her. *Lord, bring her to Yourself. Whatever it takes.*

He'd never given a direct witness to Claudia. Why not? Bill leaned back in his seat and watched the others line up for a turn at the computer station. Was he afraid he'd offend her, push her away? That she wouldn't like him if he spoke about God too much? That she'd scorn him? He wasn't afraid to face fanatical terrorists in the tropical jungle, but the prospect of seeing derision in Claudia's features cowed him.

Had Claudia's regard become more important than obedience to the Almighty?

Bill closed his eyes for a moment, letting that settle on his heart.

Lord, I want to please You. As much as I admire Claudia, I don't want to get into a relationship that will draw me away from You. Protect me from myself if that's what I need.

He inhaled deeply, and a resolve came over him. He wouldn't initiate contact with Claudia again. And if she communicated with him, he would respond clearly and firmly. He would tell her what he believed was most important in this life and the next.

TWENTY-ONE

"What do you mean, they're not here?" Claudia tried to stare down Captain Byron T. Pendergast, U.S. Navy, but apparently the captain had practiced that ploy as much as she had, possibly more.

"Please sit down, Ms. Gillette." Pendergast indicated a canvas folding chair, and Claudia reluctantly eased onto it. She was exhausted, and the outside temperature topped ninety degrees. The two fans humming in the captain's office on the deck of the *USS Caleb A. Davis* didn't make a dent in the heat. They just moved it around in waves.

"I have all the proper credentials," Claudia said, nodding toward the envelope she had placed in his hands.

"I see that, but the unit you've been authorized to…interview… has left here."

She tried not to let her smile slip. "I was told they'd be in Saipan. I'd hoped to travel with them. That clearance document says I—"

"The Navy doesn't usually embed journalists in its fighting units, ma'am."

"I'm aware of that. But this is not 'usual.' This is a unique case."

He shook his head. "The unit has left Saipan. The best course I see is to turn you back from here."

She stared at him. "But, an *admiral* agreed to this."

"Yes, ma'am. I understand. But the unit's operations are fluid.

Their plans change at short notice. They have to strategize according to a lot of variables—the weather, the situation in the target area, local politics—many, many factors. And this time they decided they needed to strike earlier than planned."

"Strike?"

His jaw twitched. "They moved out ahead of schedule."

"For…"

"For their ultimate destination, which I can't reveal to you."

Another staring match. She could see he wasn't going to budge.

A sailor came to the doorway, and the captain raised his chin, indicating permission to speak.

"Sir, the harbor master's aide is here to see you."

"In just a minute." Pendergast glanced at Claudia. "No, wait. I'll come out there and speak to him." He rose and plucked a file folder off his desktop. "Excuse me, Ms. Gillette. I'll only be a moment. When I come back we'll see if we can arrange accommodations for you and a flight back to Guam in the morning."

Her resolution swelled and hardened. Guam, indeed. No way.

A rogue thought skipped through her mind and then came back and hovered. Pendergast knew where Commander Dryden's unit had gone. That information must be somewhere in this room.

She stared at his computer. No. Absolutely not. If she were caught touching it, she would find herself in water so hot she'd vaporize. But papers lay on his desk.

She shot a glance toward the door—or hatch, or whatever they called it on a ship—then rose and leaned over the desk. Requisition Form N7209. Phooey. Nothing good there. What was this? Hmmm. Looked like some junior officer's report of a training exercise. Nothing to do with Dryden's unit.

She looked around, and her gaze riveted to a map on the side wall. Was it possible in this era that a man used the old-fashioned, low-tech method of tracking his subordinates? She strode to the wall and stared at the map. Guess not. It was a blow-up of the Marianas and surrounding sea, but no colored pushpins told his secrets.

Dryden used this port as a jumping off point for...where? It couldn't be too far away, could it? And why hadn't they left from one of the large Navy bases in Guam or Okinawa? Secrecy, she guessed. And she was right in the middle of it. Putting a journalist in the unit right now could blow their mission, that's what Pendergast was saying.

Something fluttered in the back of her mind. She closed her eyes and tried to picture the map she'd studied after receiving her travel documents—tried to trace the curve of Pacific nations that cupped gently around and to the west of Saipan and the Marianas. Japan, Korea, China, Taiwan. The unit could be headed for any of those. But why not leave from Okinawa or Tokyo?

The Philippines, Indonesia, Papua New Guinea, and thousands of smaller islands. She backtracked. Bill had been to the Philippines at least twice. The worst time of his life happened there, he'd said once. And he'd come from a training exercise in the Philippines when she met him in Okinawa in June. Would they go back? If so, why?

She'd checked up on the clues he'd let fall. American military personnel were in the Philippines, in an advisory capacity. Supposedly the United States was forbidden to take a role in combat there. The Philippines was a friendly nation, and the U.S. had sent thousands of troops for bilateral training exercises in the jungle during the last few years. They practiced all the things Bill had mentioned in Okinawa, and more.

But there was more to it than training, she was sure. She'd read about the fight against Islamic insurgents. Several strong groups were making the current president's life miserable. In the rural mountains and jungles of the southern islands—Mindanao and a score of smaller isles—they raised support for their causes and meted out terror on those who stood against them. If the rebels got together to oppose the government, anything could happen.

Could Bill's unit be going in as part of another "training exercise" That was aimed at disrupting the insurgents' activities?

Just recently—within the last six months—there had been an

incident. Some scientist had been snatched. He'd done Nobel Prize quality research in…what field? She hadn't heard much about it, but then last month there was a brief article in the newspaper saying the Philippine government was trying to negotiate his release. If he'd been released—or killed—that would have made the news.

She opened her eyes. How far was Saipan from Manila? A thousand miles? More? It was as good a guess as any.

From outside the office came the murmur of voices. She might have a few more minutes. Resuming her seat, she pulled her satellite phone from her carry-on. It took several seconds for the call to go through, but at last she heard her assistant's cautious greeting.

"Mya!"

"Yeah?"

"What time is it there?" Claudia asked.

"Quarter past six."

"P.M.?"

"Yeah. I just got home. What do you want?"

"The name of that scientist who was kidnapped in the Philippines."

After a prolonged pause, Mya said, "What are you talking about?"

Claudia sighed. Mya wasn't stupid, but she was a topnotch journalist's assistant, not a journalist, for a reason.

"Sometime last spring, or winter even, a brilliant scientist was kidnapped in the Philippines. They don't know who did it, or they didn't when I read about it. They suspected terrorists would use him as a bargaining chip. I almost think his family was grabbed along with him."

"Dr. Gamata," Mya said.

"That's it! You remembered."

"No, I used my computer while you talked."

"Great. I'm stuck on a boat in Saipan, and the captain wants to send me home. Give me anything you can on Gamata. And tell me where in the Philippines the worst clashes with the Islamic insurgent groups have been this year."

She jotted notes furiously for three minutes. Pendergast's step in the doorway alerted her. "Thanks, Mya. Call you later." She slid her phone and notepad into her bag and stood to face the captain, smiling.

"So, Ms. Gillette, I'm going to send you over to our civilian liaison, who can help you with transport. You'll probably have to spend one night in a hotel, courtesy of the U.S. Navy, but we'll get you out of here as quickly as possible. I do apologize for the inconvenience." He gestured toward the door.

"I think not, sir. I came to do a job, which the U.S. Navy authorized me to do. I'm not going back to the States."

"Oh?"

"No, sir. You can get me transport to the Philippines to join Commander Dryden's unit, or I'll arrange it myself."

His chin came up. "And how would you do that?"

"I don't expect I'll tell you if you write me off, sir. I do have permission to accompany the Gold Team, and it's not specified that I stay behind when they leave Saipan."

He stood eyeing her dolefully for several seconds. "The orders I received pertaining to your project didn't mention any destination beyond Saipan."

"I can't help that. If it's a duplicate of what I received, it says I'll join the unit in Saipan. You're telling me it's too late for that. Very well. I'll join them someplace else. It doesn't say I can't accompany them to another location. And I have permission to spend up to a week with the unit and interview the team members. My documents say so. It seems clear to me that I was to join them here and stick with them wherever they went, in order to portray a more accurate picture of what they do."

"I can't allow you—"

"Sir, it's not up to you. The Navy allows it."

His eyes narrowed and he stood still for another long moment. "If you will wait outside, Ms. Gillette, I will put in a call to my superior about this."

Claudia could see that more debate would get her no further with this man. He'd made up his mind. There was a slim chance his superior would come down on her side. If not, she'd fly to Manila and see if she could pick up the trail there, though it seemed next to impossible without inside information. Still, he hadn't denied that the unit was headed for the Philippines. She felt she'd scored there.

She raised her chin and walked into the anteroom. The sailor at the desk smiled and nodded at her. There was only one chair available, and she took it.

The minutes ground on. Several times she thought about taking out her laptop, but as soon as she did that, Pendergast would probably pop out of his lair and tell her she was booked on a flight to San Francisco.

The sailor offered her coffee, and she accepted it. She made a foray to the restroom. After she returned to her seat, the sailor assured her that the captain had not inquired after her during her absence.

Forty-five minutes had passed when he finally came to his door.

"Ms. Gillette. Sorry to keep you waiting." He stood back, indicating she should enter once more, so she rose and walked toward him. She fancied the skin beneath his eyes was a shade darker, and he sounded tired.

She didn't sit down, but turned to face him.

"Well, ma'am, you get your way."

Relief washed over her. "Thank you very much, sir."

He nodded. "My superior was disinclined to let you go, but *his* superior felt that you might have time to do your interviews with Commander Dryden's men at a staging point, before they begin their actual operation."

"I can't tell you how much I appreciate this, sir."

He eyed her as though he hoped he wouldn't regret this later. But he'd covered his bases as far as possible. If something went wrong, he could lay the blame higher up.

"We'll send you by jet to Manila. From there you'll take a small plane to a coastal city I will not name, where your escort will connect you with some Philippine sailors. They will take you by boat to meet Dryden's outfit."

Claudia nodded.

"Ms. Gillette, if anything goes wrong, the Navy is not responsible. You are undertaking this jaunt at your own insistence."

"I understand. And if anything happens, I'll make sure everyone knows you were against this."

He didn't crack a smile.

TWENTY-TWO

0530 HOURS, AUGUST 13
BASILAN ISLAND, PHILIPPINES

Bill, Squeegee, and Heidi worked as quickly as they could in the eighty-five-degree mist to hide one of the small boats that would take them to safety later. Bill could stand rain better than heat, but rain and heat together were his least favorite conditions. He tried to visualize an arctic mission—him and Stu skiing across an ice sheet toward a Russian outpost.

Nope. Didn't work. The sweat still poured off him, soaking his uniform. They'd timed it so they arrived on shore at dawn. He could only imagine how hot it would be by noon.

When the boat was well-camouflaged from those approaching by sea, land, or air, the three of them headed back to the rocky outcropping where Dryden had Stu and McGraw, the communications specialist from the second four-man team, setting up the comm equipment. The other three men weren't back from hiding the second boat.

Bill walked over to Dryden. "We're good on Team 1, sir. The boat location is a hundred and fifty yards down shore."

"Good."

"Sir, we're all set," Stu called. "Do you want us to initiate comm with our friends?"

"No, they're supposed to contact us with their precise location. Just stand by. We're right on schedule."

Bill wondered what would happen if the local contacts had fouled up the new plan. His team had hurried and moved out of Saipan a full week sooner than scheduled when they heard that Dr. Gamata had been moved for the third time. They needed to strike before the Filipinos doing recon lost track of him again and the insurgents moved their hostages to a place where the rescuers couldn't find them.

The mist became a drizzle as the men from Team 2 returned. Dryden posted two sentries, and the rest huddled together under a rock overhang on the lower part of the outcropping, but the shelter wasn't big enough for seven of them. The radio equipment came first, so they put up a couple of thin plastic tarps for a little extra protection, but no one kept dry. The day grew no brighter as the morning progressed. They broke out the MREs and ate breakfast.

"I'm gonna move to Arizona when I retire," Stu said.

"Yeah, me too. Anyplace dry." Squeegee had found a spot where the rock face protected his torso, but his feet and legs had no shelter and were soaked.

Heidi had wormed back among a clump of shrubs behind Team 1's tarp and lay with her head on her pack. "Eastern Oregon," she said. "Hardly ever rains."

"Brownie and the guys in Algeria are probably wishing they were here." Bill scrunched up the wrappings from his meal and stowed them. They had to be careful not to leave the smallest trace of their stop here.

A few yards away, the radio crackled. Stu and McGraw dove for it. Their Philippine contacts had come through.

They listened from beneath the tarps as Stu and the commander talked to the Philippine nationals. After a brief conversation, Dryden called out, "Pack up, men. We're moving inland to meet our friends. They think they can deliver the package to us."

"I knew it," Squeegee growled. "We came all this way, and *they're* going to rescue the professor and hand him to us."

"I don't like it either," Dryden said, "but they weren't expecting us to be ready, and they think they see an opportunity. We've got a six-hour march to the meeting place. Let's move."

Bill looked uneasily at his companions. Six hours! They'd expected a two-to-three-hour march by landing where they did. They quickly packed up their equipment. Bill called the sentries in and they ate while the others wiped away the evidence of their short stay near the landing place. Dryden conferred with Bill on the exact coordinates of the new rendezvous and the optimum route.

"We'll leave McGraw and Ocalla here," Dryden said. "Since we're not doing an insertion, just a pickup, I think we can leave two men behind to keep watch. They can have the boats ready when we come back, and in the meantime they can alert us to any activity along the shore. Our friends will make their move after dark and bring us the doctor and his family."

Bill nodded. They should be reunited before daybreak, with the Gamata family in tow. They would radio for a larger boat to meet them a mile or so off Basilan.

They shouldered their packs and were about to head into the jungle when McGraw whistled from his concealed spot nearer the shore.

The others turned to peer toward him through the drizzle.

"A motor, sir."

Bill listened, and he made out the faint sound. Dryden waved them all to conceal themselves until they knew the source. Bill found himself snuggled up to Stu in the dripping bushes.

"Boat," Stu whispered a moment later.

Bill looked at Dryden, who crouched ten feet away. "Sir, it sounds like the boat that brought us."

Dryden nodded. They waited in silence as the sound of the motor grew louder. Bill was sure the fishermen hired by the Special Action Force of the Philippine National Police, who had dropped them off before daylight, were returning. When the sound grew so loud it seemed almost on top of them, the engine cut out, and a man shouted. "Hey! We got a delivery for you. You still there?"

Dryden stood and emerged from his hiding place but motioned

for the others to stay hidden. He walked cautiously toward the lookout near the water. McGraw had answered the Philippine man's call, and the low murmur of conversation drifted back to Bill and the others.

"What do you think's going on?" Stu asked.

Bill shook his head, straining to hear. "It can't have to do with the kidnap victims. Our forward contact would have radioed."

A moment later, Dryden's voice came loud and clear. "What? Absolutely not! This is insane."

So much for keeping quiet. Bill stood and eased out of his hiding place.

"I don't care who signed your documents, madam, you can get right back on that boat and go back to Zamboanga."

Did he say *madam*?

Bill took a couple of steps toward Dryden and the new arrivals.

"No, ma'am, this is not a training exercise. This is a joint military operation by the U.S. Navy and the Armed Forces of the Philippines. Your presence here can only interfere with our mission and endanger you and other people. Now, are you getting back on that boat, or do I have to pick you up and put you on it?"

Bill was close enough now to see a Filipino sailor standing near Dryden, listening to his tirade with a pained expression distorting his features. Another person was hidden from his view by Dryden's broad uniformed back, and Bill assumed that person was the target of his commander's anger.

"It makes no difference who you work for," Dryden went on. "Magazine, network TV, or the Dalai Lama, I don't care."

Bill's gut clenched in foreboding. Magazine? It couldn't be. He took another step forward.

Dryden turned toward him and swore, throwing his hands in the air. "How could this happen?"

Bill ducked, but it was too late.

"White! Get over here."

He gulped and walked toward them.

"We have an uninvited guest. Get Stuart up here with the radio. This woman claims to have permission to trek through the island with us. It's ridiculous. Basilan has been a combat hot spot for years. And we've got to move out, or we won't make our rendezvous."

Bill leaned to his right just far enough to get a quick glimpse of her. Striding toward them was a tall woman with sleek, dark hair, regal in bearing. She wore khaki slacks and a shirt that looked almost like a uniform but might have come from a shop specializing in high-end casual attire. That was all he saw before he pulled back and focused on Dryden. But it was enough.

"Yes, sir." He wheeled and dashed back to where Stu and the others waited.

"Stu, get out there. The commander's mad, and I think he wants you to patch him through to…somebody."

"We're supposed to keep silence now."

"I know. Go."

Stuart shouldered the pack containing the heavy radio equipment and hurried toward the commander.

Bill inhaled deeply and turned around to watch. The rain pattered around him. It had slacked off some, and the sun struggled to burn a hole in the clouds, but that wouldn't change the facts. Claudia Gillette had just walked into their secret op.

Heidi slithered up beside him. "What's going on?"

"We…" Bill gulped. "There's a reporter here."

"A reporter? You're kidding! From Manila?"

"No, from… Actually she writes for a big magazine out of Atlanta. *Global Impact*."

"I read that when I'm home. It's good."

"Yeah…" Might as well tell her. "She may be hoping to feature you in her article. You know—first woman in a special operational force, that sort of thing."

"Wow." Heidi squinted toward the commander and his unwanted guest.

Dryden's fury, unleashed on Claudia, the men who had brought her, and the world in general, was audible from twenty yards away and possibly a lot farther.

"He told you all that?" Heidi asked.

"No, I..." Bill stopped, unwilling to admit what he knew. It wasn't his fault Claudia had found them. Or was it? If Dryden found out he knew her...

Heidi turned toward him, and he could see her eyes widen in her tanned face. "Don't tell me she's the same woman you went off with in Okinawa."

"What—you heard about that?"

"Of course I heard about that. The guys talked about nothing else for a week at least. She's someone you know from back home or something, they said."

"Uh, not exactly back home. I met her in Norfolk." Bill tried to steady his breathing and sort out his best course of action. Should he come clean with Dryden and tell him everything? The commander didn't like convoluted explanations, and it would have to be a detailed one if he were to understand Bill's non-role in bringing Claudia to Basilan.

Who am I kidding? It's totally my fault. She wouldn't have come if I hadn't let her know more than I should.

"White!" The sound of his name on the commander's lips made him shudder.

Heidi patted his arm gently, and he marched forward.

Claudia watched from beneath lowered eyelids as Bill approached a second time. He had to have recognized her by now, even though they'd had no chance to greet each other. Bill avoided looking directly at her, keeping his eyes on his leader. Apparently he wasn't going to acknowledge her. All right, she could play that game.

Dryden turned as Bill arrived at his side. "White, move the men back. Some idiot allowed a reporter to fly out and join us, thinking she could play Barbara Walters in the middle of a covert mission."

"Yes, sir."

Dryden gave a curt nod. "I've got Stuart putting in a call for me. We'll straighten this out, and then we move. We'll need to make up some time."

The Filipino sailor who had escorted Claudia cleared his throat. "Excuse me, Commander. We need to leave immediately."

"Oh, no you don't. You're not going anywhere without this civilian."

The sailor glanced toward shore and the boat that waited for him. "But, sir, we have orders to make a quick drop and then return to port. This is a highly active area for the insurgents, and we—"

"I know it. Do you think I want to stand here arguing? As soon as my superior tells this woman she has to leave, you can go. Unless, of course, she'll leave with you now of her own free will."

Claudia threw back her shoulders. She hated the thought that she might have delayed a truly important mission, but no way would she give up this story after all she'd been through to get here. She wouldn't get a second chance to observe the unit on a covert operation, especially now that she'd enraged the commanding officer.

"No, sir, I won't do that."

"Thought so. Stuart?" He whirled toward the radio man.

"I'm trying, sir. Getting a lot of static. They may be jamming us."

Dryden addressed the Filipino again. "Your commanders have been very cooperative, and we're doing our best to get your government out of a sticky situation. But do they really think we'll take a civilian along, and a woman at that? Not to mention that she's a reporter? This is a classified detail."

"I'm sorry, sir. She's an American, and her documents indicate she received clearance for this operation."

"Yeah, well, when I find out who authorized it, heads are going to roll."

All right, that's enough. Claudia lifted her chin. "Commander Dryden, I assure you that I went through proper channels for my clearance. I can also promise that I will not undermine this mission in any way."

"Proper channels." Dryden spit on the ground. "Know what I think? I think you knew someone, or you dazzled some junior grade officer and talked him into sliding this through for you when his boss was in a mellow mood. That's what I think."

"You're wrong, sir. It's true that an officer cut through some layers of red tape for me, but—"

"Tell me he's not a relative."

She felt the blood rush to her cheeks, thankful that she'd bypassed Pierre in her quest. "No, sir, he's not. I'd met him once before, when he saved my sister's life. It's a long story. But I didn't go and seek him out for this. We ran into each other again by accident, and he seemed happy to help me do this. He felt it would honor the unit and bring the Navy some good PR."

"Who's your sister?"

Claudia threw a quick glance at Bill. He was staring at the ground. "Marie Belanger."

Dryden turned his head slightly, observing her with one eye. "I remember that case. Her husband is a training officer in Norfolk now."

"Yes, sir. I suppose you know him."

"Of course I know Lieutenant Belanger. He's a good man."

"But he's not the one who helped me get here. Pierre had nothing to do with this. And neither did anyone in this unit."

Just for a second, Bill's gaze met hers. He winced and looked away.

"Sir," Stuart said, "I've got Captain Pendergast's aide, but they've left Saipan."

Dryden hurried to the microphone and registered his displeasure without giving away any particulars in case their transmission was being intercepted.

"I copy that, sir, but the captain says it's late to be grousing. He traced this thing up two levels and got nowhere. Over."

"I don't care who authorized this," Dryden growled. "Undo it. We're sending the package back to you. Over."

"Negative. We've moved position and cannot take delivery, sir."

Dryden bowed his head for a moment. Claudia looked at Bill and decided she could whisper to him. The Filipino sailor would hear, but probably not the preoccupied commander or the radio man.

"I didn't mean to cause any trouble. Honest."

Bill opened his mouth and then glanced Dryden's way and closed it.

Poor guy. Can't decide whether to pretend he's never seen me before or jump to my defense.

"I understand," she whispered. "I won't bring this back to you."

His almost imperceptible nod irked her. She'd figured Bill for a red-blooded American hero. And he was afraid to admit to his CO that he knew a woman he'd called his friend? A woman he'd kissed in magical Okinawa only two months ago? He'd shot her cherished memory full of holes, and now he couldn't even look her in the eye.

Dryden's voice rose. "Well, you just take it up another level, you hear me? This is critical."

The aide's voice sounded tired and faint. "I can't do that, sir. Our orders were to proceed with embedding the…package."

Dryden snarled something at his radio operator. All was quiet for thirty seconds, and then Stuart succeeded in securing another connection for Dryden.

"Belanger, that you?"

Claudia jumped and turned to stare at Dryden's rigid back. He'd actually patched through to Pierre in Virginia? Unbelievable, the arrogance of the man.

A feeble "Yes, sir" came, sounding as though the transmission originated on Neptune.

"I want to know what your wife's sister is doing mucky-mucking my top secret op."

"I…I don't know anything about it, sir. I can't…" Static crackled from the radio.

Stuart fiddled with the switches. "We lost him, sir."

Dryden swore and walked the three steps back to where she stood.

"Ms. Gillette, it seems the admiral who signed your clearance assumed we'd be in Saipan all week, preparing for this op. When things changed in the field, we moved our action up a week, but he didn't know that."

"That's regrettable in some ways, Commander," Claudia said, "but in others, it's terrific. I'll get to observe your troops in action, not just in training and preparation."

"No, it's not good." His voice rose again. "We do our best to keep our ops secret, and what do we get? I'll tell you. We get saddled with an aggressive reporter who can give us up to the enemy without even trying." He swung around and glared at the sailor. "Tell your crew to stand by to take this woman back aboard."

"I have a right to be here," Claudia said as the Filipino moved toward the boat. She made no attempt to soften her tone now.

"White—" Dryden rounded on Bill. "I don't care if it takes the whole team, you get her back on that boat. That's an order."

"Yes, sir." Bill grimaced at her and turned to jog away. The commander ignored her and went back to the radio.

"Sir—" The radio man spun and stared toward the shoreline.

Dryden let fly a string of curses. On the sun-dappled green water, Claudia saw the hull of the boat receding. When its engine started, the boat was already fifty yards from land.

TWENTY-THREE

"What's wrong, buddy?" George Hudson flinched as his best friend blasted him verbally via cell phone from five thousand miles away. When Pierre paused for breath, he said softly, "Okay, settle down. Take a deep breath and tell me what happened."

Pierre ground out one word. "Claudia."

"Cl... Oh. You mean Marie's sister. Miss Gillette."

"Yes, I mean the in-your-face, behind-your-back, glory-grabbing reporter, Claudia Gillette. If I'm ever in the same hemisphere with her again, I will strangle her."

George sucked in a breath and put on the slowest, calmest drawl he could muster. "I'm not sure that would be the best course of action, Pierre. Actually, I find her quite charming. Now tell me exactly what she's done to you."

"To me? To *me*? You mean to the United States of America!" A heated melee seemed to follow this statement, as though Pierre were grappling over the phone with a Ninja.

"George? It's Marie."

Ah, the sweet voice of sanity. George sat down on the edge of the bed. Rachel came to the bedroom doorway and arched her eyebrows. They were supposed to leave for the airport...three minutes ago.

"Hi, Marie," George said, shrugging helplessly at Rachel. "It's great to hear from you kids. Pierre sounded a little upset just now, but he didn't tell me what's going on."

"It's my sister. You remember Claudia?"

"Sure, I do. Beautiful woman. I saw her in New York a few weeks ago. Did she tell you?"

"Yes, she did." Marie paused. "We're wondering if that has anything to do with her being in the Pacific theater now."

George sat still for a moment, processing. "Claudia did tell me she wanted to write an article about a special forces unit, and I did take her request to Admiral Truax."

"You *what*?" Pierre was back on the phone.

George flinched and pulled the receiver from his ear. He counted silently to ten and then put it back up. "Pierre?"

"*C'est moi.* I thought you hung up."

"I might do that if you scream at me again."

"I am not screaming."

"Says you. Now let me get this straight. I did Claudia a little favor, helping her get clearance to interview some troops, and now you tell me she's making a hash of some secret op."

"That's right. We love Claudia, but she has no clue the trouble she's causing me."

"Is there anything I can do?"

"It's not what you can do, it's what you did already."

"Where is she?"

"I can't tell you over an insecure phone connection."

"Right. Well, is she hurt?"

"No, she's just making things difficult for one of our teams."

George sighed. "I'm sorry, *mon ami.* Frankly, she's a big girl. Let her sort it out."

"You're right. I shouldn't have yelled at you. It's just that I'd told her to back off. I feel as though she sneaked around to get permission without my knowing it. She used you, George."

"So? She was up-front about it. Writers use their contacts to get the information they need. What she asked me for was perfectly legitimate. She wanted to put her request before someone who had the authority to grant it. I delivered the message. That's all. It shouldn't cause you any problems. If she's in trouble now, let her deal with it."

"Commander Dryden just called me—"

"Dryden? Don't know him."

"I train his teams. He just called me from a combat location to rake me over the coals. I'm afraid he'll…" Pierre sighed. "Never mind. I'll work it out."

George gritted his teeth. "Good. I don't mean to sound like I don't care, Pierre, but Rachel and I are about to fly to Oregon to spend some time with her folks."

"You're taking leave?"

"Yes, I am. Thirty days, as a matter of fact."

Pierre whistled softly.

"I know." George chuckled. "Unbelievable, isn't it? But we haven't seen her parents since Christmas. Now that Rachel's out of the Navy and we're…well, you know. We're expecting. She wants to see her mother, and so we're going." He looked up. His wife stood in the doorway again, tapping her wristwatch.

"Rachel is still training the sea lions, isn't she?"

"Oh, yeah. She's working as a civilian now." George stood up. "Look, buddy, we've got to run or we'll miss our flight. I'm sorry. I wish I could help you."

"No, that's okay," Pierre said. "It will be all right. I just felt so frustrated. But I shouldn't have ragged on you. If it's any consolation, I feel better now."

Rachel grabbed George's hand and pulled him toward the door.

"Good. I'll call you when we get to the mainland, okay?" George hung up and shoved the phone into his pocket. It had been a good day until Pierre's call. Now he felt rushed and guilty and at loose ends. "Sorry about that."

"What's up?" Rachel asked.

"Marie's sister is in high gear. I'll tell you about it in the car." He scooped up their luggage. "Let's go."

TWENTY-FOUR

Bill heard the shouts behind him and stopped cold. Over Dryden's raging, he heard the boat's engine puttering away. Claudia stood where he'd left her, alone in the shadow of the bamboo trees. Beyond her, Stu was silhouetted near the radio equipment staring out to sea, and Dryden marched toward the landing place.

Squeegee and Heidi slithered out of the brush and stood beside him.

"What happened?" Squeegee asked.

"The boat left the civilian here and took off without her. The commander's gone ballistic."

"White!" Dryden turned and shouted to him. "Bring your team down here. Now."

Bill, Heidi, and Squeegee ran toward the beach. As they passed Claudia, she stepped into his path.

"Bill?"

He paused only a second. "I can't talk now."

"But I—"

He dodged around her and kept going. Dryden, Stu, Heidi, and Squeegee were staring out at the departing boat.

"I am going to kill someone," Dryden said in a tight, controlled voice.

"Sir..." Squeegee stared up into the cloud-strewn sky. The sun made a brave showing, but off to the south another bank of dark clouds moved in.

Bill looked where Squeegee looked, stepping out from under the foliage. He heard another thrumming—not the boat engine.

The sudden, unmistakable whine of an aircraft engine sent them all scrambling for cover. Peering out from beneath a pine's low branches, Bill suddenly wondered about Claudia. He looked around. She still stood in the same spot, staring upward. The plane zoomed low over their landing place with a roar and then turned its nose toward the sea. They half stood to watch as it flew over the departing boat. Gunfire rattled from the boat, and they could see the tracer fire. The plane circled, and a moment later a waterspout rose near the boat.

"They're targeting the boat," Stu said. They watched helplessly. A small explosion poofed, and orange flames rose from the stern of the boat.

"Direct hit," Heidi whispered.

Suddenly the plane turned and sped toward the island.

"Take cover!" Dryden pushed Heidi ahead of him and rushed back to help Stu shove the radio equipment toward the overhanging rock face.

Bill ran through the brush, grabbed Claudia's wrist, and yanked her out of the small clearing. He shoved her into the thickest underbrush and threw himself on top of her.

"Keep your head down." He smashed his face into her back. She had no helmet, but at least his body armor could protect her, to some extent.

"I can't breathe!"

He barely heard her protest as the plane roared directly over them. As the sound of the engine grew a little less unbearable, Claudia wiggled, and he raised himself on his elbows to give her more mobility.

"That was close." She tried to shove him away.

"It's not over," Bill said grimly.

"What do you mean?" The engine noise grew louder.

"They went straight for the boat, then made a pass looking for us. Come on, move further into the woods."

"What—"

Too late. Sporadic gunfire erupted as the plane swooped over their position again. Bill pressed her down again and hid his face. A couple of the men on the ground opened fire on the plane as it skimmed the treetops. A shell exploded only yards away. Bill jumped and held Claudia down in spite of her wriggling. Another hit farther away, then another.

At last all was quiet. Bill cautiously raised his head, pushed back on his knees, and looked toward the shore. Sound returned in a jumble. He rose and tried to sort out the noises that assaulted him. The receding plane engine, moans, and shouts.

"Can I get up now?" Claudia's tone was more exasperated than afraid.

Don't you get it yet? "Wait here."

Bill ran the last few steps and made out Stu kneeling beside the commander. Before he reached them, he saw the mangled mass of the officer's lower body. Blood pooled around them.

"Dryden's hit." Stu ripped open the officer's camo shirt.

Bill knelt and put his fingers to Dryden's throat.

"I didn't get a pulse," Stu said.

Bill lifted the commander's wrist and tried to catch a sign of life.

Stu looked up at him. "Too late for him."

"Are you sure?"

"Yeah. What do we do?"

Bill inhaled deeply. "Call whoever you called before. We need new orders."

"Didn't know the guerillas had aircraft," Stuart said.

"They probably stole it. They're pretty well organized and equipped now." Bill looked down at Dryden's face, barely recognizable. He tried not to look took closely at the rest of him, but he knew they would have to deal with the remains.

One of the other men crashed toward them. "Where's Nelson? We've got casualties."

Bill leaped to his feet. "How many?"

"Ocalla's hit. McGraw's dead. I don't know about the others." Proul stared down at the commander for a moment and swore.

"Take me to Ocalla." Bill followed Ensign Proul to the spot where the men of Team 2 had clustered. Two men lay on the ground. McGraw was clearly dead. Bill focused on Ocalla, the ensign who lay moaning on the bloody grass. His chest and abdomen were soaked in dark blood.

"Heidi?" Bill called.

"We're over here," Squeegee called from off to his left. "Taber's hit."

"Where's Nelson?" Proul looked about frantically as if expecting the medic to appear between the stalks of bamboo.

"Don't know," Squeegee replied.

"Nelson!" Bill shouted.

"Here. I'm coming."

"Thank God!"

The medic thrashed his way through a thicket. Blood ran down his cheek, and one pant leg bore a dark stain as well.

"You all right?" Bill asked.

"Superficial wounds," Nelson said through gritted teeth. "The shock threw me, and I think I passed out. I'll be okay, though."

"Do what you can for Ocalla. I'll check Taber." Bill pushed his way through the brush toward Squeegee and Heidi. They'd all had extensive first aid instruction, but Nelson was the only one with advanced medical training. If Heidi's wound was serious, Bill would have to give her care over to Nelson.

Squeegee rose as he approached. "She's going to be okay, I think."

Heidi lay in the bushes, trembling and holding tight to her left arm. Blood oozed out around her fingers, where she compressed what was left of her sleeve.

Bill knelt beside her. "How you doing, Heidi? You took a little lead?"

"Yeah, but it's not that bad. I don't think it hit the bone. Flesh wound."

"I dunno. You're losing a lot of blood. Let's take a look."

She struggled to sit up, and Bill gave her a hand.

"You okay? Dizzy or anything?"

"A little woozy. Just give me a minute." She squeezed the wound, rocking back and forth and scrunching her eyes shut. "Hurts like crazy."

"I'll bet." Bill laid a hand lightly on her other shoulder and glanced behind him. He could hear a lot of talk, but couldn't sort it out.

"I'll go see what I can do over there," Squeegee said.

"Yeah, good idea." Bill managed a smile at Heidi, knowing he'd have to tell her about the casualties soon. "Look, we've all got first aid kits in our packs, but you may need some extra dressings. Let me have a look, so I'll know what we need."

"Where's Nelson? Maybe he should look."

"Yeah, when he can."

"There's other people hit, aren't there?"

"Yes."

"How bad?"

Bill gritted his teeth. "It's bad, Heidi. The commander…"

"What?" Her eyes locked on his. "Dryden's down?"

"Yeah. He's…he didn't make it."

She let out a soft moan. "Anyone else?"

"We'll get an update after I look at your arm. Come on, kiddo."

She fumbled with her buttons. He helped her ease her arm out of her camo shirt. The wound was just below the edge of her dark T-shirt's sleeve. The blood had seeped into the fabric layers, staining both shirts and her bulletproof vest.

"It's a flesh wound," she insisted.

"Okay. You may be right, but the exit wound is pretty ragged. Chewed your muscles up. We can probably stop the bleeding, but it's going to hurt a lot. And keeping it clean is going to be difficult out here."

He rummaged through his own pack for his first aid kit. "Here's an alcohol wipe. It'll sting, but it will kill surface germs."

"There might be other people who need you more," Heidi said.

"They'll tell me if they do."

Bill found sterile field dressings and applied one to her bloody arm. "I can't tell if that's exactly in position."

She sucked in air. "It's the right place." She held it while he unrolled a long strip of gauze and wrapped it around the dressing. "Is Stu okay? He was with the commander."

"Yes. I talked to him. He's fine."

She nodded. "I'm sorry, Bill."

"What are you sorry for?"

Heidi blinked rapidly. "For everything that happened in the last twenty minutes. We can't get Dr. Gamata and his family now."

Bill clenched his teeth and took out his knife to cut the strip of gauze.

"Billy Boy?"

"Yeah, Squeegee."

"We just did a head count."

"And?"

Squeegee squatted down beside him and Heidi. "Our people are okay on Team 1. Heidi's the only casualty. But Team 2…"

"Yeah? I know they lost McGraw. How's Ocalla doing?"

"Not good, Bill. Nelson's trying to help him, but it doesn't look good."

"He had his vest on, right?"

"Yeah, but Nelson told me he didn't like to wear the ceramic plates. Too hot and heavy, ya know?"

Bill froze with the knife in his hand and stared at Squeegee. He was the opposite of Bill physically—small, thin, and wiry, with dark, curly hair and black eyes. "Well, yeah, but…" No use discussing the alternatives now. Shrapnel must have cut through the vest. It was too late for Ocalla, who had exercised his options.

"So we've lost McGraw and the commander, and maybe Ocalla," Squeegee said.

"Is Nelson really okay?"

"He says he is, but his face is all bloody. Shrapnel, I guess."

Bill stood up slowly, but the jungle seemed to spin around him. Two dead, maybe three, the rest of them hardly scratched. How was that possible? "Did Stu call headquarters?"

"He's trying, but he thinks the radio is shot."

Bill sucked in a long, slow breath. "So there's seven of us left, and two are wounded."

"Eight. That reporter woman is all right. She's helping Nelson with Ocalla."

Bill tried to gulp down the boulder in his throat. He'd forgotten all about Claudia.

TWENTY-FIVE

Pierre paced the small living room, his heart pounding. The baby fussed in the bedroom, but Marie would tend to him.

"Come on, *mon ami*. Pick it up."

"Hello, Pierre."

Pierre couldn't help smiling at the sound of George's voice. "I'm sorry to call you when you're off duty."

"I take it this is business?" George asked.

"Yes. Things have gone badly with the Gold Team."

"How bad?"

"The captain in their chain of command has lost contact with Commander Dryden and his unit."

"They went dark, or something worse?" George asked.

"He said the comm specialist was trying to relay a message, and it went blank. Something about an air attack on a boat, but they'd already disembarked on Basilan." Pierre bit his lip. He hadn't meant to mention any specific locations. "Scratch that."

"Okay. How long ago?"

"A while. Not long. Maybe half an hour. I didn't say anything to him, but...I'm worried about Claudia."

After a pause George asked, "Did you say anything to Marie?"

"Not yet. She was doing the dishes when he called me, and I think she's feeding Skipper now. She knows about Claudia going out there but not about this wrinkle. She doesn't even know where they are."

"Gotcha." George sighed. "We're in the airport, and we'll be leaving for Rachel's folks' soon. Do you need me to cancel?"

Pierre sank down on the sofa. "I don't know what I need. To be honest, I was hoping you could give me some advice. It's a big mess."

"Give it some time. They may call in later and tell you that everything's okay."

"I have a bad feeling about this one. Look, I'm considering heading out myself. They may need extraction."

"You have no reason to think that."

Pierre jumped up and began to pace again. "George, I personally trained this elite team. They're the best. They've taken on dangerous assignments all over the world. Last spring they saved our bacon in Algeria, maybe averted a declaration of war. And if they need help, I'm going to make sure they get it."

"I agree, but let's wait until we know what the situation is."

"It might be too late by then. They're halfway around the world. I can't move quickly from this distance. Besides, my wife's sister is out there. I can't keep this from her. Marie is going to be frantic."

"So you need to be there with Marie. Look, we're not going to board the plane for a few more minutes. I'll make some calls and see what I can find out. I don't know what else you can do right now."

Pierre ran a hand through his hair and scratched the back of his head. "I'm not asking you to cancel your trip. I wouldn't do that. But I'm telling Marie now, and then I'm going to pack."

"What is it?" Rachel laid aside the paperback she'd pretended to be reading and reached for George's hand.

"The Gold Team. They've had some kind of trouble."

"And they called you?"

"No, that was Pierre again."

Rachel bit her lip. "I heard you say you'd make some calls. Honey, you're not doing much field work anymore."

"I know. All I intend to do is see if we can find out for sure whether the team is in trouble. Claudia Gillette is out there with them." He glanced around the passenger boarding area and leaned close to her ear. "From the sound of things, they're on Basilan, which is a snake's nest of pro-Muslim insurgents. I was instrumental in Claudia's getting clearance to interview the unit, but I didn't think she'd get dropped in the middle of a guerilla war."

"It's not your fault."

George clenched his teeth. "If this is my mess, I should help clean it up."

Rachel nodded. "You're also on leave."

George pulled her to him and kissed her. "I haven't forgotten."

TWENTY-SIX

Bill issued the necessary orders. Squeegee and Proul set off to find a place where they could bury their dead. It might be a temporary grave, but they couldn't leave the bodies exposed. He'd issued Heidi a painkiller and told her to rest. Bill pulled off his helmet and stayed at Ocalla's side while Stu kept fiddling with his comm equipment.

They'd lost a third of their original strength. They couldn't complete the op, and they couldn't let their Filipino contacts know. The bottom line was, they couldn't do anything until they got help for Ocalla or he died.

Claudia moved aside to let Bill in next to Nelson, who was still working over Ocalla.

"I've done everything I can," Nelson said, shooting a glance at him. "Not much hope now. Even if we were right outside a hospital, I don't think..."

Claudia brought a cloth soaked in water. A small towel, sage green with a designer label. It must have come from her own pack. Bill used it to swab Ocalla's brow. The man's wounds were too severe. Bill's frustration mounted, knowing he could neither help the dying man nor push the mission forward.

Claudia stood over him, watching, her clothes spattered in blood. She'd surprised Bill. She hadn't cried or screamed or even vomited. She'd stepped in and helped, without complaining. That was more than he'd expect from any civilian without medical training, especially a woman used to living high.

"Is he going to make it?" she asked softly.

He glanced up at her. Impossible to tell if Ocalla could hear them. He shrugged. "Did you see where Heidi is?"

"Yes."

"Would you mind checking on her?"

"Sure."

"Bring her closer, if she feels like moving. I don't like her being over there alone."

Claudia disappeared into the brush. Belatedly, Bill thought about the possibility of encountering snakes. Well, she lived in Georgia. She must know about snakes.

Lord, give me strength and wisdom!

Second in command was a comfortable position. Much more so than being in charge. Many times he'd led his four-man team into action, but he'd never been chief of an entire op. He didn't want to now.

Rustling foliage alerted him that the women were coming. Claudia supported Heidi with an arm around her waist. She looked ahead for a good spot to deposit her charge.

"Here." Bill got up and held a branch back. "Heidi, sit on this." He offered the space blanket from his pack. Better than nothing.

She waited, leaning on Claudia, while he shook it out, and then she collapsed on it. "Thanks, Bill." She looked over at Ocalla, and her face morphed into a study in pain. "He's bad."

"Yeah."

"I've been praying."

"Don't stop." Bill went back to his post at Ocalla's side. Nelson glanced at him and shook his head.

Heidi eased back onto the ground, and Claudia asked, "All set? I'll go back for your pack."

"Thanks." When Claudia was out of earshot, Heidi whispered to Bill, "She doesn't seem so bad."

Bill stared over at her, speechless. He could hear Stu saying, "Come in, AFP." He'd given up on reaching his countrymen and was trying to raise a response from the Philippine military, who were closer, but apparently without success.

A minute later Claudia was back. Heidi lay down against her bundle and closed her eyes. "I'm really going to be okay, White."

Bill smiled. "Sure you are. I know that." He glanced up at Claudia.

She started to say something but stopped. She peered in closer and caught her breath.

Bill pivoted on his heels toward Ensign Ocalla. Nothing had changed. Or had it? Nelson leaned forward, searching for a pulse in Ocalla's throat. Bill waited, hoping, but knowing they'd lost another battle. He felt like swearing, but long habit kept him from giving in to the impulse. He closed his eyes. Hot tears cruised down his cheeks. *Lord, this is too hard!*

He felt a hand on his shoulder. Claudia. He wanted to rip into her. The insurgents had probably seen the boat that brought her. She'd led them right to the unit. Three good men had died, not counting the casualties from the boat.

"Bill, I'm sorry. I had no idea." Her voice shook.

He reached up and touched her hand gently, just for a second.

Nelson looked over at Bill. "He's gone."

Bill stood and turned slowly to face Claudia. The pain in her face mirrored his heart. Heidi still lay with her eyes closed. Asleep already? Her chest rose and fell with comforting regularity. Maybe the meds had put her out.

Bill jerked his head, indicating to Claudia that she should follow him. He walked a few steps away, and she came with him.

He forced himself to meet her penetrating gaze. "Look, Claudia… this isn't your fault."

"That's generous of you."

"No, really. The crew of the boat that brought you here was careless."

"They were just following orders."

"But they should have taken more precautions. We came here in the dark, and…well, there were things they could have done."

She pressed her lips together in a tight line and shook her head. "If I hadn't kept them waiting while I argued with your CO—" She looked toward Stu. "He's dead, isn't he? Commander Dryden."

"Yes."

"And some other men."

"We've lost three."

"The medic—Nelson—he needs some attention too. And your friend Heidi is hurt."

Bill inhaled slowly through his nose and nodded. "Yeah. Heidi's tough, though."

"All these guys are tough, or they wouldn't be here. But I got three of them killed."

"Don't say that."

"It won't keep me from thinking it." She stared off into the jungle for a moment and then back at him. "Bill, I can't write that story now."

"You'd better! And you'd better make these guys look really good." His voice cracked. He fell silent again, trying to control his breathing. He sniffed. "It's going to take a miracle to get us out of here alive. The enemy could come back any minute, and we don't have a radio anymore. If we do get out, you'd better write the best story you've ever written."

The silence hung between them until he looked at her. She pulled her shoulders back and elevated her chin half an inch.

"Yes, sir. I'll do that. And I'll do anything I can to help you fix this. Nelson told me you're in charge now. Give me orders like you would any of the others."

He nodded. "All right. Thanks for helping with Ocalla. He was…a great guy and very talented."

"I wish I could have done more." She swiveled her head and looked at Stu. "Wouldn't it be better to send you out with satellite phones, not long-range radios?"

"They did. We brought both. But that's out of commission too.

Probably the same shell that killed Commander Dryden and took the radio out. Stu's lucky—no, that's not what I mean. Stu is blessed. God kept him alive, when he should have been killed along with Dryden."

"He's not hurt?" Claudia's eyes narrowed as she watched Jeff Stuart work on the radio's wiring.

"A small piece of shrapnel in his leg. Proul wrapped it for him."

She nodded. "Well, he can use my sat phone if you think it will help."

Bill stared at her.

TWENTY-SEVEN

Pierre paced his kitchen. His captain wasn't happy when he'd heard the news, but he'd placed Pierre in charge of getting the Gold Team out of the Philippines.

"You're closer to it than anyone else, Belanger, and you have experience working behind enemy lines. Bring those boys home."

Marie was upset, as he'd known she would be. He should go over to his office on the base, but he hated to leave her alone with the baby right now. She wanted to call her parents, but he had persuaded her to wait until they knew more about Claudia's situation. No sense putting them through the wringer if it wasn't necessary. But it was getting later. Almost nine o'clock. It might be better to alert them now than to wait until they'd gone to bed.

The land line phone rang at last, and he jumped for it.

"Hello? Hello?" He waited, fearing the connection was lost. *Please, God...*

"Lieutenant Belanger?"

"Yes."

"Sir, a call came through for you at the base, and I've been requested to send it over to your home. Is that correct, sir?"

"Yes. Thank you."

"It's a satellite call, so you'll experience some voice delay. Hold on."

An agonizing ten seconds ticked by.

"Lieutenant? This is Lieutenant Bill White. Can you hear me?"

"Bill! Thank God!"

Another pause. "It's me, Pierre. We're in a sticky situation here."

"I've put our command in Guam on the alert, in case you need help," Pierre said. "What's going on?"

"We were attacked by the insurgents. Seems they've got air power now."

"They do. I got intel today saying they stole a twin engine aircraft from the civilian airport in Isabella a few days ago. What is your situation?"

The delay caused by satellite communication nearly drove Pierre nuts, but he reminded himself what the alternative was.

"Regret to inform."

Pierre held his breath, knowing the next words would be difficult to hear.

"Five casualties. Three KIA, two injured but mobile. We lost the commander."

Pierre exhaled. "Are you engaged now?"

"Negative."

"All right. You need to move to a new location ASAP. Copy that."

"I copy. But we've got a burial detail."

"Make it quick. I'm sorry, Bill."

"Ditto."

"What about the package you received earlier?"

"The package is safe."

Pierre closed his eyes and breathed a silent prayer of thanks. "Just to confirm—the package is safe."

"That's affirmative."

"Move to a new location and call me. Move now."

"I copy."

The line went dead, and Pierre hung up. He pulled out one of the kitchen chairs and sank into it. He buried his face in the crook of his arm on the table. Three men lost, including the commander. But Claudia was safe. He could at least tell Marie that. Right before he told her he was leaving for the Pacific.

TWENTY-EIGHT

Claudia stood with the men at the edge of the grave they'd hastily dug and filled. In just a few minutes, they had carefully transplanted grass and bushes, but she could still tell where it was. It might fool a pilot flying over.

Three men in one grave. She shuddered. Bill had explained to her that the Navy would attempt to recover the bodies later. As soon as possible, but when they could openly come in with more men. Not today.

She wore a supposedly bullet-proof vest and a soaking wet camouflage shirt over her tank top. The thin, dark-haired man they called Squeegee had brought them to her and held them out apologetically.

"The Lieutenant says you need to put these on, ma'am."

She'd taken the items without question. Obviously they weren't safe yet, and Bill wanted her to protect herself by wearing the costume of war. Though how they could have lost three men wearing body armor, she wasn't sure. Head wounds? She'd seen Ocalla's wounds, and Nelson had told her a grenade or shell from the aircraft had hit right where Ocalla and McGraw stood. Other scraps of things the men had said led her to believe the bodies she hadn't seen had suffered more trauma. She was glad she'd been spared the visuals.

Squeegee showed her how to fasten the vest on with Velcro. It was too big. She shook out the camo shirt and noticed the name MCGRAW on the breast. He was one of those who'd been killed, she'd caught that much.

"I…tried to get all the blood out." Squeegee's mouth skewed and he looked away.

"Thank you." She'd put it on without further comment.

Heidi lay sleeping in the thicket, and Bill had insisted they leave her there until after their brief service. The other men—Squeegee, Stu, Nelson, and Proul, stood with stoic faces around the grave. Claudia stepped in between Bill and Squeegee.

Bill looked around at the others. "Let's pray."

They bowed their heads, and he spoke quietly, with an intensity that brought a lump to Claudia's throat.

"Heavenly Father, we commit these men to You. We loved them all, and they were good men. But You know them better then we did, and You love them even more. They're Yours now, and we ask You to take care of them and to comfort us and those at home who love them. Thank You. Amen."

She thought it odd that he hadn't asked anything for themselves, other than comfort. If God were as big as Bill seemed to think He was, surely He could send a doctor and more troops their way. Maybe an aircraft carrier.

"The Lord is my shepherd," Bill began.

Claudia recognized the Twenty-third Psalm. She opened her eyes to see if Bill was reading, but he recited from memory, staring up into the gray sky. Stu joined him, and they went on for a couple of minutes as though they'd rehearsed it. "Though I walk through the valley of the shadow of death, I will fear no evil…"

Tears streamed down Bill's face. She looked away, not wanting to embarrass him if he noticed her staring. Her gaze landed on Squeegee. He, too, had lost the battle with tears. All of them had. She felt her chest tighten. She'd never seen grown men crying before. Well, Tommy didn't count.

"…and I shall dwell in the house of the Lord forever. Amen."

"Amen," said Squeegee and Nelson.

Bill nodded. "All right, we break camp. Stu, you cached the equipment?"

"It's under Team 1's boat."

"Right. No sense lugging the radio and sat phone." Bill looked at Claudia. "You don't mind him carrying yours?"

"No, that's fine. Easier for me. I always overpack, anyway."

His glance slid to Squeegee. "Do what you can about our tracks. I know we can't wipe them all out, but it would be good if this place isn't disturbed until our crews can come get them."

"Yes, sir." Squeegee picked up a branch from some kind of pine tree and moved it back and forth over the spot where he'd stood during the prayer.

"Let's go," Bill said. "Claudia, I'm going to put you behind Stu, and if you can, I'd like you to help Heidi. We'll all do what we can for her—take turns with her pack and all that. But she might appreciate having another woman along."

"I'd be glad to," Claudia said. It would be a small thing. She wished she could do something huge for these men.

He nodded toward the helmet she held, letting it dangle by the strap. "Put that on and keep it on."

"Won't we hear the plane if they come back?"

He looked toward the trees on the landward side. "There could be snipers hiding in the woods."

He walked away, to where he'd left his pack. She inhaled deeply. She'd wanted to learn everything about Bill, but she hadn't counted on this. She put the helmet on and adjusted the strap, immediately feeling sweaty and claustrophobic. Determination kicked in. She wouldn't complain if it killed her. And she would keep up with these men. If Heidi could do it with a chewed-up arm, so could Claudia Gillette, extreme journalist.

Stu roused Heidi by gently shaking her good shoulder.

"Hey, Taber, we're ready to move. You up for it?"

Heidi blinked and sat up. With a low moan, she grabbed her injured arm and grimaced.

"Let me help you up." Stu gave her his hand and pulled her to her feet, then steadied her with an arm around her waist for a few seconds. "All right? I don't want you to keel over when I let go."

"I'll be okay," Heidi said.

He handed her a bottle of water. "Have some of this. Miss Gillette will fall in behind you. If you need to rest, tell us."

"I will."

Stu eyed her keenly and nodded. "All right then. Looks like the lieutenant's ready." He led them into casual formation behind Bill.

Claudia shivered as they passed a spot where the foliage was smeared with blood. A dark stain on the ground told where one of the men had lain. She felt suddenly cold. The clammy camo shirt chafed her neck and wrists. The body armor under it weighed her down. The new, light stuff, Squeegee had told her. Only sixteen pounds. It felt like a ton.

Heidi kept up for the first half hour. They plunged into dense jungle and worked their way uphill, away from the sea. Not nearly as rugged as Claudia's climb in Peru, but there was no path here. The vines and undergrowth constantly tripped them up. Claudia noticed after a while that Heidi had slowed and they were falling a little behind Bill and Stu. She looked over her shoulder. Nelson and Squeegee were right behind her. Nelson had washed most of the blood off his face and now sported a bandage below the corner of his right eye. Proul tailed them, looking often down their back trail.

"Is Taber okay?" Nelson asked.

Claudia reached out and touched Heidi's sleeve. "Do you need a rest, Heidi?"

She could tell Heidi hated being the weakest member of the team, but after a moment, she said, "Probably a good idea."

Squeegee gave a whistle. Bill and Stu turned around, and Squeegee waved. Bill nodded and sat down where he was. Squeegee took hold of Heidi's unhurt arm. "Lean on me, schweetheart."

Heidi chuckled. "Thanks."

"Brownie would be proud of you," Squeegee said.

Claudia wondered who Brownie was. Their commanding officer, maybe? The flush that spread over Heidi's cheeks led her to believe it was more personal than that.

They caught up to Stu and Bill. Proul removed his double pack and took up a post, leaning against a tree with his rifle at the ready. Squeegee lowered his own pack to the ground, took Heidi's off Proul's, and fastened it to his own.

"I'm really okay," Heidi said sheepishly to Bill. "I just need a little breather."

"Don't worry about it. It's natural when you lose that much blood."

Heidi leaned back. "If you think you'd do better without me…"

"No way."

Nelson went to his knees beside her. "Let me have a look at your arm, just to make sure the dressing is secure."

Bill looked all around, and Claudia followed his gaze. Were there really Muslim terrorists out there in the jungle watching them? On her way here from Saipan, she'd read all she could find online about the Abu Sayyaf Group that plagued these islands. Scary stuff. Heavily armed rabble-rousers demanding an independent Muslim state in the southern part of the Philippines. Connections to Al-Qaeda. Training camps for terrorists. She'd hoped to learn what the American and Philippine military forces were doing to counteract them. She hadn't expected to get this close.

The grim mood lifted slightly when a large, crested bird landed on a bamboo branch near them. Its white feathers were relieved only by a reddish splash on the underside of its tail.

"Is that a cockatoo?" Claudia whispered.

Heidi smiled. "Yes. A Philippine cockatoo. You can teach them to talk."

Owk! Its raucous call almost led Claudia to cover her ears.

Heidi laughed at her expression. "There are a lot of beautiful birds here."

"You've been here before?"

"Oh, yes. I grew up on Luzon."

Claudia arched her brows. "Really? In Manila?"

"No, Olongapo. My parents were missionaries."

Things began to click for Claudia. "That leads to several questions."

"Oh?" Heidi's smile seemed genuine, and Claudia decided their conversation might keep her mind off her wound.

"Yes. One, how long did you live here? Two, did that experience help you get assigned to this team? Three, do you mind if I get out my notebook?" Bill chuckled and she whipped around to look at him. "What's so funny?"

"You are." He shook his head.

"Leave her alone," Heidi said. "I don't mind."

Bill nodded and turned to Stu. "Let's get that phone out and see if we can get through to Lieutenant Belanger again."

"Heidi, you should take some more painkillers," Nelson said. He opened his pack for the tablets.

After frantic digging in the depths of her own knapsack, Claudia closed her fingers around a pen. She pulled it out along with her notebook and smiled at Heidi. "When you're ready."

Heidi accepted some ibuprofen tablets from Nelson and a bottle of water from Squeegee. She swallowed the pills quickly, handed the bottle back, and shifted her position on the ground. "I was about two when my folks first came out here. My brother was born in Manila, but my little sister was born in Montana when we were on furlough. We stayed in the field twelve years, with two furloughs of a year each, so I was sixteen when we moved permanently back to the States."

Claudia wrote as fast as she could, using her personal shorthand.

She wished she had her laptop, but realized it was safer in the hotel safe in Zamboanga. "So, you grew up speaking Spanish?"

Heidi shrugged. "We spoke English in our home, but I picked up some Spanish and Tagalog from my friends."

"Wow." Claudia scribbled. "Do you consider the Philippines your home?"

"No, not really. My folks always talked about home in Montana while we were here, so I always felt as though I wasn't where I really belonged."

"I can understand that. And when you came back here as an adult..."

"Yeah, it was a little nostalgic, especially the first time. I came two years ago to take part in a joint training exercise with the Philippine military. We got to go into metro Manila on leave and take some side trips out into the country. I managed to find a couple of the families my parents had worked with. That was neat."

Claudia wondered if that was the soggy trip Bill had termed his worst. She'd bet this one was up for the prize now. She reached up to remove her helmet. If she could just get a little breeze over her scalp, she'd feel so much better.

Bill shot a glance her way while Stu worked on making the phone connection. "Leave the helmet on, Claudia."

She looked around, feeling at once guilty and apprehensive.

Stu handed the phone to Bill, and he walked away a few steps.

Claudia kept the helmet in place, much as she was beginning to loathe it, and asked Heidi a few more questions.

When Bill returned he told them, "We need to move on soon." He glanced at Heidi. "That is, if you're ready."

"I'm ready." Heidi rolled onto her knees and took a deep breath.

Claudia extended her hand to her. "Let me help you."

Heidi grasped her hand and heaved herself upward. When she stood, Claudia hovered, anxious to be sure she'd stay steady on her feet. "All right?"

"Yes. A little stiff, that's all."

Liar, Claudia thought. She couldn't imagine making this hike with a bloody wound as bad as Heidi's. She'd been dizzy and disoriented after her undignified fall in Cusco, and that escapade had resulted in only a few bruises.

Heidi smiled at Bill. "I've met Claudia, but have you introduced her to the guys?"

"Uh…" Bill's blue eyes showed only a flicker of hesitation. "Sorry. That's Stu and Squeegee behind you. You met Nelson earlier. The man on watch is Proul. Gentlemen, this is Claudia Gillette. You may have read some of her trenchant articles in *Global Impact.*"

Claudia nodded at the two nearest men, feeling her smile to be a bit inane under the circumstances. "Hi. I'm pleased to meet you, but I wish things could have started out differently."

"Same here," Squeegee murmured, shaking her hand briefly.

Stu smiled at her. "It's been a rough morning, Miss Gillette, but don't think for a moment that God didn't have a purpose in bringing you here."

Oh, no. First Bill, then Heidi, now Stuart. I'm outnumbered.

"I got through to the base," Bill said, "but Lieutenant Belanger is traveling. I'm supposed to call his personal number in an hour. Meanwhile, let's head for the rendezvous."

"We're not scrubbing the op?" Squeegee asked. "You think we can pull it off with this few people?"

Bill's shoulders seemed to square up inside his sweaty uniform. "We can. We have to. Can't leave the people depending on us in the lurch."

"The enemy knows we're here," Stu said uneasily. "They're apt to try to stop us. I'm not saying we shouldn't go forward, but what if they're waiting for us when we head back? Or find our boats while we're gone?"

Bill inhaled slowly and met his gaze. "We knew about those risks when we started."

"Yes, sir, we did." Stu put the satellite phone away and shouldered his pack.

Bill signaled to Proul, and he trotted over to them. They set off once more through the jungle. Sweat rolled down Claudia's back, beneath the layers of clothing. The sun was high overhead now and seemed to have chased away the last clouds. She was grateful when they marched beneath tall trees that shut out its glare, but there seemed to be more bugs in the forest than out in the open. A huge lizard startled her once, darting almost under her feet. She caught her breath and jumped back, managing to suppress the shriek that lodged in her throat.

"Steady, ma'am," Squeegee said behind her. "That kind is harmless."

Ah. Good to know, even if the information came from one of those infuriatingly calm men who never panicked.

Hunger came on all at once. How many hours ago was breakfast in Zamboanga? The distant memory of fragrant, strong coffee, fresh fruit, and a flaky, cheese-topped pastry taunted her. She hadn't considered what she would eat here. In her pack resided a half-full bottle of water and a protein bar. The longer they walked, the more that protein bar invaded her thoughts.

Heidi stumbled, and Claudia jumped to grab her before she fell forward. Heidi's sharp intake of breath told Claudia that her grasp on the back of Heidi's damp uniform had yanked the fabric tight, putting pressure on her painful arm.

"Sorry. Are you all right?"

"Yeah."

Heidi was upright now, so Claudia let go of her camo shirt cautiously, prepared for the woman to pitch forward.

Bill had stopped up ahead. Claudia looked over Heidi's head. He made a couple of hand signals, and Squeegee said, "The lieutenant says we'll rest up there where he is."

Heidi began to slowly walk the last few yards. Stu had spread a space blanket on the ground. "Here, Taber, lie down for a few minutes."

Heidi threw him a wry smile. "I might never get up again."

"You'll feel better after we eat," Bill said. "Squeegee, you take watch."

"Yes, sir." Squeegee faded back down the incline a few yards and all but disappeared into the brush. Nelson sat down next to Heidi. "How are you doing?"

"I'm good, really. But I won't say no to food."

Proul opened his pack. "Lunch coming up."

"Oh, I…you weren't expecting to feed me," Claudia said.

"Don't worry, ma'am," Proul said. "We gathered extra rations from the other packs."

"Of course." She would be eating dead men's food. Claudia could tell her face was flushed, but maybe they would think it was from the exertion.

Someone touched her arm, and she turned to find Stu watching her with sympathetic blue eyes. "Don't let it bother you, will you, ma'am? It may seem crass, but it's practical. When you get out in the field, you do what will help you survive." He smiled then. "Anyhow, the commander would have given you his MRE if he were alive."

"No, I don't think he would have." She remembered Dryden's fury at her arrival.

"Well, then I'd have given you mine for sure and shared with Billy Boy."

She chuckled. "Thanks, Stu."

He nodded and turned away smiling.

Claudia felt a little more at ease. But how could they talk and joke when they'd just buried two of their closest friends and their commander?

"Whatcha thinking?"

She looked up in surprise to find Bill standing next to her.

"I was thinking about you guys. How you're all carrying on, in spite of everything that happened back there."

Bill's eyes clouded for a moment. "We have to."

"I know. I'm beginning to understand."

"If this were any other kind of op…but we need to be there tonight. If we're not, the people we're trying to help could die just because we're not there. I can't really tell you much more than that."

"Dr. Gamata," she said softly.

Bill's eyes flew wide open. "Who told you?"

"No one. I guessed. It's the hottest thing in the Philippines right now. Or maybe I should say, the most publicized event. There are probably lots of things happening that I have no clue about. But I know Dr. Gamata and his wife and son were kidnapped a few months ago, and I've seen a couple of updates on that. At first I wondered if you were here to clean out a terrorist camp or something, but I think that would need a much bigger detachment and heavier firepower than you're packing."

He nodded. "Well, I hope you understand that you might not be able to write about it when we're done. Maybe, if we're successful. If not… well, we don't want them to know anything about a failed attempt."

Claudia chewed her bottom lip for a second. It was all chapped and rough. Was her lip gloss melting in the bottom of her pack?

"Listen, Bill, I don't usually do this—no, I *never* do it—but I'm thinking this is one article I'll have to have proofed before I turn it in. I'm thinking I could let Pierre read it. I honestly don't want to spill anything I shouldn't. But I also want to do this unit justice. If you do succeed, just think! The world will rejoice with you. And I'll get to see it happen."

His brow furrowed. "You know we have a much slimmer chance of success now?"

She looked down at the ground and kicked at a twig. Stu and Proul had sat down near Heidi and were opening their rations. She tugged Bill's sleeve and stepped a few feet farther away from them.

"Bill, did those men die because of me?"

He took too long to answer, but he didn't avoid her gaze. "I don't know," he said at last. "We thought we were in free, but when the boat came back with you…"

"So the enemy followed my boat."

"Or heard about it from one of their spotters and came looking for us. But if Dryden had just let you stay, the boat would have gotten away quicker."

"Or if you'd picked me up and tossed me into the boat the first time he said it." She tried to smile, but her mouth twisted. "I'm so sorry, Bill." Her tears mingled with sweat, making her eyes smart, which brought on more tears. She fumbled in her pocket, but she didn't have a handkerchief. "No tissues out here."

Bill nodded soberly. "Sleeves."

Her chuckle was more of a sob. She raised her left arm and wiped her cheeks with McGraw's sleeve. A large dark spot on the cuff didn't blend with the camouflage. She knew it was some of McGraw's blood that Squeegee failed to rinse out. "So, it is my fault."

"No." Bill's hand rested gently on her back. "Don't ever think that. God is in control of every situation, including this one. He could have brought you in here without a hitch, easily. Or He could have made it so every last one of us got killed. Did you notice the pattern? I think they fired a shell right into the spot where Team 2 was hiding. And the one that took out the comm equipment landed right next to the commander. Right at his feet, maybe. God knew where to let them put those shells."

She felt a little nauseous thinking about it and gulped. "Three dead, two relatively minor injuries, and the rest of us without a scratch."

"Hey, come on," Bill said. "This isn't a good time to talk about that stuff. You need to eat something so you'll be ready to march again. Are you doing okay? No blisters or anything?"

"No, I'm…fine. But the food sounds good. Thanks, Bill."

He nodded. "Let's eat. After that I'll try to call Pierre."

"Does he know I'm with you?" Claudia asked.

"Yeah."

"I guess he's pretty mad at me right now."

"I told him you're safe. He made me repeat it."

TWENTY-NINE

2345 HOURS, AUGUST 12
SAN FRANCISCO, CALIFORNIA

Pierre's cell phone rang as he entered the boarding area for his next flight. He dropped his bag on a seat and pulled the phone from his pocket.

"Belanger."

A pause gave him hope, but even so his pulse raced.

"Bill White here. We're proceeding toward our goal as planned."

Pierre swallowed hard. Even thousands of miles across the ocean, with his voice tossed into space and back, Bill sounded just the same—eager, determined, a little surprised at himself.

"Listen to me, buddy. You're nuts. I repeat, nuts. You can't do this with the resources you have. I'm setting up a retreat for you." During the pause, Pierre noticed that several people were staring at him, or rather his uniform. In the civilian airport, he'd have been less conspicuous in a clown costume. But on short notice, the airlines were able to get him into the Pacific theater quicker than the Navy could. He grabbed his bag and wheeled toward the concourse, looking for a quiet spot.

"Negative," came Bill's voice, stronger than before. "We can't stand up our date, can we?"

The scientist. He was saying they couldn't scratch whatever their plans had been to recover Gamata.

"That's noble thinking, but if anyone needs to be rescued here, it's you. Can you at least wait for some help?"

"That's a negative. It's already in motion."

Great. And how would pushy, interfering Claudia figure into that? "Hey, *mon ami*, my wife wanted me to ask you especially about that package we sent you."

"Yeah, I told you it arrived intact."

"Right. Thanks. But how is it going to fit into your plans?" The wait. He found a short hallway connecting two concourses, with less foot traffic, and leaned against the wall in a niche.

"Hey, it's fine. I mean, it's sort of a non-returnable gift, you know? But it's…it's okay. James 1:17, friend."

"James… You mean the Bible?"

"You got it. James 1:17."

"Well, listen to me, Bill. I'm in charge of the party arrangements now, so if you need more music, or better refreshments, speak up now."

After the requisite pause, he heard Bill's low chuckle. "No, thanks. This party is in full swing."

Mentally, Pierre ran down the roster of men in the unit, minus those he'd learned earlier were lost. "I've got to ask you, is the missionary's child enjoying the party?"

"Oh, yeah, she's here."

"Glad to hear it." Heidi's wound must not be too serious, or she wouldn't be keeping up with the team. She knew the local language, or enough to communicate with most anybody they would meet. She knew the culture. She'd be better than any of the men at foraging in that location. And Claudia was hanging tough. "Bill, are you sure that package isn't too bulky? Is it in the way?"

"It's fine. Repeat. Package is an asset. It's not slowing us down."

"All right, then, carry on. I'm in San Fran, heading to Guam. I'll be in touch as soon as I can."

"I copy. Bon voyage."

Over the loudspeaker, Pierre heard the boarding call for his flight. With misgiving, he closed his phone and headed for the gate.

Once the plane was in the air, he took out his small New Testament. Marie had placed a sticky note on the page where they'd been reading their devotions together in the evenings. He wasn't quick with locating Bible references yet, but after a bit of thrashing about in James, he found it. *Aha.* Bill's perspective on the package brought a tight smile. *Every good and perfect gift is from above.* Personally, Pierre wouldn't have pegged Claudia's arrival as the delivery of a gift from God. He hoped Bill wasn't being overly optimistic.

2355 HOURS, AUGUST 13
PORTLAND, OREGON

"Take me with you," Rachel said.

"Aw, babe, I can't. Too dangerous." George looked from his wife to his father-in-law and shrugged. "I'm sorry to do this to you, sir." They stood by the baggage claim in the Portland airport, waiting for their luggage to come off the plane he and Rachel had just left.

Rachel's father gave him a wistful smile. "You do what you have to, George. I can't say we won't be disappointed. Mrs. Whitney will let me have it for not bringing you home, I'm sure. But we'll take good care of Rachel while you're gone."

George nodded. "I appreciate it. And I'll come back as soon as I can."

"Pierre can handle this alone," Rachel said, but her protest was halfhearted. "You could take me if you wanted to. You're not going officially."

"Well, it's not like it's a recreational trip for me. I'm going to try to connect with Pierre at the Navy base in Guam."

"Hey, the Bridgefords are stationed there. I can stay with them while you and Pierre have your outing."

"Rach, no."

Her usually soft blue eyes were stormy now. "George, if you're going to get yourself shot up, I want to be close enough to get to you before you bleed to death."

Her father clucked.

Rachel shot him a fierce glance. "I know what I'm talking about, Daddy. I won't go into the combat zone, but I want to be as close as I can safely get."

"Rachel, baby, I'm not going to get shot."

"Oh, yeah? I was there for you the last time it happened, and I'm going to be there this time."

George sighed. "Your mom will be upset."

"We'll be back inside a week. We'll still have three weeks left."

They stared into each other's eyes. George hadn't felt such de-termination radiate from her since their old, pre-marriage days of antagonism. He laughed. "Pierre was with us in the old days to keep us sane when we fought. I guess he can do it again." He stooped and kissed Rachel. "I'll get the bags, babe. You and your dad skip on over to the airline desk and buy another ticket. But I'm warning you, Guam is your limit on this op."

Rachel saluted. "Aye, aye, sir."

1730 HOURS, AUGUST 13
BASILAN ISLAND, PHILIPPINES

Bill and Stu left their packs on the ground and checked their weapons. According to the detailed map he carried, Bill figured a large rubber plantation was dead ahead. His job was to make sure his team didn't stumble onto it. The others would rest in a stand of bamboo, with Proul on sentry duty, while he and Stu reconnoitered.

Claudia was talking softly with Heidi, making more notes. The article was a good distraction for them, provided they stayed alert.

He and Stu crept forward cautiously, moving from tree to tree. About a quarter mile beyond where the others had halted, the forest thinned. Soon they stood within the protection of the jungle, looking out on the wider-spaced rubber trees. They didn't see any guards, but in the distance they caught a glimpse of a building, and Bill heard an engine—not a vehicle. Some sort of machinery, he guessed. He could see the diagonal slashes on the tree trunks and the spouts that let the latex drip into collecting bowls wired to each tree.

He tapped Stu's shoulder and motioned that they should fall back. They skirted the edge of the plantation until they were sure the team could go around it to the south and regain their original course.

Stu led the way back toward the others. They slipped quietly through the jungle, but had gone only twenty yards when a clear voice called from the shadows in Spanish, "Stop! Put your weapons on the ground."

THIRTY

1830 HOURS, AUGUST 13
BASILAN ISLAND, PHILIPPINES

Bill bent his knees slowly and lowered his rifle to the turf. His heart seemed to have misfired. As he moved, he peered intently toward the foliage in the direction from which the voice had come. Stu also laid down his rifle.

"Hands up!"

Bill obeyed, and the voice materialized into a man in worn khakis and a camo vest, with weapons and ammo hanging all over his torso. His semiautomatic rifle covered Stu, and two other men flowed out of the forest on either side of them, both pointing guns at them. They wore the same getup.

"Who are you?" The leader asked.

Bill hesitated, and Stu looked over at him.

"Are you Abu Sayyaf? You don't look Yakan."

Bill inhaled then. The Yakan were the native people of the island. "No. I am Lieutenant William White."

The man's dark eyes narrowed. "AFP?"

Again Stu glanced at him. If this man were a terrorist, he'd know on sight that they weren't members of the Armed Forces of the Philippines. Bill took courage from that. He squinted at the green and gold patches on their chests and sleeves. Not any military insignia he recognized, but they symbolized regimentation. Not a guerilla. Heidi had told him the plantation might have armed guards protecting it.

Wealthy people in the area often had private armies to keep their estates secure. Bill decided to take a calculated risk.

"No. We're United States Navy."

The man blinked at him and lowered the muzzle of his rifle. In English he asked, "What do you want?"

"Just safe passage around the rubber plantation up ahead."

The man eyed him thoughtfully. "We work for Señor Alba. You cannot come on his land."

"I understand. That's not a problem." Bill pointed south. "If we detour one kilometer that way, will that satisfy your boss?"

One of the other men said something that Bill didn't catch. He didn't think it was Spanish. He wished he had Heidi with him. Instantly he nixed that thought. If he was about to be captured, he didn't want Heidi mixed up in it. The plantation owner might very well be paying protection money to the guerillas. If so, he might turn Bill and Stu over to the Abu Sayyaf or at least reveal their presence. Of course, if he worked with them, would he need such an efficient private militia as these?

"We don't have anything against Señor Alba," Bill said. "We're just passing through."

The leader and the second man held a brief exchange in low tones. Bill looked over at Stu. He didn't dare try to communicate with him. They both had concealed weapons, but he imagined Stu was concluding, as he had, that the two of them against the three heavily armed men stood little chance of winning a brawl. They would have to bide their time and see what developed.

After a minute the leader jerked his head toward Bill. "What are Americans doing here?"

"It is nothing to do with your boss. It won't affect him."

"The insurgents are moving around a lot lately. There's something going on. And if you draw the Abu Sayyaf here, it will affect us."

"We hope that won't happen."

The man spit on the ground. "Trouble. You bring trouble."

"Maybe we're on the same side," Bill suggested.

The three men watched them in silence for several seconds.

"Show me a token of your honor, and I will give you a guide. He will take you around the rubber plantation to the place you wish to go."

Bill considered that. He'd been forewarned that bribery could go a long way out here, but he didn't have much currency, and he hated to reveal his destination to anyone.

"Just see our group around the plantation and let us go on alone."

The man raised his gun barrel. "How many people do you have?"

Oh, no. I'm not going to tell you how many, or where. "If one of your men will guide us, we will meet him here in half an hour."

The leader looked at his wrist. "Your watch."

"What?"

"Give it to me."

Bill hastened to do as he was told and held it out to him. It was replaceable, a small sacrifice.

The leader took it and held it up close in the twilight. He grunted.

"It's not the best," Bill said, "but it's decent. It's waterproof, and it has a stopwatch and an alarm and a world clock."

The man's eyes squeezed up a little, as though he was trying to make sense of the unfamiliar words. He nodded and shoved the watch into the pocket of his flak vest. "Go get the rest of your men. One of our guards will meet you here and take you the best way."

The three faded back into the jungle.

Stu let out a pent-up breath. "Think he was straight with us?"

"Hope so. I think they're here to keep the ASG off Alba's land. They'll welcome anything we can do to throw the guerrillas off balance. If we put some heat on the Abu Sayyaf, maybe they won't bother the plantation for a while."

They retrieved their untouched rifles and hurried back toward the others. When they left the dense jungle and could walk side by side, Stu said softly, "Miss Gillette seems to have held up pretty well."

Bill smiled grimly. "Yes, she exceeded my expectations."

"Well, I've got to say, you two don't seem very...friendly."

"Are we supposed to?"

"Hey, just clobber me if I'm out of line, but...well, after Okinawa, I figured you two were tight."

Bill was silent for a moment. "Okinawa was an anomaly."

"A which?"

"It was like...if we got done here and we stopped in Manila and you ran into a girl you used to know in high school. Wouldn't you want to go out with her and talk about old times?"

Stu arched his eyebrows and shrugged. "If she looked like Claudia? Sure. Are you saying you're not...more than friends?"

Bill sighed. He supposed Claudia would still claim him as a friend. But he hadn't claimed her for one that morning, when she disembarked from the boat. Maybe she wouldn't consider him worthy of her friendship anymore.

"It's not serious between us," he said reluctantly. "Never has been."

Stu nodded. "Too bad she barged into this situation."

"Yeah."

"Well, God knows all about it." Stu didn't speak glibly, and Bill knew he meant every word.

When they got back to the others, the team had eaten. Bill and Stu quickly downed their MREs and explained their arrangement with Alba's private army.

"Their man will take us south and make sure we give the rubber plantation a wide berth," Bill told them. "At the speed we're going, we should be at the rendezvous point by 2100."

"And we expect contact when?" Squeegee asked.

"At 2200. I was afraid we'd be late, but we've made good time. This morning Commander Dryden estimated we had a six-hour march. He figured we'd be in place by mid afternoon. Well, it's taken us longer than that, but we started late, and we haven't gone as fast as we would have if we were all in good shape."

Heidi ducked her head.

Claudia smiled at her. "It's okay. You've done great."

"Yes, you have," Bill said. "And, Nelson, I know you're suffering too. Your leg wound may be minor, but I'll bet you're feeling it."

"You'd be right," Nelson said.

Bill nodded. "So keep ahead of the pain with your meds, you two. Another couple hours of walking, okay? We should be in place shortly after full dark, and we'll wait for our friends."

"What if these men you met up with aren't trustworthy?" Squeegee asked. "What if the minute you left, they alerted the Abu Sayyaf?"

"Then we're toast." Bill shouldered his pack and picked up his rifle. Every muscle ached, but he knew rest was still hours away.

When they approached the rubber plantation, Stu tapped Bill on the back and motioned forward, indicating he would go first to the place where the guards had stopped them. Bill patted him on the back and let him go. The other five bunched around him.

"We wait," Bill whispered. "If they've got a troop out, we'll know it soon." He watched in the direction Stu had gone, but it was almost full dark now, and he couldn't see more than a few yards away. No one asked what they would do if Stu didn't come back, and he was grateful.

Stu appeared all of a sudden, walking swiftly toward them, his rifle slung over his shoulder. Behind him came a dark-clad figure. It was not the leader who had talked to Bill earlier, but he hadn't expected it to be. He was sure several others would covertly observe their passage, however.

"Hello," Bill said quietly.

"Speaks Spanish," Stu told him. "Name's Pacorro."

Bill switched to his spotty Spanish and asked if he could take them around the south boundary of the plantation.

"Si," said Pacorro.

"Had to give him my watch," Stu said. "He was jealous of his friend, I guess."

They set out behind Pacorro, through the dense woods. After half an hour, they came out on an open hillside, and Pacorro pointed ahead, down into a valley. "Follow the river and you will come to the sea three miles down. Or cross up here where it is small and shallow." He shrugged. "Depends where you want to go."

Bill nodded. "Thank you." He handed Pacorro a 200-peso note from his small reserve of Philippine money. It wasn't much—less than five dollars—but the guide's eyes gleamed in the starlight.

"Gracias." He was gone, into the night.

By the time they arrived at the meeting place—a hillside overlooking a ravine with a stream in the bottom—Heidi seemed near exhaustion. She made the last hundred yards supported by Claudia and Stu. They stumbled into the ruins of an old stone building. Part of one wall still stood above the foundation.

Bill told Nelson to make Heidi comfortable and get some sleep himself if he could. He gave Proul and Stu the task of digging a trench at the side where the wall offered them no protection. At first light they would clear some of the brush off the hillside above their fighting position.

"Squeegee, you and I will take the first watch."

"Yes, sir." Squeegee took off his pack and grabbed his rifle.

Bill took one last look around the camp. Stu hovered near Claudia, helping her smooth out a place to spread her light blanket and stomp away any snakes before she lay down. It was chilly now and would get colder in the night. Stu would take care of Claudia, though. He appeared to be offering her his space blanket. And Claudia had a few extra clothes in her pack. She'd probably be warmer than the rest of them tonight.

Bill found a spot where he had a good view on three sides and stood unmoving for half an hour, his back against the trunk of a broadleaf tree, peering into the night and wondering how he felt about Claudia now. He knew he couldn't let thoughts of her completely take over his mind. The others were depending on him and Squeegee to spot any interlopers.

But he couldn't exclude her from his mind. His impressions of her had changed in the last twelve hours. Before, she was a gorgeous, smart, inviting woman who should be out of reach, but did her best to discreetly convince him she wasn't. This morning he'd restructured his opinion of her when she landed on Basilan. He'd perceived her then as a ruthlessly ambitious woman who would sacrifice their friendship and several lives to further her career. Now he wasn't so sure. Her sincerity had nearly won him over. What was holding him back? She'd said she would do anything she could to support the mission. He believed her, but her motives weren't so obvious. Was it only because she wanted a story? Or because she believed in their cause? Or because she felt guilty for her part in the attack? Or was she still hoping to impress him and draw him into a relationship?

That wasn't going to happen. The promises he'd made to God long ago had faded in importance for a while. Dazzled him, she had. But now he saw her with a clear eye.

He didn't see how he could trust her completely or how he could look at her as other than an unwanted civilian endangering their mission and personnel. If they failed in their purpose, it must not be because he let Claudia distract him. Let her flirt with Stu if she wanted to. He would concentrate on the op. And afterward, if they got out of this alive, he would say goodbye and not contact her again.

He shifted his back against the tree trunk. The sky was full of brilliant stars. A light breeze wafted in from the sea, folding about him on the hilltop. The leaves undulated above him. He moved out and walked cautiously around their camp toward Squeegee's post.

Squeegee rose silently from the bushes ten feet ahead of him. "Quiet around here."

Bill nodded.

"I'll go around the other side," Squeegee said.

Bill went back to his own post and waited. Fifteen minutes later Squeegee glided up to him. "Clear. Quiet in camp."

"What time is it?" Bill whispered.

"It's 2245."

Bill winced. The rendezvous time was long past.

Squeegee left him again, and Bill waited in the darkness. The occasional call of a bird or monkey sounded from the trees, and the intermittent breeze rustled the foliage. When it paused, he could hear the murmur of the stream below them.

Midnight must be near, but without his watch, Bill couldn't be sure. His head ached, and he sagged against the tree. He'd go to sleep on his feet soon. Time to change the watch.

He eased back into the camp behind the broken foundation and woke Nelson and Stu. After telling them where Squeegee was and where he had stood most of his watch, Bill found his pack and settled down with his space blanket under him.

Sometime later—how long, he didn't know, but his head still ached—he startled awake and sat bolt upright. Heidi was bending over him. "Lieutenant, we've got company."

THIRTY-ONE

0300 HOURS, AUGUST 14
BASILAN ISLAND, PHILIPPINES

Claudia awoke to gentle voices. Heidi stooped over Bill's form in the dark, and Bill sat up. He fumbled for his rifle and helmet. "Who?"

"It's our contacts," Heidi said. "They don't have Gamata."

He stood and followed Heidi to the edge of their camp. Claudia rose and tiptoed along behind him. Two men waited there near the broken wall with Proul. In the moonlight she could see that they wore ragged civilian clothes. They might be local residents, or she supposed they might have come from farther away just to try to rescue the Gamatas. One carried a rifle. The other held a machete loosely in one hand.

"I'm Lieutenant White." Bill shook each man's hand.

As one of them stepped aside, Claudia realized a third person stood behind them. A head shorter than his escorts, the boy looked up at Bill and extended his hand.

"Santi Gamata, sir."

Bill caught his breath. He shot a glance at one of the Filipinos. "Dr. Gamata's son?"

"Yes, sir."

"Where are the parents?"

"We…couldn't bring them." The Filipino man's gaze slid away from Bill's. "We were able to overcome the guards and help the family escape, but a band of the rebels came after us. They took the doctor and his wife away from us by force. We had only six men, and we lost one. They outnumbered us. Ten men, at least, and heavily armed. We dared not shoot as they ran away, for fear we would hit the hostages. We decided to get the boy away safely while we could."

Bill let out a long, slow breath. Too late now to say they should have waited for his unit to arrive. They would have to make a new plan. "I'm sorry about your friend."

The man nodded.

"Where are the rest of your comrades?"

"They wait for us, watching the trail."

"Do you know where Dr. and Mrs. Gamata are now?"

"Not for sure. They were taking them to a new location. But the boy heard some things that give me ideas."

"Come sit down," Bill said. "You must be tired and hungry. We can give you something to eat. Can you show me on our satellite map where you think they are going?"

"Yes."

Bill looked into the boy's dark eyes. "Santi, how old are you?"

"Thirteen, sir."

"Are you hungry?"

The boy hesitated. "Yes, sir."

"We'll see what we can do about that. I'm so sorry that your parents did not escape with you. We'll do everything we can to release them."

"Thank you."

Bill turned and nearly smacked into Claudia. "Dr. Gamata's son?" she whispered.

He nodded. "Ask Heidi if she thinks we can spare a few rations."

"Will the kidnappers come after the boy?"

"I doubt it. The doctor is the real prize, and they still have him and his wife."

Bill led the two men and Santi around the end of the trench, to a sheltered spot within the old foundation. Heidi seemed to have disappeared into the night. She and Proul must be on watch now. Stu rose from where he had been sleeping as Claudia approached him.

"Bill asked me to try to get some food for them."

Stu turned to his pack. A couple of minutes later he offered the newcomers some of the packaged food. The two men refused it, but Santi accepted an MRE with a quiet, "Thank you."

"He told us he has not eaten since breakfast," one of the men said.

"Did they feed you all right for the last few months?" Bill asked.

Santi shrugged. "Not so good. Sometimes we had enough rice and fruit and fish. Other times, I think they forgot."

"I'm sorry about that. Maybe later you can tell me more about how things have been for you." Bill had brought out his map and spread it before the men, shining a flashlight on it. "We're here."

"Correct." One of the Filipino men pointed to a mountain valley in south central Basilan. Stu leaned in over Bill's shoulder to look. "They had them here in an old house for the last month."

"How far away is that?" Bill asked.

"Twelve, maybe fifteen kilometers. It is an abandoned village. The rebels overran it two years ago, and no one lives there now, but the Abu Sayyaf use it for shelter when they are nearby. They had the Gamatas nearer to Mangal at first." He pointed to a town on the southern coast. "But when the AFP harried them, they moved the hostages."

Claudia wondered, if the family had been imprisoned so near the sea, why couldn't Bill's unit have sailed in then and hit the kidnappers. Perhaps intelligence hadn't known their location at that time. It seemed to her that would have been easier than tramping for hours cross-country through the jungle to the abandoned village in the hills. Oh, well. Likely Bill knew things she didn't.

"A group of Abu Sayyaf is here." The man pointed to a location deep within the jungle. "Their training camp is near the river. But I do not think they took the hostages there, unless our confrontation made them change their plans."

"Where do you think they are headed now?" Bill asked.

"They were going this direction when we met up with them." The man traced an imaginary line on the map. "We fought here. This is where they overtook us. Santi heard them say they were going to a place near the ocean."

"Is that right?" Bill asked the boy.

Santi, who had been quietly devouring his food, met his gaze. "They said an old fortress. Near the water."

Bill's eyes crinkled. "How old? I mean, aren't the historical places more or less tourist spots?"

The man shrugged. "The guerilla activity has pretty much ruined the tourist business in Basilan. We used to get Americans and Spanish and Dutch coming to Isabella, to the resorts. Australians, Japanese. They would swim and hike and play golf and spend money. It is a beautiful island, is it not?"

"Yes, it is," Bill said.

"But now... Now they say when you get off the ferry, you will have a gun in your face. People are afraid to come here. They stay near Manila. South of Luzon is too dangerous, the travel agencies tell them."

The man's bitterness surprised Claudia. Had his own family suffered from lost income because of the dearth of well-heeled tourists?

The second man spoke for the first time. "There is an old fort here." He indicated a point on the southwest coast. "The Spanish built it, maybe one hundred fifty years ago. It is abandoned and very much in ruins. It is away from the better roads and the places to stay and to shop. Not many people go there."

"You think the insurgents are taking Dr. and Mrs. Gamata there?"

The man looked at Santi. "The boy said their guards laughed and said they would be closer to the leader's home now. They won't have to go so far to watch them and deliver food and supplies."

"And your people know who this leader is and where he lives?"

The first man frowned. "We do not *know*, but we suspect. One of the Abu Sayyaf leaders, Juan Cabaya, was driven out of Isabella two years ago."

Bill nodded. "I've read about that. We've all seen pictures of Cabaya."

Claudia didn't think she had run across the name in her hurried research.

"His house was bombed, and the AFP chased him out of town," The Philippine man said. "Since then he has moved around. He has several camps in the jungle, besides those I showed you, and more on the other islands, where young people go to find him and work for the cause."

"Meaning an independent Islamic state?"

"Yes. But we have learned that he has placed his own family on a farm here." He pointed to the map again. "And the old fort my friend spoke of is only twenty kilometers from it."

"So that would be convenient for Cabaya and his men."

"Yes. They could keep an eye on the hostages easier. When changing guards, it would be a short journey. Bringing supplies in would be simpler because they could drive to it with a truck. If the AFP has not bothered Cabaya too much lately, perhaps he feels confident that he can use the fort and not trouble himself so much over Gamata."

Claudia drew in her breath, prepared to speak, but closed her mouth. This was not her affair and not her place to ask questions. But Bill looked at her keenly.

"What is it, Claudia?"

"I'm sorry. I just wondered, have they asked a ransom for the Gamata family?"

Bill shook his head. "Not a monetary one."

The Filipino looked up at her. "This woman is part of your militia?"

"No, but it's all right. She is authorized to be here." Bill actually winked at her. Claudia could hardly believe it and was still pondering its significance when the man spoke again.

"I'm amazed they still find it worthwhile to hold him hostage," she said.

The man shrugged. "I think the rebels hoped that Dr. Gamata's research and knowledge would be useful to them. However, three months after they captured him, they made their first move to negotiate."

"Perhaps they don't have the facilities needed to apply the doctor's research to their effort," Bill suggested.

"As you say. They are still in the rebellion stages, and they are not in a position to manufacture sophisticated biological weapons."

"Biological weapons?" Claudia stared at the man. "That's what Dr. Gamata was working on?"

"He is an aerophysicist," Bill said.

"That is correct. He designed new missiles that are more accurate than any our government has ever had. We believe the Abu Sayyaf would use his missiles to distribute tropical disease pathogens. A laboratory in Celebes was broken into last month. Research is done there on diseases, but no harmful cultures were taken. If the Abu Sayyaf could get ahold of the germs and start a plague in Manila, let us say, and half the population were wiped out, then the Muslims could do pretty much whatever they pleased in this part of the country."

Bill nodded pensively. "Yes, and if those pathogens were widely dispersed among populations with no immunity to these diseases, we could suffer terrible epidemics in America, Europe—wherever they wanted to cripple a society."

"Exactly. When Gamata was kidnapped, no ransom was demanded. They want him to work for them. We're afraid they are using him to make biological weapons."

"Weapons of mass destruction," Claudia said. She made a mental note to come up with a less cliché way to describe the deadly potential of the disease germs. "They could transfer him to another place where he could have a fully equipped laboratory. Someplace outside Basilan."

Bill nodded. "We've thought of that."

"So have we," The Philippine man said. "We have tried to keep them buttoned down pretty tightly to prevent that. But our troops are spread thin, and in the jungle there are too many ways the guerillas can get the best of us. And we can't ask for outright help from America."

"It's all unofficial, as far as we're concerned," Bill agreed.

"The Armed Forces of the Philippines have been very active lately," Their new friend said. "That is to say, since the spring. We hoped to make more progress by now. But the last month or two, other demands have drawn the president's attention, and the pressure has not seemed so great on the insurgents."

"And here we are, trying to pluck their prize from their hands." Bill looked at Santi. "Given the information you have, it seems that old fort is the best guess we can make as to the new location for the hostages."

Claudia said, "They haven't asked for a ransom, but you said they moved to negotiate. Have they made demands in return for releasing Dr. Gamata?"

"No demands the Philippine government can meet," Bill told her. "They want two imprisoned Abu Sayyaf leaders released and a council to address working toward secession. They want a promise of an independent nation for Muslims."

"Right here?"

"Not just Basilan," Bill said.

The more talkative Filipino nodded. "They want Mindanao and everything south."

Claudia whistled softly.

"Exactly," said Bill.

Stu scratched his head. "I don't know, Lieutenant, this move down from the hills looks suspicious to me. They could be taking Gamata closer to a point where they can ship him out of the country."

"I was thinking the same thing." Bill frowned at the map. "If they took him out of here and sent him to Libya or Afghanistan or

Syria...anywhere in the Muslim world, really. Well, that might be bad. Very bad."

"My father does not want to help them," Santi said. "They beat him several times. My mother and I thought he would die, those first few weeks after they took us. They would come and get Father and keep him for hours. When he came back, he was all bruised and bloody. He wouldn't wake up for a long time. And when he did, he told us they wanted him to make bombs for them that would spread germs in the cities." He frowned and looked down at his empty MRE package.

Bill had shut off his flashlight. Santi's eyes glistened in the darkness, reflecting a little moonlight. *Such a horror for a boy,* Claudia thought. She wondered, too, if she would get to write the Gamatas' story when she left Basilan. It was a much bigger, more immediate story than the one she'd come to find. But would it have a happy ending?

Santi yawned.

"Hey, buddy," Bill said, "let's find you a place to sleep. You must be tired." He looked over at Stu. "How about finding Santi a place to lie down? I'd like to discuss our plans a little more with these two gentlemen."

The two locals looked at each other, and the first one said, "We must go soon. Felipe and I must rejoin our comrades. We hope to retrieve our friend's body and take him home to his family."

"I understand. Is there any more information you can give me before you go? The terrain between here and the fort, for instance. Landmarks? And are we likely to run into a guerilla camp?"

Ten minutes later the two Filipino men slid away into the darkness. Claudia realized she was cold and dug into her backpack for a sweatshirt. She shoved aside the folds of a cotton sundress. What was she thinking when she packed that? The sweatshirt fit snugly over the Kevlar vest but under McGraw's uniform shirt. She was glad for the extra layer. The breeze felt damp. Not more rain, she hoped. She'd had enough of that.

"Bill, are we going after the Gamatas?"

"Of course. That's what we came for."

"Now?"

He inhaled slowly. "I think I'll send two men for recon. If the hostages aren't at the fort, it would be wasted energy for us all to trek down there. We've less chance of running into guerillas if most of us stay here and let a couple of scouts do the legwork. It will also give us more time to rest."

"You must be exhausted."

He shrugged. "I'll live."

Still, she calculated he'd had only three or four hours of sleep after a grueling day. "You won't go, will you?"

He stood silent for a long moment, leaning on the wall and looking out over the dark hillside. "I want to, but it would probably be smarter for me to stay here and sleep. Squeegee and Proul are fresh."

"What about Nelson?"

"I don't want to push him. That leg wound."

Claudia glanced toward where Squeegee and Nelson lay sleeping. "I thought it wasn't serious."

"Depends on your definition of serious. Out here the risk of infection is very high. And hiking all day with any kind of wound isn't what the doctor would recommend."

"True." She studied Bill's face in the moonlight. "I feel so... honored...to be a part of this."

He said nothing.

"What?" she asked. "You think I'm a foolish romantic, don't you?"

"No. I was wondering how you'll feel if we fail."

She stood beside him, watching the shadows stir in the breeze. "I'll still want to write about it. This whole day—I mean yesterday—has been so bizarre, so intense. I'm not really sure yet what it all means, but I feel vital. I'm part of something critical. Maybe not to the world in the end—maybe we're exaggerating that in our minds. But for the Gamatas, at least, what we do now could make all the difference."

"I feel it too," Bill said. "God brought us here. There's no doubt in my mind."

"The unit, you mean? Or does that include me?" He'd said something to that effect earlier, but she still wasn't sure she accepted his theory.

After a long pause, he said softly, "I don't like to admit it, but God definitely wanted you here. If it were up to me, you wouldn't be within a thousand miles of here. But that's not the way the Lord was thinking. It seems crazy to me, but…here you are. I just hope we can keep you safe and get you back to the States in one piece."

"I guess, to follow through on your logic, if God wants me to live through this, I will."

He smiled for the first time all day. "You got me. But, Claudia…"

"What?"

"I told you before. You might not be able to write about this."

"Oh, I'll write about it, you can bank on that."

"If the Pentagon orders you to button your lip, you'll have to do it."

She scowled at him. "You know what? I'm too tired to think of a good comeback. But I *will* tell this story, one way or another."

"Forget it."

"Never." She looked over to where Santi had lain down and curled up on his side, seemingly ready to sleep anywhere, anytime. Stu was rigging an impromptu shelter over the boy. "But don't stress over it now, Bill. If we don't get out alive, it won't be a problem. Save your worry for when we're standing on the deck of a Navy ship."

His penetrating gaze was not that of a happy man. Claudia noticed a shadow move over his face. The moon had disappeared behind dark clouds. She felt a scattering of raindrops plunk on her head.

"Help me put a shelter up for you." Bill hurried to his pack and pulled out the versatile lightweight space blanket they all carried. "Near the wall? Or would you rather sleep in the trench?"

"No, thanks. I'd rather be up here in the air." She helped him stretch the fabric diagonally between the top of the ruined stone wall and the ground. Bill tied the top corners to broken masonry and pegged the bottom to the ground. The wind tugged at it.

"What will you do without your blanket?" she asked.

"Nothing yet. I've got to go bring Heidi in. Then I'll wake the others for a powwow."

He was gone before she could say anything, but that was just as well. Anything Claudia said right now would be pointless. Might as well leave him alone to plan the next stage of the rescue.

She pulled her own thin, waterproof sheet from her pack and shook it out. Probably McGraw's. It didn't feel like a real blanket, but experience told her it would conserve her body heat. After crawling in under the flimsy shelter, she wrapped herself in the blanket and huddled against the wall. They couldn't start a fire. That was a given from the start. A sudden downpour drummed on her roof. Water poured in between the wall and the edge of the covering. She pulled the blanket up over her head and sat in misery, watching water sheet off Santi's shelter and pool on the ground.

Nelson jumped suddenly, moaned, and rolled over. He pulled the edge of his own ground cloth over his face. Claudia was beginning to understand why Bill's memories of the Philippines were so unpleasant. Though they had avoided typhoon season, the monsoons still blew over the islands, bringing with them copious rains. She pulled her feet up and hugged her knees. Was God really out there, moving them around like action figures? Had He sent her to Basilan to help rescue the Gamatas? Or was this all a colossal blunder put in motion by a handful of idealistic men?

THIRTY-TWO

1400 HOURS, AUGUST 14
GUAM

George watched the door where passengers who had disembarked from the San Francisco flight came into the Guam International Airport. Pierre stepped through it and spotted him and Rachel standing under the sign directing arrivals to the baggage claim area.

George felt a surge of pride. The tall, handsome lieutenant turned heads, and George knew he was as competent as he looked. His protégé, his friend. A dazzling grin lit Pierre's face as he scooped Rachel into his arms and kissed her cheek.

"Chérie, it's so good to see you!" He then turned to George for a bear hug and emerged smiling. "So you beat me."

"Yes, by a couple of hours. We've rented a car and arranged quarters for the night on the base."

"And tomorrow?"

"That depends on whether you can communicate with Lieutenant White or not." George led him toward the baggage carousels, holding his wife's hand. "When was the last time you heard from the team?"

"Yesterday. That is, when I was in San Francisco. Sorry. I'm a little jet-lagged."

George nodded. "Do you want to attempt contact once we're away from the airport?"

"Bill knows I'm en route. I asked him to call when he could. But I can try to raise them."

"You said they have a satellite phone?"

"Yes," Pierre said, "but it's not the one issued to them. That one's shot. My sister-in-law showed up with one of her own. When she realized the team's comm equipment was ruined, she offered Bill White the use of her phone."

"Bill White?" Rachel grabbed the sleeve of his blue uniform. "Do you know this man personally?"

"Sure. Why?"

"Because I trained with an Ensign Bill White in Seattle, right before I went to Frasier Island. He got sent to Alaska, and I lost touch with him."

"Well, we weren't exactly getting mail every week on Frasier," George said.

"What does he look like?" Rachel bounced on her toes.

Pierre watched the baggage carousel as the belt began to move. "Uh, tall, solid guy. Blond hair, blue eyes. My age, a hundred and ninety pounds. But he's a lieutenant now."

"That's him!" Rachel's eyes gleamed. "I'd love to see him again."

"Well, you won't," George said sternly. "Not unless we bring him back to Guam."

"Oh, come on." Rachel dredged up the pout that had driven him crazy on Frasier.

He reached over and pulled her close against his side. "No way, babe. You're staying here with Clay Bridgeford and his wife."

She kept the pouty face but snuggled against him. "Since it's you, I guess I'll obey orders. But you know I'm qualified for this op."

Pierre grinned. "I'll say. But, you know, Rachel, you're not active duty anymore, and besides…"

His quick glance at her stomach brought a laugh from Rachel. "I'm just teasing you guys. I wouldn't take this baby into a combat zone."

"You got that right." George stooped and kissed her.

"There's my bag." Pierre stepped forward to grab his sea bag.

"He looks wonderful," Rachel said. "A little tired, maybe."

When Pierre returned, George steered them toward the exit. Rachel insisted on sitting in the backseat so the men could talk. She leaned forward eagerly and inserted a comment into the conversation now and then.

"I told you they've lost Commander Dryden and two other men," Pierre told him as they approached the naval base. "Bill said there are a couple of other minor injuries. Lieutenant Taber took a bullet or a shell fragment in her arm, but it was an in-and-out. If she were at a hospital, I'm sure she'd be fine, but the risk of infection out there is scary."

"Did you say Taber?" Rachel asked. "Sounds like another old friend."

"I'm sorry, sweetheart," George said, glancing at her in the rearview mirror. "I knew Heidi was part of the Gold Team, but I didn't tell you before. I just didn't think it was necessary at that point."

Rachel nodded. "I understand. But you said she's injured, Pierre?"

"Yes." He looked keenly at George. "How much does your wife know, George?"

"Just that one of our special forces units is in a bad spot and may need us."

"You don't have to tell me any more," Rachel assured him. "I'm a civilian now, and I wouldn't be privy to that information even if I were still active. I'll stay here on the base and wait for you if you go to help them. But if there's anything I can do—anything—just tell me. Heidi is very dear to me."

"Old friend from basic?" Pierre asked.

"Don't you remember?" George eyed him in surprise. "She's the one Rachel was always writing to from Frasier. I was jealous of Ensign Taber, until I found out 'he' was a woman."

Rachel laughed. "When you told me that, I thought I'd go hysterical. She was on the *George H. W. Bush* when I sailed out to Frasier, Pierre. She's the one who introduced me to Christ."

"Oh, yeah. You did tell me about her."

"I'll always love her," Rachel said. "She gave me a Bible and wrote to me faithfully. She's come through Pearl Harbor a couple of times in the last two years, and we've managed to see each other."

Half an hour later, George left Rachel in their borrowed room at the home of his friend, Captain Clay Bridgeford, near the base. He walked with Pierre to the billet he'd arranged for Pierre in the visiting officers' quarters.

"So is Rachel really okay with staying here?" Pierre asked as they popped open cans of cola.

"Oh, yeah. I told her she couldn't come along unless she promised to wait here for us and not beg."

Pierre's rich brown eyes sparkled. "She's so much fun. I remember taking her fishing with me, and all she wanted to do was wade in the tide pools."

George smiled, thinking back to the stress-filled days on the island that somehow now seemed idyllic. "Let's see if we can contact Lieutenant White now. What do you have to do?"

"That's easy. Just call Claudia's sat phone." Pierre took out his cell phone and keyed it in. He waited, his eyes focusing somewhere on the closed drapes that covered his bedroom window.

George sipped his cola. He didn't really want to go back into combat, but the idea of dropping into the jungle of Basilan excited him. Pierre had a handpicked team of well-trained men—the other half of the Gold Team—that could accompany them if they had to go. But he knew the folly of considering this a lark. It was serious business—the kind where one mistake could mean death.

"*Bon nuit, mon ami,*" Pierre said into the phone.

George sighed in relief. White was on the other end of that connection, and they would get some news now.

"So, my friend, what news do you have for me? The party went well?" Pierre's face went grim. "No, listen to me. You need more… No. I don't think you should do that under the circumstances." He listened for half a minute and then shook his head. "So, it is too late.

You're telling me it's already underway... No. I think you should pull back and wait. We can get there in twelve hours. Eight of us—no, ten... All right. Yes, I hear you. Phone me again, then, in—" Pierre consulted his watch. "In three hours. I'll need to know where you are buying it."

He hung up a moment later, and George arched his eyebrows. "More trouble?"

Pierre sat down heavily. "He says they can't wait. He's sent a couple of friends to shop for the item. That means he's sent out scouts to confirm the hostages' location. He said they couldn't buy it at the first store they went to, and they need to go to a different shopping district."

George frowned. "They've moved Gamata again."

Pierre took a gulp from his soda can. "That's not all. Bill said something about getting part of what he needed. I think he means they got one of the hostages, but not all. He must be close to their location, and he's afraid to speak plainly on the sat phone, but something's up."

"When did they plan to make their move?"

"Early. Before midnight last night. Something went haywire, I'm sure of it. They're still in the danger zone, and this business about having to go to a new store. I don't like it, George."

"Do you think we should go down?"

Pierre let out a heavy breath. "I do. Rachel won't like it. I know Marie won't when she hears about it, but I'm afraid Bill's going to be left high and dry. Dryden's gone. These are my men now, George."

"All right, then. Captain Bridgeford can get us a jet to Manila."

"Not Zamboanga?"

"Maybe. I was thinking we could take a smaller plane from Manila."

Pierre took out his hand-held computer. "Well, once we're at Zamboanga, we'll have to decide if we want to jump in—"

"Too risky."

"All right, then, a boat. The AFP has a tight group of fishermen they work with. They can get us a fishing boat. But it will be slower than parachuting—"

"The rebels would shoot us before we landed. You know they would."

"Maybe." Pierre ran a hand through his glossy dark hair. "All right. We fly to Zamboanga and take a boat. But if they're clear around the south side of Basilan, which is where I think they are, maybe we can take a Navy boat part way and meet the fishing boat. I think that's what Dryden and his team did. It would be faster and more secure."

"Set it up," George said.

"Will do. But there's one more thing."

"What's that?"

"One of the last things Bill said to me, which I think was significant, was that the only item he'd been able to pick up so far was a toy."

George leaned back, thinking what that might mean in terms of a skilled tactical force on a clandestine mission. He cocked his head to one side. "Do you know what that means?"

"I think it's the boy. They've got Gamata's boy, but not the adults. In which case they've got a harder job—keeping him safe while they rescue his parents."

THIRTY-THREE

1300 HOURS, AUGUST 14
BASILAN ISLAND, PHILIPPINES

"What time is it?" Bill asked Claudia. He and Stu both missed their watches.

"A little after one o'clock."

"Thanks." Eight hours. Squeegee and Proul had been gone a full eight hours. It was the middle of the day, the most dangerous time to travel in hostile territory. He leaned on the shattered wall, staring into the trees.

Claudia turned away and walked over to Santi. She took the food containers from his lunch and stowed them in her own pack. Bill had noticed her doing little things like that without being asked. She was making good on her word and doing everything she could to help his team. But would it be enough?

If Squeegee and Proul had been caught...

Lord, You're in control. Thank You for that. Please help me not to worry. Show me what I should do now.

A low whistle came from where he knew Nelson was posted on sentry duty.

"Get down," Bill whispered to Claudia. She dropped behind the wall and huddled next to Santi.

Heidi was just finishing her MRE, and she looked toward him and silently laid aside the remains of her meal, reaching for her rifle. Stu was on duty in the jungle on the ridge a little above them. That accounted for everyone except their two scouts. Bill waited, his heart thudding in his chest. He crouched behind the wall and rose on his toes just enough to peer over it in Nelson's direction. The sentry was still invisible among the trees, but Bill thought he heard footsteps. He held his breath.

A moment later, Squeegee and Proul came trudging into view. Bill let out his breath and rose. He hopped over the wall and ran to meet them.

He didn't have to say anything. Squeegee gave him an exhausted smile. "We found them. They're not in the fort. They're in a building near it. Some kind of storage building. It looked like maybe it was part of a government-maintained historic site at one time. I think the place where they're holding the hostages was part of that—for equipment or something like that."

Bill walked along between the two until they were within the shelter of the wall again. "Did you eat?"

Squeegee shook his head, and Proul said, "Too busy staying alive."

"What happened?" Bill asked.

Squeegee sank to the ground and rested with his back against the crumbling wall. Heidi and Claudia moved closer, and Santi also sat forward with rapt attention.

"We went in before dawn and crept all over the old fort," Squeegee said. "We had to be really quiet, of course, so it took us a while to search it all. There were old dungeons, and we sort of expected they'd stash the Gamatas down in them. But there was nothing there."

Proul took up the tale. "Then we came out just about sunrise, and I saw someone moving through the bushes. It was pouring rain then—"

"Yeah, we know," Heidi said with a rueful grin. Although the sun now beat down cheerily, the ground was still spongy from the plentiful rain that had fallen in the night and morning hours.

"So then we had to move even slower," Squeegee said. "We wanted to find out where they were and what they were doing, but without them getting a clue we were there."

"Of course," Bill said. "Did you manage?"

"We did. Once we located the building a few hundred yards away, it was a waiting game. Four men came out and left in a truck. Then all was quiet. But we didn't dare move in." Squeegee leaned his head back against the stonework. "Longest two hours of my life. I kept thinking, *We're nuts. They're all gone, and this has nothing to do with Gamata.*"

Bill waited, knowing the story wasn't over. Santi, on hearing his family name, inched toward them. Claudia moved aside to make room for him between her and Heidi.

"So what happened?" Heidi asked.

"We very cautiously made a circuit of the perimeter of the building," Squeegee said. "There were four windows, all boarded up, and the one door. We weren't sure whether to risk it or not, but finally Proul moved from the spot where the brush grew closest to the structure, up against the wall near one of the windows. I stayed back to cover him."

"It was no good, though," Proul said. "I couldn't see anything. I listened a long time, and I was about to give up, when I heard something inside. So I sneaked along to the next window. I was able to peek in between the boards."

"What did you see?" Claudia asked.

"Nothing."

Heidi slugged Proul on the shoulder.

He shrugged. "Well, I didn't. But all of a sudden I heard someone crying quite close to me—but inside, you understand."

Bill eyed both men closely. "Mrs. Gamata?"

Santi leaned toward them, his face filled with anxiety.

Proul looked at him and spoke as if his words were only for the boy. "I heard a man say in Spanish, 'Don't cry.' He said it several times, but not in a mean way. And then he said—I'm sure he said, 'Santi is safe. Remember that.'"

The boy inhaled deeply, and tears streamed down his cheeks.

Bill rubbed his hand over his stubbly jaw. "They're still together then. I was afraid they'd take them to separate locations. Santi told me this morning they'd threatened to do that."

"No, I'd say they're still together," Proul said. "I didn't see any guard there. All the time we worked our way around the outside of the building, we didn't see anyone. Not after the truck left, that is. I was thinking I'd get back to Squeegee and suggest we storm on in there."

"No," Bill said. "There could have been a dozen men inside."

"Well, it was tempting." Proul scrunched up his face and shrugged. "Then I heard someone open the door and slam it."

Squeegee grinned. "He scrambled back to where I was so fast, I almost thought he was one of those lizards." He sobered and looked to Bill anxiously. "We saw two men come out into the yard. We didn't dare try to get closer, and I couldn't hear much of their conversation."

"They said Cabaya," Proul insisted.

Squeegee nodded. "That's right, Bill. I heard it too. They said Cabaya's name. Something about Cabaya being angry." He shook his head. "Maybe we should have tried to take them and get Dr. Gamata and his wife out right away, but the guerillas left at least two guards behind with the hostages. There could have been more inside. I thought it was too risky to try anything without our full force."

Bill nodded, although "full force" was almost a joke now. Instead of nine men, they had five, one of whom was limping—a wounded female operative, a civilian who might be brilliant but would be clueless in a firefight, and a thin, fearful boy who had been half-starved for months. At least levelheaded Squeegee had kept Proul from doing anything too rash. Time to make some decisions.

Claudia watched Nelson carefully peel away Heidi's bandage and wipe the wound with a damp bit of gauze. Heidi flinched but said nothing, craning to see the wound. Claudia handed him a package marked "Sterile Dressing."

"After I wrap this, I want you to take another dose of antibiotic and some more ibuprofen," Nelson said.

Heidi nodded.

"I'll get you some water," Claudia offered. That was something she could do without getting in anyone's way or messing up Bill's plans. Fetching things and helping keep Santi occupied seemed about the extent of her usefulness so far on this jaunt.

"Oh, right over there in my stuff," Heidi said.

As she unclipped a canteen of water from Heidi's pack, Claudia noticed it was less than half full. Her own supply was low as well. She gave Heidi the canteen and walked over to the wall where Stu was now lounging, looking out over the hillside.

"Think that water in the stream down there is safe to drink?" she asked.

He turned with a smile. "Not without purification tablets. Do we need to restock before we set off again?"

"I'd hate to disrupt any plans you guys are making, but we don't want to get caught without water."

"True. I know the lieutenant wants us to wait here a few more hours before we move. I could take the canteens down there and fill them."

Nelson left to take up sentry duty with Bill. Proul and Squeegee were already asleep in the shade of a staked-out space blanket. Stu poured what water he and Heidi had left into Claudia's plastic bottles and slung the empty canteens over his shoulder.

"Are you sure you should do this?" Heidi asked. "There's not much cover between here and the stream."

"It's a cinch. We've got the sentries, but if it will make you feel better, cover me."

Heidi leaned on the wall holding her rifle as he set out in a zigzag course down the hillside. He made use of the low bushes growing there and paused between moves, looking all about. In just a few minutes he was at the bottom, filling the canteens. It took him slightly longer to hike back up, but in a surprisingly short time, he rejoined them grinning.

"There you go, Lieutenant Taber. One purification tablet, if you please." He handed Heidi her canteen. She laid her gun down and went to her pack for the tablets.

Claudia took out her small notebook.

"What's that?"

"Notes for my article about the unit."

"You're writing about all of us?"

"Of course." Claudia slid down with her back against the wall, until she sat on the ground and her legs stuck out in front of her. Bad choice. Almost at once she felt the cold dampness on her seat. "So tell me about yourself, Stu. Where are you from?"

"Upstate New York."

"Yeah? How long have you been in the Navy?"

"Five years."

He was cute in a grim sort of way, she decided. He told the same kind of corny jokes Tommy did, only without the foul language.

They spent a tranquil hour talking about home and the Navy and what they'd be doing if they weren't on Basilan. Heidi joined them midway, and Claudia noticed Santi watching them from the corner of his eye.

"Come on over and join us, Santi," she called.

He gave her a shy smile and came a little closer. He kept quiet, just listening. Claudia took lots of notes during the conversation, slipping in a deeper question now and then to Heidi or Stu, but mostly Heidi. The article was shaping up, she thought with satisfaction. She could hardly wait to get back to her laptop.

"Do you mind if I snap a few pictures?"

"You're carrying a camera around?" Heidi's eyebrows shot up under the brim of her helmet.

"Yes, a small digital. Is it all right?"

Heidi shrugged and looked at Stu.

He grinned. "If some admiral said you can, what do we care?"

Claudia popped off a few shots. Stu seemed to love striking comic poses for the camera. Claudia let him—she could delete the silly ones later. "I'd like to get some action shots, but I guess we're not moving out until after dark."

"Right," Stu said. "Have to wait until the optimum time. Less chance of being discovered if we go at night."

Claudia nodded. "You should take a nap, I guess."

"Yeah." Stu sounded less than enthusiastic. She could almost read his smile: I'd rather stay with you.

"I don't mind resting all day," Heidi admitted. "This shoulder wound has taken a lot out of me. I'd like to just curl up and sleep for a week."

"You should lie down. I'll work on my story." Claudia watched as Heidi crawled under her improvised shelter and settled down for a nap.

"Weren't you up half the night on sentry duty?" she asked Stu.

He grinned at her again. "Comes with the turf, sweetheart. But I guess I could use a little shut-eye." He sprawled under the low wall with his rifle under his hand and closed his eyes.

Claudia leafed back through the notebook, reviewing her hastily jotted impressions of Basilan and the notes she'd scrawled after the attack. It seemed ages ago. She looked up and saw Santi watching her closely, his dark eyes thoughtful. She smiled, and he smiled back.

"What are you writing?" he asked.

"An article for a magazine."

"About the soldiers?"

"Yes." She wondered if she should tell him they were actually sailors, not soldiers, but then she would have to explain about the special operations force. Ordinarily, boys his age would know all about that. But she didn't know much about Santi's background, and he'd been in seclusion for six months. Maybe he wouldn't understand. "Would you like to be in the article?"

He shrugged and stared at her.

Claudia crawled over a couple of yards and sat near him. "Have you ever heard of *Global Impact* magazine?"

He shook his head.

"Well, it's a topnotch news magazine. Very influential in America. And I'm one of their writers." She smiled at a sudden thought. "Are you hungry again?"

Santi looked up at the sky. "It's not time to eat."

"Well, I just happen to have a somewhat squished protein bar in my pack. I brought it all the way from Atlanta." At his blank look, she explained, "That's in America." She took it out of her pack and held it out to him. "Here. You can have it if you want."

"Don't you want it?"

"No, I'm doing fine on the MREs, odd as that seems. But I figure you've been hungry for a long time."

"Thank you." He took it and stared down at the bright wrapping.

"You can eat it now or save it for later." She thought he might like having control over something as small as deciding when to eat again.

He studied her face for a long moment. "Did you come here because of my father?"

"No, I just came to write the article about the military unit. I had no idea I'd get to meet you. But I'm glad I did. And now it looks like I might get to meet your parents too. I think your rescue could be the biggest story my magazine has published all year."

The boy smiled. "My father is very important."

"Yes, he is. Lots of people have been working to find out where your family was hidden."

His smile drooped. "We didn't know if anyone cared. We waited and waited, but no one came to help us."

"Lots of people care, Santi." She touched his arm lightly. "Lots of important men and women in America and the Philippines have been working out plans to find you and rescue you." She grinned. "And here we are. At least part of the plan worked."

"I'm glad they got me, but…" He looked down at his hands.

"Are you worried about your parents?"

He nodded.

"I'm sorry. But Lieutenant White and the others are the best in situations like this. If anyone can get your parents out safely, they're the ones."

Santi nodded, his lips pressed together in a thin line.

"I have an idea." Claudia changed her position and curled her legs under her. "Why don't you tell me all about what happened when your family was captured. Then, after we get your parents and get out of here, I can write it all up for a magazine story, and everyone can read about it. They'll know how brave your father was and how he and your mother looked after you all the time you were kidnapped."

Santi raised his head and studied her again. "They wanted Father to work for them, but he wouldn't help them."

"That was very noble of him."

"Yes. He told Mama and me that they might…do bad things to us. He said they had caught us to make him obey them. That they might hurt us if he refused. But Mama and I both told Father not to do it."

Claudia stopped writing. "What did they tell him to do for them?"

"They brought papers and a computer and a calculator. Some lab equipment too. They wanted him to grow germs and put them in grenades. Something like that."

"What did your father do?"

"He pretended to do what they wanted. But he told them it was not working. He didn't want to hurt people, so he pretended to be working, but really…" He looked at her suddenly. "You can't tell anyone until he is free. If you write about it now, they'll kill him and my mother."

Claudia laid her hand on his shoulder and said gently, "I wouldn't do that, Santi. I won't even write that in my notebook. Because I wouldn't want the wrong people to see it if something went wrong.

But maybe, when this is over, you and your folks could all sit down with me and tell me everything. Then we could do a big story, and everyone will know what you went through and how your father kept from doing what the bad people wanted him to do."

The boy nodded.

"What do you think you're doing?"

She jerked around at the harsh voice. Bill White was leaning on the wall, glaring at her.

THIRTY-FOUR

"I won't let you use that boy for your own profit." Bill scowled at Claudia, willing her to back down. She had risen and now faced him over the wall that came up slightly above his waist. From below, where he sat in the grass, Santi stared at them with huge, worried brown eyes.

"That's a low blow. I'm not *using* him. I'm going to tell his story to the world when this is over. The free world needs to know how the other half lives."

"Oh, right. This whole article thing is so altruistic. What are you pulling down a year? A hundred grand? Two hundred?"

"I can't believe you said that."

"You can't? Well, it's true, isn't it? You exploit people to keep up an easy lifestyle. You don't care if the story you publish ends up hurting Santi and his family, or even if you tell our enemies how our covert units are organized or how we fight, so long as your readers are entertained and you get paid."

The hurt in Claudia's eyes stabbed him. Had he gone too far? The anger that surged up in him could be blamed on stress and fatigue. He had no right to lay it all at Claudia's door. Maybe she had no clue how badly she could damage their ability to infiltrate enemy lines. Maybe she really did think she was helping people by enlightening her readers. And maybe—just maybe—he had overreacted.

He opened his mouth, but she had already turned away. She stalked across the small area of their camp and busied herself with her pack. Bill watched her, telling himself to breathe deeply and slowly, wondering if he ought to apologize. Claudia dumped everything out of her pack and started putting it back in, one piece at a time. She seemed to have enough clothes in that knapsack to stock a boutique. The sick feeling and the bitter taste at the back of his throat told Bill he had some damage control to do, but he wasn't sure he was ready.

Stu rolled over and yawned. He sat up and watched Claudia too. Bill wondered if he'd heard their exchange. He went around the wall and into the camp. He woke Proul and sent him out to stand guard. When Proul had left, he grabbed his pack and chose a spot as far from Claudia as he could get.

It was hot, typical of the middle of a Philippine day. Probably it would rain again later. He unbuttoned his shirt. The thought of removing his flak vest was tempting, but he settled for opening the Velcro side closures and letting some air through. He spread out his space blanket and stretched out on it, laying his helmet beside him, but his mind whirled much too fast and furiously to let him rest.

He never should have let himself get so involved with Claudia. Not that anyone else would think he was committed. It all looked very innocent. A few e-mails, a couple of calls, prayers for a casual friend. Only Bill knew his heart was engaged. That kiss back in Okinawa complicated things. Definitely a bad move. He couldn't let Claudia take first place in his life—he knew that. But did she know that? He should have kept things much cooler.

What ailed him that night? Normally he could subjugate his feelings without acting on them. But with Claudia, he'd lost his head.

He sighed and rolled over, facing away from her and the others. It could have been worse. But now he had to face her. If only he could have written her a nice, long e-mail—no, a real letter—and explained to her why his faith prevented him from a serious relationship with her. That's what he should have done. It was so plain now, he could have kicked himself. Instead, he'd yelled at her.

She hadn't asked why his treatment of her had changed. Despite what he'd told her yesterday, she probably figured he blamed her for the attack and the death of his comrades. How could he explain to her that being around her made him want to throw out all the careful schooling he'd put himself through for years? Made him want to ignore God's laws. That was scary. He wished he could handle the situation better, but whenever he got close to her, he wanted to reach out and fold her against him and assure her that he cared for her deeply. Well, it wasn't going to happen.

He knew he wasn't going about this well, but with all he had on his plate, he felt he was doing the best he could. If they got out of this mess, maybe he'd have another chance to talk to her seriously. And he wouldn't let her beauty or her personality sway him.

Claudia laughed.

Bill froze and listened. Her musical chuckle came again, and he couldn't stop himself from turning over and rising on his elbow to look.

Stu was sitting close to her, fiddling with some flowers or something. Oh, great. He was making her a necklace, like a tropical version of a daisy chain. Claudia bestowed her heart-stopping smile on Stu and let him lift the flower chain over her head.

Bill lay back, very still, watching the sky. A few clouds drifted over. He had no business feeling angry. That lump behind his breastbone was all in his imagination.

He rolled to his feet and bent to snag his canteen. It was nearly empty.

Stu looked over at him and smiled, giving a short nod. Bill couldn't respond. He just turned away and tipped up the canteen to catch the last swallow.

When he looked again, Stu had risen and was sauntering toward him. Bill dropped the canteen beside his pack. When they headed out after dark, he'd have to fill it at the first opportunity. Stu was only a few feet away. *Leave me alone, Stu. Just leave me alone.*

"Feeling better?"

"Not really."

"You should have slept more."

Bill shrugged, and Stu stepped closer.

"Kind of hard on her earlier, weren't you, buddy?"

That took the wind out of Bill's sails. He gave up the righteous act and allowed his shoulders to slump. Stu was not the kind of friend he could keep up a front with. They'd grown close over the last two years, and Bill expected nothing less than honesty from him. Stu walked around him until they faced each other, but Bill still had his back to the camp.

"Claudia's not the enemy, Bill."

Bill gritted his teeth, knowing that what he said now would set the tone for his relationship with Stu for at least the rest of this mission. He could snap at him. He could pull rank and humiliate him. He could brush it off. He could get defensive.

What could Stu possibly know about the burden he carried on his shoulders, now that Dryden was dead? He alone was responsible for the men of his team, for Claudia, and for the Gamata family. It was up to William O. White Jr. He could call the op off right now, give up on the rescue because it was too dangerous, and whisk Santi away to safety. But he wouldn't do that.

"Just drop it."

"Hey, come on, Billy. She hasn't done anything to you."

"What do you know about it? You're all caught up in her now. Do you even know what we're doing tonight?"

Stu looked hurt. "Look, I'm just trying to make a bad situation a little less scary for her. We could all be killed tonight. You want her brooding about that? Is that it?"

"So you'll just laugh away the afternoon and pretend our purpose doesn't exist? Will that help?"

Stu frowned at him, as though trying to feel the way to sanity.

"Bill, is there something you want me to do? Can we plan it any better? I thought it was just a waiting game now. Keep low and wait for the best time to go in."

Bill couldn't look him in the eye. He chewed his upper lip and looked past Stu, toward the trees above.

"What is it?" Stu caught his breath, and Bill looked at him. "You're not... Billy, you told me you weren't serious about Claudia. I didn't mean to... No, come on. You're not...jealous?"

He wouldn't get mad at Stu. He could control himself that much, even though his friend was siding against him and had spent half their idle hours flirting with Claudia. Bill let out a big sigh. "Stu, I don't want to get into it. I happen to think Claudia is a risk."

"Of course she is, but she's doing what she can to lessen that risk. She'll help us in any way she's capable of, to make this op work."

Bill looked down at the ground and bent to pick up his helmet. "It's my job to get her home alive and to rescue the Gamatas after a botched attempt has put their captors on alert."

"That's right." Stu watched him cautiously for a long moment, his brows crinkled. "But we're here to help you, Bill. This is a team, remember."

Bill nodded. Guilt flooded over him in a wave that threatened to choke him. "You're right. I'm sorry. I'll apologize to Claudia. I just... How do I know she's not pumping you for classified information?"

"What?" Stuart laughed. "She's not a spy."

"No, and I don't think she would consciously endanger our troops. But it could happen. She could spill something critical. Don't you get it?"

Stu blinked at him. "I don't know what to say. I can't believe you're so strung out about this."

Bill ran a hand through his sweaty hair. "Can I have a minute alone, please? There's Someone else I need to talk to."

"Sure. Hey, why don't you give me that canteen? I'll fill it for you."

Bill fought what felt like tears coming on. "That's okay, buddy."

"No, I'll do it. I've been down for water once before, and it was a cinch. I'll get Nelson's canteen too and top them both off for you guys."

"Thanks." Bill handed over the canteen.

Stu clapped him on the shoulder with a nod and turned toward where Nelson's pack lay against the wall, near where Santi drowsed. Claudia sat a few yards farther away, studying her small notebook. Bill was sure she'd heard most of the conversation, but she was avoiding his gaze.

He inhaled deeply. *All right, Lord, I blew it. Thank You for sending Stu along. I'd probably be all to pieces without a reminder that You're here, controlling all of this. And I know You can work in Claudia's heart too, Lord. Please help her. Not just about the article, although I'd appreciate it if You caused her to exercise discretion there. But…she needs You, Lord. Please help her to see that, in spite of my clumsy way of handling things. Forgive my anger. Give me another chance to show her Your love.*

He walked slowly toward her. Stu had gathered three canteens and was rounding the end of the wall and heading down the hillside. Bill realized with a shock that Stu was right. He was jealous, if only slightly, of the easy banter he'd observed between his friend and Claudia.

Claudia had done far better than he'd hoped she could on this expedition. She hadn't complained once about the long march, the heat, the bugs, or the rain. He'd almost convinced himself she was a feminist yuppie, only out for her story. And why? It had to be for the money and the glory, didn't it? Yet she'd helped Heidi get her clothes on and off over her painful shoulder and had seen that everyone was fed on time. Yes, she'd asked questions, but she'd stopped whenever he told her there were things he couldn't reveal. And if he were honest, he'd have to admit her treatment of Santi was probably good for the boy. She had tried to help him cope.

She looked up as he approached. Bill paused and pulled in a breath, trying to think how to voice his thoughts. He regretted the things he'd said, the things he'd thought. He'd misjudged her.

Wisps of her dark hair straggled from beneath her helmet, and the camo shirt was crumpled and dirty after two days in the jungle, but she still dazzled him. Her big, brown eyes watched him warily, as though she feared he would lash out at her again. He wished he could undo the last hour.

She spoke first. "Pretty crummy of you to get mad at Stuart. He didn't do anything."

"Claudia, I'm sorry." He spoke softly, hoping Santi and the others wouldn't hear.

She raised her chin and continued to eye him thoughtfully.

Bill stepped closer. "Look, I shouldn't have come down on you like that. You're a professional, and you did say you'd let Pierre or someone okay your article. I know you'll honor that. I had no business getting mad at you, or at Stu either. Can you forgive me?"

She nodded and licked her lips. "I'm sorry too, Bill. I never wanted to cause you any grief, or any extra work or worry."

"It's not your fault we're in this pickle."

She hesitated. "If you say so."

"I do."

Three quick shots burst out from the jungle below. Bill's heart lurched.

"Get down!" He clapped his helmet on as he ran the three steps to the wall and crouched behind it. Claudia, Heidi, and Squeegee crowded in beside him. That accounted for everyone but the two sentries, Proul, and Nelson. Except Santi and...

He stared down the hillside, searching. It took only seconds to spot the mound by the stream bank, but it seemed hours. Amid the grass and low bushes lay an unnatural mound.

"Stu!" Claudia clutched his sleeve.

THIRTY-FIVE

"What happened?" Squeegee asked.

"Sniper," Bill said.

"They got Stu." Heidi looked at him with huge, frightened eyes. "Bill, we've got to get Stu and bring him back up here."

"We've got to take that sniper out first."

"What if it's more than a sniper?" Squeegee asked. "What if it's a whole pack of guerilla fighters?"

"Where are Proul and Nelson?" Claudia asked.

Bill studied the edge of the jungle. "Proul should be a little above us, up there." He pointed up the hillside into the bamboo. "Nelson's on the other side."

"They might have got Proul," Squeegee said, searching for movement.

Bill knew that they had to find out how strong the enemy was or they were doomed. He looked Squeegee over. "You and me?"

"Good." Squeegee checked his equipment and nodded. "I'll check Proul's sentry post first, and you go around above?"

Bill thought about it for a second. "I can't see a better way. Not enough cover down the hill."

"Wait a minute." Claudia grabbed Bill's sleeve as he passed her. "You guys can't go out there."

He stared down into her eyes. "We have to."

Heidi laid a hand on her shoulder. "Don't worry, Claudia. It's what we're trained for."

Claudia's mouth hung open as she looked up at him. "Bill, you…" She stopped and pressed her lips together.

"We'll be careful." It sounded stupid, even to him. "Heidi."

"Yes, sir?"

"You're in charge here. If Nelson or Proul comes in, make them stay with you."

"Yes, sir."

He looked at Claudia again. "Keep your head down, and keep Santi out of sight. Take him into the trench with you until it's safe."

She nodded. He hefted his rifle and turned away.

"Bill!"

He looked back. Tears washed Claudia's cheeks as she crawled toward him. A pang of regret shot through him as he watched her keep her head below the level of the wall as he'd said.

"What?" he asked.

"Is everything okay between us? I can't let you go and wonder."

Oh, those eyes. "Yeah, we're good."

She put her hand up and touched his face. He grabbed her fingers and gave them a quick squeeze. "We'll be back."

Claudia watched the two men crawl quickly but stealthily up the hill through thick brush toward the tree line. She leaned back against the wall, gasping. Heidi crouched beside her with her rifle at the ready.

"Will they bring Stu back?" Claudia asked, trying not to sob outright.

"Yes. If they can."

Bill and Squeegee disappeared into the foliage on the ridge.

Santi peered out from beneath the shade of Stu's space blanket. "Is Stu… Is he dead?"

"We don't know," Heidi said, and Santi nodded gravely. "Crawl over here and get down in the hole, Santi. The lieutenant said for you and Claudia to stay in there, so no one can see you if they're watching from the jungle."

Santi crawled out, bringing his blanket. He wormed swiftly to the edge of the trench and flipped into it. Claudia joined him, but stood with her elbows on the grass at the edge of the hole, watching with Heidi up the hill.

She was amazed at the coolness with which Heidi and Santi carried out Bill's orders. Of course, both had seen more violence than she had. Still, Heidi and Stu were close friends. Wouldn't she at least shed a few tears for him? Maybe not until business was taken care of. Claudia remembered times when she'd felt that way herself—holding back tears of frustration. But not grief. Grief had to work its way out.

She dashed a tear from her cheek. "What will Bill and Squeegee do?"

Heidi hesitated. "They'll try to get behind the shooter. But he may be gone already."

"And if there's more than one?"

"Then we'll know soon."

Claudia settled down to watch and listen. *No more gunfire. Please!* The thought filled every cranny of her mind for a long moment, but then her logic took over. *Who am I asking?*

The worst thing, she supposed, would be that whoever shot Stu had gone to bring back his friends. She wished she'd asked Bill for a gun. If things got desperate, she and Santi had no weapons with which to defend themselves.

A few seconds later, Heidi stiffened, and Claudia followed her line of sight up the hillside. A figure moved cautiously out from the trees. Claudia realized it was a man in camouflage, darting from the trees to a bush a few yards out. She could barely breathe, let alone talk. She watched with Heidi, and when the man moved to another clump of bushes, Heidi relaxed.

"Proul. He's okay." She turned and slowly scanned the area to either side. Claudia knew she was watching for anyone who didn't want Proul to make it to their position.

It took him several minutes to get down to the camp. Claudia urged him on mentally, but realized his extreme caution and snail's speed were warranted. When at last he arrived, he flung himself behind the wall, panting. Heidi reached over and squeezed his shoulder.

"What's going on out there?"

"I heard the shots. I didn't know what to do, so I stayed put. Squeegee came a few minutes ago and told me they got Stu. He said he and Bill would work their way around to where they think the shots came from, and he told me to get down here with you."

Claudia looked up the hill again. "What if someone gets up there above us and we don't have a sentry? They could fire down on us."

"True," Proul said. "But we need to know where all our people are, and…" He glanced at Heidi.

"We need to protect Santi," she said. "If they've come to get him back, we can't let that happen."

"Right. We're not taking any chances with the boy." Proul rolled over and hopped down into the trench. He shouldered his gun and looked out the side of the foundation, while Heidi continued to scan the hillside.

Claudia could see sweat dripping down Proul's cheeks and the back of his neck. She stretched to reach her pack and pulled it down into the trench beside her. She unclipped her canteen and offered it to Proul silently. He took a deep swallow and handed it back with a grin, then went back to watching.

Claudia went back to her place beside Santi and leaned on the edge of the trench. *This isn't happening.*

She felt a gentle pat on her shoulder and looked up into Heidi's clear green eyes. "God is still up there. He knows all about this, and He'll show us what to do."

"I wish I had your faith," Claudia said, realizing as she spoke that she meant it.

Heidi smiled, scanning the terrain. "You can. We'll talk later. But in case we don't get to have a long chat, just trust Jesus, Claudia."

Claudia gulped and considered that. An all-powerful God who could save them from this predicament was one thing, but Jesus... Whenever she visited her family nowadays, her sisters tried to talk to her about God and the Bible. Marie and Pierre had even dragged her to church on that last visit. Her parents had started attending church too, according to Lisa. Marie had brought up the subject of Jesus several times, but Claudia had brushed it off. She preferred to be accountable to no one except herself and sometimes her superiors at the magazine.

Now, staring at the trees and looking for movement that she hoped she wouldn't find, she did a fifteen-second rumination of her life. She'd taken risks before. That big gorilla in Uganda could have killed her, but the danger was over before she'd had time to think about it properly. Now she was looking death in the eye. This could be it. For the first time, she considered that she might not get home again. No one would know if they all died out here on Basilan.

Stuart! She tried to swallow down the painful lump in her throat. She liked Stu! He was a great guy. Funny and sweet. Had she encouraged him to take the risk of going after fresh water? She hoped he was alive down there.

This is when people who believe in God pray, she told herself. She felt very alone.

George sat at the Bridgefords' kitchen table drinking coffee with his wife on a Saturday night. Not his usual weekend pursuit, but this weekend was far from normal. His bag was packed and waiting by the front door.

"Let me go to the airfield with you." Rachel's vivid blue eyes, peering at him over the rim of her cup, jogged the practical side of his brain. Why on earth was he leaving her behind and going into danger?

"It's probably better if you don't," he said. "Stay here and get to bed early."

"Like I'll sleep."

"You need to. For the baby."

Her smile was a little strained. "You don't have to go, honey."

"Yeah, I do." He let out a sigh. He was getting a little old for this. It had stopped looking like an adventure. Pierre had introduced him that afternoon to the other half of the Gold Team, who had flown in directly from Algeria without a break between ops. But they were high from success in their mission in North Africa, and now they were gung ho to help their friends out of this disaster. They all looked so young! Even the newly promoted Lieutenant Browne looked as though he only needed to shave once a week or so.

Rachel nodded and sipped her decaf. "I knew you'd say that."

"You do understand?"

"Yeah, I do, babe." She scrunched up her face and squeezed out another smile. "This is why I love you. Once you commit to a person or a mission, you'll never renege."

"I can't let Pierre carry the weight of this alone. It's partly my fault that his sister-in-law is out there."

"No, it's not." She said it calmly, a simple fact she had stated before.

"If I'd thought about the ramifications, I never would have put the request in for her. Never."

"I know. But it's still not your fault."

George looked at his watch. "I'll call you from Manila. After that it's iffy."

"Okay."

They both stood, and George rounded the table and took her in his arms. "Pray for us."

"You know I will," she whispered.

He kissed her gently, then with a bit of ferocity. "We'll be back soon. All of us. You can take that to the bank." He stepped back and gave her tummy a quick pat. "Be good, little guy." Rachel blinked rapidly. "You're not going to cry, are you?"

She shook her head. "Just remembering the first time you kissed me."

"Yeah. I almost ruined my career for you." Did she wish he'd quit the Navy then, and that they were off on a ranch somewhere raising quarter horses now?

"I know you have to do this," she said. "And I'm glad you and Pierre will be there for each other."

He kissed her again, quickly, and turned to grab his camouflage pack. He was wearing camos for the first time in two years, and it felt odd not to put on his cover—the hat he always wore with his uniforms. The helmet Pierre had brought him was in his bag. He wouldn't need any other headgear on this op.

He opened the door and glanced back at Rachel. She was keeping up a brave front. "I love you."

She nodded. "I've never doubted that. God speed."

⁂

"Do you think the sniper found us because Bill and I were arguing so loudly?" Claudia looked straight into Heidi's green eyes. "Is *this* my fault too?"

Heidi's face melted.

Oh, no! Now I've made her cry. She liked it better when Heidi kept her emotion bottled up.

"No, I don't think that." Heidi sniffed and stared toward the jungle, blinking. "It's nobody's fault."

"But God wouldn't want someone like Stu to get shot, would He? Stu is a Christian."

"Yes, he is. But we don't always understand God's purpose."

Claudia scowled at the bamboo jungle for a long minute. It

glistened with moisture on its leaves, so that it almost seemed to be weeping. "I'm not sure I like that philosophy, Heidi. Too fatalistic. Isn't God supposed to rain blessings down on the people He loves?" Pierre and Marie's pastor had said something like that in Norfolk, but Claudia had been too busy sneaking glances at Bill from the corner of her eye to listen well. Bill! Was he out there bleeding right now in the soggy, crummy jungle? "I made Bill mad, and he yelled at me. He let his guard down. He's not normally like that."

"No, he's not. Bill's under a lot of pressure. Our commanding officer…"

"Yeah, I was there," Claudia said bitterly. "That's my fault too. So now Bill gets all the blame if things go wrong, and it sure isn't his fault."

"Well, it ain't yours," Proul said.

Claudia figured he'd said *ain't* to get her goat. Or maybe he lapsed into bad grammar instead of swearing.

"Right. It's not my fault, and it's not Bill's fault, and I know it isn't yours or Heidi's or any of the other guys'. So whose fault is it?"

Proul shrugged.

Heidi kept her eyes on the far trees. "It doesn't have to be anyone's fault, Claudia. It's just the way it is."

"But if God controls everything, why would He make this happen? It stinks."

"Yeah, I'm with you," Proul said. "Where's God when we need Him?"

"He's here," Heidi said softly. "He's right here, so close. He loves us, whether you believe that or not."

"Can He get us out of this?" Proul asked in a hard, challenging voice.

"Of course He can. If He wants to."

Claudia let out a puff of air. "So if things go right, God did that for us, and if they go wrong, He let it happen to teach us a lesson or something?"

"I don't know why He allows bad things to happen. He doesn't always show us His reasons for doing things. But I do know that if I…" Heidi glanced down into the trench, where Santi crouched and listened. "If today's my last day on earth, that's okay. I know where I'm going. But I'm a little worried about you guys."

She didn't sound smug or pious. Claudia studied Heidi's profile. She really believed it. So did Bill, she was sure, even though he'd lost his temper with her. And Stu. She'd watched them bury their friends and give thanks to God. It seemed a little creepy. And yet…

"Tell me about Jesus."

Heidi stared at her for an instant and then returned to her vigil. "I'd love to. What do you want to know?"

THIRTY-SIX

1800 HOURS, AUGUST 14
BASILAN ISLAND, PHILIPPINES

Bill darted swiftly from one tree to another. He scouted ahead, then looked behind him just in time to see Squeegee flit into the spot he'd left ten seconds ago, behind a stand of bamboo. They'd come down the hillside in a circuitous path through the jungle and were below the level of the team's fighting position. Soon they would be on the level of the stream. He'd seen no signs of an enemy, though he and Squeegee had looked carefully for evidence of men's passing.

He picked another spot to head for next—toward the lighter verge of the forest, where the sunlight came through the foliage. He inhaled and ran, careful where he placed his feet. Just because they hadn't met the sniper yet, didn't mean he wasn't out here.

He was almost to his new refuge—a clump of undergrowth beneath a large hardwood tree—when he spotted something odd, out of sync with his knowledge of the terrain. The color wasn't quite right. The shape wasn't right either. Just before he slipped behind his cover, he saw movement that definitely wasn't right.

A man in dark clothing swung toward him and let loose with a semiautomatic rifle. Bullets plunked into the other side of the tree trunk and into the duff to Bill's left, among the bushes. His heart hammered in the silence that followed the barrage of gunfire. Cautiously, he took a glance over his shoulder but saw no trace of Squeegee.

Bill squashed himself as small as he could behind the tree and willed his body to be still. He'd never been good at waiting games, but his training had helped a lot. He stayed motionless and listened. After a few seconds, he was sure he heard careful steps, so quiet they might be nothing more than a tree snake slithering along. He sent up a quick prayer, knowing the now-or-never moment was imminent.

A sudden thrashing and thud on the ground startled him. All was quiet for a moment, then he heard rustling.

"Bill?" came Squeegee's quiet voice.

Bill peeked from behind the tree trunk. A few yards away, he could make out Squeegee's lithe form, standing over the still body of a man.

Bill hurried to him, scouting all about as he did.

"How did you get around him so quickly?" he whispered.

Squeegee gave a half shrug. "Guess I was too scared to slow down. I think… Yeah, I think he's dead. You might want to check." He looked a little green, Bill thought, beyond the reflection of the foliage.

"Sit down, Squeege." He quickly examined the dark-skinned man on the ground. Squeegee had neatly impaled the guerilla with his seven-inch knife blade. Bill's first thought, as he saw the hilt sticking from the man's back, was that he must be still alive, but closer inspection showed that the blade had certainly penetrated the heart. He picked up the man's rifle and glanced over at his friend. "All that practice paid off, I guess."

Squeegee had remained upright and was watching the jungle for more movement. His dark eyes never rested on one spot long. "Lieutenant Belanger will be proud." He glanced at Bill. "Why don't you look around a little and see if he was alone."

Bill nodded and stood the dead man's rifle against a nearby tree. He scouted all about the place where he'd seen the man crouching and in a spiral outward, until he was sure the man had come alone and no one else was within shouting distance, at least.

He slipped back through the trees to where Squeegee waited. "All clear."

"Should we leave him here?" Squeegee asked.

"His friends might find him."

"All right, I'll haul him over to the edge of the woods. Proul and I can come down and get him after dark."

Bill nodded. "We'd best bury him near our camp, so they don't find him before we're done here."

At the edge of the trees, Bill went prone and crawled slowly out from the cover of the forest. He didn't like leaving its protection, even with Squeegee behind him. The idea was for Squeegee to stay within the tree line and cover him while he made his way out to Stu. It had been almost an hour since Stu went down, and Bill's gut feeling said it was too late to help his friend.

When he was in the open, he looked up the hillside. He could barely make out the jagged remains of the wall. A flash told him the rays of the sinking sun had found metal. He'd have to tell Heidi to be more careful.

He spotted Stu's body on the stream bank and crawled along faster. *Lord, if there's any chance...*

Stu had his body armor on. He looked uncomfortable, crumpled in an unnatural position, with his helmet keeping his cheek from settling flat on the ground. Blood covered his cheek just below the brim of the helmet. The dark stains also soaked Stu's right pant leg and the ground under him.

Bill put his fingers to Stu's throat and prayed for a pulse. Faint and thready, it was there. He waited a few extra seconds to be sure he wasn't feeling his own blood pulsing through his fingertips.

He looked back toward the forest and motioned for Squeegee to come. His friend ran out and joined him. Bill looked up the hill and saw that Proul had jumped the wall and was coming down the hillside to cover them. He should have stayed under cover, Bill thought, but all the same, he was glad.

He handed Squeegee his rifle and heaved Stu over his shoulder. Squeegee had the dead guerilla's gun too. They slowly made their way up the hill. When they reached Proul, he handed off his rifle to Bill and took Stu from him. They quickly covered the remaining ground to the fortified position behind the wall. Proul laid Stu on the waiting blanket Heidi had spread.

"Nelson didn't come in?" Bill asked.

Heidi shook her head.

"See if you can do anything for Stu. I'm pretty sure I got a faint pulse. I'll go out for Nelson. I think we'd better tighten our formation. So far as we know, that guy was alone."

"You got him?" Proul asked.

"Squeegee did. After dark, we'll go get him and bury him. But I think we'd better all stick tight."

"No sentries?" Heidi asked uneasily.

Bill looked up at the sky. "We'll leave here in two or three hours. In the meantime, if someone did warn the guerillas we're here, we'll be better off together. I don't want them picking us off one by one in the woods. And if no one else knows we're here, it won't matter."

"All right." Heidi already had Stu's helmet off and splashed water on his face to clear the wound.

Bill walked over to the trench and looked down into it. Claudia and Santi sat in the bottom of the four-foot slot, staring up at him.

"Can we come out now?" Claudia asked.

"You're safer in there."

"Is there anything I can do to help with Stu?"

"Maybe." Bill glanced over at Heidi. Proul and Squeegee were again observing the terrain from behind the wall while Heidi worked. "Heidi can probably use your help."

The gratitude in Claudia's eyes sent a wave of longing over him. Would they ever be back in the normal world again—the world where you could walk across the street and not worry that someone was out to kill you?

"I'm going to get Nelson," Bill said softly, hefting his rifle.

"Want me to come?" Squeegee asked.

"No. Stay here."

Bill headed out again into the darkening forest. He tried to calm his apprehension. Nelson was okay. He'd believe that until he learned otherwise. Proul hadn't seen anyone, and if Nelson had, they'd have heard his weapon fire. Unless the guerillas took him down silently, the way Squeegee killed the man who'd shot Stu.

He approached Nelson's post with extra caution, not only in case an enemy had replaced his friend. Even if Nelson was all right, he must have heard the gunfire and spent the last hour and a quarter on edge, wondering what had happened and whether to leave his post or not. Bill didn't want to become the victim of a man with a nervous trigger finger.

He slipped through the trees as quietly as he could, but even so, he made tiny sounds. *James Fenimore Cooper was wrong,* he thought. *Even Indians made a little noise.*

Nelson suddenly popped from behind a mahogany tree. "Hey, Lieutenant. What gives? Did you guys have trouble?"

"Yeah. Everything all right here?"

"All clear, but you scared the wits out of me, sneaking up like that."

Bill gave him a tight smile. "It seemed advisable under the circumstances."

"I heard shots, and then nothing. I was starting to think something really bad went down."

"Come in to the camp with me. We need you, and anyway, I want us all back there before full dark."

"Sure. Is someone hurt?"

"Stu was getting water, and he got hit."

"Bad?"

"Yeah. Squeege and I went out and picked off the sniper, but we're not a hundred percent sure he was alone."

Nelson gritted his teeth. "Let's go."

Pierre and George leaned on the rail of the boat, staring into the blackness ahead. Pierre tried not to think of home and Marie. Tonight's work would need his full attention.

"You sure this is the right place?" George asked as the boat nosed in toward the dark, forested shoreline.

"It's the closest uninhabited place to where they last called me from that we can land, *mon ami*. I have only the GPS coordinates from last night."

"Okay. How far a hike to that spot?"

Pierre frowned in apology. "Twelve kilometers at least. Maybe a little more." He was glad he'd stayed in shape, training with the men he instructed. He wondered if George was having second thoughts. The commander looked to be in fighting shape, as he had since the day Pierre met him, but how much training was he doing these days? "You sure you're up for this?"

"I'm sure. Just because I've got ten years or so on you, doesn't mean I can't hike anymore."

"It's rough going."

George just nodded. A few minutes later, he pointed to a cluster of lights. "Thought you said this area was uninhabited."

"It's a Yakan village. No way of knowing on short notice whether they support the insurgents or not. We'll get well beyond their territory before we land." Pierre looked over at the group of men further down the deck watching silently. Teams 3 and 4 of the Gold Team. He hoped they weren't leading them into a trap.

"I think we should go now," Squeegee said.

"No, it's not completely dark yet," Heidi put in, looking to Bill to settle the matter.

"They know where we are," Squeegee insisted, as though that was the only thing that mattered.

"We don't know that," Bill said. "If that guy wasn't alone, the others got away. But we didn't see any sign that he had backup. Look, I tried to call for some input from higher up, but I couldn't get through to Lieutenant Belanger or anyone else in our chain of command."

Heidi touched his arm. "I think we should pray."

Proul looked a little uncomfortable, but Bill said, "Good idea. Proul and Squeegee, stay alert." Nelson was still working over Stu with Claudia's assistance, and Santi was huddled in the bottom of the trench. That left Bill and Heidi.

They bowed their heads. "Heavenly Father, show us the best course now. And please…" Bill swallowed hard. "Help Stu."

"Amen," Heidi whispered.

"Now what?" Proul asked.

Bill looked around at them. "We need to move. It will be dark in an hour. I think we should find a new position that's more easily defendable, and stash Claudia and Santi there while we go after his parents."

"What about Stu?" Heidi asked.

"We'll take him and leave him with Claudia while we try for the Gamatas."

"Shouldn't he keep still?" Heidi's eyes were solemn as she looked toward Nelson and Claudia.

"Let's see what the doc has to say." Bill walked over and crouched beside Nelson. "Can we travel?"

"We, or are you talking about Stuart?"

"I meant him."

Nelson nodded and inhaled through his nose as he wrapped a dressing around Stuart's leg. Claudia held his supplies for him. "Well, I'll tell you. The head wound isn't too bad of itself. A graze, really."

"But it knocked him out," Bill said.

"Maybe. But he lost a lot more blood from this leg wound."

"Did it hit an artery?"

"Not the major one, but a lot of smaller vessels. I'm not sure he'll make it, Bill. And if we try to carry him very far on a stretcher, it could stress him more and put us all in danger." Nelson taped the gauze down and leaned back to look at him. "Maybe we should just leave him here in the trench tonight."

"No." Bill could see the logic, but there was no way he'd go off and leave Stu unconscious with no one to defend him. "I won't do that."

Nelson nodded. "I wouldn't either. But it is an option, and if you'd said to do it, I'd go along."

"Well, we're not leaving him alone. But I don't think we can take him far through the jungle."

Bill turned and called softly to Squeegee. His friend came over and bent low beside him. "What's up?"

"When you scouted ahead to the fort, did you see a place along the way that would make a good, defensible position?"

Squeegee's dark eyes narrowed for a moment. "Yeah, there's a place where there were a lot of rocks in the woods. Rough going, but a lot of cover."

"How far?"

"A mile or so."

"Can we carry Stu that far?" Bill asked Nelson.

The medic sighed. "I hate to, but...it probably won't make much difference to him. He's critical, Bill. I seriously doubt Stu is going to make it through tonight without advanced medical care and a blood transfusion. But it will slow the rest of us down, and make us more vulnerable."

Bill was silent. When he looked up, it was Claudia's face he focused on. He realized suddenly that she had remained silent. The opinionated woman he thought would freely give advice on any topic was keeping quiet. His respect for Claudia inched upward. He'd been wrong about her in so many ways. She did know when to let the military do its job, after all.

"This will affect you, Claudia," he said. "Any thoughts?"

"I'll stay here with him, or I'll help carry him. Whatever you think is best, Bill."

"We gonna go get that body?" Squeegee asked.

Bill nodded. "Yeah, let's you, me, and Proul go bring him in and bury him. We'll take a look around again, and I'll make my decision then."

By the time the grave was dug, Bill's fatigue had caught up with him. He wondered if they'd wasted precious energy to bury their enemy. Rain began just as they finished. It felt good for the first few seconds.

"Bring him over here, and let's get this done," he said to Squeegee. He waited, holding his entrenching tool—a Navy-issue folding shovel. They'd taken their body armor off. Digging would have been nearly impossible with the movement-restricting vests on. They ought to put them on again, but somehow Bill couldn't care.

Before Proul and Squeegee could bring the guerilla's body to the hole, Nelson walked out to meet him.

"How's Stu doing?" Bill asked.

Nelson shook his head. "He hasn't regained consciousness, and I don't think he will. His breathing's gotten very shallow. I've got Claudia bathing his face with cool water, but that's mostly for Claudia's benefit."

"Should we make a stretcher?"

Nelson hesitated, then released a sigh. "Wait an hour to fill the dirt in the hole."

Bill grimaced. "Oh, man."

"I know it seems crass." Nelson peered at him in the starlight. "If he dies, and I think it's only a matter of time, we can't leave his body exposed."

"We'll be back in a few hours."

"If we're successful."

"Well, yeah." Bill looked down into the empty grave. "I hate this." His voice broke, and tears flooded his eyes.

Nelson rested his hand on Bill's shoulder. "I'm so very sorry. We all love Stu. He's a great kid. But I'm especially sorry for you."

Bill wiped his face with his sleeve. "I really hate to bury him. I'll probably have nightmares. Man, don't you ever wonder if we made a mistake and… What if one of the guys we buried on the beach wasn't really dead?"

"Don't go there, Billy. There was no doubt. Don't torture yourself like that."

Bill wiped his hand over his scratchy face. Sweat. Grime. Blood. Would he ever be clean again?

"Okay. I hate to wait, because the delay could put us at the fort too late to move in."

"I know. You need to make your move in the dark."

Bill nodded. "I guess we can't help it." Proul and Squeegee came, lugging the guerilla's body between them.

"One hour," Nelson said. "I don't think it will be more."

Bill sat with his back to the wall. Everyone had insisted he rest, but his mind raced so fast he couldn't sleep. He had put his vest on again at Heidi's insistence, and they'd taken Stu's off and put it on Santi. The boy now slept curled up beside Bill, with his head on Bill's pack.

Dear God, let something good come out of this. At least let us save this boy. If not Stu, then, please, let us get the professor and his wife. Dear Lord, don't let this all be for nothing! He reached out and very gently touched Santi's black hair. *Let this boy grow up and do some good in this world.*

"Doc?"

Claudia's grim voice startled Bill. He held his breath and Nelson crept over to Claudia's side and checked Stu's vital signs.

When Nelson sat back on his heels and his shoulders slumped, Bill knew it was over. He said something Bill couldn't catch, but Claudia stood and stumbled a few steps away and put her hands to her face.

Bill pushed himself up, levering off the wall. In three strides he was at Claudia's side. When she saw him, she let out a sob so mournful it wrenched Bill's heart. He reached for her and pulled her in against him, drawing her head down on his shoulder.

"Hush," he whispered, rocking her a little as she wept. "We're going to be okay."

"It's my fault," she gasped.

"No, no. Don't say that. Don't even think it." He knew he spoke the truth. He would never blame this one on Claudia. He'd reserved that load of guilt for himself.

THIRTY-SEVEN

0030 hours, August 15
Basilan Island, Philippines

The last mile was the hardest—through the vine-laden jungle and mostly uphill. The rain had eased up, but the ground was slippery. Pierre pressed onward, and the eight men of the Gold Team followed in grim silence. Now and then he reminded himself to check on the commander, but good old George seemed to be holding his own.

They stopped to rest on a ridge, and Brownie checked their position for Pierre.

"Their camp should be dead ahead, sir. Point-eight kilometers."

"I doubt they're still there," Pierre said. "White was determined to carry out the rescue. They probably moved out hours ago."

His scouts came back to intercept him when they were almost on top of the location.

"Someone's ahead of us, sir," The tall, thin specialist named Williams reported.

"White's team?"

"I don't think so. They're heading the same way we are, and they posted a sentry at the edge of a clear area. We almost ran over him."

"He didn't see you though?"

"No. I wouldn't have seen him, either, but he's having a smoke."

"Not our team, then," Pierre said with certainty. Bill's men wouldn't smoke while standing guard, especially not if there was a chance an enemy might be in the area. It was the mark of an undisciplined force.

"Should we do more recon?"

"I'd hate for them to spot us," Pierre said.

Williams nodded. "I can get back to the same place I was when I spotted him and see what happens."

"Be extra careful," Pierre told him reluctantly. Now would not be a good time for a clash with the insurgents. Williams and another man faded into the night.

"What do you think is up?" George asked.

"I think it's Bill's camp up ahead and some guerilla troops found it. I just hope Bill and his people moved out before they came along."

Twenty minutes later, Williams was back.

"They've cleared out, sir. O'Neill is waiting up ahead, keeping watch until we get there. We're pretty sure they all left, heading west."

Pierre and the rest of the team followed Williams through the forest. They came out on a steep hillside. Ensign O'Neill had halted at the tree line.

"There's some kind of structure out there, sir." He pointed. "The activity seemed to center there."

"All right. Let's go. Fan out."

George took three men down below the structure, Browne took two higher up the hill, and Pierre took Williams and O'Neill with him, heading straight for the dark bulk. As they approached it, he realized it was the ruins of a building—the wall Bill had told him was part of their defensive position the day before. He checked suddenly as a black void opened before him.

"Halt!" His heart hammered as he realized he stood on the edge of a four-foot-deep trench. "Be careful. It looks like White and his men dug in here."

A low whistle from up the hill drew him to Browne's group.

"What have you got?"

"It's all soft here, like it was dug up."

Pierre nodded. "Well, there's an open trench below."

"Wonder why they filled this one, and not the other one?" Browne eyed him in the moonlight. "Maybe a grave here?"

Pierre's mind had jumped to the same suggestion. He hesitated only a minute. "Open it, but be quiet."

Ten minutes later, Browne climbed out of the hole. "It's Jeff Stuart, for sure. And I'd say a guerilla. No tags, non-standard clothing and gear."

"Fill it back in for now." Pierre touched George's arm and led him a few steps away. "I'm thinking we should hurry. The men Williams and O'Neill saw are probably following White's team."

George lifted his helmet just long enough to run his fingers through his dark hair, then replaced it. "I agree. They may need us now. We'll come back here afterward and do what we have to. But we'll need to proceed with extreme caution. If the people between us and White are Abu Sayyaf and they realize we're tailing them, it could get nasty."

≪∘≫

"We're maybe a couple of miles from the fort, Lieutenant," Proul whispered.

Bill couldn't help smiling as he tucked his GPS unit back into his pack. "Two-point-seven kilometers, to be exact."

"Oh. Right. What do you suggest?"

"We need to make sure Claudia and Santi are secure before we go on." Bill had looked over the first place Proul had suggested for stashing the two civilians, but it was so far from the target that Bill didn't like it. If the team didn't succeed in their mission, Claudia and the boy would be without resources. He'd decided to bring them closer to the shore so they'd have a better chance of getting help if they needed it. This hillside seemed a better spot to him.

Squeegee and Nelson scrambled down from the rocky rise on the side away from the sea.

"There's a little cave up there. Well, more of a rock overhang," Nelson said.

"But there's bushes in front of it," Squeegee noted. "So long as they're quiet, no one would know they were there tonight, and maybe not in daylight."

"Okay. We probably won't find a better spot." The others had bunched around him. Bill looked at Claudia. "You and Santi come up there with me and Squeegee. We'll get you settled and leave most of our stuff with you. Then we'll try to cover our tracks so that anyone coming through here won't look for you up under the rock."

They climbed to the diminutive cave. Bill decided it was a better spot than the one he had rejected. It was far better concealed and off what seemed to be an occasionally used path.

"This is good," Claudia said softly. "We'll be fine. Right, Santi?"

The boy nodded, but he said nothing. His dark eyes gleamed in the starlight.

"We'll hide the packs up above you, but I want you to keep this with you." Bill handed her the satellite phone. "If we're not back by daylight, call someone."

"Who?"

"I programmed in Lieutenant Belanger's personal number, but I doubt he's getting cell phone service now. I also put in my supervisor in Guam and my commander back in Norfolk. You should be able to get somebody. If you can't get through, try climbing to a high point."

"Right." Her chin took on that determined set. "Bill, leave me a gun."

"I'm not sure that's a good idea."

"I own a nine-millimeter pistol, and I'm experienced with hand-guns."

He stared at her, but she didn't blink. "Is that for the wild jaunts you take?"

"No. It's for the streets of Atlanta. I have a permit."

He considered her request for a moment, opened one of the

packs, and took out Stu's pistol. "This is a Baretta M92F. It holds fifteen rounds."

She took it and held it up to look it over. "I guess if that's not enough, nothing will be."

Bill looked over at Squeegee. "Give me a second here."

Squeegee took Santi's arm. "Come on, buddy. Let's get you situated."

When they were busy settling the boy in under the rock, Bill looked down at Claudia. "I hate to leave you here. It goes against everything I know."

"We'll be fine. I promise we won't leave this spot until daylight, unless you come back. And then it will only be if we have to in order to contact someone."

Bill nodded. "Okay. The shore is only about half a mile that way." He pointed south. "And there's a Yakan village about three miles northeast of here."

"That close?"

"Yes. They're generally of Muslim persuasion, but I don't think they'd hurt you. As a last resort, you could go to them and plead lost tourist. But I really think Pierre is coming out here to pick us up. The last time I talked to him, he was on his way to Guam. So don't give up hope if we don't come back. He may be coming down to Zamboanga, in which case he could come in with a boat and pick you up."

"Do you think that Santi and I could backtrack to the place where I first caught up with you? Where we were attacked?"

"Probably. You'd have to go slowly and be cautious. We have small boats hidden there. One to each side of the landing spot. But I think your best bet would be to call someone and have a boat come around here to get you."

"But if you don't come back…"

"Yeah. The jungle could be full of guerillas by morning if they mow us over. They won't like the idea that a squad of Americans came to snatch their prisoners." He gulped and looked away for a moment. There was so much he wanted to say to her. "Look, Pierre was probably right when he said we shouldn't attempt to complete the mission."

"He didn't order you to stop?"

"No, but…I have no idea what we're heading into. I don't like it. But we've got to try. Claudia, I'm sorry about this mess. I'm sorry about a lot of things."

She reached up and turned down his collar. "Well, I'm sorry about some of it too. But I'm not sorry I'm here. I can take care of Santi while you finish the job you started."

Her closeness and her quiet encouragement built up his resolve until he almost felt they could do it. "You take care. And if we ever get back to the real world, we'll have to sit down someplace dry and quiet and have a long talk."

She smiled. "You'll be back. I'm counting on it. I've been learning about God and what He can do. This is what He brought you here for, Bill. He'll see you through. Now, go. Bring Dr. Gamata and his wife out safe."

Looking down at her, he believed success was possible. And how much had she learned about God? He knew she'd had a serious talk with Heidi earlier that evening. Heidi had clued him in on that. How deep was Claudia's change of heart? He touched her cheek for an instant, and her eyes glittered.

"Thanks." He stepped aside.

She huddled into the crevice with Santi, and Bill helped Squeegee arrange the brush in front of them and sweep away the signs of their climb.

Squeegee and Proul led the team to the old fortress. All seemed quiet within, but they quickly searched it to be sure. When they'd finished, Bill took up a position outside the outer masonry wall, facing toward the building where the Gamatas had been eighteen hours earlier. He couldn't see the building, but the men assured him it was less than a quarter mile away, through the dense jungle.

Heidi wanted badly to be part of the recon team that investigated their target, but Bill convinced her that Proul and Squeegee, who were already familiar with the terrain, should go first. While they forged ahead, he made sure Nelson gave Heidi another dose of antibiotics and some ibuprofen. No matter what she told him, that shoulder wound must be killing her. Bill intended for Heidi to take as small a role as possible in the confrontation ahead.

They waited mostly in silence, and the night sounds resumed. The rustling leaves, the insects. Were Cabaya's men out there waiting for them?

Nelson slapped at a mosquito. "I s'pose you two are praying."

"Always," Heidi replied.

"How's your leg?" Bill asked.

"Okay. I'll be glad when we're done with this and I can rest. I guess you will be too, huh, Taber?"

"Yeah." Heidi stood leaning against a tree with her rifle at rest in her arms.

Bill heard a twig snap and reached to touch her arm so she wouldn't say any more. A moment later, Proul stood beside them in the gloom.

"Hey, you're back quick," Bill said.

"It's like we thought. They're in there. We could see a light through a crack in the boards covering one of the windows. But there's a guard out front, near the door, and there could be more inside. There's a truck parked out front too."

"Where's Squeegee?"

"Stayed in position, just watching. I'll take you to him."

"Right." Bill checked his gear and sent up a last silent prayer. "Let's move."

THIRTY-EIGHT

Claudia tried to find a comfortable spot on the rough rock surface. It wouldn't be so bad if it were level, but the rock floor sloped downward toward the opening. She and Santi found it best to sit with their backs to the wall, facing out, with their shoes planted firmly to keep them from sliding out of their hiding place. Claudia's toes felt a little sore inside her hiking boots. Santi wore holey sneakers—probably the same shoes he was kidnapped in six months ago. She fumbled in the dark to find a place flat enough for the sat phone to rest without sliding down the incline.

"Are you okay?" she asked when they'd been alone an hour.

"Yes, ma'am."

"You can call me Claudia." They sat for a few minutes in silence.

A sudden cry from the woods startled Claudia. She caught her breath and steadied herself.

"Monkey," Santi said.

She chuckled and put her hand to her heart. "Thanks for telling me. It scared me."

"It will be light soon."

She looked out and decided the jungle around them was less black than it had been. She could make out individual bamboo trees.

"It's going to be okay, you know. They'll get your parents, and we'll go meet the American sailors, and they'll take us away from here."

Santi nodded.

"Where did you live before they took you?" she asked.

"Manila. My father did his work at the university there."

"I'm sure you'll be home again soon. Or maybe your parents will want to move somewhere safer. I'm sure your father could do his work in America if he wanted to."

Santi turned his head, and Claudia realized she could see his face easily. Dawn really was coming. His dark, straight hair peeked out from below the too-large helmet Bill had instructed him to wear—Stu's helmet.

"Do you believe in God?"

She eyed him in surprise. Having grown up without brothers, she'd supposed boys didn't have serious thoughts like that until they were older. But Santi seemed a pensive boy. He'd probably had little to do but think these past few months. She considered how she should answer.

"I'm beginning to," she said at last.

He shifted to a different sitting position, so that he partly faced her. "We used to go to church in Manila. I learned about Jesus. But since we were kidnapped, we haven't had any worship or anyone to talk to. When I heard that girl soldier—Heidi—talk to you about Jesus, I was glad."

"Were you?"

"Yes. It makes me happy that the people who are helping us are Christians."

"Well, Santi, I'll tell you the truth. I used to think church and Christianity and Jesus were pretty hokey."

"What's that?"

"Uh, it's like a joke. Not real. But after the things I've seen out here and learning more about God and why Jesus was here on the earth in the first place, it's starting to make sense to me."

"That's good."

"Are your parents Christians?"

"I'm not sure. When I tried to talk to my father about God, he didn't want to talk. I think he wonders why God would let us be taken by the Muslims, and maybe that made him not trust God."

Claudia nodded. "I'll tell you what. I'll trust God to deliver your parents today if you will."

"You mean, God will help the soldiers get them and bring them back here?"

"Yes."

"Okay."

Claudia smiled uncertainly. "Do you…want to pray?"

Without comment, Santi bowed his head and shut his eyes. "God, please help Heidi and Lieutenant White and the rest. Help them to get Papa and Mama and bring them here, and please don't let anyone else get shot." After an extended pause, he added, "And keep Claudia and me safe. Amen."

Claudia had not closed her eyes. She had sat watching out into the jungle, hoping she would not see any movement other than the gently swaying leaves and the fluttering of birds' wings. But as she heard Santi's simple prayer, her heart ached.

"Thank you," she said. "I think God was listening."

He nodded, his face sober, but his mouth creaked open in a big yawn.

"Maybe you should sleep," she suggested. "I'll watch for a while if you want to rest."

"I'm not sure if I can without falling out of the cave."

He managed by lying diagonally across the shelter. Claudia lifted his feet and laid his smelly sneakers in her lap with a reassuring smile. Within five minutes he was out. She kept her vigil as the day broke and light filtered down through the forest ceiling. If Bill did not return soon, it would be time to try to contact Pierre. Bill had said to do that if he did not return by daylight. That was now. She didn't want to wake Santi. And if she tried to call, any nearby enemies might intercept her transmission. She decided to give Bill and his team a few more minutes before she attempted contact.

"God," she whispered, "if You're real, please do the things Santi asked. Please don't let this boy's faith be disappointed."

Bill directed Nelson and Proul to circle the building inside the cover of the trees. He left Heidi where Squeegee had been, and he took Squeegee with him to approach the front of the building. He checked his weapons and put in his earplugs. Dawn was upon them as Squeegee darted from the trees across a few yards of open terrain and flattened himself against the wall of the building. Bill gave him a thumbs-up. After a short wait, Squeegee tiptoed toward the corner of the front wall while Bill moved cautiously through the brush until he could see the front entrance and a dirty, dilapidated utility truck.

The guard sitting on the stoop looked half asleep. He leaned with both hands on his rifle, his head to one side. As Bill watched, he yawned and consulted his wristwatch. Bill waited until he slouched again and moved forward a couple of yards so that he could see all the open area clearly and would have a clean shot past Squeegee when his friend made his move. Across the clearing he saw nothing. He wished he knew where Nelson and Proul were, but if he could see them from here, then the guard would be able to see them too.

Squeegee looked toward him. Bill hated this moment—the last possible instant when he could call it off. He sent up a quick prayer and gave Squeegee Brooks the nod.

His buddy popped around the corner of the building, leading with his gun barrel.

"Drop the gun." He repeated the command in Spanish, but before his words were out, the guerilla had pivoted toward him, swinging his gun up as he turned.

With no other option, Squeegee squeezed off three quick rounds, and the man went down. All was deathly still. Was it possible they had left only one sentry in plain sight in front of the building? Across the open area where the truck was parked, Bill saw Nelson part the foliage. He raised one hand in a shrug. Bill waved.

Nelson and Bill met Squeegee on the steps. Heidi and Proul knew they were supposed to hang back and cover all approaches to the building. Squeegee had removed the prone guard's rifle and was checking for other weapons. Bill looked at the door. It had an old-fashioned iron thumb latch and a newer lock that looked like a deadbolt. He and Nelson each took up a post on one side of it, and Bill tried the thumb latch. Locked. Why wasn't he surprised?

Squeegee straightened and tossed him a key ring with two keys on it. One looked like a car key—probably for the truck. Bill inserted the second key carefully into the lock and turned it. The tumblers in the lock clicked. He and Nelson plastered themselves against the door jambs. Squeegee lifted the latch and threw the door open, dodging aside. A spray of bullets erupted from inside.

Squeegee hit the ground beside the steps and rolled. Their recon had told them the Gamatas were most likely in a room farther back in the building, on the west side. Bill looked at Nelson and nodded. Nelson tossed a smoke bomb in. Almost at once, coughing and thrashing movements could be heard. Nelson patted a grenade on his belt, but Bill shook his head. He looked at Squeegee, who was on his feet again, rubbing his shoulder. Must have taken a bullet on his vest. He pointed along the side wall and drew a box in the air with his finger. Bill nodded, understanding the option they'd discussed— Squeegee and Heidi would try to open the window of the room where they suspected the Gamatas were held, gaining access to the hostages and a flanking movement on the guards.

As Squeegee disappeared around the corner, another round of gunfire spat through the open doorway. Bill pulled a stun grenade from his belt, and Nelson nodded.

Bill pulled the pin and tossed the grenade inside. He and Nelson crouched and covered their ears, knowing what would come next. The three seconds seemed interminable, and the subsequent flash of light and booming noise made Bill jump, even though he'd expected it and wore earplugs. Nelson leaped up and beat him inside, carrying the 12-gauge shotgun in the ready position. The trick was to strike before the enemy reoriented after the light-and-sound blast. Bill was right behind him. The thick smoke swirled, cutting their vision to a few feet.

One Filipino man inside had given up and thrown his empty hands over his head.

"Don't shoot! Don't shoot!"

Nelson grabbed him by the collar and heaved him out the door just as another man leaped up from behind a chair, firing wildly as he rose. Bill shot back, and the man went down.

Leaving Nelson to deal with the prisoner, Bill picked up the dead man's pistol, tucked it in his belt, and headed into the hallway beyond the front room. He threw open a door on the left side of the hallway and cleared the room. When he reached the second door, he flattened himself beside the jamb and shoved the door open. A barrage of bullets whistled past him as the gun's reports rattled through the building. He had one more stun grenade left, and he started to pull it from his belt. Before he could get it free, more shots erupted from inside, and he heard the thud of running steps. Instinctively he backed down the hall.

The next few seconds were all noise and smoke. Bill fired indiscriminately at the figures that emerged from the side room. One fell in the doorway. The second ran toward the front room. Bill caught his breath and approached the fallen man and kicked an Uzi submachine gun out of his reach. As he patted the man's body for more weapons, he heard shots fired outside.

Lord, protect my people! Bill realized that if his enemies had used the prisoners as human shields, he probably would have killed them because he'd had no time to think or verify his targets. He rolled the man over. He was far too young and well-fed to be Gamata.

Bill held his rifle at the ready and headed for the door he thought led to the room where the prisoners were held. He stood well to the side and thumped on the wooden panel with his knuckles. "U.S. Navy. Open up."

Silence from within. What if more guards were inside with the Gamatas? He heard a sound like nails being ripped out of boards and a small scream. He tried the door latch and found it was unlocked.

The middle-aged couple inside turned toward him and gasped. The man jumped between Bill and the woman. A quick glance showed Bill that beyond them, the boards had been torn from the window, and Heidi was already halfway through the frame.

Bill lowered his gun and held up his hand.

"Easy. It's okay. Dr. Gamata, I'm Lieutenant William White, U.S. Navy. We're here to take you to safety."

"Americans?"

"Yes, sir. We're here to help."

"Our boy?" The man croaked.

Bill smiled. "Santi is safe. We'll take you to him now."

Heidi stood up inside the window. "All clear out front, sir."

"Excellent," Bill said.

Heidi smiled at the Gamatas. "Then, sir, if you're ready…"

"One moment," The professor said. He quickly gathered some papers off the small table and shoved them into a plastic bag. With trembling fingers, he sealed it and slid it into a soft briefcase. His wife grabbed a pack from the floor near the sleeping mat. Bill couldn't help noticing how thin they both were—and how old they looked to be parents of a thirteen-year-old boy.

"Hey!" Proul stuck his head in the window. "We gotta move, Bill! Nelson's prisoner keeps saying Cabaya is coming, and I hear a motor."

Bill hustled the couple down the hallway, grabbed the dead man's Uzi, and herded them out the front door. Two more bodies sprawled in the yard. Nelson was jogging toward him from the edge of the gravel road.

"Did you get the one that got past me?" Bill shouted.

"Yeah. Had to take him down." Nelson gestured toward one of the prone forms.

"Where's your prisoner?"

Nelson pointed behind him. "I tied him to a tree. He says his boss is on the way. Should I have shot him?"

As he spoke, the crunch of tires on the gravel reached Bill's ears. There wasn't a second to remove the bodies of the two guerillas in the yard. And Cabaya's surviving man would tell him how many there were and how recently they had left.

"Let's move!" Bill jerked his head toward the corner of the house. Nelson ran past him. The others had just reached the tree line. Squeegee went ahead into the jungle. Heidi and Proul followed, assisting the Gamatas. Bill watched around the corner of the building as a large, stake-body truck pulled in and a dozen armed men leaped from the back. He turned and ran after his team. Nelson was at the end of the line, trying to hurry the weakened couple into the jungle.

"Go, go," Bill said urgently. "Nelson, we'll make a stand. Here, inside the tree line."

The two of them found solid cover and huddled behind tree trunks. They peered out, watching for men to come in pursuit. The sounds of their team faded as they hurried away.

"I've got a grenade left," Nelson said.

"All I've got is one stun grenade."

Nelson swore.

"I also got one of their Uzis," Bill said. He slung his M16 over his shoulder and held the Uzi. "I don't know how many rounds are left."

A squad of six men appeared at the side of the house, scanning the woods.

"Let them get close," Bill said under his breath, not moving.

Nelson waited, ready to pull the pin on his grenade. Some of the men apparently entered the building, and he heard distant shouts.

Suddenly he wondered if he'd let the nearer six get too close. He could see their faces clearly. It would only take one bullet on the mark to wreck their mission.

"Now!"

As Nelson drew back his arm, Bill locked eyes with one of the guerillas. He could tell exactly when the man leading the pack saw him through the foliage. His dark mustache twitched, and he swung his gun barrel in Bill's direction. Nelson, the pitcher for his high school baseball team, made his throw. As the grenade flew through the air into the center of the cluster of men, Bill and the guerilla exchanged gunfire.

Something hit Bill and knocked him backward as he saw the man he'd fired at fall and three of the others lifted by the shock of Nelson's grenade. Bill hit the ground hard and lay gasping.

"Billy Boy! Come on! Get up!"

"I'm okay." He panted and grabbed Nelson's hand. Nelson pulled him to his feet. Bill's chest and shoulder screamed with pain.

"Go!"

"Not without you." Nelson glanced frantically back toward the building. "Can you run?"

"Maybe." Bill could see the back of the building through the leaves and bamboo stalks. Two men were climbing cautiously to their feet. A man in a drab uniform raced around the far corner, yelling in Spanish. Three others followed him. The first man waved his arms and shouted at the others. He ran straight toward Bill and Nelson, dodging the wounded men scattered on the ground. The other men followed the leader. His dark hair flew as he ran forward. His eyes glinted with hatred.

"Cabaya," Bill said.

Nelson seized the Uzi from Bill's hands and fired with abandon through the bushes. When the gun was empty, he threw it down and latched onto Bill's sleeve.

"Now or never, Billy!"

Bill turned with him and ran after his squad.

THIRTY-NINE

0500 HOURS, AUGUST 15
BASILAN ISLAND, PHILIPPINES

Pierre paused and listened, watching keenly ahead of him. They'd moved fast for the last hour, and he was sure they had nearly caught up with whoever was ahead of them. He motioned Browne to him.

"They're just ahead of us."

Browne nodded. "Think we can surround them?"

Pierre shrugged. "I don't know how many there are."

"No more than six, I think."

Pierre looked over at George, who had come up beside him and was breathing deeply but seemed to be all right. He arched his eyebrows, and George nodded.

"Extreme caution," George said. "Remember the intel we got this morning."

Pierre and Browne both nodded. They were only a few miles from a village suspected of being an Abu Sayyaf training camp. This jungle swarmed with terrorists just looking for a fight. It would be wise not to do any shooting unless they had to.

They hurried on, still cautious, fanning out from the trail. Pierre thought he heard someone moving before him and redoubled his caution.

A faint shout from up ahead startled them all. Pierre signaled Browne and his men to follow and darted forward.

Suddenly he saw moving figures ahead of him. He slipped to cover behind another tree, then another. Ahead, through the trees, he saw a wooded hillside. A dark-skinned man was holding up a camouflage pack, as though it were a trophy. Someone touched Pierre's arm, and he turned to find George standing very close to him.

"Looks like they found a stash," George whispered.

Pierre nodded. "I'm thinking Bill's outfit cached their supplies. We must be near the hostage site."

Claudia's heart thudded so fast she feared it would burst. She reached for Santi and grabbed his hand. Santi squeezed her fingers like a little crab trying to cut them off.

They could see the guerilla soldiers a few yards away, searching the brush for more loot. She'd thought all the packs were hidden above their hiding place, but Bill's men must have missed one in the dark last night and left it where the intruders could easily spot it on their way through. Which begged a question: Were they just passing by on their usual path, or were they following the Gold Team's tracks?

One of the men worked his way up the slight slope toward their mini cave, beating the brush. Claudia could see his swarthy face above his beard. His dark eyes smoldered as he slashed the weeds with his machete.

If I can see him, he can see me. God, make us invisible! She cringed back against the rock and tried to make herself smaller. She avoided looking out again. Her sheet-white face would certainly claim the attention of any man glancing this way. Why hadn't she asked Bill to let her and Santi paint their faces with camouflage, the way the men did? She pulled the pistol Bill had left her from her pocket.

Heavy steps, muffled calls, and chopping sounds. A shadow fell over the opening to their hiding place. Claudia held her breath. Dirty olive drab pants, a gun stock.

She flipped the pistol's safety off and held it in front of her. Santi's eyes were huge with fear.

The man stooped and looked in at them. He reached in and seized Santi's ankle and pulled him out in one jerk. He must not have seen the gun in the shadows. Santi thudded to the ground with a yelp. Claudia held her breath. He would grab her foot next and pull her out.

"Stop!" she shouted.

He peered in at her, and his eyes focused on her and hardened. She caught her breath. Now? She couldn't do it. Could she?

Another man came up beside him. Too late! Or was it? Santi must be lying on the ground. She couldn't see him. How many of them were there?

The man grasped her ankle.

Now!

She pulled the trigger. The report hurt her ears, and the small space filled with acrid smoke. The grip on her ankle tightened. Claudia braced herself, but a powerful yank pulled her from the cave. Her breath rushed from her lungs as she hit the ground.

She gasped for breath and stared upward. The peaceful leaves of the jungle waved above her, revealing just a hint of the brilliant blue sky beyond. She realized in rapid succession that her ears still rang from the repercussion of the gun, her back and elbows hurt, and she had lost her grip on the pistol.

Two men stood over her. "Where are the others?" one asked.

The other said something she didn't understand, but the first man bent and peered into the small cave. She must have missed him when she fired, and the bullet ricocheted off the rock near the opening. She was lucky it hadn't hit her or Santi.

Although the other man kept his rifle pointed down at her, he too focused for a moment on the cave. Claudia used that instant to look around. Santi lay on his side in the grass a couple of feet away, staring at her. His huge eyes screamed his terror.

He snaked his hand out, and she thought for a second he was reaching for her, but then she saw the pistol, hidden in the weeds between them. Santi was wiggling his index finger, pointing toward it.

She looked up. The man guarding her said something and kicked her thigh, but not very hard. The man checking the cave stepped backward, almost treading on Santi, and the boy rolled quickly away.

In the moment the men were distracted by Santi's movement, Claudia closed her hand over the pistol and clapped it against her side, shielding it from their view with her body.

One of the men reached down and grabbed her collar, hauling her to her feet. She managed to stay turned away from him so he didn't see the gun. Four other men, farther down the hillside, were looking up toward them. When she stood, one of them let out a cheer, and they began to climb the slope.

FORTY

"Was that a gunshot?" Pierre looked to George. The blast had sounded muffled, too faint for the men in the woods ahead of them to have fired.

"Small caliber, maybe?" George edged forward, and Pierre crowded close to his elbow.

Half a dozen men in mismatched clothing converged on a spot behind a patch of brush on a rocky hillside. Pierre spotted an AFP uniform shirt amid camouflage T-shirts, khaki pants, and ragged jeans. All carried rifles. Only two wore helmets.

"What's going on, sir?" Browne asked at his elbow.

"Not sure yet. They may have found our team's supply cache."

Pierre caught his breath. One of the men had hauled what appeared to be a prisoner to his feet and shoved him forward.

Browne swore. "That's our camo uniform."

George took a small monocular from his pocket and trained it on the group. As they watched, another prisoner was manhandled to his feet. He stood only as tall as the first one's shoulder and was dressed in shorts and a flak vest over a T-shirt.

"We've got to move in," George said. "That's a kid."

"The toy store package?"

"Could be."

Pierre looked at Browne. "Take two of your men." He motioned to his right, up the slope. Browne and two of the team members slid away from them, and Pierre motioned the rest of the men forward.

Six against one. Claudia's hope shrank from ant-sized to a mere germ. She saw that the man holding his gun trained on her held her satellite phone in his other hand, regarding it curiously.

Her guard shoved her toward his friends. She nearly tripped and fell down the hill, but caught herself. The other swarthy man pulled Santi to his feet and pushed him over beside her.

Were these the same insurgents who had kidnapped the Gamata family? She'd gathered from what the team had told her and her research en route that the Philippine jungle crawled with angry young people intent on overthrowing the government. Abu Sayyaf, the Moro National Liberation Front, the Moro Islamic Liberation Front, and even the New People's Army, which seemed to be a holdover from the outlawed Communist Party of the Philippines. But did the terrorist groups ever work together? Her hasty online research hadn't gone that deep.

God, help us! Protect Santi. Keep Bill and the others safe. Muslim insurgents would never believe she was an innocent civilian. At the least, they would use her to bargain with their enemies. And what about Santi? Did they know who he was?

She looked over at the boy. "Do you recognize any of these guys?"

Santi shook his head.

"Quiet!" The man nearest Claudia glared at her and poked the muzzle of his rifle into her side. The other man spoke and nodded toward her. Her guard frowned and peered keenly at her face. "Take off the helmet."

Claudia hesitated. She didn't think she could do it with one hand, and if she exposed her right hand, she would reveal that she had the gun. The idea of dropping it in the weeds flashed through her mind, but there was no way they could miss that, now that they were all staring at her.

"They just figured out you are a girl," Santi said.

The man beside him put his gun to Santi's head.

"Shut up," the man nearest Claudia said.

Claudia looked at him, trying to keep her breathing steady.

The other man said something in the language she couldn't fathom, and Santi let out a whimper. His dark eyes met her gaze with pleading.

Fear and anger flared in Claudia's heart. They were threatening Santi, she was certain. Without further thought, she whipped her hand up and fired at the man holding Santi. He flew backward into the bushes. She grabbed Santi's hand and ran toward the trees, across the slope, expecting any second to feel a bullet catch her.

They'd gone only a few yards when gunfire erupted behind them.

"Run, Santi!"

He gasped but kept pace with her. They ran into the bamboo trees, but she didn't stop until Santi tripped and sprawled on the forest floor.

She looked back but couldn't see anyone following them. Another barrage of automatic weapon fire burst out, just beyond the edge of the woods.

"We've got to keep going," she gasped.

Santi struggled to get up. She reached out to help him.

"You still have the gun?" he asked.

"Yes. Come on."

George led his squad up the hillside, their rifles spitting out nonstop fire. Most of the guerillas turned to fight them at the first shot, for which he was grateful. It gave the two prisoners a chance to reach the trees and hide. If only the one hadn't been so rash as to fire on their captors! He suspected from the size and build that it was Heidi Taber who had shot the guerrilla who threatened the boy. But would Heidi have been that stupid? Surely she would have given up her weapons and submitted to capture peacefully, relying on a rescue. Unless her teammates had already been cut down.

A sudden thought flickered across his mind. Could that demon in camouflage possibly have been Claudia Gillette?

He dismissed the rogue idea and concentrated on clearing the hillside without firing near any of his own men.

One of the insurgents held out for several minutes, shielded by a large rock, but Ensign O'Neill circled around and got him. At last Pierre, George, Browne, and the other seven men stood victorious before the little cave.

"Good job," George told them. "That's what I call teamwork."

"I only saw two people run away," Browne noted.

"One was a kid," George said. "I'm betting it was the Gamata boy."

"And a woman," Pierre agreed with a nod.

"Taber?" Browne asked.

"Or Miss Gillette," George said.

Browne's eyebrows shot up. "That person was in uniform, Commander. You think it was the lieutenant's sister-in-law?"

"It's possible. Come on. We need to find them."

"They don't know we're here," Pierre said.

Browne shook his head. "Oh, I'm sure they heard us."

"Well, they probably realize someone attacked their captors. But they don't know who we are. They're probably terrified right about now."

George turned to look at the men's faces. American kids, decked out in camouflage face paint and uniforms, heavily armed. Even in their regalia, they looked boyish to him. "All right, men, listen up. We're now hunting for two civilians who headed west, but probably haven't gotten far. They're scared. We need to let them know we're their friends before they meet up with more guerillas, and before they have a chance to start taking potshots at us."

FORTY-ONE

0600, August 15
Basilan Island, Philippines

Claudia and Santi sat panting behind a screen of feathery leaves. Claudia watched the back trail while Santi scouted forward.

"We can't be that far from Lieutenant White and his men," Claudia said. "It was only two or three kilometers, I think, to where your parents were held captive."

"What if the bad guys heard the gunshots?" Santi asked. "Do you think they would hurt my parents?"

"I don't know." She tried to breathe slower and deeper. Sweat ran down her forehead into her eyes. A mosquito landed on her jaw, and she slapped at it. She remembered what Nelson had said about disinfecting every scratch or bug bite to avoid infection. As if she could think about that right now, even if she had the first aid kit with the disinfectant. Which she didn't. She didn't have the sat phone, either. Her spirits drooped. If she had the phone, she might be able to contact Pierre, wherever he was. But it was back there in one of the terrorists' hands.

"I think we should keep going west," she said.

Santi's eyes were troubled. "What if we miss Lieutenant White and the others? We could walk right into the kidnappers' headquarters."

She sighed and scraped sweat off her face with her free hand. "What did that guy say to you right before I shot him?"

Santi blinked at her. His mouth drooped. "He said he'd as soon kill me as take me with them."

"I figured it was something like that. You don't think they were part of the kidnap gang?"

"I don't know. I didn't recognize any of them, but I didn't get a good look at all of them. The two that found us—I'm sure they weren't ever our guards when I was with my parents. They usually just left one or two men with us. Once in a while, a woman would come. But it was usually men. Not them, though."

She nodded. "So these guys might be part of their outfit, or they might be from a totally different group."

"There are lots of terrorists on Mindanao and Basilan."

"Right. So I think we should keep moving."

She heard a crack, like a stick breaking, and froze. Too late! Santi gasped and squeezed down next to her, clutching her arm. She peered through the foliage, wondering how close she should let them get before she opened fire.

"Hello!"

It was a decidedly American voice. Her hand shook as she tried to hold the gun steady. Rustling. Footsteps.

She squinted against the sweat that stung her eyes. A bright scrap of fabric waved from behind a patch of underbrush. Santi caught his breath.

"A flag."

He was right. A hand protruded from the brush, waving a diminutive American flag.

"Claudia? Are you there?"

"Pierre!" She parted the branches as she rose and ran toward him.

"Hold your fire!" A fierce-looking man with black and green slashes of paint on his face stood and waded through the brush to meet her. She wouldn't have recognized him in his jungle camos, but his crooked grin was unmistakable. She threw her arms around Pierre's neck and hugged him, feeling the hard plates of the body armor between them.

"You're really here!" Tears gushed from her eyes, but she didn't try to stop them. There were times when a woman could cry with pride. She leaned against him, suddenly trembling all over.

"It's okay, chérie."

She couldn't hold back the sobs. He had come all this way—thousands of miles—for her. All right, not just for her, but she was the one he embraced and comforted first.

"*Chut, ma belle-soeur!* You are scaring the boy."

She sniffed and pulled back a little, realizing she still held the pistol in her hand behind his neck. "H-here." She held the gun out and let him take it. Turning toward the place where she'd been concealed a moment earlier, she called, "Santi, come out. It's all right."

As her young friend came hesitantly from behind the bushes, she sensed movement on both sides. More men hedged them in, smiling as they approached the little group.

"Miss Gillette! It's a pleasure to see you again."

She whirled and stared at the man who spoke. "Commander Hudson?"

He grinned and extended his hand. "Yes, ma'am."

Shaking his hand in the jungle gave her a surreal feeling. Santi touched her elbow, and she looked at him. "These are my friends. Commander Hudson." She pointed to George, and he nodded and smiled at Santi. "Lieutenant Belanger, who is married to my sister."

Santi stared up into Pierre's warm brown eyes with awe.

"And…I don't know these other men, but I assure you they are friends. Gentlemen, this is Santi Gamata."

"I can't tell you how happy we are to find you safe," Hudson said. "Where are Lieutenant White and his men?"

"They went on to try to rescue Santi's parents. The lieutenant assured me they would be back by dawn, but as you can see, they haven't returned."

"We should probably move you to a new location," Pierre said.

"But Bill and the others left their equipment where Santi and I were hiding."

Pierre nodded. "We can pick it up, but we're fairly close to an insurgent training camp."

She frowned. "The Abu Sayyaf?"

"Yes. And indications are they're closely connected to Al-Qaeda. No one we want to get close to."

"All right, what do you suggest?"

Pierre looked at Hudson. "I'd like to take six of my men and go meet Lieutenant White."

"Fine. I'll take the other two men, Miss Gillette, and Santi back to where we had our little altercation. We'll pick up the stashed gear and meet you...where?"

"There was a place a couple of miles back where they were going to hide us," Claudia said. "Bill White decided it was too far from where he was headed. There were lots of rocks in the woods."

"I know where you mean," Pierre said, and Hudson nodded.

"We'll wait there." The commander eyed Claudia for a moment. "The scene back there isn't pretty. Tell me where all the equipment is, and we'll get it. You and Santi can wait below."

She was thankful for that. The carnage on the hillside before the cave must have been horrific. "Did you have any casualties?"

"Just one minor wound," Pierre said. "But he'll be okay, right Eliot?"

"Yes, sir," one of the men said. Claudia noticed that he had a bandage on his hand, but the man's grin confirmed Pierre's assessment.

Eliot and a stocky man named Abrams accompanied Claudia, Hudson, and Santi back to the site of their battle. Claudia gave instructions. Even from the path below, she could see several bodies lying on the hillside. She was glad for once that she was a woman and not required to go with the men as they moved among the dead reclaiming the Gold Team's belongings. She asked Hudson to look specifically for the satellite phone, and a few minutes later, he put it in her hand.

An hour after parting from Pierre and his squad, they reached the place where they had agreed to meet. Hudson posted the other two men as sentries, and settled down with her and Santi, offering them a meal. She opened her MRE, surprised that she actually looked forward to eating it. Santi wolfed his rations, and Hudson also began to eat his breakfast.

The commander asked Claudia to tell him all about their expedition, and she told him everything. She managed to describe the initial attack without betraying her contrition and sorrow, but when she reached the telling of Jeff Stuart's death, she began to weep. She stopped trying to talk and bowed her head, with one hand on her aching forehead. Hudson slid over beside her and draped his arm across her shoulders. He waited in silence until she regained control.

"It's always a horrible thing to see a human being killed," he said. "But when it's someone you care about, and someone who's fine and diligent and idealistic, well, then it's excruciating."

"Stuart was like that." She sniffed. "He was a terrific guy. I hate to think of him buried out there with that terrorist." She shuddered, and Hudson squeezed her shoulder.

"We'll get him and take him home, don't you worry about that. And remember, it's only his body. I didn't know Stuart personally, but from what Pierre has told me, he was a great guy, and he trusted in Jesus Christ. He's all right now, Claudia."

She pulled in a shaky breath. "He and Bill White were good friends."

"Yes. Pierre told me last night that Stuart was the type you want at your back in a rough situation."

She sobbed again. "It was so senseless. He was getting water! We weren't in a shootout or anything like that. He went to fill the canteens, and that monster killed him."

"Claudia, I know Pierre and Marie are Christians. Are you a believer?"

She looked up at him through her tears. "I...I am now. Just... since yesterday, really."

The commander looked off toward the trees and smiled. "That's good. I'm relieved to know that. You need to exercise your faith now, even though it's still young and weak. Trust God in this. He will use this event—including Stuart's death—for some good of His own devising. We may never know what that is, but God will be glorified."

She thought about that. "Do you think…"

"What?"

"I came here so…so cocky and self-righteous. Lots of people told me not to come, but I was sure I knew what I was doing. It was my right to be here. I forced myself on Commander Dryden and his men. And then he got killed, and almost half his team. I feel like it's my fault."

"Of course you do."

She looked at him in surprise. She hadn't expected him to agree so easily.

"Claudia, it wouldn't be natural if you didn't feel some guilt and remorse. That doesn't mean it's justified."

Santi wriggled and reached out a hand. "Excuse me, sir."

Hudson looked over at the somber boy. "Yes, Santi?"

"Do you think Lieutenant White had trouble getting my parents from the Abu Sayyaf? He didn't come back when he said he would, and I wonder if he and his men… Do you think they're all right, sir? I've been praying very hard."

George eyed him thoughtfully. "I can't say for sure, but I believe God will honor your prayers, Santi. We've got a lot of people praying right now for your parents' safety. If you like, we can ask God together to bring them and Lieutenant White and the others back here alive and well."

"Thank you. I'd like that."

"All right, then. And after we pray, I'll go and stand watch so one of the men can come and rest. Will you have an MRE ready for him?"

"Yes, sir."

Claudia bowed her head with Santi and listened. Hudson's confident prayer calmed her. He stayed on good terms with the Lord, apparently. She found assurance that God would answer his petitions.

FORTY-TWO

Bill and Nelson caught up with the rest of the team much sooner than Bill wanted to. Mrs. Gamata moved slowly, and he knew her pace might get them all killed. Her husband seemed a little more fit, though he limped.

Heidi flashed him a relieved look. "We heard more shooting."

"Yeah. Cabaya had a dozen men with him. We stopped a few, but the rest may be following us." Bill put his hand up to his chest, but the rigid plate in his vest kept him from massaging the area that hurt. Every breath was painful, but he knew he would recover from the bruising.

"These folks can't march long," Proul warned him. "They'll need to rest often."

"I ought to examine them," Nelson added.

"We can't stop now." Bill sent Proul to scout ahead while he and Squeegee hung back and watched their back trail. Nelson and Heidi helped the Gamatas move forward as quickly as they could. When they'd gone half a mile, Mrs. Gamata stopped, panting.

"I'm sorry," she wheezed.

"Taber, what have you got in your bag of tricks for these folks?" Nelson asked.

Heidi produced two small, brightly-colored packages of fruit chews.

"Perfect," Nelson said. "Eat these and rest for a minute." He passed

Dr. Gamata his canteen. "This is purified water. It may taste a little funny, but it's safe, and you both need to hydrate."

He left the couple under Heidi's watchful eye and walked the few yards back to Bill's position almost noiselessly.

"How are they really?" Bill asked, still watching the spaces between the trees before him.

"Weak, hungry, dehydrated, and scared. But thankful."

Bill nodded. "We've got to keep moving."

"I know. I think their willpower will take them a long way."

A moment after Nelson left his side, Heidi approached Bill. "I didn't get a chance to tell you, but when you went into the house back there, I heard some muffled noise. It sounded like shooting, but a long ways away."

"And?" Bill studied her face.

Heidi frowned and shrugged. "It seemed like this direction, but I couldn't be sure.

Bill nodded, not wanting to connect the dots but knowing he had to be realistic. If the enemy was ahead of them as well as behind…

"Okay, we need to move." He signaled Squeegee to follow, and the little group resumed its journey. They adjusted their pace to Mrs. Gamata's. She walked like an elderly woman, though Bill supposed she wasn't much past forty.

"I could carry her," Nelson whispered to him as they marched.

"If necessary. Not yet."

Proul, who had been scouting, came dashing back toward him, more concerned with speed than silence.

"There's someone up ahead, sir."

"Hostiles?"

"Don't know."

Bill signaled the others to wait and followed Proul forward cautiously. Staying behind cover, they inched ahead. Bill prayed with each step, wondering what to do if they were caught between bands of insurgents.

A whistle reached his ears and he tapped Proul's shoulder. They stood still and listened.

A tune floated through the jungle, and Bill grinned at Proul in relief. "Yankee Doodle!" He looked over his shoulder and gestured to Heidi. "Get up here, Taber, and pucker up."

Heidi was known as the best whistler in their company, after Stu. Her clear, confident notes sailed out. Amazing grace, how sweet the sound.

Camouflaged figures appeared before them, arising from several hiding places much closer than Bill had imagined they could be. His fatigue must have dulled his senses more than he cared to admit. *Thank You, Lord!*

"Bonjour, mon ami."

He stared at the jaunty figure. "Lieutenant Belanger?"

"C'est moi."

Bill rushed forward and gripped his friend's hand. "I can't believe you got here this fast."

"Not just me. You are among friends now."

Brownie almost knocked him over. "Billy Boy! Tell me you completed the op, man!"

"Oh, yeah. We sure did. But it's not over yet. I'm afraid we've got a pack of Abu Sayyaf on our trail."

"Then let's roll."

Bill looked to Pierre. "We thought we heard gunfire a while back."

"You did. A band of hostiles found Claudia and the boy, and we had to engage them."

Bill's chest ached as he searched his friend's face. "Are they okay?"

Pierre's smile flashed in the shadowy jungle. "You think six terrorists could keep Claudia down?" He turned to Browne. "Get your comm man over here."

When Ensign Resin brought him a radio, Pierre put in a call to George Hudson. "Hey, *mon copain,* we've met up with the shoppers." He looked at Bill. "You want to tell him?"

Bill's hand shook as he took the radio. "The packages are safe."

"Excellent," came the reply. "I'll see you at the place my buddy and I agreed on."

Pierre gave swift orders, and they tightened their ranks, putting the Gamatas in the middle of their party, and moved out.

They reached a steep spot in the trail, and Bill extended his hand to Gloria Gamata. "Not much farther."

"Thank you."

It took them another half hour to get back to the place where Bill had left Claudia and Santi. All the while several of Pierre's men haunted the back trail, watching for Cabaya's men.

When they reached the hillside, the Gamatas stood in shock, surveying the bloody ground and the half dozen bodies.

"You are certain my son is safe?" Dr. Gamata asked Bill.

Bill again looked to Pierre for the official word.

"Absolutely, sir," Pierre assured him. "We'll be with him and Commander Hudson and the others soon. When we get there, we'll rest a while, but we don't dare stop here too long. Are you able to keep going for a while?"

The scientist eyed his wife. "Do you need to stop?"

"Not here." She shuddered and turned away from the sight.

Bill and Pierre's men quickly looked to be sure George and his companions had picked up all the cached equipment.

"We can't stop to bury these men," Pierre told Dr. Gamata. "I wish we could, but the longer we stay in this territory, the greater the chance we'll meet more hostile troops."

"Let us go on," Dr. Gamata said.

Bill nodded. "If necessary, we can carry your wife."

"No, no," she said. "I can walk."

She looked so frail, Bill wondered how far she could take herself. Heidi offered the couple more water and another packet of sugary snacks. Bill was convinced the family had been nearly starved, partly for the convenience of their captors and partly to keep them too weak to resist or attempt to escape.

A short time later, one of Hudson's sentries hailed them. As they trudged into the temporary camp, Santi rose and ran toward his parents. Without a word, he flung himself into his father's arms. After a long moment, Dr. Gamata released him, and Santi turned to embrace his mother more gently. He was taller than she, and she clung to him, crooning under her breath and reaching up to stroke his hair.

Bill spotted Claudia, standing next to Commander Hudson but watching him as he approached. He lifted his hand in a curtailed wave, and she smiled. Relief washed over him. She and Santi were alive, and she could still smile.

Bill introduced the Gamatas to Hudson and Claudia.

"Thank you," Dr. Gamata said, pumping Hudson's hand. "We are honored that you did this. Your men have sacrificed much for us."

"The honor is mine, sir," Hudson replied. "You're past the worst of it now, but we're not quite home. We'll do our best to get you off this island and to a safe place."

Mrs. Gamata's tears flowed freely as she grasped the commander's hand. "You saved my son's life. The lieutenant told us that Santi and the young lady would probably have been killed had you not come to their aid. My husband and I will never forget this."

"Well, Lieutenant White?" Hudson asked, looking Bill in the eye.

Apparently he wasn't going to leap into the command position. Bill glanced at Pierre, but he too waited expectantly.

"My team needs a short rest and some food."

"There are enough of us that we can defend this position if we need to," Pierre said.

Hudson nodded. "It's nearly noon. We don't want to stand still for long, but probably the Gamatas could use a break too."

Dr. Gamata nodded. "Thank you. If you think it is safe."

Bill looked at Claudia. "Perhaps Miss Gillette and Taber can help Nelson make our guests comfortable. After my men have eaten, we can change the sentries. How many are on duty now?"

"Two," said Hudson.

"Let's make it four."

"Good call," Pierre said. "We don't want any surprises."

With all those in camp breaking out their MREs, Pierre, Bill, Hudson, and Brownie stepped to one side for a confab.

"What's the status of the Gamatas?" Hudson asked.

Bill winced. "Not good. Mrs. G. can't move very fast."

"Claudia and the boy are all right?" Pierre looked to Hudson who nodded.

"Traumatized, I'm sure. Who knows what Santi has seen in the past six months? And he saw a lot today. More than was good for him. But he's not hurt."

"I'm glad you could bring his parents back to him," Pierre said to Bill.

Hudson looked toward where the reunited family sat on the ground eating together. "If we can get back to the pickup point without another clash, I'd say this was a good day's work. Do you think the Abu Sayyaf are still on your tail?"

Bill shrugged. "Seems like they'd have caught up with us if they were. We busted the doc and his wife out, and one of the guards told Nelson that Juan Cabaya was on his way. We barely got the Gamatas out the door when a truck with at least a dozen men came in. We streaked it into the woods. Nelson and I hung back and gave them a few licks. I'm pretty sure we saw Cabaya himself at the end." Bill rubbed his shoulder. Now that he'd stopped running, it hurt like crazy.

"You okay?" Pierre asked.

"Yeah. I'm fine. I took a bullet to my vest, I think." He smiled. "Nelson grabbed the Uzi I took off one of the guards and let the rebels have it. Then we booked it."

Hudson's eyebrows wrinkled. "Maybe you got enough of them to make the others think twice about following you."

"Could be. I think we took out at least three with a grenade."

Hudson nodded. "There's a chance they gave up pursuit."

Pierre looked toward the spot where they'd emerged from the jungle. "If not, they could be sneaking around, watching us right now. Lieutenant White, what's your strategy now?"

Bill massaged his sore shoulder. "Have you got a boat standing by?"

"Yes," Hudson said, "but after our little firefight back there, I called and told them to stand off. They decided it would be safer to extricate us from the point they initially dropped you."

"Right. I guess we trek for the beach, then." Bill looked back toward the Gamatas. Claudia was deep in conversation with Santi and his mother. She glanced up and caught his gaze. She smiled, just a ghost of the smiles he dreamed about, but it renewed his resolve. This op had to succeed, for the Gamatas, for the free world, and for Claudia.

FORTY-THREE

1900, AUGUST 15
BASILAN ISLAND, PHILIPPINES

Claudia couldn't understand how Mrs. Gamata kept going. The last hour of the trek was torture. When Lieutenant Browne came back from his recon mission and told them they were only a few hundred yards from the beach and that it appeared to be clear of hostiles, she almost collapsed. If she could just drop right there and close her eyes...

When she looked ahead, Mrs. Gamata was still hobbling forward, clinging to Heidi Taber's hand. That did it for Claudia. She wasn't giving up, no matter what.

While the men reassembled their gear and Resin, the comm man, contacted the man in charge of their transport, she flopped down in the grass near the Gamata family. Bill ordered Heidi to rest too. Claudia noticed that Heidi's mouth was set in a grim line.

"How's your arm?" she asked.

"It's a little uncomfortable. I'll be glad when we get to a real doctor. Not that Nelson's not good, but..." Heidi's gaze bounced away.

"I'm sorry." Claudia moved closer. "Is there anything I can do for you?"

Heidi's green eyes spoke of pain and determination. "Maybe you could ask Nelson if there's any more ibuprofen in the supplies we left here?"

"Sure." In spite of her screaming muscles, Claudia pulled herself to her feet. Never, in all the mountain climbing and wilderness trekking she'd done, had she felt so near exhaustion. She found Nelson close to the shore, rearranging the packs the men had recovered.

"Hey, doc, I think Heidi's kind of sore. Do you have anything she can take to ease the pain?"

"Just seeing what we've got."

"How's your leg?" Claudia asked. She hadn't noticed that he still favored it. Was his wound healing, or was she merely oblivious to others' needs?

"It's not bad," he said. "But Taber… I'm a little concerned that she might have some infection." He glanced around at the others. "Maybe Brownie's team brought something stronger."

He left her, and Claudia gazed out at the placid sea.

Pierre joined her a few minutes later.

"Whatcha thinking about, chérie?"

"A hot shower. Coffee. Makeup. E-mail."

He chuckled. "We're going to put out in the small boats as soon as the men are ready. Our contact can't reach us for another hour or two, but I feel like we're sitting ducks here."

"Like we all were two days ago." She shook her head, but nothing had changed when she focused again.

"Yeah, well, Lieutenant White still thinks Cabaya and his outfit may try to stop us. The sooner we're off this island the better."

She looked around at the buzz of activity. "So much has changed in two days. It seems like a year."

Pierre draped his arm about her shoulders. "I'm sorry you had to go through all this."

"Me too. But we got the Gamatas."

"Yes, we did." They smiled at each other.

"Can I take this stupid helmet off?"

"Best to wait. You've seen how quickly they can attack."

She nodded, the gruesome memory of Stu's murder flashing across her mind. "Right. Better sweaty than sorry." Another image flitted at the edge of her brain. "Pierre?"

"Hm?"

"I think maybe I killed a man. One of those Muslim terrorists that pulled Santi and me out of the cave this morning."

"We saw you."

She looked at him then, her brown eyes broody. "If I'd known how close you were, I wouldn't have shot. But we didn't see you."

"Duh. Camouflage works."

She couldn't help a little chuckle. "As it was, all I could think of was to get Santi away from them. And as soon as we started running, I heard all that gunfire. I thought they were shooting at us. But I guess...it was you they were aiming for."

"And us aiming for them. To make sure you and Santi got away."

"I might have killed you in the woods. I was shaking like a leaf."

"You kept your head. I'd say you did everything right, *ma belle.*"

She smiled. "Have you talked to Marie?"

"Not yet. When we're off Basilan."

"She must be wild with worry."

"Perhaps a little, but...she has the peace of God."

Claudia nodded slowly and raised her chin. "I'm talking to God now."

"That's super."

"Do you think... Can He block out the memories, Pierre?"

His smile nearly broke her heart. "I'm afraid you'll always remember. It won't go away. But God can still give you peace. Trust Him."

"I do."

He squeezed her shoulders and left her, and she turned toward the sea again. She understood for the first time what Marie endured. Could she love a man who spent his workdays fighting terrorists?

She tried to home in on her story and plan the lead, but so many divergent thoughts came to her that she gave it up and just watched the sky darken. More rain? Or was it time for sunset? She looked at her watch. Maybe a little of both. They faced east, so she couldn't see the sun, but the shadows of the trees and hills of the island stretched far out over the cove to meet the ocean.

Someone touched her arm, and she jumped.

Bill smiled apologetically. "Hey. Time to load the boats. We're heading home."

Bill sat in the stern with Pierre, holding on to the gunwale and letting Squeegee pilot the boat. They had decided to leave the wrecked radio equipment and leftover rations behind, as they were already overloaded. The two small craft that had originally brought nine men in now carried nineteen people: Brownie's entire team of eight, Bill's remaining five, the Gamatas, Claudia, Belanger, and Hudson.

The family sat together in the second boat, under Brownie's command. The scientist held fast to the satchel filled with the research notes he had salvaged. Bill had offered to put it in the boat's food locker, but Dr. Gamata didn't want it out of his grasp.

A larger vessel had already set out from Zamboanga to meet them. Bill hoped that when they were aboard, the Gamatas could have a little privacy at last and perhaps a little rest.

The waves seemed to be increasing, and the small boats lunged through them with the grace of a rhinoceros on roller skates. The wind buffeted them, and he figured it was only a matter of time before the low, gray clouds dumped their load.

Eliot, in Brownie's boat, yelled across the water, "They're two miles out, sir. Contact in twenty minutes."

Bill nodded and waved.

"So Claudia did all right," Pierre said near Bill's ear.

"Yeah." He looked toward where she sat, near the prow of his craft, with Heidi. "She's helped a lot, and I think she truly cares about Heidi and Santi."

"The boy would be dead if not for her."

Bill considered that. "Well, we couldn't have left him behind if she wasn't there to stay with him. Who knows what would have happened?"

"You know she shot one of the guerillas, right?"

Bill stared at him. "You're joking."

"Am I laughing?" Pierre leaned close. "I saw it with my own eyes. The terrorist puts a rifle barrel to Santi's temple, and cool as you please, Claudia whips out a pistol and shoots him. Then she grabs the kid's hand and drags him into the woods. Meanwhile, we charge in blazing for a diversion."

"Brownie said you guys killed them all."

"All but one. First blood belongs to Claudia."

"Does she know?"

"She knows. She talked to me about it right before we shoved off."

Bill inhaled carefully, thinking about it. "Are you sure her bullet killed him?"

"Pretty sure. We didn't do an autopsy."

"Right." Bill shook his head. She hadn't mentioned it, but then he hadn't had much of a chance to talk to her.

"Pray for her," Pierre said. "She also told me she's trusting in God now. I hope it lasts when she's out of danger."

"She's been talking to Heidi quite a bit. Stu too, before he was shot."

Pierre nodded. "She's avoided religion like she would a skunk until now. She'll need some good teaching. We'll encourage her to get into a good church. Maybe Marie can send her some Bible study books too."

Bill shut his eyes for a moment. *Thank You, Lord! Make her faith deep and genuine. And if You can use me to help her grow, I'm willing. Just don't let me do anything stupid that will hold her back.* He immediately thought of the kiss they'd shared in Okinawa. Had he misled Claudia by taking things too fast? And what about his coldness to her when she landed on Basilan?

Brownie yelled to them, "Philippine naval vessel dead ahead."

Bill opened his eyes and peered into the twilight. He thought he saw a light in the distance, but they plunged down into the trough of a wave and he lost his focus. Above the wind and the throbbing of the little boat's motor, he heard a louder whining. His pulse rate doubled. Every sailor in the boats turned and faced upward, searching for the source.

An airplane soared out from over the island and swooped down toward them. Bill couldn't be sure in the darkness, but he thought it was the same plane that had attacked them when they landed.

Several of his and Brownie's men opened fire on the plane with their rifles. Strafing stitched across the water from above, throwing up splashes in a line that missed Brownie's boat by only a few feet.

As it soared away and banked, Hudson yelled, "Make it good, boys!" He shouldered his own M16 assault rifle, waiting for the plane to come back within range.

Lieutenant Belanger's weapon of choice was a Heckler & Koch MP5 submachine gun with an optical sight. It rattled out rounds so fast that Bill felt sluggish as he fired his rifle, tracking the plane and aiming ahead of the fuselage.

It dove low and dropped a package neatly between the two boats. When it hit the surface, the bomb exploded, sending up a wave that rocked the boats so violently it nearly swamped them. When they regained relative stability, Bill looked over the waves. Brownie's boat, containing the Gamata family and six team members, had capsized in the rough seas.

FORTY-FOUR

2020 HOURS, AUGUST 15
BASILAN ISLAND, PHILIPPINES

Claudia clung to the rail of the boat, hoping she could keep from being flung over the side. Her hands were freezing, and saltwater soaked her clothes. The boat rose on another swell, and an ear-splitting crack drew her attention. The attacking plane threw off several large pieces of debris and plummeted toward the sea, trailing smoke.

A glance over her shoulder showed her Pierre, half standing, bracing himself against the thwart where he'd sat, his gun still pointed toward the plane. He pumped his fist in triumph.

Then Claudia saw beyond him, on the dark waves, the hulk of the other boat bobbing wrong side up. Her heart leaped into her throat.

"No!" She pointed. Pierre turned and looked where the rest were staring now.

"Cut the engine!" Bill barked rapid-fire orders at Squeegee, and the boat came about so quickly that they were almost caught sideways by another big wave.

Another drenching crest slapped Claudia. She held onto the side rail and screamed a prayer into the wind. "God, help!"

She coughed and stared at Bill. He was standing up in the boat, stripping off his flak vest and helmet. Nelson and one of the other men in their boat followed suit, and within seconds the three men had dived into the water. Pierre laid his gun down and ripped off his cartridge belt and body armor. Commander Hudson slid into Squeegee's spot at the tiller, and Squeegee too prepared to dive in.

Already several people were clinging to the edge of the capsized boat, but it was so unstable in the waves that holding on to it was difficult. She saw Santi try to climb on top of the boat and then slip back and under the surface of the water. He bobbed up again, and Nelson reached him with a few strong strokes. He looped his arm around Santi's chest from behind and swam with him back toward their boat.

Claudia edged along the gunwale to meet them and reached for Santi's hand. She grasped it, and the boy leaped upward.

"Easy," Nelson cautioned. "You don't want to swamp this boat too. Go slow, buddy."

Heidi moved to the far side of the boat to counterbalance the extra weight. Santi wrapped one arm over the rail. Claudia tried to lift him, but it was Nelson's boost from below that sent him flopping into the boat. Nelson hung on to the side for a moment, then took a deep breath and turned back.

"Are you all right?" Claudia asked Santi.

"Yes." He was shivering. Heidi had already pulled a blanket from a pack and wrapped it around his shoulders.

Claudia heard a shout and turned her head. The Philippine transport—a sixty-foot gunboat—was nearly upon them, and its sailors were lowering a small boat. She looked the other way, toward the capsized craft, and saw that the men of the Gold Team had successfully flipped it over in the water. Two were inside and bailing.

Another figure swam toward her, and she recognized a dripping wet Dr. Gamata.

"Santi," he called when he was within two yards.

"He's safe," Claudia assured him. "Let me help you."

"My wife—" Dr. Gamata swiveled in the water and looked back.

"Let the men help her," Claudia said. "Take my hand and climb into the boat, sir."

Hudson managed to hold the boat fairly steady, but Gamata seemed too weak to climb over the side. He clutched the rail, but as each wave lifted the boat, he struggled to maintain his hold.

"I need help," Claudia called.

"Lieutenant, take the tiller," Hudson shouted.

Heidi took his position, and the commander came to Claudia's side.

"Go sit on the other side, by Santi."

Claudia took one last look at Dr. Gamata and obeyed. She settled beside the shivering boy and put her arm around him. "Your father's okay," she assured him.

"What about Mama?"

"I don't know." Claudia noticed that his trembling lips were bluish. "That other boat will pick us up, and we'll get warm soon."

Santi nodded, staring out over the dark water.

To her amazement, Commander Hudson braced himself and, taking advantage of the rhythm of the waves, hauled Dr. Gamata into the boat in one concerted lift.

"Hey! Give me a hand." Another man swam toward them, side-stroking and pulling an inert form.

"I got you, Billy," Hudson said, leaning over as far as he could without laying the boat on its beam ends and dipping the gunwale under the surface.

Hudson had formally addressed Bill as "Lieutenant" all day. After this crisis, would they all be on a nickname basis, Claudia wondered? No, he would always be Commander Hudson.

She crawled toward Dr. Gamata where he lay panting on the deck.

"Sir, come over here with me and Santi and help balance the weight."

He peered up at her, then nodded and crawled toward his son. A moment later Hudson laid a form down between the thwarts. Water streamed from the body.

A sudden moan from Dr. Gamata informed Claudia that the person Bill had rescued was his wife.

"Gloria!" He clambered to her side.

Claudia unbuttoned her jacket and handed it to Hudson. He laid it over Mrs. Gamata, and Claudia turned to find her pack and dig out more clothing.

The small Philippine Navy boat pulled alongside the boat that had been capsized. A Philippine sailor cast a line linking the boats together and gestured for the people still in the water to come to him.

Claudia wanted to help Bill and Commander Hudson, but the boat they were in still plunged up and down in the waves, and she knew the best thing she and Santi could do was sit still.

Commander Hudson bent low over Mrs. Gamata.

"She's breathing," he told her husband. He looked over the gunwale. "Bill, do you want to come aboard?"

"I'm fine," came Bill's voice. "I can hang on here, sir."

By some miracle all nineteen people clustered on the deck of the gunboat half an hour later. Claudia could scarcely believe they hadn't lost anyone in the air attack or the dunking most of them had taken. The Gamata family was hustled below to receive care from the physician on board, and all the sailors who had been in the water were taken to a large cabin where they could wait in relative comfort to be checked over.

Claudia gratefully accepted the loan of a warm jacket. She shed her helmet and McGraw's camouflage shirt and bulletproof vest and let the cool wind ripple her hair. Bill found her leaning on the rail near the stern in the mist. He'd had a chance to dry off and put on a clean uniform—someone else's, a little short at the wrists and ankles.

"Hey, Claudia. Don't you want to get out of the weather while you have the chance?"

She smiled. "Kind of crowded in the cabin."

"This will probably turn to bona fide rain in a minute." He held out one of the two paper cups he held. "Black coffee. You want some?"

"I'll love you forever for this." The aroma and the warmth that spread to her hands from the cup lifted her spirits so much that she decided not to try to analyze Bill's reaction to her playful words. She nodded toward the lights on the ship's boat as it pulled away from the side. "We're not under way yet, and I wondered why. Does that boat out there have anything to do with it?"

"Yeah." Bill rested his weight on the rail beside her. "Dr. Gamata lost his packet of research."

"Oh, no!"

"Oh, yes. Our men dumped a lot of gear in the water too, but nothing irreplaceable like the doc's notes. Lieutenant Belanger and Brownie and Commander Hudson are trying to pinpoint where the boat capsized and take precise GPS coordinates. Hudson thinks if we can come back within a few days and dive, there's a chance we could find the package."

She stared at him. "How deep is it here?"

"I don't know. But Dr. Gamata said he had his notebooks in a waterproof bag inside his satchel. He's hoping his research will be readable if we can recover it."

"Couldn't he reconstruct it?"

Bill shrugged. "He wrote some of the notes before they captured him. They had him take his laptop along, but later it crashed and they didn't replace it. He says he had written a lot of the most important things in his notebooks, and there are also a couple of flash drives in the satchel. If those are readable, he'll be in business when he gets to a new lab."

"Wow. I thought he didn't have anything with him that the Abu Sayyaf could use."

"Actually, he says he had a lot of his most critical research along, but he managed to convince them he couldn't do what they wanted him to do without more data and equipment. He stalled them for months. When the AFP started putting the heat on them, the rebels had to keep moving him, and there wasn't even a pretense of him working on the project for the last six weeks or so. But he had all that data and managed to preserve it."

"And now it's on the ocean floor."

"Exactly. But we're not that far off shore. It's probably recoverable."

Claudia nodded. "That's exciting."

"The Philippine Armed Forces have already promised to come back here with enough of a presence to keep the insurgents at bay while we recover our dead. If they'll stand guard while we dive for Dr. Gamata's package too, I think we have a good chance of winding this operation up successfully."

"We got the family out, anyway," Claudia said.

"Yeah. That's the most important thing. But Dr. Gamata feels like he failed because he lost the research." Definite raindrops spattered them, and Bill looked up. "We're in for it. Come on inside."

FORTY-FIVE

The Philippine sailors turned over to the Americans the cabin that served as their mess deck and lounge. Bill ate the scanty cold meal they provided and watched Claudia across the room. He had to remind himself often not to stare. He hadn't let himself observe her at leisure before, and the temptation nearly dumbfounded him. Even after three days in the jungle, she looked good. And she had a way of making people laugh.

The men of the Gold Team eagerly gathered around her, peppering her with questions about her work. She told them stories that kept them all laughing as the boat chugged back toward Zamboanga.

After a half hour as the star attraction, though, she seemed to have had enough. She left them with a dazzling smile and settled at a corner table with Heidi, where the two of them talked quietly for some time. Bill couldn't catch their words, but Claudia's face held an earnest look. She smiled gently now and then, but mostly she seemed to be questioning Heidi. Funny. It was the first time he'd seen her interview someone without a notebook and pen in her hands.

When the two women bowed their heads, he sat very still, forgetting his no-staring rule. They were praying together, he was sure. A tear glistened on Claudia's cheek. They opened their eyes, and Heidi reached to squeeze Claudia's hand, and they both laughed.

Bill walked out on the deck and leaned on the rail again. The rain had ebbed to a drizzle.

Nelson came up the ladder and nodded to him.

"How are the Gamatas?" Bill asked.

"Better than I expected. Santi is asking for Claudia." Nelson went into the cabin.

Bill inhaled deeply and shrank into the shadows. A moment later, Nelson, Claudia, and Heidi emerged from the cabin and went below. The two women were chattering together like childhood friends.

Thank You, Lord! If there's any way I can help her, please show me.

"Lieutenant White is keeping a close watch on you," Heidi murmured as they went down the stairs.

Claudia smiled. She'd noticed Bill's almost constant gaze on her. "I think we're still trying to figure each other out."

"Oh?"

Nelson stopped at a doorway and stood back. "Here you go, ladies."

"Thanks," Heidi said, and they stepped inside.

Mrs. Gamata reclined in a bunk on one wall of the tiny cabin. Her husband and Santi sat on a bench nearby.

"Claudia!" Santi bounced to his feet with a grin.

"Hi! How are you doing?"

"Much better now," his father said, rising. "The doctor and Nelson checked us all over."

"The doctor gave Mama some medicine," Santi added.

"That's good."

"But Papa's seasick."

Dr. Gamata smiled wanly at the women. "They tell us we will be in Zamboanga very soon, and that I can go from there back to Manila, or to the United States."

"Which will you do?" Claudia asked.

"I don't know yet."

"Go to America, Papa." Santi grabbed his father's hand. "I don't want to go back to Manila. Claudia said if we go to America, she'll introduce me to all her friends and take me horseback riding."

Claudia felt her face flush. "I'm sorry, Dr. Gamata. I didn't mean to get your son all stirred up. When we were alone together, we talked some. I like your son, and I meant everything I told him. If you ever do come to the States, I'd be happy to host your family for a visit and take Santi to some of my favorite places. But I wasn't trying to influence him against the Philippines or your choice."

Dr. Gamata shook his head and smiled. "He is a boy. A thoughtful boy, it is true, but he does not understand all the variables we must weigh."

"Of course."

Mrs. Gamata lifted her hand and beckoned Claudia to her side.

"I hope you're feeling better." Claudia grasped her hand gently.

"Yes. Thank you for helping Santi. He has told us what you did for him."

Claudia's mouth went dry. She didn't want to remember those moments when she agonized over whether or not to pull the trigger.

"I...you're welcome."

The dark-haired woman lay back on the pillow. Her face bore delicate lines of past beauty, but now she seemed frail and exhausted. Claudia wondered how she had walked so far through the jungle today.

Mrs. Gamata looked up at Heidi. "And this is also a friend."

"Yes, ma'am," Claudia said. "This is Lieutenant Taber."

Mrs. Gamata smiled at Heidi. "You came in through the window and helped us on the march."

"Yes, ma'am, I did." Heidi eased closer to the bunk. "I'm so glad it worked out and your family is together again."

"We are free," Mrs. Gamata whispered.

"Yes, ma'am."

Dr. Gamata cleared his throat. "Miss Gillette, Commander Hudson has explained to us who you are and why you came to the Philippines. I know you haven't asked us, but if you wish to write about our experience, we would be honored to give you our story."

Claudia glanced from him to his wife. Both were smiling. "Oh, sir, that is the most generous thing you could give me. I had made up my mind not to ask you. It seemed to me that you needed privacy, and this isn't the time to pester you with questions."

He shook his head. "We owe you our boy's life."

"I wouldn't want you to feel you had to repay me. I only did what I felt I needed to do, for myself as well as for Santi. I didn't expect anything in return."

"I know." He pulled Santi to him and stood with his arm around his son's shoulders. "And I understand that when we return to the world, there will be news stories, whether we want them or not. Our privacy will be at an end, at least for a while. There is no one we would rather have break the news of our rescue. I'm assured you are a fine writer and that you will handle the details with sympathy and discretion."

"I'd be honored, sir." Claudia looked at Santi, who was grinning at her. "There's something I want to tell Santi. I brought Heidi here for a reason. Well, she wanted to see you, but—"

"Heidi was good to me too," Santi said to his father. "She gave me food and a blanket, and she told me about when she lived on Luzon."

Heidi chuckled. "Yes, I spent much of my childhood in the Philippines. My parents were missionaries here."

"And she's sort of a missionary herself," Claudia said. "Heidi has explained a lot of things to me, Santi. Things about God, and how His Son, Jesus, came to die for us. I think I understand now how my sin kept me away from God. But I'm a Christian now."

Santi's brow furrowed. "So…you don't think it's hokey anymore?"

"What?" his father asked, glancing anxiously at Claudia. "What is this 'hokey'?"

She laughed. "It means fake. Not real. And you're right, Santi. The only hokey thing was my attitude toward God. I refused for a long time to admit I was accountable to anyone. I've always been big on independence and self-sufficiency. But out there in the jungle, I realized that I hoped someone bigger than me was in control. And all the things people had told me—Heidi, Lieutenant White, my family—kind of jelled for me. For the first time I saw myself as nobody. Just…a sinner with no future beyond this life. I wanted to tell you, Santi. Heidi helped me see it all so clearly."

"Santi and I have talked about God sometimes," his mother said softly. "He is a good boy."

Dr. Gamata looked into Heidi's face. "I'm afraid I discouraged him somewhat. I found it difficult, during the last few months, to think about God. I did talk to Him once, though."

"You did?" Santi asked, pulling away from him a little and staring into his face.

His father nodded. "About a week ago I asked God, 'If You are real, then why do You not help us?' And then the other night, when they moved us and the soldiers came and we thought we were free… and then the Muslims took us back again. That night…" His face clouded.

"We thought we had lost you forever," his mother confessed with tears bathing her face.

Heidi found a tissue in a wall compartment near the bunk and handed it to her. "I'm so sorry you had to go through that, not knowing Santi was safe with us."

"We heard the explosion and the shooting, and then you came to the window and tore the boards away," Mrs. Gamata whispered. "I thought at first you were one of them. The Abu Sayyaf. But my husband said, 'Gloria, that is foolish. Why would the Abu Sayyaf rip the boards off the window?' And then I saw that you were a woman. An angel in camouflage clothes."

Santi grinned. "Funny angel, Mama."

His father said slowly, "Not so funny. You were God's answer to my prayer."

Claudia felt the sting of tears in her own eyes, and Heidi's also held a sheen.

"Would you mind if we all prayed together now?" Heidi asked.

Peace washed over Claudia as she closed her eyes.

FORTY-SIX

All the way from Basilan, Claudia had pondered how to present the Gamatas' story. During their short stop in Zamboanga, she retrieved her laptop and extra luggage from the hotel and called Mya, Russell, and Marie.

She had strict orders from Russell Talbot—get the story to him by eight tomorrow morning, Atlanta time. Rather than holding it for the next week's magazine, he would offer it to every major news service, and it would be all over the TV broadcasts by nightfall.

When the taxi let her off at the airport with her baggage, George and Pierre were waiting for her.

"Where is everyone?" she asked.

"The Gamatas are getting ready to fly to Manila," Pierre said.

"Oh." Claudia felt bereft, though she barely knew the family.

"Did you get everything you need for your article?" George asked.

"I guess so."

"I think we can catch them at their boarding gate if you want to say goodbye."

She looked up into his sober gray eyes. "Thank you, Commander. I'd like that."

Santi saw them coming and ran to hug her. "I hoped we would go to Atlanta and ride horses!"

Claudia laughed and squeezed him. "Maybe sometime. I'm going to miss you."

Dr. Gamata and his wife walked over to them, smiling. "I hope we meet again, Miss Gillette," The doctor said.

"Me too. Thank you so much for letting me interview you all."

He nodded. "I will call you when we have a number where you can reach us. I want you to be able to contact me if you have any more questions."

"Thank you so much. Gloria, take care." She hugged Mrs. Gamata briefly.

"You too, my dear. We will never forget you."

The soldiers protecting the family closed in around them as they headed for the gate. After a final wave, Claudia went with George and Pierre down the terminal to where military planes landed. She'd seen no sign of Bill, but just as she, Pierre, and George mounted the steps to their plane for Guam, he and the rest of the Gold Team showed up.

She sat beside Heidi on the flight and encouraged her to talk about her military service for the article on the team. Heidi would definitely be the star of that story.

Bill came back to their row once during the flight and leaned on the back of the seat ahead of them.

"How are you doing?"

"Tired," Claudia said.

He nodded. "I think we'll all sleep well once we land in Guam. Do you have a place to stay?"

"I'll get a hotel room. What about your team?"

"Oh, Uncle Sam will put us up at the base."

He lingered a few more minutes, making small talk, and then ambled back to his seat next to Squeegee.

When they landed in Guam, George Hudson left them, and Pierre escorted Claudia to her hotel.

"I'll be staying here until we get our casualties out," he told her at the door to her room. "I may be able to see you again tomorrow."

She stretched to kiss his scratchy cheek. "Thank you so much for all you've done."

He nodded gravely. "Don't forget your promise."

"What? Oh, you mean the article."

"If Commander Hudson has time, maybe you should let him read the one about the Gamatas."

After a shower and complete change of clothes, she collapsed into bed and slept deeply. When she arose in the morning, she expected to perform as well as usual and whip out at least two articles before dinner. Instead she felt sluggish and all at loose ends. She decided to let the magazine splurge and ordered a hot breakfast from room service. While she ate, she thought over the massive amount of information she'd accumulated. She wasn't sure how much to put in the story about the rescue. Should she describe the trek through the jungle and the cost in human lives? Or zero in on the Gamatas and begin the tale with the infiltration of the building where they'd been held?

She deliberately put off the article about Heidi and the special operations unit because the Gamatas' story was more urgent. But even there she had some misgivings. She could make heroes out of this bunch, and they deserved it. But how much of the truth would the Navy let her publish? Russell would be furious if he knew she'd agreed to let them censor her. Another nagging thought was her underlying motive. Writing the article in first person would draw the readers into the adventure, but did she want to do that to make herself look daring and heroic?

She sighed and stared out the window. At least it wasn't raining. She wondered what Bill was doing today. He'd almost hovered over her on the trip back, which surprised her. He'd been cool to her early in this trip, but she'd hoped he was only maintaining his professional distance during the operation. Toward the end she'd sensed an empathy, but it hadn't warmed her the way his friendship had before Basilan. She tried not to think of Okinawa and how it felt when Bill held her in his arms and kissed her. She shook her head and turned back to the computer.

An hour later she was still stymied. She'd begun the kidnap victims' story twice and then erased what she had typed. She gave up and called Commander Hudson's cell phone number.

"Why don't you join us for lunch?" he asked.

"Oh, I don't want to impose," Claudia said. "I just thought you might have some insight. I'm not usually so at sea when it's time to write the story, and I only have eight hours until my boss goes to his desk and expects my story to be waiting in his e-mail box."

"It's okay," Hudson assured her. "We're staying with friends, and Ellen asked if we wanted to invite anyone over. Pierre is busy today, but I'm sure she wouldn't mind if we put an extra plate on for you."

Getting out of the hotel room proved invigorating. Claudia's brain seemed to recharge from both the change of scenery and the stimulating company. She liked George Hudson's wife, Rachel, and Ellen Bridgeford. The two women invited her to go shopping with them that afternoon. It was tempting, but Claudia knew she had to finish at least the first article. She relaxed for an hour, enjoying the home-cooked meal and easy conversation, but while Rachel and Ellen cleaned up the kitchen, George invited her to join him in Captain Bridgeford's study to discuss her problem.

He listened quietly as she laid out her thoughts. "There are just so many directions I could take this, sir. I've never felt so inadequate."

"May I suggest something?" He sat in a recliner, holding a steaming cup of coffee, and she felt at ease with him.

"Of course."

"Let's pray about this, and then I'll give you my perspective."

It seemed so obvious that Claudia sat motionless for a moment. "Why didn't I think of that?"

"Your faith in Christ is new, Claudia."

"Yes, only in the last forty-eight hours. I'm sure it sounds foolish, but I didn't even consider praying about my work."

"You can take anything to God now."

She knew at once that he was right. God was available, not just to save lives and thwart terrorists. He would help her with her ethical quandaries, and even with her relationships. Bill had told her once or twice that he prayed for her. Suddenly it seemed as though the pieces of a fiendish puzzle slid into place. She could pray for Bill. She could pray for the Gamatas' well-being, for Heidi and Brownie's relationship, and also for help in her work.

"Do you think God will show me how to write this?"

George smiled. "I do. That and a lot of other things. You need to get into His Word, Claudia. Study the Bible. Go to a good church."

"It seems a bit daunting. So much I need to do."

"Take it one step at a time. Do you have a Bible?"

"No."

"Rachel and I will get you one before we leave here."

"Oh, you don't need to. I can get one. After I finish my article, that is."

His smile grew. "Let us do this. You've got enough to worry about right now. And, Claudia, we'll be praying for you after we leave here too."

"Thank you, sir." Funny how she would have sneered at that a few months ago. Now the promise warmed her.

He prayed then, and his words soothed her. When he was done, she went over all the major points of the story with him. George sat back in his chair, his chin on his fist, listening.

"I don't see a problem with any of that going public," he said. "We want the world to know that American forces freed the Gamatas. If you tell some of the details, it will make the readers more sympathetic."

"You don't see it as exploitation?"

"Why should I? Dr. Gamata gave you permission to use their story."

She bit her lip, trying to avoid the thought that troubled her most. "Sir, do you think…"

"What is it?"

"I feel so guilty. I know God has forgiven me, but I can't shake the idea that the Gold Team wouldn't have been attacked if I hadn't come."

"You can't know that. I suspect the insurgents knew something was up but not specifically what. Remember, the Philippine soldiers had tried to rescue the family the night before and botched it. The Abu Sayyaf got the best of them. They got Santi away, but it was a wonder none of the hostages were killed. This rescue mission was in the works for a long time, Claudia. I don't think you should claim all the blame for the conflict it caused."

She felt tears rush into her eyes. Maybe it wasn't her fault that Stu was dead. She hoped not. "I still plan to do the article I originally came here to write, but I'll save that for after the one about the Gamatas is done. My intention all along was to profile Heidi Taber in our magazine. Do you think I'll be spilling too much information if I tell how near the team came to annihilation?"

George inhaled and let his breath out slowly. "The enemy could make use of some of that information. They might incorporate it in their anti-government and anti-American propaganda."

"Would they…retaliate? Against the Philippine military or against other political prisoners?"

"I really couldn't say. But I think Lieutenant Taber's story is worth telling. She's a courageous woman."

Claudia leaned toward him and looked into his eyes. "I'm thinking…This would be a real first for me, but I'm thinking I could print a little bit about her faith. Just a few lines. Let her tell how her belief in Christ carries her through the tough parts of her job."

"I think that's a very good idea."

Claudia stood and extended her hand to George. "Thank you so much. I think I'm ready to go back to my hotel and do some writing now."

FORTY-SEVEN

Bill raised his hand to knock on Claudia's door. He remembered Okinawa and the fancy resort where she'd stayed. This hotel was less ostentatious, more utilitarian. And Claudia...she was less dazzling now. He'd seen her in blood-smeared camos and muddy boots. And she'd held up through the whole op. Maybe they could go beyond the dazzle and find a better rapport.

He knocked, sending up a quick, silent prayer. The chain inside rattled, and she threw the door back.

"Bill! I was afraid I wouldn't see you again."

The eager light in her eyes struck him so hard it almost robbed him of his breath. "Hi. Are you busy?"

She leaned against the door jamb and crossed her arms, still smiling. "I just sent off my second article, and let me tell you, it feels good."

"Hey, that's great. Are you going to stay here tonight?"

"Yes. I've been thinking I should tell my assistant I'm ready to have her book a flight for me back to Atlanta. But I wanted to make sure I got the stories written while I was still here near the source."

"How long will you stay?"

She shrugged. "My boss wants me back yesterday. What's up?"

He grinned. "You're gonna love this. Do you know what Rachel Hudson does for a living?"

"Yeah, I do. As a matter of fact, I ate lunch with her and the commander yesterday, and she told me quite a bit about her job at the Marine Mammal Center in Hawaii. She was in the Navy, but they continued her position when she retired."

"Separated."

"Whatever."

He chuckled. "You are *mellow* today. You're usually so particular about correct word usage."

She straightened. "What's this about Rachel?"

"The sea lions. They're bringing them here."

"What?" Claudia's face expressed the surprise and delight he'd hoped for. "Why?"

"To dive for Dr. Gamata's research."

Her jaw dropped. "Of course! When? I'll have to call Russell."

"So you can do a story?"

"Absolutely. This is a chance in a million! To see them in action, doing a real recovery job, not just a training run. Oh, Bill, this is great!" She dashed inside, leaving the door wide open, and grabbed her cell phone off the desk. Ready to make the call, she asked, "When will they get here? Is there time for Tommy to fly out for pictures?"

"They should be here tomorrow, and the next day we'll head back to the Philippines. Captain Pendergast is arranging it now."

She lowered the phone and frowned at him. "Pendergast?"

"You know him?"

"We met."

"He's in charge of the logistics for this one. We'll have a combined force of American and Philippine naval forces. Rachel Hudson will be in charge of the diving op while a joint force…"

He stopped suddenly and stared at her. He hadn't meant to link the diving expedition to the recovery of the bodies in her mind.

"What?" Her smile faded slowly. "Are they going to get Stu and the others?"

"Yeah."

She blinked. "I'm glad."

"So…you want to go, right?"

"Oh, yeah, I want to go."

"Great. I'll add you to the list we're giving Pendergast, so he'll be sure you have a berth."

"Thanks."

"Claudia…"

"Yeah?"

"I'm glad you're staying. I…" He felt the blood rush to his face. "I was hoping I'd get to see you again. Talk to you."

She eyed him silently for a moment. "I'd like that too. Do you think it's possible? What's your schedule like?"

"Well, this recovery op comes first, of course. And then Squeegee and I are doing some work for an orphanage in Barrigada. Heidi too, if the doctor says she's fit."

"Where's that?"

"Not far from here. We're taking a few days' leave before we go back to the States."

"What about today? Tonight?"

He winced. "I'm on duty. I'm sorry. I'd really like to do something with you."

"Well, maybe when this is over."

⚬⟿

Claudia went on deck with Pierre as their ship approached Basilan. The sun sparkled on the calm water, and she put on her sunglasses. "I hope the coordinates they took were accurate."

"Me too. When that boat swamped, the gear could have scattered over a fairly wide area." Pierre shot her a smile. "It's too bad your photographer couldn't make it."

"Yeah, but the guy we have on loan from the base at Guam seems to know what he's doing. And he's going to do the underwater shots too. It was kind of nice of the Navy to agree to let him do the pictures for my article."

"Well, this is a big deal for us," Pierre pointed out. "If we're successful, the Pentagon will authorize releasing some of his photos to the news services."

"I know. That's the part I don't like. They'll probably come out before my article. So I have to do a really super, in-depth piece." She looked up at him. "Did you talk to Marie this morning?"

Pierre nodded. "She's eager for me to get home. I told her I'm heading her way as soon as we see this through."

"How's Skipper?"

"Fussy last night."

"Teething?"

"She says it's early for that."

Rachel Hudson came on deck carrying a bucket of fish for the two sea lions. Her protégés were housed in a large cage on the foredeck.

"Time for lunch?" Pierre called.

Rachel grinned. "This is just a snack. I'll give them the rest when they've earned it."

Claudia and Pierre walked over to watch her feed the big animals. Kanga, the older female sea lion, had more diving experience and a good track record. Reggie, the younger male, was a bit smaller and less steady, but Rachel's pride in him was evident.

"He'll go a little deeper if I ask him to," she promised, flipping Reggie a fish. "He's got that youthful exuberance. I wouldn't say he's reckless, but he'll try a little harder sometimes. When the older sea lions want to give up, he's always ready for one more dive."

The ship slowed, and a helicopter lifted off the deck. Pierre scanned the horizon. "We're near the spot. They'll try to locate the exact spot for us and mark it."

Ten minutes later, the circling chopper hovered a quarter mile away, and one of the men inside threw out a flare. George hurried over to them.

"That's it, Rachel. You ready?"

"I sure am." She picked up the duplicate briefcase they had

used to teach the animals what they were to look for on the sea bottom.

Claudia watched in fascination as the sea lions came out of their cage and slid down a chute into Zodiac inflatable boats. In the boat with Reggie went Rachel, her husband, a sailor, and the photographer. Kanga went in the second Zodiac with two sailors and the trainer who had accompanied the sea lions on the trip from Hawaii.

Claudia and Pierre had a perfect view of the diving operation from the ship's deck.

"What if it's too deep?" Claudia asked.

Pierre shrugged, watching Rachel fix the harness and line to Reggie. "We're close enough to the island that it should be okay. The charts we have show a depth of sixty to one hundred feet in this area."

While Rachel and her team got the sea lions ready, Claudia watched as their escort ship—a larger vessel carrying Bill's unit and a platoon of Marines to aid them in recovering the bodies of the Gold Team's fallen men—moved away from them. It sailed in closer to the island, and Claudia felt a little queasy. They were going back to the landing spot where Dryden and his men were buried.

Kanga dove first, then Reggie. Each time they submerged, the sea lions carried in their mouths a bite plate with a clip, attached to recovery lines. Rachel had explained to Claudia that if the sea lion found the object it was trained to recover, it would push the clip onto a handle or other part of the object, pull to test its secure attachment, and then let go and resurface. The people in the boat could then pull up the object.

When Reggie and Kanga resurfaced still holding the clips, Rachel and her helpers took the bite plates, praised the pair, and threw them each a fish. Rachel held up the dummy briefcase so they could look at it. Then they dove again. The photographer got in the water with his special camera equipment.

"What if they can't find it?" Claudia asked.

"That's very possible," Pierre said. "It was choppy that night, and they may have drifted quite a ways from where the boat capsized before they took the GPS reading. Gamata's briefcase might have floated a ways before it settled. We just don't know."

On her third try, Kanga attached her clip to something. When the sailors pulled it in, a camouflage backpack dangled from the end of the line.

"That's one of our men's packs," Pierre said. "I wonder how they knew to get that. I thought we were only after the briefcase."

"Rachel told me yesterday that she prepared them to pick up other stuff from the boat too. That way if they didn't find the briefcase right away, she said they could at least recover some of the lost gear, and it would tell us we were in the right spot."

"Makes sense."

Over the next hour, the two sea lions recovered two more packs, an M16 rifle, a boot, and a helmet. The pauses between dives grew longer. Rachel, the other trainer, and Commander Hudson stroked the sea lions' heads and spoke to them after giving them their treats.

"I wonder if they're getting tired," Claudia said.

Reggie clamped his teeth on his bite plate, pushed away from the Zodiac, and lunged beneath the surface again, pulling out the line. They all waited. Rachel removed the harness from Kanga.

"I guess Kanga's finished for the day," Pierre said.

Reggie's head broke the surface fifty yards from Rachel's boat, but instead of heading for Rachel, he flipped and dove again. The people in the Zodiacs talked and pointed. The sailor in Rachel's boat eased it closer to the place where Reggie had dived.

A minute later he popped up again beside them, without the clip. Hudson began hauling in the line. When the object attached to the clip came up, Rachel fished it out of the water and held it high. Claudia let out a whoop as Rachel waved the dripping briefcase.

FORTY-EIGHT

At the airfield Claudia hugged Pierre for a long moment. "Kiss that baby for me, and Marie too. I'll see you all at Lisa's wedding."

"Are you sure you're going to get home in time?" Pierre asked.

"Oh, yeah. I've got two weeks. I'm only staying here a few more days. As soon as Bill gets back from delivering Dr. Gamata's research to him, he and his crew are going to do that charity work for the orphanage. I'll get some pictures for a short write-up in the 'Make a Difference' section of the magazine, and then I'm out of here. My boss has lined up a TV interview for me in Atlanta next week, and I've got another interview scheduled. But I will be at that wedding."

"Okay, we'll see you in Maine." He kissed her cheek and walked to the gate holding out his boarding pass. He looked back and waved, and then he was gone. Claudia drove back to the hotel feeling a bit lonely. George and Rachel Hudson had left an hour earlier for Hawaii with the sea lions, after which they planned to visit Rachel's parents in Oregon—their original vacation plans.

But Bill would be back tomorrow, she reminded herself. She looked forward to some time with him, however brief. Quality time. But when she'd said that to Marie on the phone, Marie had said something like, "Quality time is a myth, whether it's with kids or husbands. It's simply not a substitute for *quantity* time."

Claudia was a little taken aback to hear a mother say that. "Well, yeah, I suppose," she'd replied, "but you take all the time you can get with them, and you try to make it count, right?"

"Of course," Marie said. "I didn't mean that a short time with Bill won't be significant. I just wonder how you think you and he can ever have a meaningful relationship if you're both on the road constantly."

"Well…I'm sure if we get to that point, we'll figure something out." She'd believed it when she said it, but now Claudia was having doubts. What if Marie was right? What if she and Bill couldn't land in the same hemisphere often enough to fall in love? They were both nearing thirty, and neither had sustained a long-term relationship. Ever.

Her first impulse was to deep six that whole train of thought. But when she entered her room and saw, lying on her bed, the beautiful leather-covered Bible Rachel and George had given her, she thought of another way to deal with the question.

"I'll take it to God," she said aloud. "So there, Marie!"

Bill was pleased that Nelson decided to join his crew in building a playground at the orphanage. It would help them not to miss Stu so much, and it would make the work go faster. It took them, Heidi, and Squeegee three days, with a little help from Claudia, to finish.

At first Claudia was more of a diversion with her camera and her constant questions. But by the afternoon of the first day, she was wielding a paintbrush too. The children stood and watched them work whenever their house parents allowed it.

When they took a break for soft drinks, Bill hovered near Claudia. "You've got green paint on your nose."

She smiled at him. "Good thing I won't be in the pictures. Thanks for letting me do this."

"You mean write the story about us?"

"No, help you build the playground."

"Hey, I never turn down help." But he knew Claudia's help was more significant than anyone else's could be. Her participation in the project implied her approval of his ministry. He watched her with a new peace in his heart. Claudia's belief was genuine. That meant she was no longer off-limits.

The urge to ask her out tickled his psyche. Were they ready for another change—one he hoped would be for the better?

Heidi suggested a movie that night, and they all ended up going together. He would rather have been alone with Claudia, but it was okay. Better than okay. He held her hand during the movie. The second night his crew was asked to have dinner with the orphanage adminstrator, and they couldn't say no.

When he got back to his quarters that night, he called Claudia. "I missed you."

"I missed you too," she said, "but I got the first part of my story written, and I caught up on my e-mail and made a few calls."

On the final afternoon of the project, when the last swing was hung and all the rough edges on the playground equipment were sanded, they held a grand opening and let the children run wild for an hour, trying out all the features. Monkey bars, slide, jungle gym, sandbox, and tunnels. The kids had a blast. So did Bill and his crew, playing with the kids. Claudia took about a thousand pictures.

That evening was their last night on the island. Claudia would leave on a commercial jet in the morning. Bill and his crew would catch a military transport later in the day.

When Claudia hopped into one of the "big kid" swings, Bill moseyed over behind her. "Having fun?"

"I sure am."

He gave her a gentle push. "Are you free tonight?"

After a couple more pushes, she dragged her feet and stopped the swing. She twisted around and faced him. "Yes, I am."

The options were limited, but with a few inquiries, Bill found a school concert. Claudia seemed to enjoy it—largely pops and a few patriotic tunes. Afterward they strolled along the beach near her hotel. Claudia paused to slip off her sandals and carried them dangling from her hand. The breeze rippled her skirt and her waves of dark hair. Bill reached for her hand.

"Claudia, I haven't said much about your faith, but I want you to know that it makes me very happy."

Her bewitching smile was even more alluring in moonlight. "Thank you. I know it doesn't really count how I *feel*, but...it feels right. Like going home and sleeping under one of my mother's quilts in my old bedroom under the slanted ceiling."

He squeezed her hand. "I thought you wanted to get away from all that."

"I did. I couldn't leave Maine fast enough. But I'm finally seeing that roots aren't all bad. Call me a slow learner. But it's not just nostalgia. God isn't just a nice addition to my life. He's necessary. How could I not see that?"

"He showed you in His own time, I guess." They walked along in silence for a few minutes, passing other amblers. "Think we can get together once in awhile, after we're back in the States?"

"We can try." After a few more steps, she added, "I'll be disappointed if we can't."

Bill stopped walking and gently tugged her around to face him. "Me too. Let's make it happen."

He bent to kiss her, and she met him halfway. None of the guilt he'd felt in Okinawa assailed him, and he wrapped his arms around her, pulling her in, warm and soft, against him. She stayed close, holding him with her head nestled on his chest.

"My sister's getting married in two weeks. Have you ever been to Maine?"

"No."

"Could you? I mean...it's the one time I'm sure where I'll be for a while."

"Yes. I've got combat leave. It started with this extra time in Guam, but we've got thirty days."

"What a luxury. I'm in the wedding. I'll warn you, Lieutenant

Belanger will be there. The groom is his brother. I think Pierre is the best man. So you'll have to behave yourself."

He chuckled. "Not a problem. You all can show me how a big French family celebrates."

"That could be fun. What about your family? You haven't told me much."

Bill shrugged. "Not much to tell. My folks are both gone. I have a brother, but I only see him now and then. He's in the Navy too."

"So you chose the same career."

"Both Navy but very different careers. He's a chaplain."

He kissed her again. The perfection of it renewed the achy visions of a life he'd begun to think he could never have. A cozy home, a fireplace, rowdy family reunions, precious children, and an enduring love. "Claudia!" He buried his face in her hair and clung to her.

She rubbed his back and sighed, a sound of absolute contentment. Then she eased away from him. "We ought to go back, I suppose."

He kept his arm around her waist, not wanting to lose the intimate contact, not wanting this night to end.

When they reached the steps to the hotel, she slid her sandals on, holding on to his arm for support as she bent over. They were alone in the elevator, and he pulled her into his arms again. At her door he kissed her once more. She emerged with shining eyes and a bittersweet smile.

"Two weeks isn't forever," she whispered.

He nodded. "E-mail me the details. You know—where I should fly to and all that."

"Yes." She pulled him down and captured his lips again, and Bill lost himself in the joy, wishing his life could be a series of such moments.

FORTY-NINE

After the meal was under way at the wedding reception, Claudia left the head table and slipped into a chair beside Bill at one of the family tables. She tucked her billowing pink chiffon skirt around her legs.

"Hello, gorgeous," Bill said with a contented smile.

"Ha! I still can't believe Lisa chose such a froufrou design for the bridesmaids' dresses. I mean she wears coveralls every day, for crying out loud! Wouldn't you think she'd pick something just a tad more practical?"

Bill grinned at her. "Maybe that's exactly why she chose it. To show everyone she's not all business."

"Hmph." Claudia traced the gold stripes on the sleeve of his dress blue uniform with her finger. "Having fun?"

"Oodles of it. Matthieu here just told me how you beat him at the fishing derby a few years back."

Claudia made a face at Pierre and André's brother, who sat on the other side of Bill. "And I was going to say something nice about you to my adorable cousin, Kathy. You can forget about that, Matthieu."

"Where?" Matthieu asked, scanning the room.

"Ha! Ask Marie to introduce you."

"Feeling a little snappish, aren't you?" Matthieu shot back.

"I'm always this way when I have to wear pink, with shoes dyed to match."

Bill laughed and slipped his arm around her. "I don't suppose you can disappear anytime soon?"

"Afraid not. Pictures."

He nodded, his lips compressed in resignation.

"Do you really have to leave tonight?" Claudia asked. "You only got here yesterday, and I didn't think your month was up."

"I know." He glanced around, but the others at the table were immersed in their own conversations. He leaned in close. "We've got a new op next week, and there's fancy high-tech equipment to train on. I've got to stay on top of things."

"Aha. Can't let Squeegee and Nelson know more than you do, eh?"

"Right. I'm the CO of the unit now. Under soon-to-be Lieutenant Commander Belanger." He smiled and reached for his nut cup, tossed a peanut into the air, and caught it in his mouth.

"How's everyone doing?"

"Not bad."

She eyed him thoughtfully. The day before, on the ride back from the airport, he'd confided to her that he had returned to Norfolk before his leave was over and undergone mandatory psychological evaluation. All of the special force were required to take it after losing a member, it seemed, and the Basilan op had given them multiple reasons to see the shrink.

"Your job doesn't leave you much of a personal life."

"Well, yours doesn't either."

They eyed each other dolefully.

"Heard anything from the Gamata family?" he asked.

"Santi e-mails me all the time." Just thinking of the pensive boy made her smile. "He still hopes his father will come work in America."

"It might happen. Things are not getting better in the Philippines." Bill reached for his water glass.

"Oh?"

"Since we left, Cabaya's been up to no good."

"So it's official? You didn't kill him."

Bill shook his head. "He's pretty much taken over the town of Akbar and made it his base of operations."

"On Basilan?"

"Yes." He sipped his water and set the glass down.

"I'm glad most of you got to go to the memorial service for Stu," Claudia said softly. "Wish I could have been there."

Bill nodded and inhaled deeply. "It was intense, but I'm glad we went too. Of course, you were traipsing around Greece last week."

She smiled. "Oh, the nasty assignments I pull. Four days interviewing lesser royalty in the Aegean islands."

Bill squeezed her. She laid her head on his shoulder for a moment, wishing they could escape the crowd.

Matthieu tapped his fork on his water glass repeatedly. Other young people all across the hall—and Claudia's Grandpa LaChance—took up the clatter until André, at the head table, stooped to kiss his bride. Everyone cheered.

Claudia grinned and clapped with the rest of them. André was perfect for Lisa. The two of them would be supremely happy in a life that, by Claudia's standard, would be boring. But who was to say what constituted success? They would no doubt live in contentment. Their grand adventures would be replacing the ancient wiring in the old farmhouse they'd put a down payment on and teaching a new generation of Belanger babies to talk with a Maine accent. What was wrong with that? The glow on Lisa's face this moment outshone Claudia's satisfaction when she won the IPET award.

She felt a tear trickle down her cheek. Bill reached over and caught it with his finger, his empathetic smile reaching deep in his blue eyes. Claudia's return smile was a bit watery. *But that's what weddings are for. Right?*

Her mother edged between the tables to find her and bent over close to her ear. "I know you're right where you want to be, sweetheart, but we'll need you for the pictures now."

Claudia sighed and pushed her chair back.

"May I watch?" Bill asked.

"It will be boring."

"That's all right." The smoldering look in his eyes told her he'd rather sit alone on a hard church pew watching her pose with her sisters for formal photographs than be anywhere else in the world while she did it.

She touched her fingertip to his lower lip. "All right, come on then. And when it's done, we'll get out of here. We only have a few hours left."

They didn't get away for two more hours, after the pictures were snapped, the cake was served and the bouquet was tossed and caught by Pierre and André's younger sister, Elise. At last Claudia hugged Lisa goodbye, and she and Bill sneaked away.

He drove her to her parents' home and paced the driveway while she ran up to change out of the cumbersome pink gown. She pounded down the stairs in a pair of capris and a striped top.

"Quick, let's go before anyone else comes home." She dove into the passenger seat of her rental car, and Bill got in on the driver's side.

"Where to?"

"Do you want to change?"

"Well…"

"If you do, head over to Belangers'." Somehow Pierre's parents had found a bed for Bill in their rambling but crowded farmhouse.

Half an hour later, they sat on the dock at a lakeside cottage belonging to a friend of the Gillettes. Claudia dipped her feet in the cool water.

"Are you sure the owners won't mind us being here?" Bill fumbled with his shoelaces and put his sneakers on the dock beside him.

"No, they've moved back to town. But they let us come out here all the time. This is where I learned to water-ski." She kicked the surface of the glassy lake, sending a spray of droplets out several yards. "Do you really think we can manage to keep seeing each other? I mean…I really like you, Bill." She swallowed hard. What she really wanted to say was that she loved him, but Bill hadn't used the L word, and her own faith was new and untried. The casual way she'd thrown that word around in the past seemed flagrantly trifling now, almost irreverent. She didn't even know yet what God expected of people in love. Did she need some sort of probationary period, before she got into a new and possibly permanent relationship? A time to learn more about God's expectations and her own potential to meet them? And had she already gone too far by kissing Bill and cuddling up to him as though he belonged to her?

"I hope we can." He draped his arm over her shoulders and gazed out over the water.

At the far end of the lake, a motorboat hummed along, but most of the summer people had left. A breeze rippled through the warm air and ruffled his blond hair. Claudia couldn't resist reaching up and brushing back the strands that fell on his forehead. He turned into her arms and pulled her to him for a tender kiss.

"Aw, Claudia," he whispered in her ear. "What'll we do if we can't? I don't like this."

"But you can't give up your job."

"No. Neither can you, I suppose."

"Well…" She sighed. "I've got lots of obligations scheduled. The magazine has invested a lot in me." They sat in silence for a long minute, and she dared to ask, "How much longer do you have in the Navy?"

"At least eight years."

She cringed inwardly. "How can a man survive eight years of doing what you do? I was lucky to survive three or four days."

His rueful smile told her nothing would change, but he kissed her nose and said easily, "Not lucky. God protected you."

"I knew that. Really. I'm just not used to putting it that way, but of course He did."

He nodded and watched a bird swimming out from a marshy area down the shore. "He's watching over me. If He wants me in special ops, He'll keep me there. Look at that. Is it a loon? I've never seen one before."

"Yes." The sun settled lower behind the trees, throwing a golden light across the woods on the opposite shore. The loon's eerie call echoed across the water. "I suppose we'd better get back and pick up your luggage and head for the airport."

Bill pulled her closed and twisted his wrist so he could see his watch without removing his arm from her shoulders. "It takes an hour, right?"

"Yes."

He sighed.

She looked up at him timidly. "We can pray about it."

"Of course."

"How will you...I mean, what will you say?"

He shrugged. "These past two weeks I've been asking God to let me be here, and He did. I've also been praying that we can go on and maybe work toward being together more. If He wants that, it will make me very happy."

"And if He doesn't?"

"That's why we need to be careful, Claudia. Until we know."

"That's what I thought."

FIFTY

4:00 P.M., MARCH 7
JAKARTA, INDONESIA

Claudia and Tommy entered the hotel together, carrying their equipment. They stopped at Tommy's door. While he dug out his key card, Claudia held his camera bag.

"Thanks." He swung the door open. "You want to get supper together?"

"Sure, why not?"

"Ten minutes?"

She grimaced. "I think I want a shower."

"Half an hour then?"

"Yeah. That's good."

She went to her room, turned on her laptop, and skimmed the e-mails that had come in during the day. Bill's stood out in green type. She'd programmed the computer to color all Bill's messages green and Russell's red.

Change of plans re Fiji. We have a new op. Can you call me? WOW2

Disappointment washed over her, followed by resolution. She closed her eyes for a moment. *Lord, You know what's happening. If You want us together, You can work this out.*

In the six months since Lisa's wedding, she and Bill had only managed to see each other twice, though they'd tried several times. In early November, they'd arranged a brief meeting in Istanbul with Tommy in tow, after Bill did a mission in Iraq. Claudia and Tommy were doing a piece on Ottoman Empire mosaics, but she'd ditched the assignment for a day. And just after Christmas she'd spent a weekend at Marie and Pierre's home. Bill had spent every off-duty moment with her. But since then they'd had to make do with calls and e-mails.

Claudia had finally convinced Russell to let her pursue her story idea about birth and child care in Indonesia. He'd dismissed it at first, but after Claudia unearthed some statistics about the differences in prenatal care and childhood diseases in Indonesia and the United States, he had relented and let her go. She had coordinated her trip with Bill's scheduled training exercise in Micronesia, and when they both were done, they would meet in Fiji for three glorious days. But now it seemed Uncle Sam had once more thrown a monkey wrench in their plans.

She keyed in his cell phone number and prayed for a good connection.

"Hello?"

She grinned from ear to ear. "Hi, sweetie!"

"Hi." He sounded smug—settled somehow, in contrast to her own inner turmoil.

"What's up?" she asked. "You're not gonna make it?"

"Can you cancel the hotel without a penalty?"

"I think so."

"And rebook your flight?"

"Well...Where are you going?"

"We. It's where are *we* going, I hope."

She wrinkled her brow. "What's better than Fiji?"

"Manila?"

"What?" Her brain whirled. "You guys are going to the Philippines again? And why are you telling me? It should be a secret, shouldn't it?"

"Did you get an e-mail from the Philippines?"

"I don't know. I think I saw one from Santi, but I saw yours and opened it first, and—hold on." She went back to the computer and scrolled down through the messages. "Hey, it looks like Dr.—you know, our mutual friend—sent me something." She had learned early on not to mention specifics when she talked to Bill. She clicked on Dr. Gamata's message and caught her breath.

Claudia, I have made the decision at last to visit your country. I have been offered a temporary teaching position at Johns Hopkins University and unlimited use of a well-equipped lab there. We all hope to see you soon. We'll contact you with more details later. Sincerely, A. G.

"I can't believe it, Bill! They're really going to do it."

"Yes. Without saying too much, let me just tell you that my friends and I have a special job to do. We'll be transporting a package from the mall to your neighborhood, so to speak."

"And I can meet you at the mall?"

"Sure. You can even go a day early and hang out with your buddies if you want."

She smiled. A day with the Gamatas before Bill and his unit escorted them to Baltimore. And once they were in the States, she ought to be able to arrange another visit with them.

"That sounds good. But you'll be working when you get there."

"I think I can get a few hours free. It's not three days on the beach, but…"

"I'll take it!"

"Great. I can't give you the details right now, but I'll send you several e-mails, and you can put the pieces together, okay?"

"Sure. And if it's more secure, send one of them to my work address."

"Affirmative. I'll see you soon, Claudia."

She smiled at his wistful tone. "Can't wait."

"Okay, hang up and see if you can fix that reservation. Get yourself a room in Manila. My uncle will put me up."

Yeah, Uncle Sam. Well, at least she would get to see him. She let him go reluctantly and made three more calls to cancel the two hotel rooms in Fiji, rearrange her flights, and give Mya a heads-up about her change in schedule.

A knock on her door startled her. Tommy. With a sigh, she grabbed her sweater and purse. So much for a hot shower.

1900 HOURS, MARCH 9
MANILA, PHILIPPINES

Bill sat opposite Claudia in a dim restaurant off a main artery in downtown Manila. A transport glitch had delayed his team twenty-four hours, but he was finally with her. He was stuck in his khaki uniform, but she didn't seem to care what he wore, so long as he was actually here with her.

"You're the best, Claudia. I was afraid we'd miss each other after all." He picked at his rice and fish sauce, wishing he'd ordered something else. "How did you get an extra day out of your boss?"

"I didn't tell him. Remember, we were going to do three days in Fiji."

"Yeah." Bill compressed his lips. "I wish I could make that up to you."

"You can't help it when they change your orders. I know that."

"True. But it seems whenever we think we can spend some time together, one or the other of us has to cancel. I'm really getting tired of this."

She blinked rapidly, and her eyes took on a dangerous sheen.

"Hey, I didn't mean it that way," he said quickly. "Claudia, really. I'm not sick of *you*. I'm sick of not being able to be with you."

She grabbed her glass and took a sip of her diet cola. When she put it down, Bill reached across the table and took her hand.

"I'm so very sorry."

"It's not your fault. I don't blame you."

"But it's not fair to you, and you've been so good about it. I know you must be disappointed."

She looked away. "Well, sure. Aren't you?"

"Very."

Claudia sighed and picked up her fork. "We have a few hours."

"Seems like that's the most we'll ever get. Do you—" He stopped. They'd been together fifteen minutes and already he had her on edge. Better to enjoy the moment and talk about this later.

"Do I what?"

"Forget it," he said.

"No, let's talk about it." She wiped her lips on her napkin. "If we're ever going to be anything but pen pals, we have to deal with this."

"Okay. I was going to say, do you plan to keep doing the same type of work all your life?"

She lowered her lashes and concentrated on her food for a moment. At last she glanced up. "I'm not sure. I like it, but I might consider a less hectic career if the perks were good enough."

Perks like a high salary, Bill wondered, or like the freedom to get married and settle down?

In the back of his mind, he couldn't help wondering if God had purposely disrupted their plans to keep them from having three unchaperoned days in a tropical paradise. Even before he and Claudia had decided to try to make their relationship work, he'd determined to keep it pure. Maybe Fiji would have been too much temptation. He wanted to believe they would have handled it maturely. But he'd never been around Claudia much without her family or Tommy Knowlton.

"So what happened to Tommy?" Bill asked.

"He went home. He still thinks I'm with you in Fiji."

"You didn't tell him about the change of plans?"

"I didn't see any point in it. Besides, he wouldn't believe that we weren't going to share a room in Fiji. Why should I tell him what I'm up to?" She laid down her fork and pushed her dark hair back. "Look, this is nobody's fault. Let's make the most of it. I spent yesterday and today with the Gamata family, and I love them. I think it's wonderful that Dr. Gamata asked for your unit to escort him to Washington."

"It's an honor. And it will bring a sort of satisfaction to us all, to see them well and thriving in America."

She nodded. "Santi is very excited about it. I told him that if they can't visit me in Atlanta, I'll come to Baltimore once they're settled and find a place where he and I can ride horses."

Bill chuckled. "Santi is quite a boy."

"Yes, he is. And he's got his father's mind. I'm glad he won't have to grow up here, Bill. He's scared all the time. He told me that when he goes to school, he runs all the way. He's afraid someone will jump out and shoot him or kidnap him again. And every afternoon, he's on edge until he gets home and sees that his mother is all right."

"I'm sorry he has to live with that fear."

"It makes me sad."

"I hope the extra guard we gave them tonight will help him feel more secure."

"You have people with them now?"

"Yes. Because their trip has been publicized, I decided to post a two-man watch with the family until it's time to take them to the airport tomorrow. Brownie and Ellis are over there right now, outside their apartment. Taber and Nelson will relieve them at midnight."

Claudia nodded, her lips pursed. "I'd feel claustrophobic if I lived in a gated community the way they do. I guess they lived in a single-family home in the suburbs before, but they didn't feel safe."

"Well, the wall around the apartment complex would be a small barrier for anyone who seriously wanted to get at them, but I'm sure it's a help psychologically."

She crumpled her napkin and tossed it on the table. "Can we go somewhere else? Do you mind?"

"Not at all. Let's go." They left their unfinished food on the table. Bill paid for the meal, and they went out into the urban dusk. The air was cool, and the city smells assaulted him. "Where do you want to go?"

"I don't know. Just…somewhere else. I've got a rental car at the hotel if you want to drive somewhere, but I walked over here to meet you."

He took her hand. "Which way?"

She nodded south. "It's only three blocks." They walked along the sidewalk at a leisurely pace.

"I have a suite. If you don't think it's too…" She turned and faced him, letting people dodge around them. "Please, Bill, we need a place to talk. I won't do anything to lead you on."

"Okay." Her words would have amused him if he hadn't heard a catch in her voice that suggested underlying turmoil. Did she think he considered her a temptress? He didn't know the city well enough to suggest another place where they could talk in privacy. They reached her hotel and went into the sitting room of her suite. Claudia took off her jacket and gestured toward the sofa. "Have a seat. I can make coffee if you want some."

"No, I'm fine." He took his hat off and laid it carefully on the end table.

They sat for a long minute, watching each other guardedly. Bill cleared his throat. At the same moment, Claudia started to speak.

"Go ahead," he said with relief.

"Well, I just wonder if this is working. Even when we're together, we're not. We always have other obligations. It's…not the way I imagined it could be."

The ache in Bill's chest deepened. "Are you saying we should stop trying?"

"I don't know." She looked anywhere but at him.

"I don't want to give up," he said.

"Neither do I."

He could hear the unspoken *but*. "Look, I have another eight years at least in the Navy, Claudia."

"Where in there are we supposed to be together?"

"Wherever we can, I guess." His voice cracked a little, and he pulled in a deep breath.

She opened her mouth, then closed it.

He stood up and walked over to the window. The view of the harbor must have cost the magazine a fortune. The running lights of a yacht leaving its mooring slid slowly seaward, like his hopes of a future with Claudia. "Maybe you're right. Is there a point in continuing a relationship that has no future except a pot of tea together every few months in some foreign port? That's what you're saying, isn't it?"

"What strategy would you use if you wanted to change that?" Her voice sounded unnatural, strained, and too neutral.

He turned and looked at her, but she wouldn't meet his gaze. "Well…marriage for starters. And a wife who wouldn't mind moving around for a few years or waiting for me while I was off on field work." It surprised him a bit that he'd put it out there, but he couldn't retract it now, and he didn't want to.

"That…sounds rather dull for the wife, if she can't have a career to keep her occupied while her husband's gone."

Bill ran his hand through his hair. "How about if the wife wrote articles that let her stay home more or that let her schedule her travel to coincide with his cruises and special ops?"

She said nothing, and his heart squeezed. He strode across the carpet and went to his knees beside her.

"Claudia?"

Her brown eyes glistened with unshed tears.

"Your sister makes it work," he whispered, grasping her hands gently.

She sniffed. "I'll think about that."

"Okay." He guessed that was the best he could hope for right now. "Do you want me to leave?"

"No. Oh no, Billy." She lifted her hands to his neck and pulled him toward her. He leaned in and kissed her and then pushed himself up onto the couch beside her. She came into his arms willingly, but he tasted salt tears on her lips.

His cell phone rang insistently as he kissed her, and after the third ring, he leaped up and dredged it from his pocket. "Yeah?"

"Lieutenant, we've got trouble."

"Where?"

"The target. Come quick."

He snapped the phone shut and reached for his hat. Claudia had stood and was staring at him with huge, frightened eyes. "What is it?"

"The Gamatas. I've got to go. How often do the buses run?"

"Take a cab," she said. "It's much faster."

He gritted his teeth. "I'm not sure I have enough cash."

She grabbed her purse and jacket. "Come on!"

"Cl—"

She was already out the door.

FIFTY-ONE

She drove. It only made sense because she'd driven from the hotel to the Gamatas' apartment several times in the last two days. Bill seemed fidgety, but he refrained from giving instructions.

"When we get there, just drop me off at the gate and go back to the hotel," he said.

As if. She braked for a stoplight. "Do you know what's happened?"

"Not really. I don't want to put you in danger, so if you can just let me out and keep driving...You don't even have to park."

We'll see when we get there, she thought, but aloud she said calmly, "You just do what you have to when we get there and don't worry about me."

"You'll stay out of things, won't you?" He eyed her warily. "You really shouldn't have come."

"I'm here." She set her mouth and concentrated on her driving. Bill said no more.

She pulled up before the gate of the apartment complex. Nelson and Taber waited for him outside the stone wall. The wrought iron gate was open, with no gatekeeper in sight.

Bill leaped out of the rental car. Claudia lowered her window and sat still.

"What happened?" Bill asked as Heidi and Nelson strode toward him.

"Several irregulars tried to storm the building," Nelson told him. "Ellis and Browne were on duty like you said, even though Dr. G. said he didn't need us until we were ready to go to the airport tomorrow."

"Anyone hurt?" Bill asked.

"Not that we know of. Brownie's in radio contact, and he and Ellis have the family barricaded in the apartment. He said he took one hostile down near the elevator in their hall. We're afraid that civilians may be in the way, though."

Bill stood to one side of the gate with them, sheltering behind the wall and looking into the courtyard of the apartment complex. Claudia strained to hear what he said.

"Any chance of evacuating the buildings?"

"We're trying to reach the manager," Nelson said. "About a dozen people came running out just as we arrived and said someone was shooting in there."

"Okay, do we know how many hostiles, or how they got in?"

Heidi pointed to the gate. "When we got here, the gate was open and the guardhouse was empty. Either the guard let them in and vamoosed, or they got rid of him somehow and forced their way in. We haven't found a body, though."

"We don't have a count," Nelson added. "Brownie thinks at least six. Maybe a lot more."

"How many men do we have?" Bill asked.

"Just us so far, but the rest of the team is on the way from the base," Heidi said. "Estimated arrival, five minutes."

"I could go in and do some recon on Dr. G.'s building," Nelson said.

"Let's wait. You've got contact with Brownie now?"

Heidi handed him her radio. Bill put the handset to his ear. "GT-1, this is WOW2."

"Roger that," came Lieutenant Browne's voice.

"Conditions there?"

"Stable at the moment."

Bill, Heidi, and Nelson looked toward the street and Claudia watched in her rearview mirror as a light military transport truck drove up behind her. Men in khaki work uniforms piled out of it and hurried toward Bill. He held a quick council with his team, and then the Gold Team dispersed inside the walled compound.

Claudia checked her mirrors. The truck was still directly behind her small rental car. She doubted she could get past it, even if she wanted to. She got out of her car and walked back to the truck. There was no one inside and no keys. Great. Too bad the driver hadn't parked it part way through the gate. That might serve as a deterrent to the insurgents if they tried to leave the complex in a hurry.

She eyed the gate critically. Was this the only entrance? There must be a service entrance too. Had the insurgents driven boldly into the city and right into the complex, or had they come stealthily on foot? If they had driven, they would have a hard time getting out this gate past the vehicles. And maybe she could make that task just a little bit harder.

FIFTY-TWO

Bill and Squeegee sneaked across the back parking lot of the apartment complex, trying to stay out of the direct glare of the security lights. They crouched behind a dumpster and watched the corner of the Gamatas' building until Nelson appeared, waved, and retreated out of sight. Two men were already climbing the fire escape. Two more men—Williams and O'Neill, Bill thought—were ready to join him and Squeegee when they approached the back door. The four of them met at the rear entrance and tried the door. It was locked.

They waited by prearrangement. If all was clear, Heidi and a squad of three others would go in the front and open the back door for them. Those three included Nelson and two of the new team members brought into the unit since Basilan. Bill hoped he hadn't made the wrong call. Maybe he should be leading the assault through the front door, not Heidi. But she needed combat leadership experience to carry her up the next step in the ladder of rank. He contacted Lieutenant Browne on his radio.

"Let's have an update, Brownie."

"They're right outside the door. I'm surprised they haven't busted in yet."

"I don't hear any gunfire," Bill said.

"After the first commotion, we engaged them briefly. One of their men is down. I saw at least four more outside the apartment. We've dug in, so to speak. They tried to ram the door, and I fired on them. They've been quiet the last few minutes."

"I copy." Bill knew Brownie probably had the Gamatas stashed in the bathroom or the kitchen, whichever had the fewest windows and doors. He and Ellis were doing all they could to prevent entry.

Bill put his ear plugs in. A minute later he heard gunfire inside the building. No more waiting. He nodded at Squeegee, who promptly shot out the lock on the back door.

They entered a dimly lit hallway. The gunfire had ended, but Bill heard shouts from the front of the building. He and his three men advanced cautiously, using the urban combat methods they'd trained on for years. He recognized Heidi's voice and called out to her before rounding the corner into the front entry.

"Clear," Heidi replied.

As Bill came into her line of vision, Heidi was covering the front entrance with her rifle while three others ran up the stairs. Two men clad in black clothing lay motionless near the bottom of the stairway. Proul and another man stood guard beside the elevator.

"Up you go, Bill," Heidi said. "There are more on the third floor."

"Civilians?" he asked.

"I've got four men clearing them out on this level and the second. Anyone on the third floor is at high risk."

The Gamatas' apartment lay on the third level, so Bill was not surprised that most of the attackers had gone up there. He passed Heidi and led his three men upward.

Fresh gunfire erupted above him, and he ran up the second flight of stairs. Nelson and two other men were bunched at the top of the flight, exchanging gunfire with unseen shooters in the hallway beyond. A heavy volley of fire rattled out, and one of the men dropped his weapon and thudded down on the steps.

"Ricci, you okay?" Bill reached the man's side and crouched to examine him.

The young man rolled over and pushed himself up.

"Yes. No. I think I'm hit." He held his forearm, and Bill saw blood oozing between his fingers.

"O'Neill, take him down to Taber." Bill helped Ricci to his feet and let him squeeze past him. By the time he'd reached Nelson's side at the top of the stairs, Nelson had thrown a smoke grenade into the hallway.

"Ready?" Nelson asked.

Bill extracted a hand grenade from his belt, pulled the pin, and threw it around the corner. They ducked against the wall, covering their ears. Immediately after the explosion, they dove into the upper hallway, mindful of their friends' positions. Two men lay injured where the grenade had blasted out a large section of floor and side wall. At the far end of the hall, the two Americans who had scaled the fire escape were entering through the frame of the shattered window.

Bill couldn't believe the two injured insurgents were the only enemies remaining on the third story. The others must be in one of the apartments. He pulled out an ear plug and called Brownie by radio.

"Any hostiles in there with you?"

"No, we're good."

Squeegee scowled at him. "Where'd they go? There had to be more than this."

"Maybe not." Bill contacted Heidi. "Taber, you status quo?"

"Affirmative."

One of the new men stopped beside a door near the far end of the hall, several yards beyond the Gamatas' front door. "Lieutenant! This door was forced open."

They entered the apartment cautiously and found an elderly man unconscious on the kitchen floor. "Nelson!" Bill shouted.

The medic hurried to his side.

"See if you can help this civilian." Bill turned to help Squeegee clear the other rooms of the apartment.

Bill took one door leading from the kitchen, and Squeegee took the other. Bill's was the bathroom, and it took only a moment to make sure the shower was clear.

Shooting burst out in the next room. Bill ran back into the kitchen. Nelson still knelt beside the unconscious civilian, but he had his rifle trained on the other door. He nodded at Bill, and Bill hugged the wall between the two doorways.

"Squeegee?"

No answer.

Nelson stood and shouldered his rifle, in position to shoot over Bill's head. Bill tossed a smoke grenade in and whipped around the door, aiming from a crouch toward the window. A man was just climbing over the windowsill. He jerked his head up and fired a pistol at Bill. Recognition caused Bill to falter a fraction of a second. Nelson began to shoot above him. Cabaya's expression went from hatred to shock. His hand wobbled as he tried to steady his aim on Bill. The rebel squeezed off one round, but it went wild and struck the ceiling as Cabaya slipped over the windowsill and downward.

Bill and Nelson charged to the window and looked cautiously down on the parking lot at the rear of the building. A body sprawled on top of the dumpster below, where Bill and Squeegee had hidden ten minutes earlier.

"They must have brought a rope in case they needed a quick escape route and rappelled down." Nelson said.

Two dark figures were running toward a van parked between other vehicles in the residents' parking area. Bill's heart sank when he realized he'd left no one guarding the gate.

He considered following them down the rope, but discarded that idea. He'd make a lovely target against the wall.

Bill turned from the window and saw Squeegee struggling to rise from the bedroom floor. "Tend to Squeegee!" He ran through the apartment, past two other men. "Come with me!"

They raced down the stairs. Heidi flattened herself against the wall as he dashed past her. "They went out a window," he spat out without stopping. He sprinted for the gate. The van tore around the curved drive, veering for a short distance onto the lawn, and rushed away from him. It accelerated as the driver made for the gate. Bill dropped to his knees and fired his rifle at the rear of the vehicle, low on the frame, hoping to hit the gas tank or tires.

A tremendous crash shocked his eardrums as the van slammed into a dark bulk and pushed it forward. A smashing crunch of glass and metal ended in a shower of debris.

Bill jumped up and ran with his men toward the wreck. He was vaguely aware of a knot of spectators huddled against the inside of the stone wall. The streetlights near the gate showed him that the van had shoved through the closed iron gate and hit a small, red car, pushing it smack into the front of the transport truck his men had arrived in. With horror it dawned on him that the car was Claudia's rental.

A flash of fire and noise hurled him backward. Flames soared upward from the demolished vehicles.

FIFTY-THREE

1050 HOURS, MARCH 9
MANILA, PHILIPPINES

Proul ran over and knelt beside Bill. "You okay?"

"Yeah." Bill sat up and tried to catch his breath.

"Whatcha want me to do, boss?"

Sirens split the air.

"Someone's called the Manila police and fire, I'd say." Bill pulled in another gulp of hot, smoky air. "Call our contact in the Philippine Army ASAP. Tell Taber to make sure Browne and Ellis and the Gamatas are okay. We need to get them to a secure location for the night. And Squeegee's hit. Make sure he gets an ambulance if he needs it. We've got to thoroughly search that building. Make sure no other civilians were injured and that we cleared out all the insurgents."

"Will do." Proul ran back toward the apartment building.

Bill stood slowly, staring at the fireball. He walked gingerly toward it. The intense heat stopped him twenty yards from the gaping hole in the fence where the gate had hung.

Claudia.

Bill jogged along the inside of the stone wall until he'd left the searing heat behind and leaped to the top. His ribcage hurt as he strained to balance and climb over the row of iron spikes along the wall. The leap to the ground jarred his ribs and he paused to catch his breath and rub the sorest spot. He straightened and strode toward the burning vehicles. Spectators had gathered across the street, and he flanked the crowd, searching. If she'd been too stubborn to leave when he told her, anything could have happened.

Lord, I refuse to think she was in that car. Please, God!

He found her on the other side of the driveway, leaning against the wall a safe distance from the fire, watching the flames die down. Bill quickened his steps.

"Claudia!"

She turned toward him, her brows arched and her lips slightly parted. When she spotted him, she smiled and ran toward him, her arms wide.

"Thank God you're safe!" She catapulted into his arms.

"I'm fine." *That was stupid,* he thought. *She can see that I'm fine.*

"I heard a lot of shooting and what sounded like a bomb."

"Grenade. But we're okay."

"All of you?"

"Yes. But I almost had a heart attack when I saw your car doing an imitation of a flapjack—a burning flapjack, I might add."

"That's a crepe suzette." She laughed. "Pretty neat, huh? I got the gate closed and turned the car sideways right in front of it. It was a tight squeeze, but in my driver's ed class, I was the best at parallel parking. I sat that baby endwise, right between the gateposts. Of course, the rental company doesn't have to know I did it on purpose."

He squeezed her so hard that her breath whooshed out.

"I love you."

She went suddenly still. "Really?"

"Yes, and I don't know what to do about it."

"Don't you worry. We'll think of something."

He pulled away. "Yes, we will. But I've got to speak to the local authorities and get back to my men. You won't be safe in this crowd. Go back to your hotel, please. I'll worry if you don't."

She hesitated.

"Claudia, let me do my job."

"Okay. I'll go back and call the car rental agency."

Bill walked toward the police car that had pulled up a few yards away, thanking God with every step. A crew of firefighters sprayed down the remains of the smashed vehicles, and Brownie squeezed out through the gate and past the wreckage.

"Bill! Everything okay out here?"

"Yeah. What about the package?"

"All safe."

"And Cabaya?"

Brownie stared at him. "He was here? In person?"

"The guy who fell out the window in the back." At Browne's blank look, Bill shook his head. "You weren't there. I'll ask Nelson. Is Squeegee okay?"

"Nelson said he might have a broken rib. He's sending him to the hospital if we can get him out of here. Heidi finally got hold of the apartment manager. They're going to open the service entrance for emergency vehicles." Brownie eyed the still smoldering van. "I take it someone was in that thing?"

"The last two terrorists."

"You mean the last two until next time."

"Right." Bill sighed. "Go on back and make sure they check out the guy on the dumpster. I'm sure it's Cabaya. I've got to talk to the police."

FIFTY-FOUR

9:00 A.M., MARCH 12
ATLANTA, GEORGIA

Mya was lurking near the elevator when Claudia got off.

"Welcome back!" Her assistant held out a mug of coffee.

"Thanks." Claudia juggled her purse and portfolio so she could accept the mug.

"Russell wants you to go to his office as soon as possible. All the wire services picked up your story on Juan Cabaya's death and the attempt on Dr. Gamata. The board wants more, and Russell finally seems ready to let you call the shots on the slant."

"Okay. I want to visit the Gamatas next week in Baltimore, after the doctor settles in at Johns Hopkins. Can you set up my travel? Oh, and can you tell Tommy I want to talk to him about the art for the Jakarta story?"

"Uh…Tommy won't be in today."

"Why not?" Claudia reached her cubicle and set her coffee and bags on her desk. She turned to look at Mya, who hovered in the entry, chewing her bottom lip. "What's up?"

Mya shot a glance over her shoulder and stepped closer. "Tommy's in jail."

Claudia froze in place and opened her eyes wide. "For real?"

"Uh-huh. Russell had a conniption yesterday and refused to bail him out."

Mya's voice rose barely above a whisper, and Claudia automatically lowered hers to match. "What happened?"

"Driving under the influence. Of what, I'm not sure. Russell is so mad, he wants to fire him. But Bob Kingsley's sticking up for Tommy, since he's so good at his job when he's…you know. When he's actually doing it."

Claudia nodded and sat down. "Wow."

"The board is going to hash it over this afternoon, I think."

"Meanwhile Tommy sits in the slammer?"

Mya gulped and looked toward the cubicle doorway again. "He was supposed to be arraigned this morning, so he may be out. I don't know. They may have kept him. This is really bad, Claudia."

Trust Mya to state the obvious.

"Okay. I'm glad you told me."

"But you won't let on to Russell that you know?"

"Mum's the word. If he wants me to know, I'll let him break the news."

"Thanks."

Mya left her, and Claudia took a moment to compose herself. *Dear Lord, help me sort this out. And show me the right way to respond to Russell. And Tommy…God, I don't know how to pray for him.*

FIFTY-FIVE

3:00 P.M., MARCH 23
ATLANTA, GEORGIA

"So Tommy's okay now?" Bill asked.

"I wouldn't say he's okay, but he's back at work finally. He's a little subdued. The board told him one more infraction and he's fired."

"Maybe this is what he needs to bring him around."

"Maybe." Claudia's mind wasn't really on Tommy's troubles now. It was on the news Bill had just dropped on her. "I'll miss you."

"I'll call you as soon as we touch down on American soil."

"You'd better." Claudia chuckled, but her heart was heavy.

"Keep praying about this," Bill pleaded. "There's got to be a way."

"I will." She licked her lips and resolved not to let the tears filling her eyes appear in her tone. "It's just a drill you're going on, correct?"

"Please—an allied training exercise."

"Oh, right."

"Dummy charges only. I promise."

Her lungs ached from the effort of breathing and not crying. "And you're not going near the Philippines."

"Not even close."

"Okay." She hated the whimper that crept into her voice. She wanted to be able to send him off with a bold, reassuring *I love you*, but the last two weeks had taken her to the depths of discouragement. Since they'd parted in Manilla, she hadn't seen Bill, and now he was leaving for a six-week cruise to the Marianas for a naval exercise. When it was finished, they would have been separated two months. Again. And the end wasn't even on the radar, let alone in sight. The Gold Team would return, not to Norfolk, but to Seattle, their new home port.

Ever since she'd begun praying that they could be together, obstacles had blocked that from happening. She couldn't help sniffing as she grabbed a tissue from the box on her desk.

"You okay?"

"Yeah. Yeah, I'm fine."

"You don't sound fine."

I'm not! I hate this! "No, really, I'm fine. Just…be safe. Have fun. All that."

"Yeah." He sounded uncertain.

"Oh, Bill, this stinks!" After a long pause, she said cautiously, "Bill? Are you still there?"

"Yes. I just can't think of anything to say."

When they hung up a moment later, after unsatisfactory goodbyes, Claudia put her head down on her desk and wept quietly, trying not to let the tears fall on her keyboard. A gentle hand on her back caused her to jump and whirl around in her swivel chair. She *never* cried at the office.

"Hey." Mya shifted her weight from one foot to the other. Her eyes were large and apologetic. "Sorry."

"About what?"

"Whatever did this to you. Was that…your Navy guy on the phone?"

Claudia nodded and dabbed at her face with the tissue. "Is my mascara all smeared?"

"Yes."

"Great."

"He, uh…didn't break up with you, did he? Because I've never seen you so…" Mya gulped and pasted on a smile. "Russell has some ideas for you. Can you see him at three thirty?"

Claudia glanced at the time in the corner of her computer screen. "Sure."

Mya nodded and patted her arm. "I'll tell him. Wash your face."

As she turned away, Claudia yelped, "And we're *not* breaking up."

"Of course not." Mya's parting smile was a little forced.

Claudia grabbed the first thing that came to hand—the tissue box—and flung it at the far wall of her cubicle. She sat staring at it, her teeth clenched.

All right, God. You're the one running the show. Everyone tells me that. Bill, Heidi, Marie, the pastor of the church I found. So nothing I do can change this, I guess. If You want Bill to be at least three thousand miles from me forever, that's what will happen. But could You please tell me why? It's just so hard.

She wondered if Marie knew about this. Pierre must. He supervised the Gold Team. Had he told Marie? She picked up the phone.

"Well, hi! What are you up to?" Marie's upbeat greeting sent Claudia's spirits even deeper down the mine shaft than they'd already fallen.

"Not much. I—"

"I was just going to call you! I've got some big news."

"Oh?" Claudia didn't feel like playing guessing games. "What is it?"

"Skipper's running. You know he's been walking for a couple of months? Well, now he's running. Oh, and we're moving to Seattle."

Claudia stopped breathing. This was not a mine shaft. It was a hole through the center of the earth. "When...?"

"In about a month."

"No, I meant, when did you find out?"

"Today. Pierre called me from his office a couple of hours ago. I know it's a long ways away, but I think we'll like it. He'll have his promotion, and he'll oversee a bigger training program, and—"

"And the Gold Team is going with him."

Marie was silent for a moment. "Well, yes."

"Bill told me. He didn't know you and Pierre were going too. Or if he did, he didn't mention it."

"I'm sorry, honey. I know you care a lot about Bill."

Claudia sobbed out a little chuckle. "I barely get to see him, anyway. Look, I have a meeting in about five minutes, and I need to freshen up first."

"All right." Marie sounded a little hurt and confused. "Claud, we can't help it when the Navy reassigns its people."

"I know. I love you. Kiss Skipper for me. Bye."

She hurried to the restroom with her makeup case to repair the damage her tears had caused. How could things go so far south in two weeks?

Bill's last words to her in Manila had been to ask whether she had thought about his so-called strategy. It amounted to her working less and vegetating in crummy base housing while he saved the world. Her reply?

"Have you considered taking a less dangerous job?"

He didn't have a straight answer. Pierre had switched to training special forces units. Surely Bill could do something like that. Okay, so Pierre was tearing up roots again and moving to Seattle too. But he wouldn't be getting shot at.

"I'll pray about it," Bill had replied. His stock answer.

She sighed and returned to her cubicle to leave her makeup case and grab a notebook. Bill would be based in Seattle for at least the next year. Was that progress? She'd prayed diligently about their future since the Basilan op. Instead of letting them be together, God was prying them farther and farther apart.

Pierre and Marie and their precious little boy were going too. No more weekends at their loving, cracker-box home in Norfolk.

And Tommy was on probation. If she lost him, how long would it take to break in a new photographer? She'd probably get stuck with that obnoxious Desiree Milton. All she was good for was still lifes. She had no sense of composition in an action shot. And Russell would probably insist they save the magazine money by rooming together wherever they went.

As she walked toward the door to Russell's office, Claudia made up her mind to go to Baltimore next weekend to see the Gamatas. After that she would spend every weekend with Marie and Pierre until they left the east coast.

She paused by the door to the small room designated as a library and took a deep breath. *Okay, Lord. I know I'm being selfish. If You're truly good—and deep down, I believe You are—then You won't cut me off from everyone I care about. Even Tommy. Lord, You need to help him get his head on straight. I've tried, and I can't do it. And Marie is putting the best face on things. Another move will be hard for her, but she's supporting her husband, and that can't be wrong. Make things easy for her.*

She felt a little better, having considered other people's needs, if only for a moment. She raised her chin and walked to the editor's door.

"Come in, Claudia. Let's talk about the breaking news stories for the April editions. Salli's doing a story on education reform for the April 4 issue."

That seemed a little tame to Claudia, but she said nothing.

"For you, how does an exclusive interview with Raul Castro sound?"

"I like it."

"Terrific. You'll fly to Havana Tuesday and meet with him Wednesday. Home that night."

"That quick?"

"They don't want you hanging around Havana very long. It's a coup for us that they're letting you in at all."

"Okay, I'll take it. But only if Tommy goes with me."

Russell scowled, swiveling his chair back and forth. "All right. And for the week after, can you squeeze in a trip to the flower market in Amsterdam?"

She curled her lip slightly. "How about a profile of women of Tashkent?"

"Tashkent?"

"You know, Uzbekistan. The Great Silk Road. Genghis Khan. I'd like to see how their women are treated today."

Russell frowned at her. "Sounds to me like a story that would make a lot of Muslims angry."

She shrugged. "All right, but not the flower market thing. I'm not a green thumb sort of person."

Her mind was still on Bill. Fifteen minutes later she had agreed to do a piece on the shrinking big cat population of India and another on Kenyan beadwork artists. She left Russell's office clutching her notebook and leaned against the library door jamb.

Lord, why am I so apathetic? I love my job.

Her gaze fell on the rack of professional periodicals. A new issue of *Editor & Publisher* drew her into the room. She picked it up and flipped to the back. Lots of "help wanted" ads. She tucked it and an issue of *Broadcast Journalism* under her arm and headed for her desk. As she passed Tommy's cubicle, she called, "Hey, Tommy, we leave Tuesday for Havana."

FIFTY-SIX

Bill sat down at the computer in Commander Hudson's den and connected to his mail server. As the messages flooded the screen, he sat back with a no-doubt silly smile on his face. Even though he'd told Claudia he probably wouldn't be able to communicate with her for six weeks, she'd sent him about a hundred e-mails.

He quickly set up a new outgoing message.

Claudia, I'm in the U.S. of A. again, but only made it to Hawaii so far. We leave for Seattle in the A.M. Commander Hudson heard we would be here at Pearl tonight and invited me and Brownie and Taber to have supper with him and Mrs. Hudson. They are wonderful people, and he is letting me use his computer. I'm just starting to open your messages now. More soon. Bill

Rachel Hudson poked her head in the doorway. "Coffee, Bill?"

"Thanks."

She set a steaming mug on the computer desk and smiled. "Looks like you've got lots of e-mail. Take your time."

He began at the bottom. No sense reading them out of order. Most were short snatches. *I'm going to Cuba. I miss you. Tommy's been warned to stay sober or else. I'm going to Baltimore. Santi and I went horseback riding. He and his parents are adjusting well. I miss you. Tommy's portraits of RC are fabulous. I'm going to India. I saw a tiger in the wild. I spent the weekend at Pierre and Marie's and helped them pack. I'm going to Kenya. I miss you.*

By the time he was halfway to the top, his heart ached. Same animated, gorgeous Claudia, always on the move, full of passion. Would he ever get to be with her?

I heard about a job on the West Coast. It would be a drastic change, but maybe it's time. He read that one twice. Did he dare hope it might mean they'd be closer together?

I applied for the job, and they want me to go out for an interview. I'm nervous. If you get this, pray for me. He paused then and there to send up a petition for her, though the message had been written more than a week earlier.

The next message tore his heart to shreds. *Tommy was fired today. Can you believe it? His portraits of Raul Castro are absolutely haunting. You know they'll win a gazillion awards. And they fired him. I feel so alone here. I miss you.*

The next one was more upbeat. *Tommy got on with* Newsweek, *but he's going to rehab first. I think he's going to be okay. I hope so, anyway. Keep praying for him. And guess what? Lisa and André are expecting!*

Finally, a message dated yesterday. *I'm flying out for my interview. Pray hard. Maybe we can connect for our famous pot of tea in an airport.*

Bill inhaled deeply. If only they *could* see each other. He would send one more message, but she might not get it until after her trip. Still, Claudia usually took her laptop with her. He hoped she would see it tonight. As he reached for the mouse, a new message slid in. He smiled and opened it.

Bill, I love you. Call me!

His pulse galloped as he checked his watch. It was midnight on the East Coast, but she must be closer. California, maybe. He took out his phone and dialed her cell number.

"It's me," he said when she answered.

"I got it. Billy, I got the job. The pay's about the same, but I won't have as much vacation. They're really eager to get me, but I'm nervous about it. It will be worth it, right? Bill? Bill?"

He laughed. "Slow down. I just came from six weeks of booming guns and military speak. Where are you?"

"Oh." She hesitated. "I didn't want to get your hopes up. Otherwise I would have told you."

"Baby, you're not in Seattle?"

"If you mean Seattle, *Washington*, yeah. That would be the one."

Bill closed his eyes and let peace and joy slide over him from head to toe.

"Are you still there?" she asked.

"Oh, yeah. I love you. Which magazine are you going with?"

"Well, it's…not a magazine."

"The *Seattle Times*?"

"No. It's a TV station. And I'm really ignorant about broadcast journalism, so they're giving me a crash course before I go on-air. But the people are all so friendly, and they keep saying I'll do a great job."

Bill swallowed hard. "What exactly… Claudia, you're going to be a TV reporter?"

"Yes. Well, sort of. I'm…anchoring the nightly news. Starting June fifteenth. I'm not doing a network show or anything. It's only a local broadcast. It's… I mean, is that okay? You don't mind, do you? I didn't consider that you might not want me on television every night. Do you? Bill, say something."

He scratched his head. "I… Can you live with that? Being in the same place all the time, I mean."

"We'll see. And they might let me do some location broadcasts."

Bill's chest began to ache again. Within a year, a national network would probably entice her to New York. "I'm flying into Seattle tomorrow. We land at 1400. Can I see you then? Will you still be there?"

"Yes. But I'll have to fly back to Atlanta the next day and put in my resignation."

"What's your hotel? I'll get settled at the base and pick you up for dinner."

Claudia waited in the lobby, trying not to fidget. In her mind she went over all the reasons why Bill should love this turn of events. At the top of her list: It will mean they could be together part of every day that Bill wasn't off on a military operation.

She wished she'd taken a suite, but the television station was paying for this trip, and they'd set her up in a regular room. Best to meet Bill in the lobby.

He strode in through the door and halted, looking around for her, squinting at the change in light. Dress blues and gleaming black shoes, she noted. Flowers too. She stood and took a step toward him. Another man in uniform had also entered and stopped beside Bill.

When Bill noticed her, he turned and said something to the other man and then hurried toward her. His eyes sparkled, and she automatically reached for him. He whirled her in his arms and planted half a dozen kisses in her hair.

He set her down and handed her the bouquet. "I tried to get hibiscus, but I guess that's too exotic here."

She looked down at the mixed tulips and carnations. "They're lovely."

"So are you." He looked long and deeply into her eyes.

His sun-bleached hair invited her touch, and she reached up to slide her fingers through it in the back, where it was short and tickly. "I missed you so much," she confessed.

His smile grew. "I gathered that. I read every one of your e-mails last night."

"Oh. That must have been an overdose."

"Not at all." He looked over his shoulder and beckoned the other man. "I hope you don't mind, I brought someone to meet you."

As he approached, Claudia looked the stranger over. His hair was almost the same color as Bill's. He was nearly as tall, and he had the same straight nose, firm jaw, and blue eyes.

"You're Ben."

He grinned and took her hand. "And you're Claudia. Hope you don't mind my horning in on the reunion."

"Of course not. Bill met my family last fall, and I've wanted to meet you. Can you have dinner with us?"

"No, I wouldn't do that to Billy."

"I wouldn't mind," Bill said, "but I know you've got other plans."

"Right." Ben smiled at Claudia again. "I may be out to sea the next time you come, but my ship is home ported here now, and I have a feeling we'll see quite a bit of each other in the future."

He left with a jaunty wave, and Bill looked down at Claudia. "Is there a place we can talk? Before the restaurant, I mean."

"Well…"

He looked around the large lobby. "There's a corner over there that's out of traffic. Do you mind?"

She followed him to a loveseat set back behind a partition and partially screened by a large plant. They sat down and he reached for her hands.

"I guess you've thought about how restricted you'll be if you take this job. They won't be paying your way to Peru and Tibet and all those exotic places you love."

"That's true, but I've reached a decision. Maybe it's because I'm getting older, or maybe it's because I don't feel so restless since I've believed in Christ. I'm not really sure why, but I think I'd rather have a stable home life and…and love than continuous adventure."

"Love is good." Bill slid his arm around her and eased closer. She caught the tiniest whiff of aftershave. "Are you sure you can sit still for a while?"

"It's going to be a challenge to learn a new business. That will hold my attention for a bit. And I'll have Marie close by. Yes. I want to do it. That is, if you can stand me being on television."

"Are you kidding? I'm so proud of you." He went down on one knee beside her. "Claudia, I don't want to wait another minute to do this. I love you insanely. Will you marry me?"

She sat still for the space of one sweet, achy breath, letting the words hang golden in the air.

"Yes. The sooner the better."

THE END

ABOUT THE AUTHOR

Susan Page Davis is the author of several novels, spanning categories such as historical, mystery, young adult, and romantic suspense. A former news correspondent, she and her husband, Jim, are the parents of six and the grandparents of five Susan and Jim make their home in Maine.

Visit Susan at her website: www.susanpagedavis.com

Also by Susan Page Davis...

FRASIER ISLAND

After specialized underwater training, Ensign Rachel Whitney of the U.S. Navy is posted to a remote island in the North Pacific, a tiny scrap of rock guarding a highly classified secret. She could love her new assignment if her commanding officer, Lt. George Hudson, weren't so difficult to please.

Despite George's first reaction to her presence on the island, Rachel sets out to prove she is perfect for the job. She doesn't dream of being a heroine—or falling in love— but when word leaks out about the prize they are guarding, Rachel and George find that they have few resources besides each other and their faith in God to thwart an enemy attack that could endanger all of America.

FINDING MARIE

Marie Belanger knows nothing about the covert assignments her naval lieutenant husband goes on from time to time, but she's pleased that their tour in Japan is at an end. What once seemed an interminable assignment is finished, and now Marie and Pierre Belanger can think about a Stateside posting and perhaps even starting a family. While Pierre wraps up his duties, Marie plans a brief visit to her family home in Maine.

But life turns upside down when Marie unexpectedly finds a computer flash drive in her carry-on luggage at the San Francisco airport. Moments earlier the woman she had been sitting with on the plane from Tokyo had been murdered. Suddenly her journey from California to Maine becomes a nightmare as Marie is forced to run for her life. Pierre, afraid for his wife, contacts his best friend, Lt. Commander George Hudson, and together they set out on a search for Marie that spans the country. Yet as hard as they try, they keep finding themselves one step behind their enemies, who are just one step behind Marie.